VIGILANTE

SHELLEY HARRIS

LARGE
PRINT

First published in Great Britain 2015
by
Weidenfeld & Nicolson
an imprint of the Orion Publishing Group Ltd

First Isis Edition
published 2016
by arrangement with
Orion Publishing Group Ltd
An Hachette UK Company

A catalogue record for this book is available
from the British Library.

ISBN 978–1–78541–199–1 (hb)
ISBN 978–1–78541–205–9 (pb)

Published by
F. A. Thorpe (Publishing)
Anstey, Leicestershire

Set by Words & Graphics Ltd.
Anstey, Leicestershire
Printed and bound in Great Britain by
T. J. International Ltd., Padstow, Cornwall

This book is printed on acid-free paper

To
Seth and Caleb,
for whom I would leap tall buildings
and
Loz, whose superpower will save us all

"We have made you a creature neither of heaven nor of earth, neither mortal nor immortal, in order that you may, as the free and proud shaper of your own being, fashion yourself in the form you may prefer."

Giovanni Pico della Mirandola,
Oration on the Dignity of Man

"Housework is work directly opposed to the possibility of human self-actualisation."

Ann Oakley, *Housewife*

VIGILANTE

Jen   looks
afte   s like
son   to a
fan   she
dec   ay to
the   being
mu   nalin
rus   do it
aga   . The
ma   ation
of   p by
self   Jenny
soo   orate
wh   ather
tha   s the
bad

Prologue

I was a critically-acclaimed novelist living in Hampstead. I was the one who turned down the Booker — remember that?

I was an actor. I made my name in that movie about the marijuana farm in Yorkshire, the film that won the Palme d'Or. You may recently have tried to buy tickets to my West End play.

I was a high-profile civil rights lawyer. You know those shots of Ramirez walking free in 2002? Look just behind him — the woman in the red jacket? Business-like hair, quiet pride? That's me.

I was a war correspondent who made her name in the Gulf.

I was a chef who revolutionised Britain's eating habits.

I was a politician.

I was an artist.

I was a master criminal.

Except I wasn't. I was a housewife and I ran a charity bookshop, and I was a sore disappointment to myself. There's no other way to start this story than that: I was sick of my life, and eventually I got so sick of it that I became a superhero instead.

This is how it happened.

CHAPTER
ONE

Before I was a superhero, you could have walked into my life at any moment and I'd have been tidying up. Sorting, discarding, relocating: it was my life's work. And it was exactly what I was doing the night I discovered Elliot's secret.

I was alone in the house. Elliot was in London at a design awards ceremony. His company had won a couple of years previously, and he was hoping for a repeat. He'd told me not to wait up. Our daughter, Martha, was staying overnight with a friend — I can't remember which one now. In any case, they were both out and I was in, amidst the mess remaining from their activities the previous night. I was alone and could do a proper job. The trick was to start with the kitchen. Once that was clear I could move out from it and colonise the other rooms. I stacked the dishwasher and ran it. I wiped the counter. Elliot had insisted on a wooden worktop, which you have to keep constantly dry. Inevitably I hadn't managed, and the butler's sink was edged with greying, rotty bits. I plugged my mobile into its charger. I cleaned the floor around the bin with a wet cloth.

Then I had to deal with the kitchen table. It acted as a sort of vortex, sucking in all the things that weren't properly tied down: books, bills, lone socks, junk mail, DVDs, Post-it notes with baffling single words on them ("timings!" or "bibber" or, once, "dog?"). The notes had usually lost their stickiness, detaching from their original surface and falling to the floor, where they'd be rescued and dumped on the table. As they unstuck from the fridge or cupboard or counter, their significance became unstuck too. They would be found days later, meaningless, amongst the take-out pizza menus, the labels cut from new clothes, the milk bill, the free paper, the spare keys.

The table required a system, and I had one. Music first; in the absence of Elliot's commentary I could listen to anything I wanted. I started with Bowie: *Ziggy Stardust*. At seventeen I'd listened to the album constantly. I was years too late, the charts stuffed with hit-factory clones by the time I discovered it. But most nights I'd fall asleep with Ziggy on my record player, waking in the morning to that vinyl heartbeat, the needle skating round the edge of the label.

Wastepaper basket brought through from the lounge, paper recycling box from outside the back door, both put next to the table for easy access. I cleared a space in front of me.

I was very good at this. The system had taken years to perfect, and I could usually get through a substantial pile before "Moonage Daydream" started. The work needed a certain decisiveness. I cleared enough space for two piles (In-tray and Redistribute), and started sorting through. The rule was that everything had to be filed the first time I looked at it. Letter from school? In-tray. Election leaflet? Recycle. Flyer about self-defence classes (*you have a right to feel safe!*). I wavered, thinking of Martha, at fourteen old enough to need them; I stuck it on the In-tray. Charity plastic sack binned, hairgrip redistributed, and so on.

When I heard "Moonage Daydream" I was back in my teenage bedroom, lying still in the dark, the room around me blocks of grey and black, a sliver of light under the blind. The record was quiet enough that my parents couldn't hear, and if I put on my school uniform in the morning, it was only so I could fool them that I wasn't the one who'd made earthfall the night before in platforms and a catsuit: my hair feathered, glitter on my cheeks.

I looked up and saw myself reflected in the darkened windows which gave out onto the garden, my face bisected by the strut of the window frame. I was wearing one of Elliot's T-shirts, adorned with a logo he'd done for a client. That was what he designed: logos, websites, stuff like that. Packaging, sometimes. This one was for a manufacturer of posh hairbrushes, and it reminded me of the kind of drawing Elliot used to do, back when he was going to be an artist; stylised locks of hair curling, Beardsley-ish, across my left breast. My own hair was pulled back into a ponytail, fastened with one of the red elastic bands which the postman used to wrap our letters with. I thought about falling asleep at seventeen. I thought about waking up at forty-two. By the time "Starman" came on I'd sorted the lot, and the Redistribute pile needed to be put away. I scooped it up but a set of keys slithered under my arm and fell with a crash. When I retrieved them a book toppled from the pile, landing facedown on the floor so that I had to lower myself gingerly to pick it up. *Hey Martha, love ya grrrrlll!* the inscription said on the flyleaf. It was signed in a scrawl, Isabel K Rogers written underneath in neat capitals. I'd seen the cover everywhere — Soviet-style block lettering, a yellow insignia. All the kids were reading it this year; used copies had started to come into the shop already.

I climbed the stairs, and I could see it even before I reached the landing: my daughter's chaos, filling her room, overflowing, a towel heaped across the threshold, a jacket dumped on the banister. Inside, her desk was covered in magazines and books: a couple of history texts, my copy of *Fingersmith* bookmarked with a sweet wrapper on a late page.

Fingersmith: she had taste. It was one of my favourites, and it made sense for her in other ways, too. I had worked out already — was pretty sure, at any rate — that Martha was gay. Lesbian. Actually, I didn't know what language was OK to use. I worried about it sometimes; *lesbian* sounded so pointed, somehow. But *gay* was for men really, and I thought she might be insulted if I used it for her. Elliot's work partner, Yaz, he was gay. A gayer, actually — that was what he said: I'm a total gayer. Queer? Could I say queer? I didn't think straight people were allowed.

I couldn't discuss any of this with Martha because she hadn't told me yet and there was, of course, always the possibility that I was wrong. I couldn't discuss it with Elliot, also in case I was wrong, and in case he felt hurt in ways I couldn't anticipate. It's a funny thing, but you don't know how you'll react; you think you'll be really cool. I'd thought of grandchildren, right away. I was ashamed of myself afterwards. I'd picked up Martha from a school field trip in Year 8, and there she was getting off the coach with all her mates, and I noticed something incredibly subtle — a compounding, actually, of all the subtle things I'd been noticing for years, things I'd registered subliminally. Something to do with the way she dressed compared to the other girls, the way she did her hair, the way she looked at the boys, not a giggle in her, not a switched-away glance. I think I would describe it as *comradely*. I thought: my girl's a lesbian. I remember leaning back against my car for a bit of support, slipping on the sunnies I'd just taken off, trying to look as if I was relaxing. The other parents were already moving forward to greet their kids but I stayed there an extra moment, the open window at my back, "Love Train" coming from the radio. The first thing: grief, and I hadn't even known I wanted grandchildren. Forty years old, and all I could think about was the grandchildren I wouldn't have. Later I remembered that lesbians have babies: of course they do, all the time. But that had been my first thought, before I got in there and started talking sense to myself.

So, Martha was gay. She was, possibly, a total gayer. More pressingly, she was untidy. There was a collection of mugs in her room, the fluid within them supporting rafts of mould at different stages of growth. There were three plates scattered with the remains of Marmite toast. Martha liked hers spread mouth-strippingly thick and she always left the crusts. The floor was all shoes and crisp packets, knickers and jewellery. Even the noticeboard above her bed was a mess, crammed with photos of her and her friends, silly drawings, an ancient swimming certificate. One corner of a poster ("I refuse to become what you call normal") had peeled free and bowed forward under the weight of Blu-Tack. I left the book on her bed.

Martha's window had the best view: our tiny garden, and the tiny gardens of our neighbours, and the houses backing onto us. It was dark and there was a smattering of lights on in the other houses. I opened her window, pushing my head and shoulders out into the muffling night silence. For a few moments it was quiet indoors too, a pause between songs. I breathed in the cold and closed my eyes. Then, somewhere below me, there was a rustling.

I opened my eyes and held still, stopping an exhale mid-breath. It was too dark out there to see anything, and too bright inside. I turned off the light, easing down the switch so it didn't make a click, and waited for my eyes to adjust. In the kitchen "Lady Stardust" began, rising in stereo, up the stairs and out of the window beneath me. I waited, lulled, while the darkness resolved into its multiple densities: shed, path, fence. There was an alleyway running along the bottom of our garden that gave access to all the back gates. I could see the wavering line of my neighbours' fences, punctuated by trees, following the alley's course right the way down to the Duke of Cambridge at the end of the road.

"Lady Stardust" was about Marc Bolan, Mum would tell me, and then she'd sigh and say *what a waste*, and it was only after I'd had Martha that I thought to consider that she'd been a new mum herself when that album came out, her future crash-landed in her arms. I didn't think about it at seventeen though, and if I had, the thought would have slipped from me without the slightest resistance. The world would be mine, I knew it. On weeknights I'd rehearse, at weekends I'd snog boys at the Irish Club discos; I knew one of them would come up trumps. And in between I did my homework like a good girl. Belt and braces.

Bowie was wailing downstairs and nothing moved in the garden. Maybe it had been a hedgehog. People said urban foxes came out after dark, but I'd only ever seen them in nature documentaries, foraging in shades of grey, their eyes glowing white. I waited a minute or so more, long enough to be sure that the only noises were unremarkable ones, the ordinary soundscape of a small town closing down for the night. I shut the window.

In the study it was Elliot-world. I put his headphones on the desk and took a moment to appreciate the room's quiet order. No strewn clothing, only the broad expanse of his monitor, the squat wooden speakers, the framed posters of his design campaigns. This was the part of the house which was always tidy. Elliot had kept the Victorian fireplace in this room, blacking the grate and restoring the tiles. There were photographs on the mantelpiece; Elliot's grandparents, him and Yaz, him and me on a beach in full scuba gear trying to kiss, leaning towards each other, our masks clashing. I recalled the weight of the aqualung, how hard it was to move on land; in the ocean, we shook off gravity. I'd sheltered with him next to a cluster of rocks, Hammerheads tooling through the water above us, white-bellied and sad-mouthed. I remembered later, changing in the hut, the seams of the wetsuit tracking pink down his body, the smell of neoprene and sweat. I remembered my own body too, effortlessly mine back then, loosened and disinhibited by drama training, uncomplicated in ways I didn't yet know to be grateful for.

Tucked behind a photo of Martha as a baby there was one of me, taken the year Elliot and I met. Rubbish picture really — wonky, off-centre, the only badly-designed thing in the room. I'm standing in front of Jules's transit van. It's some godawful hour of a grey morning and I'm feeling dreadful in the wake of another heavy weekend, a midweek comedown in progress. The van doors are open behind me so you can glimpse a flash of colour inside: costumes and bits of scenery. We're off to some school to do palatable, truncated Shakespeare. Elliot got up that early just for me, to see me off and take the picture. I've spotted that he's raising the camera and I'm pouting and sticking two fingers up, but I know exactly what I was thinking: how unbelievable it was that he was here, that he was *still* here after six months. How he was kind and fun, how I didn't know those two things could co-exist for any sustained period. How — just a tiny thought this, a batsqueak — how I hoped I matched up.

Not much tidying to be done in the study. I checked the floor, the bookshelves, the desk, scanning for incongruity. Just one; a book out of line, the spine protruding from the other spines around it. I looked closer: our wedding album, separated from the other photo albums and in the wrong place. Gripped in Elliot's ergonomic office chair I opened it, peeling back the tissue paper to see the first shots of me on my wedding morning: grinning, bobbed, dressing-gowned, hands resting on my belly though I hadn't started to show yet. Me, twenty-seven and up the duff, lying with bullish cheerfulness every time someone asked if it was planned. Me, five months away from becoming the *coolest mother ever*.

(She won't call me *Mum*; I'll be Jen.

She can tour with me.

People always make such heavy weather of it.)

I turned a page and a fat booklet fell out of the album. It was A5 size, stapled at the spine. Order of service, I thought, but this was something quite different, something which didn't belong.

There was a punch of colour: yellows and blues, lots of red. At the bottom right-hand of the top sheet, in a flourish quite unlike his usual signature, it said, Elliot Pepper.

It was a comic book. When I saw what was on the cover, I felt a sort of leap. I was looking at a dark street, a cobbled square bordered with old buildings. Rubbish littered the pavement. There was a scrawl of graffiti on

11

a wall. In the foreground was a streetlamp, and in the wedge of its light stood a superhero. The superhero was Elliot.

He was clad in red and black, sporting the kind of muscles that heroes are meant to have, hillocky biceps and a six-pack like oversized bubble wrap. He wore a domino mask across his eyes, but they were Elliot's eyes, no doubt about that, the grey-green of them, and the hair which stuck up above his hero's forehead was Elliot's salt-and-pepper spike. His right cheek bore the mole of Elliot's right cheek. He was called Vermilion.

Of course — that nerdish streak of Elliot's, his muttered corrections when we watched a badly adapted superhero movie, his insistence that comic books — *graphic novels* — were Art. I thought: am I in the story, too? I thought: I shouldn't really be looking at this.

I turned the page.

It began with an explosive image. Vermilion crashing to earth in a ball of fire, the foetal curl of his naked body at its heart, a streak of flame trailing across the black of the page. Then it cut to the present, and Vermilion's alter ego — Edward Porter — living in quiet obscurity as an artist in Metro City. Enter arch-villain, Necro, placing the earth in peril, forcing Porter to put on the mantle of Vermilion once more and do battle.

As a plot it wasn't inspiring. But the visuals were something else. There was Vermilion in extreme close-up, the black of his mask, a single green eye, and reflected in that eye: Necro. There was a child being snatched from its mother in a succession of images,

12

mother and child face to face, terrified, then those same faces at the edges of the frame, separated by a broad space, then the mother's scream, then her empty hand. I hoped I wasn't a henchwoman. Perhaps I was a sidekick. But there was only a henchman. Vermilion threw him from the top of a tall building, and his plunge was a skinny vertical panel the full height of the page; Vermilion a tiny figure on the roof, arms akimbo, cape swirling, the henchman a flailing dot, eighty-nine storeys through a ninety-storey drop.

This was brilliant. It was genius. Was I in here at all?

And then I turned the page. Teetering on the edge of that ninety-storey drop was a chair, and tied to the chair was a woman. She was dressed in a scrap of material cut low over the solid globes of her breasts, high across her hairless groin. Vermilion caught her just as she tipped backwards, her red mouth open, eyes wide, body about to succumb — finally — to gravity. When he untied her she clung to him, a Man Ray tear balanced on her lashes. His hands on her improbable waist, he held her close. He told her: "You're safe now."

It wasn't me. It wasn't even trying to be me. I became conscious that my lips were bunched down hard and I made myself relax. I looked away from the comic; my gaze fell on Elliot's desk, and I had a sudden urge to chuck his stupid computer out of the window, or through it. You stupid man, I thought. This is not a woman at all, and it most particularly is not a woman who has had children. Who has had *your* child!

I was shocked by the ferocity of my anger. Cool your jets, Jen, I told myself, it's only a bloody comic book.

But I found myself dumping it on the floor and grabbing my breasts to remind myself what real breasts were like, even those corralled in a bra, and grasping the fat fold of my belly — too hard; it hurt — my belly at its fattest because I was sitting down. I pushed it out to make it even bigger and looked down at it, bulging over the belt of my jeans. It's a comic book, I reminded myself. They never look like real women.

Once in a while I'd chosen to share with Elliot some of my despair over the way my body had run out of control, and every time he'd been admirably supportive: I love your body, you've always been beautiful, aren't we lucky to be growing older together? Blah blah blah. But look at this, now! This wasn't just a bloody comic book. It was a window into his desires, and this was what he wanted: big tits, tiny waist, hairless fanny. It wasn't off-the-peg porn, either. He'd designed it himself, and he wanted the stuff you cannot have without surgery and childlessness and the kind of constant attention that women like me can't give themselves.

And I don't want to, anyway, I raged, hearing his key turn in the front door. I can't and I don't want to. The door clicked shut behind him. Go on, I thought: find me, the one you've ended up with.

"Jen?"

He could come upstairs and look for me. He could see what I'd found. And I'd say . . .

I looked at the wedding album he'd hidden the comic in, and at the comic itself, dumped on the floor. I'd say that I'd looked at his private stuff, and it had made me feel atrocious. We could talk about my ageing body and how it disappointed him. We could explore my feelings, which would undoubtedly, at some point, start to look like insecurity, like paranoia.

"J?"

I stuffed the comic back where I'd found it and went downstairs.

Elliot was sitting on the bottom step. "Hi," he said. He was hunched over, picking at the lace on his shoe.

"Bit dull," he said. "Didn't get the gong." He gave up trying to loosen the lace and pushed the shoe off with the toe of the other. "Can't win 'em all." He looked up at me, singly-shod, coat on, a smile applied tentatively to his face.

"Hey," he said. "You OK?"

Through the doorway I spotted a pile of books I'd got at the shop, waiting on top of the piano to be assigned a shelf. I didn't know how I'd missed them earlier. "I'm fine," I told him, my molars grinding against each other.

"You don't look fine."

"I'm . . . well, OK. I'm not fine. I'm pissed off."

He blanched and his hand went to his chest. "Give me a minute," he said. "Bit rough. Need the Miracle Cure."

He got up and clopped past me into the kitchen, every other step silent. Alone in the hall, I picked up the abandoned brogue, yanking at the knot until it came loose, pulling the lace free, ramming the shoe into the rack under the stairs. In the middle room I scooped up the novels from the piano and put them on the

To-Be-Read shelves, shoving them into the horizontal space on top of other books. Then I went into the kitchen.

Elliot was standing, lopsided, at the cupboards, staring into them. My entrance roused him and he shook himself minutely, pulled out a glass and a sachet. "Rehidrat," he said. "Breakfast of champions."

There was a clunk as something toppled inside the dishwasher. "Yaz took it a bit hard, but I was fine," he went on. "You can't please all of the people some of the . . . you know what I mean."

He left the cupboard door wide open. On the countertop lay the torn sachet, a scattering of granules next to it. He'd not been home five minutes.

"This room," I said. "It was actually tidy a minute ago. I spent ages. Can you . . .?"

"It's lovely, J." He stepped towards me. "What's happened? What's wrong?"

"My body's like this because I've had a kid," I said, and I could see his surprise, which made me even more livid. "Don't pretend you haven't thought it. And my clothes are like this because I'd look bloody stupid cleaning in a bikini."

"Thought what? I love your body," he said, putting his hand out, placing it on the nape of my neck. "You're beautiful. Don't let anyone tell you otherwise."

I wanted to slap him a bit, just then.

"And I don't care about your clothes," he said. "Mate, where's all this coming from?"

Mate? When did that start?

"I'm not your bloody mate. I'm babe or honey."

"Honey," he said, pulling me towards him. "Babe."

"I feel horrible," I said. Elliot kissed me on my forehead. He stayed there, his skin damp with sweat, his mouth wet with Rehidrat.

"Bad night?" he asked.

"You had one too," I said, with a shameful little kick of satisfaction.

"To be honest, it's a bind anyway, the winning," he said, his words vibrating against my skull. "Expectations. Need to be free . . . to create things."

He disengaged, his shod foot tolling its thud . . . thud. Sitting down, he miscalculated, landing half-on half-off the kitchen chair. He had to reach out to the table to steady himself. After a bit of fumbling he pulled off the other shoe and dropped it on the floor. He watched it for a while.

"Go to bed," I said and then, because it had sounded harsh, and because I didn't want to be called on it: "I'm sorry you didn't win."

"Them's the breaks," he said. "Come to bed."

I put the shoe on the rack with its partner. I closed the cupboard door and threw away the empty sachet. I put the glass and spoon in the sink, ready for the next dishwasher cycle, and wiped the counter. Before I left the kitchen I turned to check that everything was once again as it should be. I looked across the room to the windows and saw myself reflected in them a second time, the window frames the borders of a panel in a comic book, and me inside them, ordinary and fat and serviceable, waiting for someone extraordinary to enter the story.

CHAPTER
TWO

Before the shop — before Allie — my life had deconstructed itself. We had moved out of London after I got pregnant, back to be near Mum, back where the housing was cheaper, and there was no point staying anyway because I couldn't lug scenery into schools pregnant, and I didn't get auditions pregnant, and Elliot and Yaz had already started to talk about setting up the business.

I cannot tell you how isolating it was. I knew two girls from school who still lived there, and motherhood had *not* put a spoke in their careers — at least, that was how it seemed to me. At any rate, they weren't around during the day. Suddenly I was living in a town I didn't recognise, toddlers thronging its streets, buggies congesting its pavements. I went to baby music classes and baby gym classes, and I don't think I or any of the women there managed to complete a single conversation. Those conversations were, anyway, about the virtues of disposable over washable nappies, about the relative demerits of their male partners and the quality of the local schools. I can remember, quite clearly, knowing that I had other things to say — and wondering if they did, too — but being somehow unable to winkle out of my head any ideas or opinions unrelated to Martha. After a while, I started to worry about what those opinions might sound like, how baseless they might turn out to be, after all these months of not formulating them, after being cut off from any evidence that might support them.

Then I had two miscarriages in quite quick succession, and found I couldn't bear to be with the other mothers as they started to pop out their second children. I began going for voiceover work, Mum looking after Martha while I made the trek into London. And then, Mum died.

I was right there in the kitchen with her. "Well," she'd just said, a prelude to a minor announcement, probably: Well, you know that shop in the High Street? Well, shall I tell you what? Well, you'll never guess. She pushed herself away from the counter and stood up a little straighter. "Well," she said, and then she frowned and touched her chest. "Oh," she said next. And then she slumped and I thought she was making a joke, as if the "well" announcement was something she was pretending to despair of, and I actually started smiling because she was making this joke with me. Then she just fell to the floor with her eyes open and her shoulder banged against a chair and the first thing, the first stupid, stupid thing I did when I reached for my dead mum, was to rub her shoulder because she'd bashed it so badly on the way down.

When I first met Allie, the only shaping force in my life was Martha and her needs, and on weekdays the two of us were alone in the whole world. I'd wander around town with the buggy, going down every footpath and back road. After a while, I could have found myself anywhere in Bassetsbury and known exactly what was round the corner. When our trek took us through the town centre we'd detour into charity shops and look through the kids' clothes. At that time Allie took in all donations, books as well. When I bought from her, I'd sometimes try to start a conversation about the novels, but to be honest Allie was never a great reader.

She learned what I liked though. I was reading a lot of Garrison Keillor: comforting small-town stories in which families come down with stomach bugs and then get over them, where fathers think their daughters are getting divorced but find out they're happily pregnant, where the plot will never take you anywhere unpredictable or scary. Those stories were a safe place for me. After a while when we came into Allie's shop, she'd have put aside a couple of titles she thought I might like, a dress or two for Martha. She knew her business, but it amounted to more than that because Allie adored Martha. I noticed how tenderly she treated her, the ways in which she'd pay attention. Martha's favourite teddy was a tiny thing: beige fur, red scarf. One day, we came in and Allie had found a child's scarf in the exact same shade of red. "Look what someone brought in!" she said, wrapping it round her. "It's just like Spencer's." That night, when Martha finally took it off, something caught in her hair and I had to disentangle it: a price tag strung on ribbon and attached with a teeny gold safety pin. Not from Allie's shop after all, but brand new, from the cashmere place in the shopping centre. I wondered if she'd wanted me to find it so that I'd know how she felt, without the awkward business of her actually having to say it.

Sometimes Allie would tell me she was just about to make a cuppa. I'd cross to the other side of the counter and we'd sit there side by side as if I belonged, Martha dozing in her buggy next to the Fair Trade shower gel or, later, rifling through the toy corner. When a customer came in and bought books I'd have a look at their selection and try to second-guess what else they might like. Allie would rummage through the shelves trying to find copies of the titles I'd suggested. Upselling, she called it.

Then one day, about two years after we'd first met, she said: "I'm looking for a new books co-ordinator. Wondered if you fancied the job."

"Books co-ordinator?" I wondered what it might be like to join the ranks of volunteers she chivvied into adequacy.

"It's . . . it's a new post. Something I'm trying. Come in next Tuesday at nine-thirty."

"Tuesday? It's Martha's first day at school. I'll be feeling a bit ropey."

"Yeah, I know," she said. "Come anyway. We'll start with a cuppa."

I think I must have hesitated because she added, as if it were the clincher: "You'll get first pick of the books."

In fairness, it *was* the clincher. And I realised it wasn't just Martha she'd been paying attention to. I'd been flying around in the dark looking for somewhere to land and suddenly there it was: Allie had lit up a runway for me.

A year later Famaid opened a second shop next door, one just for books, and Allie recommended me as the salaried manager. It wasn't what I'd thought I'd end up doing with my life, but it fitted in with school hours and it gave me a place to belong to. And when it became dull (as it increasingly did after the novelty of being back in the workplace had subsided), when it felt like an only slightly more sophisticated version of the tidying up I did at home, at least I had this recompense: a friend working right next door — my best friend, I thought in private, but never wanted to use the term with her because it smacked of primary school. I'd been given another gift too: an entire shopful of books which were mine for the reading, a shopful of exits. I could walk out of my life any time I wanted and into their worlds.

A couple of days after I'd found Elliot's comic, I was alone in the shop and waiting for my afternoon volunteer to turn up. I had a roster of twenty-five a week. That day it was Judith, conspicuous by her absence. Our stockroom was at the back: a workbench, a desk, floor-to-ceiling shelves of categorised books waiting to go out. Nothing was new here, we couldn't justify it. Me they bought for twenty hours a week, a tad above minimum wage. Everything else — the kettle, the computer, the rest of the staff — came free, and none of it in very good condition.

The stockroom was doorless, so we could monitor the shop while we worked. I was in there, at the workbench, sorting through a donation. It was largely rubbish, the books dusty and heat-warped, hollow clenched bodies of spiders littering the corners of the box. There were all sorts of other things slung in which shouldn't have been there at all: a PVC purse, a set of coloured pencils, a travel chess set. I put them all into a bag. They really belonged with Allie next door, but few donors bothered to differentiate. I'd take them across later, none of it would make much money. Still, there were other sorts of treasure to be found.

A book takes quite a time to read: days at the minimum, sometimes weeks. During that period it goes with the reader on journeys, it sits next to her bed, it accompanies her through holidays and hospital stays and bouts of insomnia, through bereavements and celebrations and long, long stretches of boredom — through life, in short. It accumulates evidence of that life, and I collected the evidence. I'd found all sorts, in my time: a recipe for veal quenelles in copperplate script, postcards ("Say hullo to the little one for me" sent in 1905, the writer long gone now, probably the little one too). Pressed flowers, a resignation letter, a wedding card containing sex advice; Allie and I had cracked up over that one, Allie rocking back and forth, silently corpsing.

A customer came in, banging the door against the window display, and I leaned back to catch sight of him: stocky and jumpered, pink-nosed from the cold. "I'm just through here," I called. "Give me a shout if I can help." He squinted past the counter into the stockroom, and nodded.

In the box I spotted a plastic toy, the kind you get free with a hamburger, and a fancy-dress mask — a little bit Venetian, black and gold — both wedged between books. The toy I binned, the mask . . . the mask pulled my thoughts straight back to Elliot's comic. I stuffed it into the bag with the other unwanted things.

In the days since I'd found the comic, I'd been reminded of it at arbitrary moments, and each time I'd charge with some complex emotion, an amalgam of anger and self-pity and embarrassment. The force of it unsettled me, and I told myself I was overreacting; Elliot had just been playing. He didn't take the comic book woman seriously, and I shouldn't either. These little pep talks proved completely ineffectual. I kept thinking I'd speak to Elliot, and I knew how you were meant to go about it. You say, *when you did that, it made me feel . . .* You abandon judgement and accusation. But what I felt seemed bottomless, and I was scared of starting to dig down into it; I was nervous of what I might find. So I kept knocking the issue back every time it entered my thoughts, promising myself that I would talk to him, I would tell him how I felt — next time, next time, next time.

In the shop, a throat cleared. My customer was standing at the till holding *A Girl's Book of Ballet*.

"Insert joke here," he said.

"I'm saying nothing," I told him. "That'll be one ninety-nine, please."

"It's for my daughter," he said. "Who shows very little interest. She takes the piss: nice toes, naughty toes." He flapped his hand, fingers pointing horizontal then vertical. "I think the wife's just reliving her childhood. She actually cares about naughty toes."

"Right," I said, handing him his change. "That's your penny."

"She should do ballet herself," he said, slipping the coin into the collection box.

"Better than living vicariously."

The man clicked his fingers. "Vicariously!" he said. "Yes! I was going to say that, but I didn't know whether you'd understand it."

My mouth hinged open. I wondered if I'd heard him properly. "I . . ." I said, as he turned at the door and raised a hand in salutation. "Hey, that's . . ." The door banged shut. ". . . massively rude!" I had to actually restrain myself from chasing after him, hauling open the door and yelling a whole load of not very classy things. *A Girl's Book of Ballet?* I've read *Les Miserables*! I've read *Crime and Punishment*! You think I'd falter at vicarious, do you? I could *vicarious* you to within an inch of your life. I could *mimesis* you from here to next Christmas! I could *discourse* you so hard you wouldn't sit down for a week!

People just think you're thick if you work in a shop. They take one look at you behind that counter and . . .

I watched as my customer slipped in between two market stalls and disappeared. They take one look at you and think they know everything.

Back to the sorting. The bloody sorting. All travel guides, this next box. I'd cleaned ours out a few years back because really, what was the point in keeping them? Two shelves reduced to one volume, a 1996 guide to Istanbul, now tucked between my recipe books. On its flyleaf was a note from Elliot: *Pack. We're off.*

These donors were sunbirds: Miami, Ibiza, Greece, the one exception being a travel guide to Sweden. The Northern Lights swirled green across its cover, this inscription on the title page: *Paddy, I will take you there. All my love always, Deanna.* So maybe Paddy was the sun-lover and Deanna yearned for something different. And in any case — you bastard, Paddy, I thought. Why haven't you cherished this book and its inscription? What's it doing here, dumped in my shop?

Deanna had killed Paddy. No, not killed him. After years of neglect she'd finally snapped, drugged his cocoa, flown him north of the arctic circle in a twin-prop and dumped him in a ... in a forest full of ... reindeer. And bears. She'd zipped him into a padded jacket and stuffed the pockets with strips of dried moose to help him survive. Which was a pity, because if there's one thing guaranteed to fill bears with bloodlust, it's the smell of dried moose. So Deanna probably did murder him after all, but at least she'd also made good on her promise; he saw the Northern Lights before he went.

I tore out the flyleaf and started on the next box: several greasy cookbooks and a pile of threadbare textbooks patently nicked from a school. Geography,

Human Biology, History. In a rush of recognition, I saw that the history textbook was the same one I'd used — the picture of Queen Victoria, the block lettering of the title. On my copy the gloss of the cover was streaked with shards of matte where I'd picked at the shiny coating and ripped it off. There was a piece of paper glued inside the front of this one, school crest at the top, motley list of names and dates underneath — the older ones in angular fountain pen, later ones in biro — and it was my very own school, Bassetsbury Girls. Checking through the rest of the donation I saw my science textbook, my world atlas, and a copy of *Jane Eyre*, my GCSE text.

Our English teacher, Miss Scull, went on peace marches at the weekend and wore her hair hippy-long, but she broke with her habitual freewheeling to make us learn by rote: "I am no bird, and no net ensnares me. I am a free human being with an independent will." Not long after Martha was born, I'd considered getting that latter sentence tattooed around my arm, just to remind myself. But I worried about breast-feeding and toxicity, and I chickened out.

The donor had signed for Gift Aid as Mrs Thompson, but the name common to all these was Amy Horrocks. She had been a year younger than me and I couldn't bring her to mind, or match her up with the woman I'd met that morning. Above her on those bookplates I saw names I did know. I got flashes of them: the girl who left early because she was pregnant, the one who used to quote *The Hitchhiker's Guide to the Galaxy*, the one who kept a photograph of Judd Nelson sellotaped to the inside of her desk.

And then I opened a copy of *As You Like It* — faded boards, the weave exposed along the spine where stringy bits of cloth had been stripped out — and it was 1989 all over again. Seventeen years old, shivering at the back of the hall in the boys' school for the first read-through. I opened *As You Like It* and it was mine, not in the way that *Jane Eyre* and the science book had been mine, but really and absolutely mine. There I was — Jenny Jordan, 6A — written when I was experimenting with a curvaceous, flourishing hand.

I was Jenny Jordan back then, and for a while I was Rosalind too, and also Ganymede. There were four of us girls, armed with copies of the script and shipped across to the boys' school. I didn't know the play, but I'd looked at the cast list and knew I didn't fancy being a shepherdess, or a country wench. I knew those characters would be funny or stupid or just marginal. So I was Rosalind, and the local paper said I was "outstanding". I went on stage each night thinking I was about to throw up, and came off resolved to try out for drama school. At the after-show party, Jacques made a move, but I got off with Orlando instead.

A clatter at the door, a new customer. There was no market for school textbooks. I threw them, one by one, into the yellow sack waiting beside me. I threw in *As You Like It*, but not before I'd torn out the page with my name on it.

I nipped to the shelves, slid my hand behind a stack of Princess Diana conspiracy theories and pulled out the boxfile where I kept my finds. The back door opened, channelling a current of cold air down the shop. I shoved the pages in and snapped the box shut, hurrying back to the workbench. The breeze swept in from the yard, past the sink and lockers and staff toilet, through the stockroom and out across the shop floor. It rustled the cellophane-wrapped cards against each other in the revolving stand and pressed against the back of the customer who was hesitating now on her way out, unsure whether to stay or go. Maybe it tipped her into a decision because she left, exiting through the front at the same moment as the back door closed.

Allie gave the handle a final tug and came through into the stockroom. You could go between our shops either way: through the back — where we shared a common yard — or the front. There were times when we had looked for each other simultaneously, circling through the shops in a closed loop, each entering the place the other had just vacated.

"You been busy?"

I thought of the vicarious man. "Don't ask. You?"

"Not bad. Got a big load of M&S stuff with a DKNY coat hidden at the bottom," she said. "Stuck it front and centre, first thing you see when you come in the door. It went in half an hour. Forty quid." She brushed her hands against each other. "That's how I roll."

I winced at her. "Really?" I said. "It's how you *roll?*"

"Thought I'd give it a try," she grinned. "I hear all the young people are saying it now."

"It might be worth checking that with Martha," I told her.

She was wearing something posh that day herself, a fiftiesish dress in the kind of pastel colours which always look better on black skin. It would be from stock; I'd known her sell the clothes off her back. Looking at her hands, I noticed she was holding a little glass cup, filled with solid purple to about halfway up. "Someone donated this," she said, sliding it onto the workbench. "Look — it's been used. Who donates a used candle?"

Lavande de Provence, the label alleged. The sides of the glass were smutted black, the wick set deep in a hollow of wax. Allie sniffed at it and held it out to me: mango with an edge of toilet cleaner.

"It doesn't smell great," she said. "But it smells better than drains. I thought it might be useful back here sometimes." Then she frowned at something over my shoulder and I turned to see Judith, my volunteer, making her way across the square.

"She's not just arriving?" said Allie. "It's three o'clock."

"She needed to go to the garden centre." I reached for one of the boxes I'd emptied, laid it on the floor and stood on it to crush it flat.

"You've got to get those vollies in line. Set up a rota, make them sign in the diary. No excuses. They walk all over you."

"It's tricky. They leave." I stamped down hard, the box surrendering as the final corner collapsed inwards.

"No they don't. Not if you create the culture."

Not if *you* create the culture, I thought. Allie had it without even trying, that quality — what would I call it? A natural authority, a restraint which meant her volunteers would always blurt out something before she did, and that something was usually in the vicinity of *yes, of course,* or *I'm so sorry,* or *I'll do that, shall I?* I'd tried copying her, but I always seemed to end up doing the blurting.

"Sorry," said Judith as she came in. "I've had a complete nightmare. I had to wait for hours at the till. Some child fell in the pond and the staff were running around like headless chickens. Sorry. Did I miss much?"

"I need a fag," said Allie.

We sat in garden chairs in front of the shed. The sky was a grey wash. Beyond our back wall, above the churchyard, a flock of birds was shaken out like a sheet.

"If I was still acting, I'd love to do Judith," I said.

Allie vented smoke up into the still air. "Do her?"

"Watch her," I said. "And then copy her. The way she hoists her bag strap higher up her shoulder when she's got a point to make." I mimed it. "The way she holds her hands cupped in front of her body, like she's about to give someone a leg-up."

"Did you used to do that?"

"When I was training we'd get sent out to watch people," I said, and Allie grinned. She loved hearing about my acting. I will confess that I didn't overplay the mundanity of those years to her. I hadn't made it entirely clear how very small-time I'd been, despite leaving drama school with big plans (tasteful ones: Donmar and the Old Vic, independent movies rather than Hollywood trash; I wouldn't sell out). In fact, the reality was pretty much as we'd always been warned; I don't know why I'd thought it would be any different for me. As it turned out, school halls were my stage, Year 9 my audience. My time on screen, that brief flicker of fame, came courtesy of an ad that, for a few months, and quite unexpectedly, grabbed the public imagination. Allie had spent her life in retail. She loved me I think, but the actor me — the old me — was the only part that came anywhere close to impressing her. I think I could be forgiven for working it a little.

"We had to observe one person closely," I said. "Then the next day in class we'd perform them for the group."

"Did anyone ever guess you were watching them?"

"Once or twice."

"What happened?"

"One bloke, I . . . picked him up. I went home with him."

"Wow," said Allie, and I was just about to make a lameish joke (really close observation) when she added: "You've never told me that," and I registered a tiny blip of resentment that she'd thought I'd told her everything, that she'd assumed she'd seen every corner of my life.

"Copy me," she said then. "Like you used to. Go on."

Somewhere, on the other side of the churchyard, a car gunned its engine. Allie looked down at her body and gave me a nod of encouragement. I leaned back in my seat, stretched out my legs and drew on an imaginary cigarette. "OK," I said, exhaling imaginary smoke, shooting a sideways look at her. "So, obviously don't take this the wrong way, Jen. But your window display looks like crap. Let me at it, won't you? I've got a fabulous idea." A slight sibilance on the s, the r more about the lips than the tongue and palate.

Allie sniggered. To hold yourself like someone is to feel like them. What did it feel like, to be her? More confident; I'd seen that coming. She took up more room than I would, as if she were entitled to the space. Right hand held up, cigarette aloft like a challenge. But here was her other arm, a gate across her chest. It felt surprisingly defensive.

She watched me, her gaze flicking between our bodies, making little adjustments. Her head bobbed a bit lower, her shoulders hunched slightly. As she brought her hands down to rest on her stomach, the cigarette poking up, away from her lovely dress, I worked out what she was doing — who she was doing. I saw, for the first time, that when you cover your belly with your hands you are drawing attention to it rather than disguising it. My mouth popped open with embarrassment and I coughed to cover it up. Allie drew her feet in under the lip of the chair. She searched my face, concentrating. Her jaw clenched, her lips pressed against each other, and I saw myself, hatchet-faced.

Not an ounce of malice in her, but *Stop it!* I wanted to say, mortified. Then I remembered I was still Allie, and flicked the imaginary filter with my thumb, winking at her as if it had been a great joke until she laughed herself out of character. In the yard of The Stag next door, something heavy was being dragged across the cobbles. Change the subject, I thought. Allie had gone out to a new pub the previous night, a place that boasted forty different kinds of sausage on the menu. It seemed like a distracting enough topic to mention.

"How was last night?"

"Good, actually," said Allie. "You and I should go there. You don't have to have sausages. Mike had kangaroo."

It was a first date. I hadn't met him and there was usually little point; Allie operated something of a revolving door policy. But she had mentioned him beforehand, and — *Mike?* I was sure she'd used a different name. Inside my shop, someone was calling out.

"Mike?" I said.

Allie cocked her head. "Hang on. Is that . . .?"

And then Martha was in the doorway of the yard and Allie was up before I was, grinning ("Emster!"), holding the cigarette behind her back as they kissed and shaking it a little to make sure I saw it in time. I slipped the stub from between her fingers and stepped on it.

"So," said Martha. "Can I stay the night with Liv?"

"Hi, Mum. How's your day going?"

"Hi Mum how's your day going can I stay the night with Liv?" She pulled her heel out of her ballet pump and the sole snapped against the ground.

"Weren't we going to watch some rubbish together?"

"Yeah," said Allie. "Watching telly with Mum. That's what all the kids want to do." I knew she thought I was a bit of a fusser with Martha, and everything I wanted to say (it's easy to be cool when you're not a parent. You try it and see how you get on) was impossible, because Allie would actually rather have liked the chance to try. There's a horrible moment when you realise the tenses have changed, when someone moves from the present perfect to the simple past. "I haven't had kids," Allie used to tell people. Now — when she mentioned it at all — she said, "I didn't". So I absorbed this little dig, while Martha offered me wide eyes and a downturned mouth.

"Don't do Kicked Puppy!" I said. I reached out and pinched her lips between my fingers. They made a squishing noise and she pulled free, wiping her mouth.

"Gross."

"Have her parents said it's OK?"

"They will." She glanced back towards the shop. "Liv and Izzy are coming by in a minute. Liv's dad's working in Chapel Road. We're going to ask him."

I checked my watch. "It's the last job of the day," I said. "You can help. The fiction shelves need to be culled and re-stocked. Do you remember how you did it last time? Put your bag in the back and I'll be with you in a tick."

"What? No! They'll be here in a minute."

"Martha Pepper, you will help me, please. When the others arrive, we'll go."

"We . . . ?"

"Chapel Road's on the way home. I'll pop in and say hi."

"No! God!" She looked at Allie, who adopted an expression of exaggerated disbelief.

"Don't make a fuss," I said. "I want to check if Ian's OK with you staying over. And I've been wanting to see that place since he bought it. Just a peek, and I'll be off."

Martha snorted and turned away. She stopped when she got to the doorway, propped her bag against her leg and rummaged for something.

"Dad said to give you this," she told Allie.

When she'd gone into the shop, Allie and I looked at each other in silence. The corner of her mouth twitched and I could see she was on the verge of teasing me. But she just sat down again, tapped out a fresh cigarette and lit it, before addressing herself to the box Martha had given her.

"Oh, my days!" she said. "These are gorgeous. Go on — first one's for you."

She handed me an invitation. Elliot had used four photographs of Allie — four repetitions of the same photograph, in fact — and lined them up side by side. He'd edited out her original clothing and dressed her, paper doll-style, in four different outfits (police officer, Bo Peep, rabbit, queen). Underneath were the details of Allie's fancy-dress party, scheduled for her birthday in three weeks' time. The prospect didn't light a fire in me. Fancy dress works in one of three ways: you're sexy, you're fun or you're clever. I'll come as Demis

Roussos, I thought. I'll come as a whale or a mattress, or a marquee.

"He's a genius," said Allie, and though I was usually the first to big him up, his infallible cheerleader, this felt like one time too many; if it's possible to feel simultaneously annoyed and bored, I would say that I did.

"I should be getting inside to Martha," I told her, but she spotted my reaction and narrowed her eyes. "Elliot's not my favourite topic at the moment," I said. "We had a . . . just a falling-out."

Allie pulled on her cigarette, her lips unsticking from the paper with a dry *pah*. "Is it time for How-Does-It-Make-You-Feel?"

"I'll tell you when I know. Maybe I'm being silly. I don't want to . . . Allie? Your date last night. Was it *Mike?* Really?"

"Mike really what?"

"You said he was called Mike, but I thought . . ."

"Yeah. Hang on — what did I say?"

"You said Mike." She frowned at me. "You did."

"Oh God," she said. "Mark, Mark, Mark! Bugger, bugger! Mark! And I probably called him that all night . . ." She gave a last, fierce drag and threw the cigarette to the ground, where it sent up a thin plume of smoke. "Mark!" she said as a parting shot, disappearing through her back door. I ground out the stub, just in case, and went in through mine.

The woman arrived as I did. She strode across the shop floor to the counter, her court shoes thudding on the

lino. There was a businessy look about her —
structured jacket, leather document case — as if she'd
turned up at the shop for a meeting.

"Glad I caught you," she said to Judith. "You're my
last."

Behind her, Martha pulled out some volumes and set
them on the floor. The woman pushed a piece of paper
across the counter. "I couldn't persuade you to put this
up, could I?"

Over Judith's shoulder, I read the headline: **HAVE
YOU SEEN THIS MAN?** There was a photofit picture —
a generic white man, baseball cap, five o'clock shadow.
His features were slightly out of line with each other, as
they are on these things. Underneath the notice
continued: **ATTEMPTED ABDUCTION AT HEATHLAND
SCHOOL**. It gave the number of a police tip line.

Heathland was out west of our town, along the valley
road. Martha's school crested one of Bassetsbury's two
hills. I calculated the distance between them and
reached across Judith for the paper.

"When was this?"

"Wednesday. It was quite shocking. We're all . . . I
thought, if people knew to look out for him . . ."

"Is the girl OK?"

She frowned. "They're asking us to stay vigilant."

After the woman left, I stuck the flyer on the side
panel of our bay window and went over to help Martha
stack the shelves. I noticed that she was doing it with a
certain amount of care. When I came up beside her she
made a bit of eye contact and let me join in without
visibly resenting my presence. This was a win.

When your kid becomes an adolescent, all the rules change. It doesn't do to fall behind the curve. In Martha's first year at secondary school, I'd turned up for Sports Day just as I'd turned up for every Sports Day she'd ever had at primary school. I knew what to do: you shout like crazy for your kid, even — especially — if she's last, even if (as one year) she spends the whole of the skipping race thrashing on the grass, entangled in the rope. You yell and cheer and take pictures, and tell her she's brilliant. That first summer in secondary school, when Martha told me most parents didn't come, I thought she was trying to save me the trouble. I thought she'd be thrilled when I turned up, because that's how it had always worked before. Her event was rowing and I had waited under the trees, where four rowing machines had been lined up next to each other. It was so hot that day, even the visitors' lanyard I'd been given was making me sweat. Out of the corner of my eye I saw Liv's mum on the footpath which runs beside the school field. I called to her through the diamond wire fencing.

"You coming in, Helen?" I asked. "Is Livvie doing this event?"

She shook her head. "I'll watch from here. She doesn't want me inside."

Then I saw Martha coming towards us swinging a bottle of water, her vest top purple to match her house colours, a crowd of people around her. Because I had been so effectively trained by those earlier years, because I was so very much behind the curve, I failed to notice that not one of those people was another parent. I went to stand next to her machine because that's what you do, and when she slipped her feet into position and braced against the pulley I shouted, "G'orn Martha!" She flashed me a toxic look and I opened my mouth again because I was here now and couldn't reasonably leave, and had to account for my continued presence. "Go on, baby!" I yelled. "Pull!" I continued like that for exactly two minutes as she heaved on the pulley, the other kids glancing from me to her. At the end she staggered from the machine, sweat-drenched, and walked off without saying a word.

Of course, I laughed about it. But the rules had changed and they kept on changing, shifting with Martha's moods. She'd always been such a predictable person, a familiar landscape I'd lived with for years. It was rarely hard to guess what lay round the corner and if something did surprise me I could always trace its origins (bad day at school, hungry, coming down with something). Now, I never knew whether I was about to step on solid ground or something cunningly got up to look like it; whether I'd keep walking or feel the whole thing give way: the lurch, the squawking fall into the dark, the graceless landing.

Out in the square, Liv had arrived. She was clutching a paper bag and perching on a bollard, her face Klimt-pale against her red hair, arm white as she raised it to wave. Martha beckoned her in, and she shook her head. Izzy would come next, and they'd be ready to go.

It was only on the way out that I stood back and saw properly what Martha had done with the books. We always had front-facers at the end of shelves — they sell quicker and break up the line of spines — but she had inserted an extra one in the centre of each row. I chose them for saleability but she had picked for colour, starting with whites and moving through yellows and oranges, to a spectrum of reds which took up the whole of the next block of shelves: scarlets, then cherries, then crimsons and violets. After that came blues, and then turquoise, and a brief run of deepening greens. The final cover was a black full stop. There was something in her meticulousness, her aesthetic sensibility, that Elliot would love, I thought. But for some reason I stopped myself from telling her so.

When Izzy arrived I was locking up, struggling to pull the door towards me and turn the bottom key at the same time. The three of them hugged. I heard Izzy say, ". . . burst in and there was some half-naked old woman in there!" and they roared with laughter. She was showing off her purchase, a strappy black top decorated with a sequinned skull. The sequins glittered as she tilted it to and fro, glittered and fell, some of them, little flashes of light as they came loose and floated down to the cobbles. Already there were dull grey circles of adhesive dotting the image, and the price tag not even off it yet. "What's new, Jenny?" she asked.

Izzy had spent four years in Seattle. When she'd come back to Bassetsbury, the new kid again, she'd brought an accent which made her a novelty in her school. Liv and Martha, tasked with helping her to settle in, had pumped her for stories of life in the States, a location whose constant presence on TV had rendered it paradoxically exotic. Two years later, Izzy was still hanging on to that accent and — despite the common wisdom about girls' friendships, about three's a crowd — they had stuck together pretty well. Liv would always have the upper hand I thought, but Martha was devoted to Izzy in ways that were oddly tender.

"I'm fine," I said. "And how are you?"

But the other two had started to walk away and she followed them, throwing her reply back over her shoulder: "Awesome!"

The girls walked ahead of me, bumping up against each other. They were dressed in the same uniform: skinny jeans, layered tops, scarves. Like a girl band designed for wide appeal, they sported three different hair colours (Martha's dark bob between Izzy's blonde ponytail and Liv's red). There were other differences too, ones which looked small but, in the heated conditions of adolescence, changed everything. They were pieces of code written into the girls' bodies: Liv's breasts, months ahead of her friends', the slight roll of fat above Martha's beltline, the layers in Izzy's hair, its good-girl straightness cut out the previous summer. Martha slid her arm around Izzy's waist and pulled her close.

It's a terrible thing to acknowledge that you envy your own daughter. At some point in the preceding years, I had transformed from Snow White into the wicked queen, and now I coveted what they had, their collagen, their dress sizes, their energy. In my youth the songs always said the same thing, even when the words

42

were different: not us, we are far too young and clever. Martha thought that, too. Her certainties mocked mine. I walked faster to catch up. I could hear Izzy laughing and Martha's voice raised in tones of protest.

The old Methodist chapel had been desanctified for years, standing derelict up a steep side street. But now there were new signs — "Another Development by ISD Holdings", "No Hats, No Boots, No Hi-Vis, No Job!" — and clean chipboard across the empty windows.

The chapel door was much as it had been: broad, solidly wooden, with a twisted loop of metal as its handle. It had been graffitied in places, and elsewhere letters had been scratched into the paint, the initials of sometime lovers. I imagined them now, amused or embarrassed by the memory of those former assignations, or still together, each wishing they could do something even half as interesting as hopping over the boundary wall of an old chapel, snogging in the porch, and leaving their names behind them. The paint itself was peeling and bubbled. I wanted to lodge my nails under the fringes of it and snap some more off.

Liv banged on the door and waited. Martha set her back to the wall and bounced gently against it, facing out past me into the street.

"When did he say he'd be here?" she said.

Liv checked her phone. "Now." She knocked again. Izzy headed off into the scrubby grass round the back. A moment later there was laughter, and Izzy's shout.

"I've found him," she called. "Check it out!" Liv, Martha and I trooped round to find her pointing up to the chapel roof, waving.

There was a figure up there, standing black against the sky, and there must have been some trick to it, some flat part of the roof we couldn't see from below, because he seemed to be balancing on the perilous sharp edge of the gable. The figure waved back and shouted something. I couldn't hear the words, just the cadence; he was on his way down.

On the ground, Ian was ordinary again: hard-hatted, dust on his jeans and boots. I went to kiss him and then realised it was inappropriate but I was halfway there and couldn't pull back. We bumped cheeks and the side of his hat dug into my temple. I rested my hands on his upper arms, their muscularity a bit of a shock, a faint erotic charge pinging in my groin. But when we separated his gaze flicked down my body and he looked away in dismissal. I fixed my eyes on the girls so he wouldn't think I'd felt any differently about him.

Liv hugged Ian, sweet-talking, landed a smacking kiss on his cheek and rapped on the top of his hat. It took all of ten seconds for him to agree the sleepover. No problem, he said, but he had something to show us first.

He took us round to the back of the chapel where there was a door open. It led into the kitchen, or what had been the kitchen. You could map the cupboards back onto the walls, lines of bare plaster where the paint finished, a tap rising out of the floor to the height of the missing sink. There was a squat tower of hard hats on the floor, and a kettle, and in the corner a pile of KitKats, Jenga-stacked. I raised an eyebrow at Ian, who mugged back at me.

"Busted," he said and for a second we grinned at each other.

The girls had gone on ahead but he summoned them back and doled out a hat to each of us. "Keep them on," he said, rapping on Martha's. "All the time. And don't play silly buggers."

We felt our way through a dimly lit hall. I could hear Izzy giggling, someone tripped and shrieked, and I called out to Martha to be careful just as I stumbled myself, knocking against something that was sticking out from the wall. "Watch yourself there!" said Ian, close behind, his hand on the small of my back. I felt it printed on me even after he'd pulled away: his palm on my spine, his fingers braced against the cushioning of fat. I wondered if he'd felt the fat. Ahead, a door opened, and then we were in the front of the building. The girls opened a final door and at last there was light.

The chapel was vast and wrecked, smelling of timber and dust and something earthy. A single plastered board stood inside the entrance, incongruously pale, incongruously square, a harbinger of the flimsy walls Ian would soon be putting up. The girls stood in the middle of the space created by ripping out everything that had once filled this room. There were pews stacked round the edges, wood panelling, lines of railing. Trails of yellow flex meandered across the floor, and twin-eyed yellow lights stood like obliging robots next to a wooden construction that might once have been the altar. On the wall above it there was an arc of lettering in relief: *O Worship the LORD in the Beauty of Holiness.*

"OK," said Ian, his voice echoing in the space. "You're going to love this." He started to issue instructions to the girls, getting them to move the lamps into new positions. I went over to the altar and squatted down to look at it more closely. I ran the sleeve of my fleece across one of the panels, rubbing at the carving with my wrist.

"Oi!" I heard him shout. There was a clatter, and I looked up to see Izzy and Martha struggling to prevent a lamp from heeling over. Ian caught it in one hand and set it straight. "Second thoughts," he said. "Stick to what you're good at, ladies."

The panelling was beautiful, a line of scalloped arches carved across its base. I ran my fingers inside the curves, feeling the knots catch on my skin. Ian was arranging the lamps in a triangle at the end of the chapel. "Hey," I called to him. "What's going to happen to all this wood?"

"We'll reclaim it," he said. "We use it for things like doors and window seats. Buyers love all that."

"OK. I just thought . . ."

"Don't worry," he said. "It won't go to waste."

Martha detached herself from the others, and came over. "Look at this," I said. "It's lovely."

She crouched down beside me, and glanced across to where Liv and Izzy were jumping up and down, trying to pull themselves onto one of the windowsills. "He's happy for me to stay over," she said.

"Yeah, I know."

"So . . . I'm fine here. I'll go to Liv's after."

I waited for her to say something else. She cocked her head towards the door. The hard hat, too big for her, slopped sideways as she did it and I was assailed by this memory: Martha was nine, we were at the park. The council had just put in a water feature, a very shallow, very broad paddling pool. Little jets sprouted from it intermittently and kids rushed to press down on them, spraying water sideways over themselves and anyone else in the vicinity. I was standing in the centre of the pool where the spray couldn't reach me, holding up my maxi dress so it didn't get wet. I couldn't do much else; both hands were occupied. Martha managed to squash one of the jets and got soaked from the waist down. I readied myself to mete out some kind of standard-issue parental chiding, but before I could say anything she'd sploshed over and was crouching next to me. She took handfuls of water and patted them down my calves. My first response (I would always be a bit ashamed of this later) was to feel embarrassed. It was such an odd and intimate thing. But she grinned up at me and kept doing it, kept sluicing water down my calves and waiting for me to see how much fun it was, and I was overwhelmed, choked up. It took every bit of acting I could muster to treat it lightly. Sometimes, in later years, I made myself remember that afternoon. I told myself: this is the same girl.

At his end of the chapel, Ian adjusted one of the lamps. A beam of light travelled across the floor and started climbing the wall.

"Go to the back," he said. "You'll get a better view."

"Please?" said Martha. "I'll see you tomorrow."

"I can't go now," I said. "It'd be really rude."

Martha's bottom lip pleated and bulged, as if she could shove me out of there with it. "I can't believe you wanted to come here," she said. "Izzy's mum didn't!"

She spoke loudly enough that Ian frowned in our direction. "You ready for this?" he asked.

Martha kept her eyes on me. "Please. Just. Go," she said. I eased up with a grunt, patting her on the shoulder, calculating that it was the most she'd permit.

"I'm sorry," I told him. "I have to go. Thanks so much for having her."

He raised his hand and Martha emitted a noisy sigh. As I turned into the side hall there was a bang behind me — the chapel doors slamming shut — and a cry went up from inside, the girls' voices raised in admiration.

Outside, the light was fading. It was the change of shift, shoppers deserting the high street while early drinkers began to arrive. I thought about Martha and my newly vacant Saturday night. I thought, just briefly, about an alternative existence in which I might be going home to her, let's say, *brother* — a kid young enough to welcome my company. I hadn't known the gender of the first baby I'd lost; it had all happened so early. The second was a boy.

I walked past the back of the old Woolworths, boarded up, still waiting for its new tenant, past the hippy shop and the newsagents and the greasy spoon café, and was almost at the convenience store when four men came out of it — boys, really, just a few years older than Martha. They wore clean trainers and had the raw look of the newly shaved. They tumbled out and into my path, so we had to dodge each other. "Sorry," we all said. "Sorry". And I noticed how they each gave me the same look, a flick-flick, just as Ian had done: a flick to register my physical presence, a flick away again. I turned round to look at them walking off, but they didn't do the same.

It sounds stupid that this should be any kind of shock, but it was. *Pow!* I was invisible. I had been visible not so long ago, walking down the street as if attention were my due, the sticky gaze of passers-by settling on my body, and this — this was all wrong. That person was the real me. I wanted to shuck off the fake one so I could be her again.

The real me wore tight, short dresses that I never had to hold in my tummy for, clumpy DMs ("Here comes Max Wall," Dad would say). Blissed out in some club and even after the comedown, days later when I knew that we didn't really all love each other, there were things I could still take for granted; a lot of the time, I'd get to look away first.

Suddenly, getting home seemed like the most tremendously important thing. I crossed over the hill road and cut down the footpath that ran behind the station. The wind barrelled along it, causing an empty crisp packet to levitate and spin in front of me. It made a skidding touchdown then took off again.

The path came out near the railway tunnel. I looked down its dark length, the opening at the other end a frame for a stretch of wall. I could see what was written on that wall — *suk my cock* — and thought of the woman who'd come into my shop and the flyer she'd given me; I felt a stirring of unease.

The mouth of the tunnel carried a sign detailing railway byelaws. A concrete rubbish bin stood sentinel. Inside, every step was a double-knock, echoing off the sides. One of the lights worked; you could see graffiti-resistant paint encrusted on the walls. Undaunted, Bassetsbury's artists had colonised the ceiling, a curve of riveted metal reminiscent of a ship's hull. There was a jumble of names: ChillBoy, Magik, Jammz. There were perfunctory drawings of penises. On the other side of the tunnel was home, and Elliot.

When I emerged, the dusk had thickened to darkness. There was a click from a streetlamp above me and suddenly I was held in a pillar of light, its sodium glare dazzling me so that I stood at its centre, my eyes shut tight, seeing nothing but my own blood.

Elliot was doing something in the shed when I got home; I could see him moving in the rectangle of its window, lit by a bare bulb. I took our party invitation from my handbag and set it on the counter where he'd see it. Slipping off my coat, I saw that one arm was clouded with a white powder, probably from the chapel. I banged away, but it was a dry cleaning job. And then I realised I'd managed to carry the bag of crappy donations — the ones which should have been next door with Allie in the first place — all the way home with me, rather than dropping it off in her shop. I sat on a kitchen chair and looked through the stuff again, wondering how much would be lost to the charity if I just binned it all. Chess set, coloured pencils . . . they might sell. The fancy-dress mask had found its way to the bottom of the bag. It was black, edged in gold braid, swoops of gold glitter decorating the cheeks and forehead. Beautiful, but not worth the trouble of saving; one side of the elastic had come untethered. If I bothered to rethread it, Allie's shop might make twenty pence.

In a moment of detachment I saw myself, hunched over a pile of tat in my kitchen, planning to fix it so that the shops might make a few extra pence. A pathetic, scrabbling figure (the memory of Allie's impersonation returned: my rounded shoulders, my defensive hands). A negligible person; someone you'd look past. I held up the mask to my eyes and it blinkered me, obscuring half of what I might see. It was nice behind there, darkly comforting. Elliot noticed me then. He peered over his reading glasses, frowning, and knocked on the shed window. I snatched the mask away and, the second I did, I hated myself for doing it. Stuff it, I thought. I don't care if he thinks I look stupid. Let him see what a real woman looks like in one of these things. Let him deal with that.

He waved. And then it happened: I had an idea.

I had an idea that changed everything.

CHAPTER
THREE

That night I went up to bed early, thinking I'd start a new novel. On my way past Martha's room, I noticed her own book splayed on the bed and hoped she wouldn't regret leaving it here while she was out for the night; there is a particular kind of panic which sets in if you're a compulsive reader caught short. I found myself wondering what sort of fictional world she inhabited these days and, on an impulse, took the novel with me. I pulled her door shut afterwards, as I always did when she wasn't at home because I hated seeing into her empty room.

I'd expected to skim-read, but was drawn in quickly despite myself. It was compelling: a dystopian future, a heroic girl standing alone to protect her sister. Brave girls, I thought, that's what Martha liked. There was never much evidence of boys and shoes and shopping in her choices. Brave girls and — was I pushing this one? — family loyalty. Maybe a yearning for siblings? No, not that. A desire for intensity.

At one point in my own childhood — I'd have been maybe ten — I spent most of a year in serial readings of *The Railway Children*, returning to the first page as soon as I'd finished the last. It was intensity I sought there: Bobbie standing small on the track, waving a red petticoat to stop the train. Bobbie jumping onto the rails as the train bore down, waving as it finally slowed, waving as it stopped and then long afterwards, until she fainted. I don't think I was any different from most girls in wanting to be Bobbie rather than her dreamy little sister Phyllis (or, a bit later, Jo March rather than Beth, or Jane Eyre rather than Helen Burns). The stories pushed us that way, towards adventure. I grew up with those narratives and then I entered adult life, and discovered I was Phyllis after all.

Downstairs, Elliot was playing his music; something on the bedside table rattled with the bass notes. I read for longer than I'd intended, until I was drowsy and the Hammond organ had faded. A door shut, a light-switch clicked. I turned mine off, too. Elliot's progress was measured in noise: the creak of the stairs, the gulp of water down the plughole as he cleaned his teeth, his whispered *bugger!* as he stumbled against the bed in the dark.

"Jen?" he whispered, reaching across to find me.

"Jen?" He rubbed my neck with his knuckle, and I realised I could predict exactly what he'd do next and wished very much that I couldn't. I caught his hand in mine and slipped his index finger into my mouth. He knew all my moves too. I found myself wondering if he was ever disappointed about that. "I love it when we're filthy," he'd told me once. I'd loved it too, but filth, when I considered it now, seemed to be mainly knackering. Instead, we had organised desire into an efficient sequence: conveyor-belt sex. How had we got here? No big bust-up, no affair or deception, just age and time and work and parenthood and all those other co-conspirators, acting upon us by increments. All the conversations that got stuck in logistics and never moved on, the drop-down lists of chores that filled my head when we were together, the endless household information that passed between us. There was no lack of love — never that. But I couldn't have predicted in those first, heady months, how unfeasibly dull love might turn out to be.

Elliot did the next part, where he moved his hand across my collarbone and down to my breasts, where his fingers snagged on my nipples and made them stiffen as if they knew their cues, too.

I shifted slightly, and his hand fell lower, to my belly, and I had to turn quickly before it spent any more time there.

"Hey, honey," he said, and we did the kissing part and I made the noises, and we did the next bit where he went down on me and I came once, and as I came I was thinking of Elliot, only of him, but Elliot in our heedless days, puckish and unfastidious, going down on me in someone's spare room at a party and me hoping that no one would come in and also hoping someone would. He tried to move me on top of him as he did one time in two, but I couldn't bear the visuals so I pulled him inside me instead. It was then that I thought of the woman in the comic, of how she might look if she were straddling Elliot (breasts high, belly flat, mouth red and open), and any desire I felt evaporated.

I did the nails thing and the shouting thing.

"Yes," I said. "Oh God, yes," and then he came.

We lay there for a bit and I asked him to push the duvet back over my side.

"Did you . . . was that good?" he said.

"Uh-huh," I said.

He kicked the duvet over and cold air puffed across my body. He leaned over to kiss me.

"Night night."

After he'd settled I stayed lying on my back, looking up at the ceiling. Outside, a train trundled in towards the station, easing to a halt with a sigh.

"Elliot?"

"Hmm?"

But I bottled it. Not even stuffed up with disappointment and self-loathing, not even in the dark, where I didn't have to look at him as I talked, could I bring myself to say: *this is how you made me feel*. So I didn't say anything at all. I said, "I love you," because it was true, and I lay there until his breathing grew slow and regular. Don't tell him how you feel then, I thought as sleep came for me, as I rolled over and clenched my fists under my chest. Don't tell him. *Show* him.

CHAPTER
FOUR

In the weeks before Allie's party, I did all the usual
jobs. I tidied up, I got Martha out of the door in the
mornings, I kept shop. They were necessary activities,
but I did them with half my attention because, in
between, I had new things to do. One afternoon I
visited a local seamstress. She worked in her spare
bedroom. There was a notice on the wall asking
customers not to let their shoes drop onto the floor as
they undressed; it would upset the parrot that lived
downstairs.

"I've got a sketch here," I said, handing her a piece of
paper. "It's not great but . . . you get the idea?"

She frowned at the image. Below us, the parrot gave
a squawk. "You want me to . . .?"

"Yes. Please." I'd coloured it in and added
explanatory notes.

She took off her glasses and rubbed her forehead. "I
once had a man in here who wanted me to sew a pouch
into his underpants," she said. "I never asked what it
was for, but I told him: I don't do that kind of thing."

The minute I'm out of the door, I thought, I'm going
to text this to Allie. She'll love it. Then I remembered

that it was all a secret for now, and that I couldn't breathe a word. A little frisson went through me.

"I don't blame you," I said. "But this is just for a fancy-dress party."

On the wall was a case of thread: dozens of cylinders arranged in a spectrum, several shades of every colour, so she could pick exactly what she needed. I reached up and popped one of them out of the holder. "This is perfect," I told her.

I toured the charity shops of Bassetsbury, only to find exactly what I wanted, exactly where I didn't want to find it: next door, in Allie's shop. I waited until she was off duty and bought it as teenagers used to buy condoms, smuggled out amongst a pile of unnecessary things, buzzing with a teenage thrill.

It was the wrong colour, but I could fix that. Two days later, Martha safely upstairs, I stuck it in the washing machine along with some fabric dye and a load of salt. I called her down for tea and we ate chicken pie together at the kitchen table, the machine churning in the background, my brilliant idea slopping about in it as we ate.

I rummaged through my kitchen drawers. I went into haberdashers' and DIY stores. I spent a long time in an underwear department before choosing the Sylph Easy-On High-Waist Brief. I knew, from previous experience, that it would simply redistribute the fat, great drifts of it higher up my belly and down my thighs, but I bought it anyway.

The shoes came last. I took the Park 'n' Ride into the next town along and spent the morning in wedges, stilettos, strappy diamanté sandals. In shop after shop I pulled off my trainers and tottered up and down, peering at the low-level mirrors running under the display shelves. When I found the glossy patents — stacked soles, flared heels, three inches off the ground — I hesitated; they were so emphatically not me. Then I thought about the not-woman teetering on the edge of that drop and remembered the point I was making. I bought them before I could change my mind.

To keep the element of surprise, I made sure I was alone when I got ready for the party. The week before, I told Elliot it would take ages to close up the shop, so I'd get changed in town and meet him there. He was perfectly happy with this arrangement. With a couple of days to go, he had shown us his own costume. He made me and Martha sit in the lounge, and disappeared out of the back door into the shed. A few minutes later I heard him coming down the garden path and through the kitchen, clanking slightly. "Close your eyes," he called, and I could hear how pleased with himself he was.

"Shit!" said Martha, when she opened hers.

"Don't say shit," I told her, but in truth she was probably understating it. Elliot was dressed in a frock coat, tight trousers, gaiters and boots. He wore a cravat but, instead of a waistcoat, it was neatly tucked into a brass breastplate, the sort you might see on a medieval soldier. He had a top hat, a pair of old-fashioned flying goggles wrapped round the crown, and more eyewear pushed to the end of his nose: a pair of sunglasses. The lenses were round, their darkened glass seeming to float free of the metal rims. There was a gauntlet on his left wrist to match the breastplate, and further metalwork in his hand: a weapon, half-Victorian pistol, half-Gatling gun, which he pointed aloft.

"Dad, that's actually cool," said Martha. Elliot grinned at her.

"What's that?" I asked. "That's . . . Victorian?"

"It's steampunk," Martha said, as if my not knowing it was an affront to her. My annoyance rose, but I pressed it down.

"OK," I said. "I knew that." But she was peering at the gun, and Elliot was pointing out some detail on it; neither of them had heard me.

"Wait till you see my costume!" I said.

"I'm sure it'll be great," said Elliot, his eyes still on the barrel.

"Can you make me a costume, Dad?" asked Martha. "Exactly like this?"

Not just annoyance rising up then, but fully developed resentment, the same old gripe: that I got to do the hard yards, the boring stuff, and Elliot got to tinker in his shed and dazzle her. I'd talked with him about this imbalance once or twice, and he'd pointed out instances of his own paternal dullness (the odd signing of a homework diary, the occasional request that she tidy up). The more patient and evidence-based Elliot got, the more enraged I became. We quickly descended into point-scoring, listing our various parental activities, me arguing that they should be weighted for tedium and unpopularity, him suggesting I needed to lighten up a bit, at which point things usually got sticky. In the end, I'd mutter something like: stuff it, it's as dull for me as it is for her. I don't know why I bother.

I hated my own martyrdom. I hated the passive-aggressive way I'd crash around the kitchen afterwards. Most of all, I hated how impossible it seemed to change anything, how unimaginable that Elliot might pay attention to the details of Martha's life, or that I might ignore them.

Now, as Martha cooed over the costume and Elliot posed jokily in it, I thought: no, really. Wait till they see me.

On the day of the party I took my costume to the shop and stowed it in one of the lockers, pushing the hasp into place to deter casual discovery. Nobody — not Allie, not Elliot, nor anyone else — would see me before I was ready to make my entrance. I worked alongside Judith for the afternoon, sneaking into the stockroom to peek at the costume whenever I could, then coming back out into the shop as if everything was normal. I sent Judith home early, closed up and marked time, working through my emails. When I got too excited to focus on them, I sat behind my till with a book of short stories and tried to focus on that instead.

When it was time to get ready, I switched off the shop lights and went into the stockroom to change. I took off my fleece, my jeans, my socks and trainers, even my bra and greying pants, so that I finally stood naked, shivering, next to the piles of unread celebrity biographies, the cookbooks nobody cooked from anymore, the unwanted ruminations of motoring journalists. I looked up and caught a glimpse of my body in the small mirror hung next to the lockers: the swell of pale flesh at the top of my arm, the furrow from my bra strap ploughing down my shoulder. I had a sudden, terrible plunge of doubt. I think I said, "Oh, no!" or something equally useless, and I stared down at my body.

And then I knew what a stupid idea this had been. You desire *that*, I'd be telling Elliot. But you've got *this*. And *this* was me, and it was something to avert the gaze from, something to laugh at. Elliot wouldn't get it, I couldn't carry it off. They'd think I was trying to be funny. Or worse — they'd think I was trying to be sexy. I sat on the chair and wrapped my arms around myself. I ran through my options: plead illness, turn up in my normal clothes. I looked at the door and imagined walking out of it, and just as the comfort of that possibility hit me, I realised I'd felt this way many times before.

Every single performance I had ever done, I'd got stage fright just beforehand and had to check the exits. On the Monday I'd filmed that TV ad, I'd turned up to the studio after two hours of sleep, jittery as hell, laying down my escape route like a ball of string behind me. But I'd put on the dress and they'd done my make-up, and I'd delivered my line. Three months later kids were saying that line in every playground in the country. And all the rest of the time, when backstage was an empty classroom or a staff toilet, when I'd fantasise about bolting into the teachers' car park, I'd grit my teeth and put on the dress, and then I'd become Titania, or Juliet, or Lady Macbeth.

So, put on the dress. Or — for God's sake — put on the pants! Put on your new bra, at the very least. I did, and then I coaxed myself into another garment, and then another, talking myself into each one until I was, finally, fully costumed. I told myself to put on some make-up and I did that, too.

The little mirror was no good so I went into the darkness of the shop, wobbling on my new heels, and moved the card stand away from the window. I stood well back, keeping my eyes fixed on the light switch, nervous of what I'd see when the room lit up and the window became a mirror. I flicked the switch. I turned.

The first thing I saw was red. Red on my lips, red lacing up the front of my black corset, red lining my black cape, framing the shape of my body. I saw what that shape was, that it was less shaming than I'd feared it might be: the *out* of breasts rendered voluptuous by the twin forces of the corset and a push-up bra; the *in* of my waist not the sharp descent I'd want — the bowed line of boning, the roll of fat between corset and skirt — but an *in* nonetheless. Slung low on my hips, a tool belt (keys, mobile phone, likely-looking knife designed for cutting cheese). My fists clenched in their satin gloves, the mask dangled from one hand.

If they do laugh at me, I thought, it won't be because I fall over, and I took a few more steps in those perilous, glossy shoes, towards the window, so I could watch myself approaching. I noticed that my shoulders were back and my breasts forward, that my chin was up. I did this a few times, back and forth, until I felt more secure.

Then I put on the mask, its curls of glitter flickering in the light. I put it on and my field of vision contracted: no periphery any more, just the figure in the window, massy and tentative. For a second I wondered: blimey, will they know it's me? And then I thought: what if it weren't? What's the difference between other people not knowing who you are, and you actually becoming someone else? In this mask, I could be anyone I bloody well wanted. The thought was exhilarating, a thermal under my cape, lifting me right out of the shop, through the back door, through the gate and into the churchyard, sending me on my way.

The churchyard was dark but bounded on two sides by roads; yellow streetlight bled in, enough for me to see the path curving between the gravestones. It was smoothly tarmacked, and as I strode up it towards the road I practised my new walk which was, in truth, more of a strut, my legs crossing slightly in front of me, my hips rolling.

I reached a good vantage point halfway up and stopped, feet planted wide, arms folded, as I'd practised. It was cold, but the cape whipped satisfyingly about my shoulders, lifted by the collusive wind. At that moment, it didn't feel such a leap to imagine myself as a sentinel, a protector, my presence alone making people feel safe and secure. I scanned the deserted streets, the shuttered shops, an alleyway, its entrance a shadowy hollow. I was ready to brave danger, to face down evil. I was ready to —

A noise among the gravestones.

I flinched. That was the first thing. I couldn't help it. Then the noise came again and I realised it was laughter. Someone hunkered down by the churchyard wall. Had they seen me flinch? I thought about pretending I hadn't heard them, just slipping out quietly, but then two hands were suddenly raised, as if in surrender, from behind one of the gravestones. A boy rose up into the half-light borrowed from the streetlamps, and then a couple of girls — hands held high, a cigarette apiece — and another boy, his face hidden in his hood. They were barely older than Martha.

"Fat Girl," said the first boy, grinning at me. "Only you can save us." One of the girls reached out a puffa-jacketed arm and slapped him on the shoulder — "Don't be a dick, Ollie" — but the other kids sniggered.

"Hey! That's very rude," I said, forcing myself to stand straight, and he laughed all over again, and my arms folded automatically over my belly.

He looked at me and then he winked at the girl. He waved in the direction of the road, and behind the flick of his hand, I was sure I caught another movement in the street beyond. "Haven't you got to go and save the world?" he said. "Or whatever?"

"Very funny," I said.

Puffa girl took a drag on her cigarette. "Let's just go," she said.

"No!" said Ollie, and to me: "I mean it, Chunky. Piss off!"

"I beg your pardon?" I took a step towards him.

He came out from behind the headstone and, again, I thought I saw something moving beyond the low graveyard wall, something out in the street. But when I looked once more, everything was still. He drew closer and I saw the wet shine of his hair, his skin heaving with acne. "Ollie," said the other boy, weary.

Ollie stepped onto the path. "I said, piss off," he told me. He lifted his hand and when it was level with my face he turned it, and stuck his middle finger skywards.

"You little . . ."

I wasn't imagining it. Behind Ollie's left shoulder, in the entrance to the alleyway opposite, there was a flicker of movement. Then I saw a boot, the hem of a coat, and there was a noise, a grunt of effort. Ollie pulled a phone from his pocket. I walked past him out of the churchyard. There was a flash — my silhouette against a shopfront — and a rattling bang ahead.

Drawing level with the alleyway, I could see what was happening. A man and a woman were scuffling against the wooden fence. He was bald and paunchy, much bigger than the woman, who was curling over to protect herself. Her long hair fell forward, screening her face. What he wanted, I could see immediately, was the handbag. It was slung across her body. She'd anchored the strap in her armpit.

"Bitch!" he said, slamming his hand into the back of her head. She staggered against the fence. My belly went solid.

The kids had followed me onto the pavement, Ollie's face twitching with every shout and blow. "Get out of here!" I told them. The woman pulled up her head trying to locate me, but the attacker got to her first, grasping her hair and wrenching her head back. She yelled out and grabbed his fist. Don't get involved. They always say don't get involved. He'd beat the shit out of me. I looked down the street both ways, hoping for the police, hoping for a security guard from the shopping centre, hoping for a man. God, he was going to kill her.

"Give him the bag!" I reached down to my tool belt and felt for my mobile.

She shouted something in a language I didn't understand, the last syllable morphing into a cry as he gave a vicious tug. He'd maim her, damage her for life. I stepped towards them: off the pavement, into the middle of the road. Why wasn't she giving him what he wanted?

"Police," I whimpered, when the operator answered.

The man reached round, panting, to where the bag hung unprotected, and started to pull it off her. She wriggled in his grasp.

"All Saints Road. There's a woman being robbed. Come quick. She's being hurt."

The man nearly had the bag now, the woman clinging to the strap as it was wrenched from her. She looked about and saw me for the first time. For a second her body, which had fought and evaded and struggled all the while, stopped moving. The strap slipped away from her. Thank God.

She looked straight at me. She called out "Help!", and then several things happened at once.

"Lights and sirens," said the operator.

The attacker flung the bag behind him, so that it hit the fence and fell down onto the path. I thought he'd pick it up and run, but he didn't. He held the woman steady and raised his fist.

"No!" I shouted.

He looked me up and down once, then he laughed — he *laughed* — and he jerked his arm back for the punch.

I can't explain what I did next. I don't think I could have controlled it. I was aware of a great roar, founded deep in my belly, ripping its way up through my guts and entering the world in a bellow through my open mouth. An electric jolt galvanised my muscles and suddenly — like a jump-cut, like the panels of a comic book — I wasn't watching the scene anymore; I was in it.

CHAPTER
FIVE

Panel 1: Superhero in the centre of the frame, fists clenched, teeth bared. Behind the mask, her eyes are narrowed.

Panel 2: The victim's mouth is bleeding, red on her chin and lips, red on her hand where she's touched her face. She's crouched against the fence. The man is stooping to pick up the handbag. In the corner of the frame, a gloved arm reaches towards him.

Panel 3: The man bats it aside. Superhero's face registers shock.

Panel 4 [Extreme close-up]: The man's mouth, sneering. [Speech balloon]: *"Oh, for fuck's sake."*

Panel 5: A scarlet shoe, sharp-heeled, kicks at the man's leg. Motion lines stream out behind it. [Sound effect]: *CRUMP!*

Panel 6: The man's open hand connects with Superhero's face. Her head skews sideways. [Sound effect]: *SMAK!*

Panel 7: [Background]: the man flees down the alleyway into darkness. [Foreground]: the light glints off the knife in Superhero's tool belt.

Panel 8: [Page-width]: At the extreme right-hand side of the panel, the man is running. He has nearly exited the frame. At the extreme left-hand side of the panel, Superhero is in pursuit. Between them is a long stretch of fencing daubed with red graffiti. Superhero shouts [speech balloon]: *"Come back, you bastard!"*

Panel 9: [close-up]: The attacker's foot catches on a manhole cover.

Panel 10: The attacker falls to the ground. His chin scrapes the tarmac [Sound effect:] *OOF!*

Panel 11: [Splash panel]: The victim sits on the ground against the fence, clutching the handbag to her chest. She looks down the path towards Superhero. Her face registers incredulity. The attacker lies face down on the ground, his cheek pressed to the tarmac, his chin bleeding. Superhero sits on his back. The knees of her tights are torn. With both hands, she bends the man's arm behind him. Her face registers euphoria.

CHAPTER
SIX

Oh God, for a few seconds I was a superhero. I was. The rush of it! A glut of chemicals slamming into my blood, a lightness in my belly, the unburdening of violence. It was a kind of frenzied passion, and when it was over the world was different.

"Are you OK?" I shouted to the woman. "Tell me you're OK."

She'd been letting out gasping sobs, pushing herself away from him, against the fence. Now she was breathing more regularly. "Thank you," she called, her mouth full of Eastern Europe. "I'm alright." She was, and I was too — better than alright. I was magnificent and powerful, righter than I'd ever been. The man snarled and wriggled, and I shoved his arm higher, puffing a bit with the effort of keeping it there.

"If you're really alright, please get over here," I said, as the man roiled beneath me. I shifted my weight forward and he said "Bitch!"

"There's nothing to be afraid of," I said, as he bucked and jerked, my own words knocked out of kilter with the effort of keeping him down. "We can do this together. We can stop him hurting anyone else." Finally, she scrambled over, letting herself drop hard onto his back, forcing his breath out in a grunt.

"Yes!" I said, craning round to look, sobering slightly when I saw the blood on her face, the blotches of mascara around her eyes. Her coat had been pulled open in the struggle; underneath she wore a blue tabard, *Spotless Cleaning* embroidered over the left breast.

"That's right," I told her. "Stay there. Police'll be here soon." Behind me there was a commotion as he kicked at her and she let loose a mother-tongue insult which didn't need translation.

I looked round for a rock or brick or fragment of broken glass — anything I might use as a weapon to subdue him. Then I remembered the cheese knife in my tool belt. It looked like a little scimitar. The curving blade was dull, but the double-spike at its end might keep him quiet for a while.

"You think you can hold me till the police get here?" he said, snorting a laugh. The woman did something — I felt him convulse — and the laugh was cut off. He twisted his head to look at us and his body twisted with it. I yanked at his arm. "It's a fucking joke," he said. "They get here, I'm away for a few weeks, then I come and find you both."

"Rubbish!" I said. I unsheathed the knife, keeping it out of the man's eyeline, and pressed the tip into his neck so that it made a little crater in his skin but didn't break the surface. Then I remembered how the nurse pricks your finger before you give blood: a single jab, quick and deep. It worked. He let out a yelp and a trail of red ran down his skin, detouring round the curve of the blade.

"You come and find us, and you'll regret it," I told him. And I called behind me, to the woman: "He's talking nonsense. You'll be fine."

The man started to rise and I bounced heavily twice, landing between his shoulders; two barks as the air was jerked out of him. I felt the woman shift. She said, "Why you dressed like this?"

I looked down at myself; one shoe had come off and was now lying next to the fence. My tights were ripped, my gloves were dirty, and my view of it all was hindered by the mask, knocked askew in the fight. My cheek burned where he had hit me.

"Fancy dress," I told her, with an odd sense of deflation.

From the road outside came the faintest click, a sound I recognised — too late — as the gear change on a bicycle. By the time I'd gathered myself to shout ("Help! In here!") a bike had already whisked across the opening to the alleyway, a subliminal image of a man pressed forward over the handlebars, a rucksack bearing down on him from behind.

"Why didn't you give him your bag?" I asked the woman. "It was all he wanted."

She snorted. "So, is my fault?"

"No! God, no." The man heaved up and to make my point, I stabbed his neck again. He stopped moving and once he was properly still, I felt her tap on my back. I risked one quick glance behind, quick enough that the mugger couldn't take advantage.

She was holding up a picture of a girl: perhaps five years old, blonde ponytail, wearing a very obviously home-knitted cardigan. "My Olenka," said the woman. "Only one." And I didn't know if she meant the child or the photograph.

In the distance, a car turning in from the hill road. "What's your name?" said the woman. I opened my mouth to tell her and it seemed entirely unlikely that my own name would come out. I was wondering what would emerge — I think I had as little an idea as she did, right then — when at last there were sirens and the man gave a lunge. I wrenched his arm towards his shoulder and he uttered a sharp cry, and then there were shouts and booted footsteps echoing off the sides of the path, blue strobing the air, and the woman called "Help! Here!" She stood and he finally shook himself free, rolling me onto the ground. I scrambled up, tucking the knife into my tool belt, and was shoved to one side by a copper sprinting past in pursuit. They disappeared into the darkness.

The woman was already being tended to by a second officer. This one was shortish, dense, filling her uniform as sand fills a bag. She was peering at the victim's bloodied face and making a call on her radio. As I walked past she holstered it and reached out to stop me. "You're a witn—" she said, easing to a stop in the middle of the word as she saw my costume. She sighed. "Witness. Wait here. We'll need a statement."

Higher up the path, her partner had come back into view, pushing the handcuffed mugger ahead of him. I'd brought him down. Me. The police hadn't been anywhere in sight.

"What's your name?" I heard the copper ask the woman, and that was when I knew I wouldn't stick around long enough to be asked the same thing. How dull, I thought — in that heedless moment, all my usual obedience forgotten — how tedious to lay claim to my name, my address. How dissatisfying to be a *witness*. Witnesses watched other people do things; I'd made something new happen. The man was in custody and the victim's evidence would see him punished. They didn't need me now. More fun by far to slip back into the dark, a masked mystery.

I took off my shoe, no chance of rescuing the other one, and started padding gently down the alleyway. I kept expecting to be called back, but the call didn't come and I made it to the end unchallenged. I turned out of the entrance and walked, then walked faster, then jogged along the road away from the scene, little stones lodging themselves into my feet so that I cried out, low and percussive, as I ran. Finally there was a shout — "Hey!" from the policewoman — and I looked round to see her coming after me. But then the attacker rushed out behind her, broken free from the other copper. She turned quickly and — one, two — felled him with intimidating economy, a swift movement of the leg, of the arm, and he was on the ground. I almost faltered — such effortless strength, she was already bending over him with a half-smile — but then she raised her head to look at me and I turned again and pelted away.

"Hey!" she called out. "Wonderwoman! You can't fight crime in high heels!"

I ran through the streets until I was far enough away. My feet were bleeding and I was retching for air. I came to a stop against the wall of a pub and I leaned there for a while, letting my breath slow down, remembering who I was.

Wondering what to do next.

CHAPTER
SEVEN

Monday morning, a slab of sun lying across the churchyard, steam rising from the damp wood of the bench. In my hand was a grocery receipt dating from July 2001, triple-folded because it was so long, inserted halfway through *The Power Of Now*. Enough groceries to feed a hungry family for a month I reckoned, which was just as well because I also reckoned that the receipt's owner had been inspired by the book to grab *now* by the horns. She'd dashed out to the supermarket and filled her family's larder, then left a note bidding them goodbye and reminding them to recycle. After a year exploring the Andes by microlight she'd returned sun-lined, wind-hardened, and never shopped for groceries again.

Allie hadn't seen me yet. She was trudging along the pavement, carrier bag in hand — milk and a paper, I guessed. She was mouthing something, talking to herself. I thought it might embarrass her to be caught doing it so I looked elsewhere, at the gravestones Ollie and his friends had hidden behind, over the churchyard wall at the bridal shop where my silhouette had been projected and just along from there, the alley where I'd been . . . quite incredible.

I was back at the scene of the crime, disguised as an ordinary woman. I'd thought there might be police tape at the entrance to the alleyway, but there was nothing. I'd already looked for the shoe I'd had to leave behind, but it was gone. It reminded me of those scenes you see on *CSI*: everything quite normal to the naked eye, but if you turned on the UV the evidence would *shine*.

Allie turned down the churchyard path and into my field of vision.

"Playing hooky, Jen?"

"There's three volunteers in there this morning. I'm cluttering up the stockroom. Come and sit down." I shuffled along the bench and she settled next to me.

"This seat's soaking."

"I know. After a while you don't notice it."

Allie put down the bag and we sat in silence. "I feel crapulous," she said, after a bit. "I didn't even drink that much. Did I? And I had all of yesterday to get over it. Fucking birthday. Thirty-seven. Can I still say mid-thirties?"

"For as long as you want," I told her.

"Every year, it's like I'm growing less . . . I don't know, robust. Maybe I'm getting too old for this."

"Sod that," I said. "You had a fabulous time, so sod it. And you were a very beautiful Josephine Baker."

Allie looked at me. "And you were a great . . . what were you again?"

Here's how you dress when you're an hour late for your best friend's party because you have temporarily become a superhero: you pull on a hippyish top and long skirt, your mind elsewhere ("Oh my God!" you

77

say, over and over again, stunned at yourself, at your daring and courage). You apply plasters to your bleeding feet and suddenly you feel weepy and you have to stop for a cry. You put on your most comfortable shoes. You borrow a scarf from your daughter's room and you're struck again by the brilliance of what just happened. You wrap the scarf round your head and borrow the glass stopper from a wine decanter to stand in for a crystal ball. When you arrive — late, buzzing, to a roomful of Michael Jackson and Winston Churchill and Elizabeth I — your steampunk husband raises his gauntlet to you in greeting. Josephine Baker pushes a glass of wine into your hand and you realise that in about thirty seconds the soaring intensity you have just experienced will mutate into a funny anecdote, and that you just can't bear to let it go so quickly. You tell yourself this isn't the moment. There will be a party, and there will be a morning after. You can tell them then.

"I was Gypsy Rose Lee," I said.

"Right," said Allie. "You were seriously on form."

I'd thought quite carefully about how to put it so she'd understand. I didn't know whether I was longing for her to find out, or dreading it — both, I think.

"Listen to me, Al," I said. "I've got something amazing to tell you." There was a rustle next to the bench as the contents of her bag keeled over. She nudged it with her foot and the *Bassetsbury Examiner* flopped out onto the path. I caught the headlines: **COUNCILLOR SLAMS "RACIST" GRAFFITI, HEATHLAND GIRL IN ATTEMPTED ABDUCTION.**

"Hang on," I said. "Pass me the paper."

I flicked through the pages. The lido was behind schedule, a councillor was retiring, the Rotarians were holding a charity lunch.

"I'm genuinely feeling quite grim," said Allie. "Tell me the amazing thing now. I need to go in."

HAVE-A-GO SUPERHERO THWARTS MUGGER

Beneath the headline was a photograph; I remembered the flash from Ollie's phone. There wasn't much to see: a dark blur stamped red where the edge of my cape lifted, the glitter of the mask, the corner of a scarlet lip. I stared at the picture, and then at the headline again, and returned to the picture, and it was like that moment in stories when someone wakes up from sleep to find that an object from their dream is lying beside them on the pillow. I gripped Allie's arm.

"Look!" I said.

She sat up and peered at the photograph. I squeezed harder.

"Shit!" she said, glancing up at the shops opposite. "That's Bride and Joy. That's right here."

I watched her, waiting for the penny to drop. "Read it!" I said.

A woman attacked in Bassetsbury town centre on Saturday night was rescued by a female member of the public — dressed as a superhero.

The victim (29), who has asked not to be named, was on the alleyway between Harewood Avenue and All Saints Road when the mugger struck. "He tried to take my handbag," she told the *Examiner*. "When I wouldn't give it to him, he attacked me."

But the man got more than he bargained for when the assault was witnessed by a passer-by dressed in full superhero garb, complete with mask and cape. Described by police as "generously proportioned", the hefty hero threw herself into the fight, eventually using her weight to bring down the attacker. She managed to restrain him until police arrived.

"OK," I said. "Hefty's not nice. But . . ."

Allie held up a hand.

Little is known about the secretive superhero, who fled the scene immediately, leaving only a shoe behind. Of her size seven saviour, the victim said: "I don't know what he would have done if she hadn't been there to rescue me."

A police spokeswoman told the *Examiner*: "It is important to show gratitude to those who are active, responsible citizens."

But she warned against vigilantism. "The police are fully trained to deal with these situations," she said. "If in doubt, dial 999."

The man will appear at Bassetsbury Magistrates' Court later today.

I worked hard not to seem triumphalist. I pressed my lips together and looked down as though I were seriously contemplating the path. I made ready to accept the acclaim with dignity.

"God," said Allie. "Bit of a nutter if you ask me!"

"Yes. And horribly violent."

"No, the vigilante," she said. "It's madness. She could have got herself killed."

In my rehearsals of this moment, I'd never imagined that response. The rescue had been such a huge thing, such a bold act. If I could just make Allie understand what it had been like, what had really happened that night . . .

But she was gesturing towards the paper as if my insanity was self-evident.

"Hero," I said, pointing at the word. "Rescue. Gratitude."

"Unbalanced," she said. "Narcissistic, dangerous," and it should have been then that I produced some extraordinary rhetorical burst, because it was all inside me, pushing to get out: the liberation, the thrill of it, the power. I'd saved the woman, I knew that for sure. If I hadn't been there in just that place, at just that time, anything could have happened. If I hadn't put on the costume . . .

"Is that what you wanted to tell me? About this mugging?" asked Allie.

"Yes!" I said. "Don't you think it's . . . isn't there something rather brilliant? About what . . . that woman did? Saving the victim?"

"Honestly? I'm finding it a bit of a headfuck. I'm sorry. I'm awful company today. I really do need to go inside, get a coffee or something."

Headfuck? Is that what Elliot would say when I told him? Allie eased herself off the bench, muttering, and sloped away through the gate into our back yard. I felt a plummet of disappointment; she'd rained on my parade. And it would be a short-lived parade because really, how often did things fall into place like this? It

81

was an eclipse, a blue moon. Unthinkable of course that I would actively go looking for that sort of trouble. What kind of person would? Not my kind. I reminded myself of the unalterable facts of my life, of Martha and Elliot (no, I thought then. I can't tell him, can I? He'd definitely think *headfuck*, just like Allie had. He'd think *nutter*). I was the good girl, the sensible one, a mother with a daughter who relied on her. Luck and adrenalin had kept me safe that night; they might not again. However incredible it had felt, however authentically heroic it had been — not a bloody metaphor for once, that "all mums are heroes" flimflam, but the real deal, actually saving someone from harm . . .

I must have sat like this for ten minutes, ruminating on all the things I wouldn't dream of doing. Behind me, in the back of the shop, was the costume (all but the remaining shoe, which I'd carried home and shoved into my wardrobe under a pile of jumpers). The rest — tights, mask, cape — I'd brought over from my place in a bin liner and secured in a locker which was padlocked fast. I'd been absolutely self-disciplined. But I was surprised the stockroom hadn't been lit up all morning, a white blaze ramming through the gaps around the locker door. I was surprised Allie couldn't hear it even now, its hum vibrating the building; the costume clamouring to be let out.

CHAPTER
EIGHT

I had a glass of wine in one hand and a paper plate in the other. Next to me, Elliot was posting sweaty chunks of cheddar into his mouth. He glanced at the clock.

"I know," I told him. "Me too. Let's stay for the presentation and then scarper." I was trying to work out how to eat my cheese and crackers; there was nowhere to put my glass.

He swallowed. "How about this?" he said. "How about we pay the PTA *not* to run these events? They'd be overwhelmed with donations. Generous, grateful parents queuing up to fund their . . . computer suite?"

"Humanities wing."

"Of course."

"I think you might be onto something." I said. There was a sally of laughter near the door. A man was handing out leaflets to a group of newcomers, his expression exaggerated as if he were talking to a baby, or a dog.

"Imagine if we weren't here," I told Elliot. "Where would you like to be?"

"In Paris," he said quickly. "In the Musée d'Orsay, looking out through the clock."

The speed of that reply, its detail. "You've thought about this before," I said.

"Yep." He slugged back a mouthful of wine, and I wondered exactly why he'd made himself the hero of that comic. There was enough in his life, I'd have said, without the need for that: a job everyone found fascinating, financial independence, a body untouched by fatherhood. Yet there he'd been, transformed into someone quite different.

"I'll tell you where I'd like to be," I said. "I'd like to be lying on a reindeer skin under the Northern Lights."

He let out a *ha!* of surprise. "Really?"

"I mean, I do actually want to go there. I don't want to go to Norfolk this year. I want to see the Northern Lights. We could go to Finland or Sweden," I said. "Somewhere like that. There are incredible places. There's an ice hotel . . ."

"That's right. It's an art project."

"It's a proper hotel. You sleep on a bed of ice. At the end of the season the whole thing melts." I could see it: me on a reindeer skin in a carved white room, the Northern Lights flailing in slo-mo above me. I thought maybe Elliot could see it too. He reached out and touched my cheek, his fingers a little damp from his wine glass.

"We always used to do that stuff," I said, leaning in to him. "Martha's old enough for something more adventurous. Let's just do it! Let's book it and go."

He started to reply, but the man with the leaflets had arrived; I saw him out of the corner of my eye, bouncing on his toes as he waited for us to finish.

"Hellooo!" he said, when we turned to him. "Lambs to the slaughter? Short straw?" This last was directed at Elliot. "Not really, not really," the man went on. "Don't mind me. Too many hours in front of the little . . . We do appreciate you coming. Who do you belong to?"

Elliot was at a loss, but I said, "Martha Pepper? She's in Year 10." The man nodded.

"Of course, I know Martha," he said. "Top girl. I'm Bill Grafton."

I recalled his name appended to Martha's History report at the end of the previous term (*very able. Should guard against becoming distracted*). He had the sort of long-fringed hairstyle I'd previously only seen on boys of Martha's age, but Bill Grafton had a good twenty years on them. Elliot gave him our names and he nodded again, then asked what we did.

"I'm a designer," said Elliot.

"I run —" I began, but Mr Grafton was already saying, "Wonderful! What do you design?"

And just like that I was ejected from the conversation. I waited for the usual feelings to march in and got ready to subdue them. I waited to feel small, to feel livid.

"I'm a brand designer," said Elliot. "We do logos, online presence . . ."

"I run the Famaid bookshop in town," I said, surprising myself by cutting across them. "Do you know it?"

Mr Grafton gave a little jump, as if he'd forgotten I was there. I watched him feel about for a reply. Finally, after a false start or two, he said, "Oh yes! Just off the High Street? Great! It's my favourite charity bookshop."

I tried not to wince. "Are you a reader, then?" I asked.

"You wouldn't think much of my reading," he told me. "I'm big on detective novels."

"So am I," I said. "So are lots of people. Actually, there are some interesting theories about why readers find them so satisfying. I love Chandler and Walter Mosley, and I adore Sara Paretsky. Have you read her?"

"No," he said. "I'll put her on my list," and I thought: bollocks you will, mate; I know a brush-off when I hear one.

"Who do you like, then?" I asked.

"Peter James," he said, then directed a question at Elliot with the air of a desperate hitcher who's just spotted a car, and they were off again.

The faint praise, the simulated interest: they were nothing new. But something else was, something I can only describe as an *absence* of feeling; an absence of all the humiliation and anger I was used to enduring in conversations such as this. There was none now, and there had been none earlier, I realised, when I'd thought about the comic. It was curious, like being medicated. You know the pain must be there, but you don't feel it. Instead, I felt . . . buoyant, as if I'd jettisoned something and was rising, as if there was an awful lot of air between me and the things that made me feel crap.

"The kids would give their eye teeth to do that," said Mr Grafton. "They always go for the glamorous jobs.

Design, television presenting, you know the sort of things."

What I'd done on Saturday night, it knocked TV into a cocked hat. It knocked just about everything into a cocked hat. Best of all, no one had the slightest clue I'd done it. There I was, standing right next to them — Mr Grafton asking Elliot to talk at Careers Week, Elliot trying to appear modest — and no one was paying the slightest attention to me. I realised then that for a superhero, secrecy isn't just about practicality or protection. It's about the thrill. It's no fun if they realise you're Superman; they have to think you're Clark Kent.

"Jen," Elliot was saying. "Could you hold my wine for a minute?" He held out his glass and I set mine down on the floor. He dived inside his jacket and brought out a business card.

"Cracking!" said Mr Grafton, pushing his fingers through his adolescent fringe. "I'll get Pete Olushola to give you a call. He heads up our Business Studies department." Someone waved from the stage.

"Whoops!" he said. "That's me. Time for the soft-shoe shuffle." He offered one of his leaflets, slipping it under my paper plate after a bit of polite faffing. "There's a Gift Aid form on the back," he said, knocking a fist against Elliot's arm.

"Who are you?" Elliot asked me, as Mr Grafton retreated. "And what have you done with Jenny Pepper?"

"What do you mean?"

"I run the Famaid bookshop!" Elliot boomed, fist aloft. "He didn't show the slightest interest, did he?"

"Haven't you noticed?" I said. "They never do."

He frowned a question, then touched my arm tentatively, as if verifying something.

"The Northern Lights," I prompted.

"What? Oh, yes. It's a great idea. But . . ." He glanced at the couple standing nearest us and dropped his voice. "It's shedloads of money. We couldn't afford it, not for a summer holiday."

"I bet we could, if we tried. Anyway, you can't see them in the summer. September's best."

The sound of a spoon against a glass, someone calling for attention.

"This September?"

"Yes. There's a cycle. They're at their peak this year."

"Lucky them. But we can't do it, can we? It's term-time. Martha's GCSE year."

I slapped my hand over my mouth. "I can't believe I didn't think of that."

Ordinarily I'd have admitted defeat: the logistics seemed to be against us, and I could see that Elliot wasn't sold on the idea. But even as I considered doing so, a part of me rebelled: why shouldn't we do this lovely, magical thing? Time was, we'd have packed up and gone on the spur of the moment, and damn the practicalities. Would the sky really fall in if we did the same again?

"Next February, then," I said to Elliot. "Half term."

The head teacher, Ms Murray, appeared on the stage, squinting into a beam of light, her shadow thrown onto a screen behind her. I looked to see where the light came from, following the revolving dust up to a ceiling-mounted projector. She started talking about the council's cooperation and the generosity of the PTA.

"February's out," whispered Elliot. "We'll be needing to kick off the Easter campaigns at work."

Mr Grafton had made his way through the small crowd and was putting on a headset. He fiddled with a laptop on a side table and a drawing of the school appeared across the screen, a slice of it jumping into the foreground, etching Ms Murray's face with roof tiles and pasting a line of windows across her body. Then he took the stage to threadbare applause, his one-handed audience confounded by the wine glasses they held.

"It's ridiculous," I said to Elliot. "Why is it so hard to get away? Doesn't it frustrate you?"

He took me by the elbow then, turning me to look at him. "Yes!" he said. "It frustrates me all the time." In that moment it was as if a door had swung open between us and I could see something quite new through it. Elsewhere, I could hear Mr Grafton telling a perfectly-amplified joke about teaching the Tudors in a Portakabin.

"What's going on?" I asked. Elliot let go of my arm and I stepped back just as Mr Grafton delivered his punchline. I heard, in quick succession, the *ting* of my heel catching the abandoned glass, the liquid crunch of it falling. "Oh no!" I said, and my cry dropped neatly into the silence.

"Don't say that." Mr Grafton's voice came at us out of the speakers and echoed through the hall. "It's my best material."

★ ★ ★

There was a kitchen in the staffroom. I made my way there through the crowd, whispering apologies as I went. Glossy parquet streaked with skidmarks squeaking under my feet. When the doors closed behind me, I could hardly hear anything from the hall.

I went over to the sink and grabbed a handful of paper towels, the sheets interleaved so that I pulled out more than I'd wanted. On my way out, I looked round: catering box of teabags, dying spider plant, photocopier. On the noticeboard, a list of staff birthdays. In the black windows, a middle-aged woman, overweight and round-shouldered. I went over to the bank of switches and clicked them all, and the lights went off row by row, a line of darkness marching across the room.

As soon as they were off, I could see outside. I dropped the kitchen towels on the floor and went over to the window, hands in front of me, feeling for obstacles. There were threads of light out there, undulating queues of cars on the hill down to the town centre. I thought about leaving right then, walking out and away, down the hill beside the glittering cars. I'd had passing urges like this before, but for the first time it occurred to me that this was something I could physically do, that no one could stop me.

I allowed myself to see it: me, walking out into the night and never looking back, never explaining, never apologising. I could feel an expansion in my chest and throat, a quickening of my breath. I let myself plot the course of that other me: from the top of the hill to the bottom, where I'd drop behind the hospital and out of sight.

CHAPTER
NINE

Day after day in the shop, as I sorted donations, pacified volunteers, tidied and binned and recycled, the costume called to me. I found myself slipping the padlock from the door of the locker when no one was around, just so I could stare at the cape and the corset and relive that night. Sometimes I'd even pop on the mask and watch myself in the mirror as I uttered the kind of witticisms I'd been too full of adrenalin to think of at the time. When the shop was busy I'd sneak glances in the direction of the locker, or find myself staring at it, gaze fixed in the state of reverie Mum used to call a Brown Study.

After the school fundraising evening, I started wondering about a more permanent solution for the costume. I could just throw it away of course, but . . . all that work, wasted? The bespoke cape stuffed into a bin, the beautiful corset never worn again. Self-evidently (I realised, with some relief) that was not the way to go. But what else to do? I could donate it to a charity shop, but thanks to the publicity about the mugging it would be quickly identified, and then so might I. Despite the pleasure I'd have from hearing those words again — hero, gratitude — applied to me definitively this time, I didn't want to be discovered. There was always a chance that Allie wouldn't be alone in her response, and I couldn't bear the thought of public humiliation. Besides, the very notion of someone else wearing the costume and being able to put it on and feel that euphoria, that power, of anyone else slipping on the mask and hearing the normal world subside, filled me with such furious possessiveness that I didn't know what to do with myself.

So it would be much better (again — *self-evidently*) to mend the costume so I could use it at some future point in the way it had been intended, as a dressing-up outfit. I'd do it when the fuss had died down. An awful thought that one, my heroism forgotten for long enough that there was absolutely no danger of discovery. An awful thought, but a sensible one, a rational one.

Of course, I'd have to try on the costume first — to inspect the damage.

The morning after I'd decided this I arrived early, long before any of my volunteers might turn up, even earlier than Allie, who often put in an hour or so at her desk before the shop opened. I chose some music (*Heroes* by Bowie, so sue me), released the padlock, opened the locker door.

It was too bright for the room. Even shoved messily into the locker, the costume glowed against the grey metal, the peeling white paint, the concrete floor. I checked the shop doors, front and back, to make certain they were secure. Then I put it on.

I hauled up the tights so fast they ripped even more. My body juddered as I yanked the laces of the corset, the gloves strained at my fingertips as I pulled them taut above my elbows. But every garment ignited a memory: my knee pressed against the tarmac when I sat on the mugger; the corner of my cape flipped over in the photograph, its flare of red. When I'd finished, I was panting. I put on the mask last of all, and let go a moan of relief. The world was framed by two eyeholes, simple and clear and controlled.

No chance of seeing myself in the window this time; I examined the costume in the little mirror, sending its gaze down my body and back up again, training it on my face, my chest, my legs. Shoeless, with ripped tights, my gloves smudged with dirt, my cape mucky, its shine dulled in patches where the satin had been grazed, I still looked like a superhero. A world-weary, battle-scarred superhero. A punk superhero who would take no shit.

Then I thought, why keep the costume at all if it remained incomplete? Because it *was* incomplete, I could see that. It wasn't just the shoe problem, though that would need to be addressed. I recalled how cold I'd felt standing in the churchyard, shoulders bare. I could fix that. It would just be a question of buying one or two things, doing a bit of mending, and the cape would need a dry clean. It would be a kind of craft project.

At my front door, a knock. I whipped off the mask and peeked round the wall: Allie. I glanced at the clock and saw that, incredibly, I'd been here for a full hour.

Cape off, and she knocked again. I pulled my jumper on over the corset and peered out once more, letting her see me, making sure I kept my skirt out of sight. I waved. She frowned. She mimed turning a key — oh blimey, of course, her key! — and I shook my head.

By the time I let her in, I was in a bona fide fluster, but I was dressed as myself again. "Cuppa?" she said. Then she stuck out her finger and tapped the bridge of my nose. "You got reading glasses, old-timer?" I brought my hand up and stroked the skin there, feeling a dent where the mask had rested against my face.

Leaving the shop later, it was as if someone had turned up the volume. There was a bellow from the Pepperpot, the covered market house that dominated our square: a trader calling for custom. I could make out his legs, denim-clad, and his trainers moving amongst the empty fruit and veg crates, treading on the cabbage leaves that had fallen to the ground.

I walked past the pound shop and the key-cutting place, past the insurance office and the chicken takeaway. Crossing Chapel Road I heard a squeak of tyres, the blast of a horn, and looked up to see a pedestrian scurrying for the pavement. Further up the street, outside Ian Donaldson's new development, a group of people had gathered, holding up placards. There was a cartoon of a bat on one of them, black writing on another. The group was shouting something, a rhythmic chant (Dad's voice in my head: *trouble in t' mill* . . .). I checked my watch. I had ten minutes before my volunteer went off shift.

The dry cleaners stood just off the High Street, next to a florist in a small cobbled yard. The space was tiny, the two shops at right angles to each other, a brick passage connecting them to the street. When I handed over the cape I watched the assistant for any signs of recognition, half-terrified he'd guess, half-wanting him to. But he just said, "Someone's been dressing up, then."

"My daughter," I told him, and he gave me a complicit smile.

Out in the yard, the cobbles were patchily glossy. I could see where they'd been washed, the spread of cleanness which had carried the dirt from the florist's to its margins in a rippled line of jetsam. I'd just stepped out when a man came haring through the passageway into the yard, knocking me out of the way. "Sorry!" he called, and I caught sight of his hoodie and grubby jeans, of the plastic bag swinging from his fist.

My hand was at my waist before I remembered there wasn't a tool belt there. I'd started running before I could think straight.

He skewed right, dashing towards the service road at the back of the yard. I set off after him, and by the time I'd taken stock, had recalled that muggers are unlikely to apologise when they bash into you, he'd crossed the next street and was running into the fire station car park.

I expected him to dash round the side of the building, but instead he made for a door at the back, wrenched it open and disappeared inside. Bonfire stink puffed out as the door swung shut. Panting, I watched him through the wired glass, darting along the rows of hunched black bundles, yellow-striped, that hung against the walls. He grabbed one and I ducked down beneath the level of the window so he wouldn't see me. When I next looked, he was gone.

The air was throbbing blue-white now. I heard someone yell, the revving of an engine, and I ran round to the front of the station, where the great red doors gave out onto the road. A siren wound up, then down again.

The doors folded back like a theatre curtain opening, and the engine nosed its way forward, its fluorescent strips blinking with the pulse of its own lights. I saw the man inside. He was dressed in black, a yellow helmet on his head, his gloved hand raised. Someone else's gloved hand slapped against it in a high-five and he laughed. I wondered how the alchemy had been performed. It was his uniform, surely? Some magic garment — the helmet, the gloves. Or, maybe, the place itself, an ordinary bloke going in one door, the hero emerging from another? Had it all happened on the concrete floor of the bay amidst the flash of the engine's lights, a trick pulled off in a dark moment between illuminations?

The sirens started again and the engine pulled out into the road. Cars parted, speeding up or holding back so it could pass, the rest of the world giving the engine passage as it sped towards danger, and rescue.

CHAPTER
TEN

The next time I did a big tidy-up at home, I came across the leaflet about self-defence classes sitting, forgotten, at the bottom of my in-tray. You have a right to feel safe, it reminded me, and now, in the light of the mugging, something snapped into clarity. It wasn't so much that the streets were dangerous — which woman doesn't know that? — rather that I didn't have to feel passive in the face of the danger. Out after dark, I was used to treating my body as a vulnerable thing in need of protection. What hadn't struck me before was that, rather than staying at home, or avoiding certain areas, or twitching with alarm every time I heard footsteps, that same body — *my* body — could be a force in itself.

I thought back to my first reaction when I'd seen the woman being attacked. *Give him the bag*, I'd yelled. I'd been exasperated when she didn't. Now I thought: why should she have to? Who made that rule? Maybe there were other ways to respond.

The self-defence classes took place at a martial arts centre across town. I arrived a little early. My teacher — Mac, I'd been told when I'd called the centre — wasn't due for another few minutes. I could see where we'd be working, an expanse of crash mats under a vaulted ceiling two floors high, but I didn't go there. Instead, I hung around alone in the waiting area, perching briefly on one of the low chairs and fiddling with the water cooler. There was a display of weapons on the wall. Beside it, a gallery of children swaddled in white, pinned into their Judo suits by oversized belt knots. An iron staircase led up to a mezzanine level, signed "reception", and a side door led into a gym. I could see bodybuilders through the glass panel, clenching their teeth, sweating as they applied their bodies to the equipment, shuddering under the weights.

Another woman arrived, dressed in proper gym gear, all new, all matching. We acknowledged each other with raised eyebrows — absolutely silent, a British greeting. Then others came, two teenaged girls arriving together, and a hearty woman in her fifties who was laughing on her mobile as she entered. "Must fly," she said, and took a seat. "Got some bashing to do." Then she giggled again, and switched off her phone.

The wall-mounted weapons were bewildering: priapic toasting forks, chains with sticks at either end, curved blades that made me think of my own cheese cutter. I went over to one of the knives and ran my finger along its blade. It wasn't as sharp as I'd thought.

I wiggled it — just gently, to see if it came off — and as I was doing so I heard the *clang-clang-clang* of footsteps on the iron stairway behind me. I turned to see bare feet descending, then tracksuit bottoms, then a clipboard and a tracksuit top, stockily filled, printed with the logo of the martial arts centre. When I saw who it was I gripped the handle in a kind of spasm and the knife came free.

It was the police officer who had attended the attack by the church, the one who had felled the escaping mugger and smiled while she did it. "I'm Mac," she said, and I was overwhelmed by a desire to run away. I slipped the knife behind my back and tried to look normal.

There was movement around me, the others stirring themselves, pushing past to greet her. I tried to think straight. The attacker had knocked my mask sideways. Was it back in place by the time the police arrived? Had I spoken after they'd got there? Would she recognise my voice? I became aware of the handle gripped hard in my palm, the moment suspended between advance and retreat.

"Come on," said Mac, turning away. "Shoes off in the dojo."

I plumbed her last glance for meaning (Recognition? Shock? Amusement?) and stepped towards the door.

"All of you," she called, heading towards the crash mats, not bothering to look back. "And put down that knife. It's for display purposes only."

I fumbled the weapon onto its bracket, and was still fumbling when I heard my name being called.

"Jenny Pepper," said Mac, pen held above the clipboard. "Jenny Pepper?" There was silence. The two older women turned to look at me. Mac's face was expressionless and I dared to hope that she knew nothing, after all. Maybe I really was just Jenny Pepper. So I said, "Yes," and she ticked my name and moved on. I took off my shoes and went to sit behind the others, head down.

As for the lesson, I can't begin to describe what a disappointment it was. We all signed disclaimers acknowledging that we were engaged in a dangerous activity. Maybe that — and the weapons — had set my expectations too high, but, rather like the knife, Mac's teaching seemed to be for display purposes only. Most of it was a lecture. The woman in the new clothes pulled out a notebook and jotted down everything.

Mac paced in front of us, talking about her experience as a police officer, about domestic violence claiming far more lives than random street violence, about how, outside the home, it was safer to avoid confrontation altogether. To this end, she suggested walking with purpose and confidence, making assertive eye contact. She talked about wearing shoulder bags with the flaps facing our bodies, about not using mobile phones or iPods in risky places. The notebook woman scribbled furiously.

"If you think someone's following you," she said. "Cross the road, go somewhere busy, knock on someone's door." I wondered which of those things the mugging victim might possibly have had time to do in that narrow alleyway. "There are many good attack alarms available," she said. "Most attackers desist upon hearing an alarm." I thought about how you'd have to scrabble for it in your bag, how you'd probably find it too late. "Always let family and friends know where you're going," said Mac.

After twenty-five minutes of this, she finally let us get up. I saw the two girls exchange looks as we rose and stretched. "If you're feeling unsafe and there are other people around, then shout!" she said. "Loud and authoritative. Say: *Are you following me?*" She lined us up at opposite ends of the crash mats, three on each side. Notebook woman shuffled so she was opposite Mac, the two friends faced each other, and I got the woman who'd been talking on her mobile.

We had to shout — *are you following me?* — at our partner and then she'd shout it back, then we'd take a step forward and do it again, until we were up close. I yelled down to my partner, who replied, and we took a step closer to each other. Are you following me? My partner started to grin. Mac shouted: "*Authoritative!* It's not a joke!" ARE YOU FOLLOWING ME? The girls announced it to each other, a neat pace forward each time. Are you following me? Until eventually my partner was close enough that, were she not a giggling fifty-something woman but, say, a mugger, she could have reached out and put a stop to my yelling. Then we were a step closer and my chest felt tight. I found I was out of breath. She screamed into my face: "are you following me?"

"Well done," said Mac. "Some need for fitness work there," and her gaze lingered on me longer than I was comfortable with. At the water cooler I kept my finger on the button while everyone sat down again. A whole cupful, chilled enough that I felt it streak down the inside of my throat, felt the cold bloom in my stomach.

101

There were ten minutes left of the lesson. "When you are out and about as lone females, the best thing you can do to protect yourselves is to use defensive behaviour," said Mac. "That means noticing things. Being aware. Look at these." She drew a handful of photographs from her clipboard and passed them round. "Tell me what you see."

Mine was a street at night: empty of people, one parked car. When you're in it, I thought, it isn't grey and black, like the picture; you're painted yellow by streetlight, and the black is really a deep blue. Sound carries more, you can hear the hum of the motorway over the hill.

I said, "Be careful of the alleyway?"

She pursed her lips and jerked her head, as though knocking my suggestion out of the way. "Look," she said, holding it up so the others could see. "Pub: If it's just past closing time, you've got drunks in the vicinity. If it's open, you've got lots of people inside, somewhere to go to if you're feeling unsafe. Car: notice that?" She pointed to the exhaust pipe, which was emitting smoke, and the driver's side, where a dark figure sat. "Occupied car, engine on. Abduction threat." She nodded at the two girls. "Notice everything," she said. "Be aware. It can save your life."

She wasn't wrong, but it pissed me off that teenaged girls should have to think like this. A pub's for meeting your mates in, a car's for skirting round as you giggle down the road afterwards. I looked over at them, a little less sure of themselves than they had been, and wondered if Mac could have played down the more lurid aspects of her doom-mongering. *Abduction threat?* I was just starting to resent her insensitivity when I remembered the attempted abduction at Heathland School. I thought of Martha and her friends, and felt a pinch of fear.

At the end, Mac dismissed us and headed up the stairs to reception. In the car park, I heard the notebook woman telling the giggler: "Didn't even do an icebreaker. No sense of lesson management."

I'd nearly reached the road when I heard a whoosh behind me and jumped to one side. A flash of reflective green, a beetle-headed cyclist: Mac. I watched as she turned right onto the street, clicking the gears as she started up the slight incline, raising herself a little off the seat. Then she checked front and back, signalled left, and steered towards the opposite pavement.

I could see what had caught her attention. Beneath the streetlight was a dark lump which fluttered in the breeze. She got off her bike, settled it on its kickstand and crouched down next to the fluttering thing. Mac reached out and stroked it with her forefinger. I saw her lips move. Then she stood up again and began to look around.

On her side of the road there was a block of flats, one of those places the council puts up for pensioners. There was a municipal lawn out front, and a municipal flowerbed surrounded by a low wall. Mac leaned over that wall now, leaned quite far. I'd have hopped over it, but she stayed scrupulously on her own side. When she pulled herself back, she was holding a rock.

103

I watched as she checked around her again, looked down at the thing and then after a moment of suspension — Mac's jaw clenching, pulling the straps of her cycle helmet tight against her cheeks — she raised the rock and let it drop onto the thing below.

A thud. Mac's lips pursed. Then she picked up the rock, shook something off it, and replaced it in the flowerbed. She glanced down at the pavement and adjusted her reflective vest, tugging it into line. Kickstand off, a nice hand signal, the way they teach you to do it at cycling proficiency, and she was back on the road.

By the time I reached the place where she'd been, Mac was long gone. I made myself look. A mash of black and red, coiled guts and feathers still shivered in the breeze. Two perfect bird feet, untouched, sticking out of the mess as if they didn't belong there.

CHAPTER
ELEVEN

I'd done almost all the work on the costume but the skirt still needed mending, a tricky job to perform in secret. I'd had a couple of abortive attempts at the shop, before deciding to do it at home. Now it was a Saturday morning, nearly lunchtime. The garden was filled with teenagers, Elliot was getting on with something upstairs, and the skirt was still hidden in its plastic bag beneath a pile of ironing on the kitchen table. There had been one interruption after another. Every time I'd got it out, I'd had to put it straight back in again, until I gave up and started reading the paper instead. A yell came from the garden and I looked up to see Liv being pursued by Dan, who was shaking something invisible over her head. He'd been a different boy on his way through the kitchen (Pleased to meet you Mrs Pepper / Call me Jenny). Now he chased Liv across the lawn while she screamed judiciously, slapping out just for an excuse to touch him.

There was nothing more about the mugging in the *Bassetsbury Examiner*, but even so I found the paper more compelling than usual. Every page offered new evidence of theft and violence, of vandalism and intimidation. Had it always been this way? The

Examiner was stuffed with bad things which should have been dealt with a long time ago.

In one article — **BASSETSBURY SHOPS SUFFER AS BUSINESS RATES BILL RISES** — a shop owner was pictured, arms folded, looking sullenly at the camera. I knew the place: Dashwood Stores, just down the hill from Martha's school. The shop could be seen in the background, its side wall a mess of graffiti, a problem so permanent that it wasn't even deemed worthy of its own story. The wall was an endlessly-renewing, endlessly-changing blackboard on which Bassetsbury's bigots could unburden themselves. There were drawings scrawled across the bricks, lettering tangled in the spaces between. We hate Packies, I read. Why is a dog better than a woman? Because it knows its master. And looming high on the wall another pneumatic, tight-waisted not-woman, her skirt flipped up flirtatiously, her blouse bursting open, her whole outfit which looked horribly similar to . . . was it . . .? I took the paper over to the window, to check in the light.

The tits-out cartoon figure was wearing Martha's school uniform. I felt a lurch of anger and glanced out into the garden, where Liv and Dan were leaning against the shed with Dan's friend Josh. Martha and Izzy were settled in the folding chairs. They'd closed their eyes as if they were catching some rays, but as I watched, Martha sneaked one eye open to look sideways at Izzy.

I had a vision of a black-gloved fist powering towards a shocked male face. Open mouth — THWAK! — bloody tooth arcing through the air.

There was a movement from outside. Martha was waving at me, pointing at her stomach. When Elliot came in I was still at the window, and I must have looked grim because he said: "Jen? Is everything alright?"

"Here," I said, shoving the paper at him.

"What . . .?"

"The graffiti. The girl. You know that's Martha's uniform, don't you? That's a schoolkid they've sexualised."

He frowned. "Not in the best taste, is it?"

"It's more than that," I said. "It's foul. It's harmful. It makes me want to . . ." I mashed my hands on an imaginary neck. I bunched my fists. I looked to Elliot for confirmation, saw his own relaxed hands holding the paper, and realised that fury was not battering against the inside of his chest. Then I noticed his black-smudged fingers, and worked out why. Half his mind was elsewhere, almost certainly with his comic book. He saw me looking and his mouth twitched. I wondered what fantasies he'd been sketching out upstairs, and part of me wanted to bundle him together with the graffiti artist and be angry at them both. But I remembered what he'd said at the PTA evening, about being frustrated, and was surprised to find in myself something like empathy. I was uniquely qualified to know just what he was feeling: naughty and secretive and Clark Kent brilliant.

I reached for his inky hand and rubbed his fingertip and some of the black came off on my own fingers. I looked at him and he looked at me, and neither of us said a word. I placed his hand on my cheek, then against the other cheek. I checked the window for witnesses and placed his palm on my left breast.

"You'll get mucky."

"I don't care."

I kissed him, a couple of semi-colons and then a nice ellipsis. There was a noise at the back door. Martha said, "Eew," and we did a full stop. When we looked round, she'd left.

"Elliot, you said you were frustrated all the time."

"What?"

"At the PTA thing, just before I smashed the glass. You said, 'I'm frustrated all the time.' What did you mean?"

Elliot put the paper on the table. "I'm not sure I said exactly that."

"I'm sure. You did."

"I was probably overstating things. I just meant I was frustrated about the holiday, I think. We're not . . . we're doing fine at work. Really." He went over to the table and picked up my mug. "The thing is, we'd all love it to be just high-end clients and big contracts. Everybody wants that. But the reality of the business is that it can be famine or feast."

"Should I worry?"

Elliot opened the dishwasher and loaded the mug. I wasn't sure I'd ever seen him do that unprovoked. "Absolutely not," he said, touching my cheek with his forefinger, leaving his print. "We're sound as a pound."

He went into the lounge and a moment later his music started up. Martha crossed the lawn and headed up the side path to the back door.

"Can I come in now without you doing something gross?"

"I don't know. I think Dad's about to sing. Take your chances."

She looked out into the garden, a reflexive teenage glance, assessing the social damage Elliot might be about to do her. In the other room, he'd started. "Martha Martha Bo Bartha, Bonana Fanna Fo Fartha . . ."

"Dad!" she called through. "Not now. Please!"

". . . Fee Fi Mo Artha! Martha!"

"Mum, can we have some lunch? Dad — please!"

But he was on his way in, chicken-heading it towards us, eyebrows jumping. "Jenny Jenny Bo Benny, Bonana Fanna Fo Fenny . . ." He made thumb-and-finger guns and aimed them at me on the beat.

"This is touching, Elliot, but . . ."

". . . Fee Fi Fo Menny! Jenny!"

I looked at Martha. "The cupboard's bare. Grab some money from my purse and get some stuff for a barbecue. Hopefully by the time you're back, Shirley Ellis over there will have gone quiet." Elliot retired, defeated. Martha winked at me and I winked back, a spread of warmth in my belly.

I pulled the skirt from beneath the pile on the kitchen table. Out in the garden, Martha galvanised her friends. By the time they were back home I'd have mended the skirt and the costume would be complete again. I looked at it nestling in the bag, lustrous, about to be placed beyond use for what might be months — even years. I would put it away, and put away everything that went with it. But it was silly, I thought, to go to all the trouble of reworking the costume without at least seeing what it looked like on. After that I'd stick it in the loft as planned. Just a quick fitting, to make sure I'd done a decent job. What harm could it do?

On my way upstairs, I looked in on Elliot. "I know it's a pain," I said. "But I have to go back to the shop tonight. I need to do a stocktake."

"A stocktake?" he said. "With donated stock?"

"Yes. It's a new head office thing. Shouldn't take long."

"On a Saturday night?"

"I should have done it last week. I missed the email."

He tapped the remote and another song started. "Do what you gotta do," he said, and I thought that it wasn't too much to ask. Half an hour, and I'd be done.

CHAPTER
TWELVE

Later, in the back of the shop, I laid out the costume: new fishnets to replace the torn ones, new blouse to go under the corset so that (on the unimaginable future occasion when it would be an ordinary fancy-dress outfit again) I wouldn't feel too chilly. There was the cape returned from the dry cleaner; the skirt mended as best I could. Finally, released from their box, my new boots. Too beautiful to be consigned to the loft, I'd wear them with my usual clothes until they were needed. Patent-glossy, steel toe-capped, laced up the front, they were the kind of boots you could run in, or kick in. Mac had been right; you can't fight crime in high heels.

Valedictory, I took my time dressing. I noticed every detail, storing it away: how a toe poked through the fishnet and I had to tweak it straight, the tight embrace of the corset, the squeak of the boot leather. One glove wasn't sitting quite smooth, my engagement and wedding rings lumpy under the satin, so I stripped off the left glove and put the rings in the coin compartment of my purse.

Strapping on the tool belt, I discovered the one thing I'd missed; the cheese knife was crusted brown with blood. I'd remembered it in comic-book primary. There was something shocking about finding blood in the real world like this, ferrous and decomposing. At the little sink I scrubbed the blade with antibacterial soap, wiped it dry on the scrap of towel we kept out back, and slipped it into the tool belt. Then I used the mirror to apply a slick of lipstick. Once more, with feeling.

I put on the mask and the world shrank to its two eye-holes, simple and comprehensible, stripped of complexity. My shoulders dropped, my breathing eased. In the window-mirror, I stood grounded, sure on my feet. I drew myself straight, I dropped my arms to my sides. There was a shout from the High Street beyond and suddenly the desire to get out there was overpowering.

I felt the town expanding around me, the shop a small dead space, a vacuum. Just a few steps and I'd be walking those streets. It seemed ridiculous to deny myself this. After all, I didn't want to fight, or take risks, or put myself in danger. I just wanted half an hour — an hour, say — to not be invisible any more, to be that incredible person all over again. It would be a hit of intensity to set against the dullness, a safe thrill. Just imagine if people saw me and had read the newspaper article, and seeing me made them feel a little bit safer. Or what if criminals noticed me and it made them hesitate? If they thought I might get involved . . . I wouldn't, I had no intention — but what if they were put off?

One time, I told myself. Just one more time, before it all stopped.

My gloves grabbed the key from the workbench. My boots took me through the back door and out into the dark. When the gate swung open, the churchyard was held in its frame for a moment and I was held too, suspended on the threshold. Then I pulled the gate shut behind me and walked out.

Slipping through the roads near the High Street, I headed west. As I walked, I could feel the different stance my body assumed in the costume. I'd thought it was the shoes doing all that, but it must have been the corset instead because my shoulders were back and my head was high.

In the houses the lights were on, yellow against the deep blue of the evening. I saw scenes through the windows: four people eating dinner around a table, a man throwing his head back to laugh, the other diners looking at each other, hands over mouths. A child at a top window waved to me. I waved back and she gave me a thumbs-up. Beneath her, the downstairs room was lit in pale blue, like something underwater.

It was just as brilliant as I'd hoped. A paramedic hooted and stuck a thumbs-up out of his ambulance window and I raised my hand in greeting (in solidarity actually, that was what I felt, as if he and I were both on the same team). At a late-opening hairdresser's, a stylist stopped what she was doing, a lock of her client's hair anchored between two fingers, scissors gaping. I walked on past the second-hand furniture shops and takeaway outlets, grinning in a way that was probably inappropriate for a vigilante. There was a difference, I saw after a while, in the way women and men responded to me. The women tended to look up quickly, register me, and glance away again. Some of the men did that, too — one of the more surprising things about being dressed as a superhero is the number of people who pretend you aren't — but when they did acknowledge me it was always with a shout, a gesture.

The costume made me bold, made me remember that I used to be bold as a matter of course. In my twenties, when men used to place a hand on the small of my back, as if I was incapable of navigating through doorways without help, I'd stop short and stare at them until they pulled away. Now, when a man yelled from a doorway: "It's my birthday! Do I get a freebie?" I stuck two black satin fingers up at him, and it was like a recovered memory.

It grew dark and I realised I must have been out for longer than I'd planned. The last shops were shut, the pubs had started to fill. I hadn't seen anyone I knew — not once. There was no one here who had to put kids to bed or cook an evening meal. It was just like it had been after Martha was born, that same weather-clock effect in reverse; most people who might recognise me would be at home now, only emerging once morning came.

At the big roundabout near the new shopping centre, cars were backed up. There were hoots, someone rolling down a window and shouting, "Is it a bird? Is it a plane . . .?" before the traffic eased, his cry tapering as the car moved off. I landed on the pavement outside a nightclub. A woman leaned against the wall and stared, cigarette in hand, elbow lodged in her belly. A bouncer looked up from examining his nails, caught sight of me and winked.

I winked back. The club pulsed with music, a relentless throbbing. Above the door, neon-blue letters glowed rakishly, a gap between them where a tube had conked out: "The dge". Three lads loitered on the pavement nearby, glancing across at the bouncer from time to time.

I'd cut down a side street and drawn level with an alleyway at the back of the club when my phone began to ring. I jabbed at the buttons, trying to shut it up, but the gloves made me cack-handed and I accepted the call by mistake.

"Hello?" I whispered.

"What?" said Elliot. "Jen? Can you speak up?"

With a shock, as if I'd dozed off and been sharply awakened, it came to me that I was really Jenny Pepper, wife and mother, in the middle of Bassetsbury on a Saturday night, dressed as a superhero. Air eddied cold across my face and I looked down at myself in a flush of embarrassment.

"I'm here," I told Elliot. On the other side of the street, two blokes stood at a fast food van, manoeuvring kebabs towards their mouths. One of them looked towards the club and I had a horrible feeling that if he saw me, he'd laugh. I pulled back into the alley. "I'm . . . busy," I said.

"Where are you?"

"The shop."

"No you're not. I've just called there. What's going on?"

"I mean . . . sorry . . . I'm out the back. I'm doing stuff in the shed."

"Why are you whisp —"

A crash as a door at the back of the club banged open, a whacking-up of the music's volume. I pressed the phone against my chest and a girl emerged, kicking the door closed behind her. When I lifted the mobile to my ear again, Elliot was saying, "Jenny? Jenny? You OK? Jen?"

"I'm fine," I said. "I couldn't hear you. The Stag's got a band in."

There was quite a long silence from his end. "Right," he said, and then he paused again. "Look, Martha's dinner. What did you want her to have?"

"Have you only just thought about this? It's really late."

The girl who'd come out was very young, Martha's age maybe, too young to be alone here at night, too young to have been let into a club in the first place. She leaned against the door and exhaled noisily. From across the street, sheltering under the canopy of the van, the men watched her.

"Any ideas?" said Elliot. I could hear the echo of our kitchen, caught the soft rasp of him rubbing his head.

"Look, there's some Bolognese sauce in the freezer," I told him. "Heat it in the microwave. Use the defrost setting. Ten minutes."

"OK."

116

The girl plucked off her shoes unsteadily, tipping first one way and then the other. She subsided, inches shorter. "Take it out of the plastic pot and stick it in something different," I said. "You shouldn't microwave food in plastic. Got to go." I cut him off in the middle of his goodbyes and tucked the phone into my belt.

Fingers hooked in the heels of her shoes, the girl started walking.

"Hey!" I called after her, and she gave a little jump and thumped her hand against her chest. "Are you OK?"

"Where the fuck did you come from?" she said. "Fucken . . . Batman. Nice cape though."

"Are you OK?"

She gestured to the alleyway: the dumpsters, the ripple of vomit at the base of one wall, the pile of free newspapers abandoned in a clump, the top one lifted by the wind which swirled in the entrance to the passage. "I'm golden, mate."

"This might not be such a great place for you to be," I said. "I don't know that it's very safe here." I stepped closer and touched her arm, but she slapped at me.

"Fuck off back to your hen night?" she said. "It's none of your fucken business?" And she set off barefoot, wincing down the pavement. I looked across at the blokes and thought of all the blokes who might loiter between here and where she was going. No fighting, I reminded myself. No danger. But what if I could just see her safe home? How wonderful would that be, to know that someone (another someone — this girl *and* the mugging victim; I wanted to punch the air at the thrill of it) was safer because of me? I waited till she'd got a bit ahead, then slipped out of the alleyway and started to follow her.

I can't claim I was a skilled tracker, but then I didn't need to be; her progress was slow. At the end of the street she put her shoes back on and clack-clack-clacked ahead of me. We made our way out of the town centre and into smaller roads, the girl's head bobbing in front, my own held high. In the event she passed unmolested and while I'd never wanted her to be scared or threatened and, while I'd promised myself not to take risks, there was a very, very small part of me that felt disappointed I would never again feel the wave of euphoria I'd experienced fighting the mugger. When the girl finally clacked her way through a back gate, up a garden path and disappeared, I thought it was all over.

I had kept her safe . . . possibly. Watched over her, at least. The next thing was to return to the shop and take off the costume, pack it away — pack away all of this strange time — and go back to being ordinary Jenny again. That was the next thing to do, but I didn't do it. Because when I turned to leave, there, high above me on the wall of the shop opposite was the cartoon schoolgirl I'd seen in the paper that same afternoon, looming and obscene, a taunt. Her skirt was flicked up and her breasts strained at the buttons on a blouse which was *exactly* like my girl's, like my child's, like Martha's.

CHAPTER
THIRTEEN

Maybe I was a little out of kilter that night, frustrated by all the derring-do I hadn't done. No — stuff that — I wasn't a *little* out of kilter. What I felt when I saw that drawing was huge, a fury which seemed to arrive in a single instant; it came to me massive and complete, destabilising. But this wasn't the sort of anger you could create all in one go. It was the sort that is laid down over years and years like sediment, each layer seeming so slight that I hadn't justified doing anything about it: the pink T-shirt Elliot's aunt had bought for toddler Martha proclaiming her a "diva in waiting", the relentless stream of toys which assumed her to be passive, the many and varied ways in which she was told that her job was to be beautiful, to be thin. I'd watched her strong little body rendered weak in her eyes — I'd done it myself, teaching her to be scared of the world outside our home, and I knew I'd do it again and again to keep her safe, until fear was a normal condition. These layers had built up, and each one looked like nothing — you could tell yourself it was nothing — until finally it reached critical mass, and I stood in front of that obscenity and knew: this was not how a human should live.

And even then, I might have done things differently without the costume on. I might have gone home and penned a strongly-worded letter to the paper, or the council, or the police. But it must have been the costume — I can only think it was that — which made me suddenly convinced that the only possible response was to take direct action instead. I would get rid of the graffiti myself. I would find a ladder, get some paint, obliterate it. I would do it right now. I crossed the road to Dashwood Stores, while behind me a light flicked on in an upstairs window of the girl's house.

Close up, the side wall was even more manky than it had looked in the photograph, woolly-edged blurts of spray paint, rudimentary representations of body parts. Ironically, the only image on which artistic skill had been lavished was that of the schoolgirl, tits and arse and mouth at your service, her body jinked in ways that owed nothing to nature. A schoolgirl, for heaven's sake! And when the men who saw this also saw Martha and her friends, did they see people who were like this *really*, or who were in some way *failing* to be like this, or people who were stubbornly refusing to conform, who wanted *showing?*

Dashwood Stores stood in its own scrubby car park. It was the sort of place which would normally stay open late, where you could buy milk and bread and chocolate. They sold papers and magazines, and the windows carried adverts for cheap international phone calls. I crunched over the gravel to look for a ladder thinking, don't get your hopes up: even if there's a ladder, there won't be any paint. In the unfolding logic of my anger, I decided I wouldn't just cover the cartoon; I'd put something of my own in its place. The idea provoked a sudden, glorious rush of triumph and, unlooked-for, the realisation that Elliot would have been brilliant at the new drawing. He'd be in his element. Then I remembered his own pneumatic woman and booted him out of my thoughts before he could colonise them.

The shop was closed, the windows concealed behind metal shutters. Above the shop was a flat, its entrance up some iron stairs, lights on behind the curtains. In the gloom of the car park, I waited for my eyes to adjust. There was an MPV, presumably belonging to the residents of the flat, and two dumpsters. I nipped behind them to see if a ladder had been stored along the fence. Then, a clicking patter from the pavement, veering off it and coming my way. A snuffle, a pant. A Labrador tugging on the end of an extendible lead. A woman's voice said: "Out of it, Bonnie." I flattened myself against the fence so the woman wouldn't catch sight of me. The dog and I regarded each other for a second before it started to bark gamely. I dropped low, the corset evacuating my breath. The walker moved on — and then she hadn't, or she'd doubled back, because there were footsteps on the tarmac.

A man said: "Emma did? She brought it into school?"

I peered out cautiously, thinking of the gold on my mask which might catch the streetlight, the gloss of my boots winking. The speaker was short, wearing a jacket and a hat like an old-time gangster's. He'd stopped at the entrance to the car park and there was a second, taller man with him — a boy; they were both boys really, carrying skateboards on their shoulders.

"In a plastic bag, Johnny!" This was the taller one. "Just brought it in and showed everyone. It was gross."

"Bats should be fucking gassed," said Johnny. He moved closer to the other lad, who took a step back. Johnny set down his skateboard on the pavement with the faintest *tak*, wheels side-on to the slope of the hill. His mate followed a beat later.

Johnny held out an open hand. "Max!" he said, when the other boy didn't react straight away. Max scrabbled in his rucksack, pulling something out of it: a cylinder. My thighs were starting to ache. Johnny took the object without acknowledging his friend. I shifted and knocked something which fell against me, digging into my side. There was a *clack-a-clack-a-clack* as the aerosol can was shaken. These, then, were the bastards. Maybe not the schoolgirl-drawing bastards. Maybe just the women-are-dogs bastards.

"Like a rat," said Max. "And its wings, all skin and bone."

The thing digging into me was a rubbery cylinder: a bike's handlebar. When I looked down I could see light glinting on the brake, the bell and the tinselly decorations I couldn't feel through my gloves. A kid's bike, so small. I remembered my back complaining as I bent over to grasp the handlebars for Martha, remembered running alongside her, hovering, just so she could feel what it might be like when I let go. Handlebars, saddle, let go. And it was no different now:

hold on, hold on, let go. Let her coast straight out into a world where she was just an object, a thing with tits.

Clack-a-clack-a-clack. "They might hear you, Johnny," said Max. There was a crack as the aerosol lid popped.

"Emma Burtonshaw," said Johnny. "She's a fucking minger, all ways round."

I started to tremble. My throat closed up and I thought, shamingly, that I might be about to cry. They could do this with impunity. They could just come here and write anything they wanted and draw those vile images and, God, I had to stay still, because if they saw me here they could do anything. They were so much bigger than me. They could haul me out and then . . . what would they do? If I was lucky they'd laugh, though that would be awful enough. They'd see me as some kind of saddo, an old frump in a cape. If I was unlucky . . .

I was totally alone, one against two. Just let them get on with it, I instructed myself, even as fury swelled inside me. Let them do anything they bloody want. Then I thought of Martha, and Liv, and Izzy, and the "minger" Emma Burtonshaw, and my anger was filling me up, more than I could bear or control. Don't think about Martha. Don't think about Martha. Don't —

"Hey," said Max, nodding towards the wall. "You reckon you can do Emma?"

And all my sensible injunctions disintegrated and I didn't care about jeering or danger; I couldn't hold back for a second longer. I emerged from behind the dumpster in a crouching shuffle, an *oof* as I straightened up, a click in my hip as I stepped forward.

"Stop!" I told him. Bloody hell, Max was big.

They jumped. "Fuck me!" said Johnny, turning his gasp into a laugh. Max started to smile.

"This is foul!" I said, moving my hands behind my back because I couldn't stop them shaking. "It's horrible. Why are you doing this . . . Johnny?"

Johnny raised his eyebrows. "Seriously?" he said, and then they both laughed, looking at each other and shaking their heads. Hilarious bastards.

"How do you think they feel, these girls? They are people! Real people! Just like you!" And I moved nearer the side wall, skirting the boys, the same leap of fear I felt when I walked through a train door, not knowing whether it would clamp shut on me.

"Who are you?" he said. "My mum?" He stepped towards the wall. I held up my hand, warding him off.

"You've got a choice. You can be a bastard or a . . . or a . . . don't be a bastard." But he raised the paint can anyway and then I was shouting. "Hey!" I yelled, and then, taking even myself by surprise: "Don't mess with me."

"Piss off," he said, and he started to spray.

I kicked him.

It wasn't the way it looks in the films, all sideways and cool, but I kicked him anyway, and it caught him on the knee, and he yelped and paint sprayed cold onto my forehead. Red mist falling — the acetone stink of it — and him lashing out in a slant of yellow streetlight. His hand punched my breast and it hurt like fuckery, so I went at him again, kicking his shins and I did not, for even a fraction of a second, give a stuff what might happen next.

"Ow!" he said, but he was still laughing. Max was too, bent double with it, bright blue hood flopping over his head. Those little . . .

"Don't you dare!" I shouted. "Don't you . . ."

Johnny moved fast. He got to me in one quick step and held me by my left arm so I couldn't pull away. He reached out to my face and I tossed my head around and bent it back, but he got the mask — *my* mask — between thumb and forefinger and started to lift it.

"No!"

I did the only thing I could think of. I brought my knee up, hard, into the softness of his balls and he cried out and let go. My mask snapped back into place. He crumpled to the tarmac, rolling out a single, extended vowel of pain.

Max leaned over him, glancing up at me to ask, "What the fuck is wrong with you?"

"Do *not* mess with me!" I bellowed again. Johnny was rising now, off his knees, on his feet, rising and walking away from me, bending to pick up his skateboard.

"And don't come back!" I shouted, but there was something wrong with the way Johnny was moving, with the way he was turning towards me.

The sound of something heavy tracking through the air. An edge, a wheel, and then I was the one creased and folded, down on the ground and emptied of breath. I saw the skateboard coming at me again, from above. I curled up against it, arms wrapped round my head. Pain fell randomly on my body, again and again, but I

125

could only focus on the necessity of filling my lungs. There was shouting — me, I think, and him, and Max yelling Johnny's name. And then the shouting and the pain became indistinguishable from each other and I couldn't help myself any more. I closed my eyes, hoping that the next blow would be to the head, so I could black out and not have to endure the rest of the beating.

Then I heard a voice.

"I am so sick of this!" said the voice.

I tensed for the next blow, but it didn't come. Opening my eyes, I saw a man standing over us, holding a cricket bat. Light fell on him from the open door at the top of the stairs (beard, glasses, blue T-shirt: the shopkeeper I'd seen in the *Examiner*). He swung the bat at Johnny, catching him in the side with a soft thump. Johnny let out a cry of pain.

"I knew you'd come again!" the man shouted. "You little shit!" He landed a blow on Johnny's leg. "Just say when you'd like me to stop."

"Stop," said Johnny, rolling onto his side.

"Because I can go on like this all night," said the man, aiming a whack at Johnny's rump. I rolled up into a sitting position and took a few trial breaths. From below us came the rumble of a skateboard being ridden down the hill: Max, leaving his friend without a backward glance.

"Stop it, you cunt!" shouted Johnny.

"Not so clever now, are you?" said the man. He lifted the bat and gestured to the street. "Go home," he said. "Go tell your mum how you got those bruises."

Johnny got up slowly, uttering little groans. He looked back at the man, who raised his bat again and took a pace towards him. Johnny stumbled backwards, scooped up his own skateboard and limped away.

The man watched till he'd dropped out of sight. "You're bleeding," he said.

"Hang on." I was having trouble getting up. He put a hand out and I grabbed it, hauling myself to my feet. I couldn't stand straight, and fell backwards against the shutters with a rattle. The man pointed to my forehead, his finger hovering near the skin, not touching me. I tapped my finger lightly there; it came away sticky red.

"It's just paint," I said, showing him.

"Are you OK? What's all this?" He gestured at my cape.

"I feel a bit sick." I kept my head down while I waited for the feeling to pass.

"Just take it slowly," he said.

"I'm alright," I told him. I was making surprised sounds each time I breathed in. "I was trying to . . . I just wanted to stop them."

"Why are you dressed like that?"

"I wanted . . ." I looked at him, at the T-shirt and jeans in which he had done the job so much better than I had in my cape and mask. "I wanted to see what it felt like," I said, and he snorted.

"Well, now you know. I'm going to call an ambulance."

The paramedics would love this. I'd be their Saturday night anecdote. "No . . . don't do that. I'm OK," I told him. "I'm fine."

Shock reduced the world to a simple sequence of actions. I'd needed to prevent him calling the ambulance. Now, I needed to leave, slowly, painfully. Halfway across the car park I saw that Max had left his rucksack and, in a nod to any future beyond the immediate moment, it struck me that this would be the only way of tracing the boys. If I wanted to get the police involved, I'd need some evidence of their identity. So, as I passed, I lowered myself to pick up the bag. Behind me, the door to the flat slammed. Across the road, the girl I'd seen home was at her window, gaping. I could hear my own laboured breaths, my own voice murmuring encouragement as I might to a frightened Martha: "Come on now, just down the hill, that's the way. Not far to go, you'll be fine . . ."

I didn't think I'd make it back to the shop. I shuffled down the hill, shivering convulsively, muttering comfort. Every time someone came near I'd shrink away from them or cross the road. If they commented on my costume I kept my head down.

Limping up the High Street — nearly there — I crossed to the quiet side, away from McDonald's and the pub. Shop after shop in darkness, but the insurance office window was a block of light. As I passed, I looked between swaying vertical blinds to see a woman standing at a desk, frowning at a document. I recognised her tabard first, pale blue, the embroidered name a dark scrawl; it was the woman I'd rescued from the mugger. She glanced up and saw me, flinched then dropped the paper onto the desk.

It was funny, but seeing her galvanised me. It didn't stop me hurting — my ribs creaked with pain, and there was a throbbing in my thigh — but some reserve of pride made me pull myself as straight as I could. I gave her a thumbs-up. She frowned and pointed to her forehead.

No. Paint. *Paint*. I slicked an imaginary paintbrush up an imaginary wall, but when I stretched high my side twanged and I had to stop. She nodded warily and I turned away.

Reaching the sanctuary of the shop, I felt all the puff go out of me. I was shaking as I unlocked the door, fantasising that somehow Allie would be there — I longed for her actually, so that I wouldn't have to do any more of the difficult things on my own. At that moment I would have accepted all the disapproval she could muster if she could also have hugged me and called me a numpty, sat me down and checked my injuries, decided what was to be done and made me drink tea. I wouldn't even care that I'd look a fool to her (and you *were* a fool, I told myself. What were you thinking, taking that sort of risk? What would you think if someone else behaved like that? That's right, Jenny, reclaim the night — just as long as some bloke is around to rescue you when things get serious.)

Alone, I sat in the stockroom, out of sight of any windows, amongst the comforting smells of dust and mildew, and thought I'd never get up again. I let myself have a bit of a cry. And then I realised I couldn't cry there all night, that I had to get myself home because there was nobody else around to make it happen.

Slowly, slowly, I peeled off my costume, my right hand protesting every time it was called upon to grip. I took stock of my injuries. I could see where the bruises would come. Across my ribs, the first blow — how could he? All that force hammering against another person? The top of my arm, where I had tried to protect myself. That terrifying animal instinct for survival, but he hadn't hesitated: on my left thigh, twice, and on the back of my right leg. Then the shock of the attack hit me once more and I needed to sit again for a minute or two, my ribs wrenching with each breath.

Before I left, I looked through the rucksack. The wallet inside told me Johnny's chickenshit friend was Max Wheeler, 18. He'd be kicking himself for losing this — wallet, keys, a couple more cans of paint, an energy drink . . . a bag of cocaine.

Cocaine. A tiny bagful, personal use only. There was a time when such a thing would have felt commonplace. Should I flush it? Hand it in, together with Max's ID? It occurred to me that giving the bag to the police might cause more problems than it would solve. For the first time, I wondered whether I had been guilty of a crime myself when I'd slipped away from the mugging without giving a statement. If I handed over the bag, surely they would wonder how I'd got hold of it, and then the story would all come out.

The dilemma chased itself round my mind for a couple of turns, until I realised I was incapable of resolving it. So I put the coke back in the rucksack, the rucksack under the desk, and my costume into a locker. I left a note for the next day's volunteers. (*Have caught a bug and won't be in for a few days. So sorry.*) Then, I set off for home.

I came in through the back gate, shattered and aching. I was counting on Elliot having a bottle of white spirit in the shed, so that I could clean off the paint before I entered the house; it was the only thing that had looked out of place once I was dressed.

The shed was nearly empty, and clean, too. There was a pile of plastic crates in one corner, and on the workbench some tools, a couple of tins of paint and — yes! — a container of white spirit. I worked at my forehead for a while with a tissue. By now I was leaning on the bench, head pillowed on my injured arm, rubbing with the good one.

I won't mince words. I felt like shit. All the way home I'd kept getting playbacks of the beating and they scared me stupid. Even walking down my own garden path I kept checking behind me. My body had been tenderised. It hurt to move even in the smallest ways; my skin would be piebald by morning. I was smeared with red paint, I may or may not have broken a rib, and I had to conceal it all from my family, who were waiting in the house for me to return from a late night pushing paper. I'd been subject to a kind of madness, I could see that now, and it would never happen again. But as I

131

looked through the shed window, up to Martha's room, I felt the tiniest jolt of incongruous joy. The thought popped up before I could squash it: just a few weeks ago I'd been standing there looking out at the world. Now, I was in it.

CHAPTER
FOURTEEN

I'd been right about the bruises. I spent the next day in bed pleading illness, while they bloomed purple across my body and pain rooted deep beneath them. In the bathroom I caught sight of my arm and it was a shocker, stopping my breath for a moment. I had to look at all the familiar things (my shampoo, lid open because Elliot had used it, Martha's razor) until I felt steady. Then I made myself look again. I was stamped with an exact facsimile of the lip of the skateboard, a magenta swoosh curling, vine-like, up towards my shoulder. I wondered how Johnny looked now and I hoped (fervently, angrily) that in between the bruises from the cricket bat, he bore some marks that I had made. Then I wondered how old he was, whether I'd hit a kid, whether I was a bastard, too.

Downstairs, Elliot was banging away at something. Martha's music shouldered out of her room and occupied the landing. Outside my window people walked into town, trains rumbled to and from the station.

Back in bed, I reached for a book and rested it on my belly, telling myself I was just about to open it, caught in memory-loops like those gifs Martha shared with her friends: me kicking Johnny, him crumpling, a single wheel and the curled edge of a skateboard expanding into extreme close-up. My heart hammered away, fear tangling with exhilaration as I relived it all. When I'd calmed down, my hands weakened and the book flopped forwards. I turned — slowly, carefully — and felt it slide onto the bed beside me, and the outside sounds switched off, one by one, until I slept again.

There was a disturbance in the light, a breeze across my skin, the sound of someone else breathing in the bed next to me.

"Mums?"

"Martha?" I reached out and the strands of her bracelet tickled the back of my hand. I opened one eye.

"Don't give me anything gross, will you?"

She was lying on her stomach, hands up to her face, cheek squashed against the pillow. I hooked my little finger into the bracelet and we lay there, attached. "I don't think it's catching," I said. "It was probably something I ate."

"Better out than in," she said, her mouth fish-pouting. "Dad said you should eat something now."

"Yeah, I probably should."

"I made toast." She started to get up.

"Oi, madam," I told her. "You're staying right here." I twitched the bracelet towards me and she gave a token huff and let herself fall back onto the pillow, face-first. On Elliot's bedside table there was a plate with a slice of toast made just the way she knew I liked it: not too well-done, shiny with butter all the way to the edge, Marmite dabbed on in tiny spots. Next to the plate was a book. I didn't need to see its title. I knew it by its colour, a Pepto-Bismol pink. It was the book I pulled out every time I was ill or miserable, the one I'd read over and over the year Mum died.

"You brought me *The Young Visiters.*"

"Yeah. I didn't think . . ." She nudged my novel, which lay between us. ". . . *The Human Stain* would do the trick."

"You might be right."

"Bet the jokes are good, though."

I laughed into my pillow, my breath rank. Martha giggled, the two of us fallen somehow into this crevice in our lives where she'd forgotten I was the enemy. This happened occasionally; I'd catch glimpses of a different Martha, the way she used to be — the way she might be again once adolescence had burned off.

I unhooked myself from her bracelet and gingerly wriggled upright. "Give us the toast, then."

She passed it over, half-stood to go, and then sat back on the corner of the bed. One bite and I was starving.

"So," she said, scratching at something on her knee. I was immediately alert: Defcon 4. This was how she always broached something difficult, with a *so*, a *well*, an *umm*, just like Mum had. It astonished me, this legacy. Martha couldn't consciously remember her gran at all, but sometimes when she spoke it was as if Mum was back in the room.

I squished the toast between my tongue and palate, sluicing melted butter from it.

"Don't go off on one," said Martha, looking straight past me and out of the window. "There's this girl at school who's being bullied."

It's her, I thought, and blood came rushing up to my face and chest, and I had to put down the plate. I tried to do it casually, as if this were a natural moment to stop eating. The pellet of toast blocked my mouth.

"Mmm?"

"It's not, like, a massive thing."

A bully, threatening my daughter. Hulk smash.

I swallowed. "The victim . . ."

"Don't call her the victim!"

Inside, I was sweaty with emotional back-pedalling, a hail of good advice falling on me: play it cool, let her trust you, empower her. But I didn't want to empower her. I wanted to go for someone's throat. "OK," I said. "Not the victim. So, your . . . friend —"

"It's not me, if that's what you think." I checked her expression for deceit, but her profile had tightened up. "Everyone goes, 'tell an adult, tell a teacher,' like that wouldn't basically get you in deeper shit. They go on about how bullies have this really bad home life, but I don't even care. And Izzy's like . . ." Martha went silent. She bit down on her lips, rolling them inwards. Whatever it was outside the window had suddenly become fascinating.

"Is it Izzy, then?" Before the sympathy, a terrible surge of relief.

Martha turned on me. "If you *ever* tell anyone, or mention it to Izzy, or anything, I will . . . hate you."

"Alright. Calm down. I won't. Of course I won't."

136

"This nasty bitch, this Zoe bitch. I want to punch her." Martha's eyes lit with an evangelical fury that was so absolutely and nakedly the same as my own that I wanted to claim kinship. "Don't ever, ever say anything," she commanded me again. "Don't tell the school because they'd just make it, like, a nightmare."

"I won't. I promise." And then, because I had to really, because she should do as I say, not as I did: "Don't punch her, will you, M? Maybe you could . . ."

"It's not that big a deal," said Martha, and just like that, the temperature changed. I could tell she regretted having mentioned the subject at all. Her pocket uttered a pre-emptive hum. The phone was out before the first bar of the ringtone had come to an end, and she was gone.

That evening I was lying cocooned on the sofa, bruises hidden beneath a comprehensive pair of pyjamas, when Elliot came in from the garden.

"You feeling better?"

"A bit achy. Hungry."

"I'll call for pizza in a minute." He toed off his shoes and kicked them to one side, perching on the coffee table so we were eye to eye. "Not like you to be confined to quarters," he said, with a somewhat unflinching gaze. I sent him back what must have been a pretty wobbly smile, and hoped like hell my story had convinced him.

"Thought I'd sleep it off," I said.

He frowned and touched my knee, rubbed it idly, and it pinged with pain. I coughed, just to give my face something to do. The more I'd thought about the things I'd done in costume, the less I wanted him to find out. I'd rehearsed a dozen different ways of explaining the compulsion I'd felt, and not one of them hit the spot; I'd started to wonder if even I understood what had driven me. Certainly, I had no chance of enlightening Elliot. I was sure his response would bounce between anxiety and ridicule. The only alternative — flat-out deception — jabbed me with guilt, but I reminded myself that what had happened that night would never happen again, never affect him, and that a few white lies were preferable to the mortification of exposure.

"You got in late," he said, and I felt a plunge of apprehension. "When I called you, you sounded . . . weird."

"I was starting to feel dicky."

He reached out to move some hair off my face, and I leaned towards him, watching to see if he believed me. His hand dropped to my arm, stroked it. A bruise flared — my purple swoosh inflaming — I winced, he pulled back, and I cursed myself.

"Oh no, don't go!" I said, placing his hands on my face. "I'm just . . . I've got that hurty skin thing. That you have with a bug."

He touched my arm again. When he passed over the bruise I controlled my expression very carefully. I watched him and was horrified to see he was controlling his, too. He had guessed — had he? He was definitely suspicious. The real possibility of discovery filled me, I was surprised to find, with more than just mortification. What I felt was bigger, a kind of grief.

Stop him, I thought. Create a diversion! So I felt for his hand and squeezed it and smiled at him, and after a couple of seconds of us sitting quietly, fingers interlinked, he frowned.

"What . . . where's . . .?" He held up my hand, squeezing the tip of my third finger. "Where are your rings?"

The rings. A slap of fright, and then I remembered.

"Blimey," I said. "That was a bad moment. They're fine. There was so much mess at the shop last night, I took them off to stop them getting dirty."

Elliot tilted his head, as if he was conducting a particularly tricky calculation.

"Honestly, it was grim in there . . . I put them in my purse," I said, when he stayed quiet. "I take them off to make pastry sometimes. I —"

He dropped my hand and I wanted to snatch at his again, to turn the conversation in a new direction. I thought of all the ridiculous things I might say to explain the absent rings, and said none of them because that would only make it worse. Instead I sat there, cobbling together an innocent expression, my last-ditch attempt at putting him off the scent.

Elliot stood up. "I'll call for a pizza," he said.

After that, all the usual things happened. He ordered and the pizza came, and we ate it in front of the telly. I pushed away my anxiety about his suspicions. Everything would be back to normal soon, and Elliot would come to see this evening as an aberration. A little while later, he would forget about it entirely.

★ ★ ★

I allowed myself a couple of days off work, shuffling round the house because it hurt more when I was immobile for long periods. On day three I saw, as I hadn't for a while, how messy the place had got, how sticky the kitchen counter was, how crowded with shoes the hall. But I found I had limited patience for doing anything about it. There had been a time — before Martha and everything that came with her — when mess was just an accepted feature of the landscape, a shared territory. But when you're at home with a kid it becomes your territory and you want to control it, and then after a while you *must* control it, because you can control so little. Then, one day you wake up and realise that you are the sort of person to whom it really, really matters that the shoes are put away, that the kitchen counter is clean.

In the aftermath of Johnny it was different, though. God, tidying was dull. Why hadn't I spotted that before? I used to find it cathartic, ridding myself of clutter. I'd experience peace in those post-housework moments when everything was in its place. Now I thought: how long does that peace last? Housework is cyclical, it fixes nothing permanently. Clear one lot of crap out of the way and soon enough another lot will move in to take its place.

So I slouched from room to room, reclaimed a few necessary things — tickets to an upcoming Casino Night at the school, a bank statement — and stuck the rest into two bin bags, divided roughly between things Elliot should have cleared up, and things Martha should have cleared up. I dumped Elliot's in his study,

Martha's in her room, thinking, stuff this for a lark, I want to read my book.

There was a poster above Martha's bed I hadn't seen before, a leather-clad girl, bobbed hair helmet-hard. I knew her, a singer who'd come out recently. And look at what Martha was reading. She'd despatched the teen novel I'd borrowed and now *Tipping the Velvet* sat on her bedside table; she was obviously working her way through Sarah Waters' backlist. The poster, the books: they seemed such obvious hints. Did she want me to guess?

This was a new idea. Was I supposed to broach the subject and make it easier for her? But if I pre-empted her and got it wrong ... bloody hell, I thought; damned if you do, damned if you don't. Because I was absolutely ready for her to come out. I would be so cool about it. In fact, I was longing for her to tell me, in part so that I *could* be cool (and because I wanted her to know things would be OK, and because the suspense was slightly killing me). I'd even rehearsed some different responses:

"That's great, love. Can you pass the biscuits?"

"Sweetie, I know. I've always known."

"I'm so proud of you!"

[Hugs. Wordless weeping.]

A few months before, a letter from a father to his son had gone viral. He'd overheard his kid talking to a friend about being gay and left a note for the boy expressing his complete acceptance of the news. There was such utter devotion and humour in this note, a part of me thought, dammit! I can never measure up to that.

I wanted so much to not fail her in this, to be everything she needed, to be perfect.

Leaving Martha's room, I noticed a new addition to the layers of paper fish-scaled on her noticeboard, a leaflet she'd pinned on top of a photo. It said, *Save Our Bats!* and underneath, *Donaldson Development Threatens Serotines*. There was a photo of something that looked like a rat, only with round, guinea pig-ish ears. It was lying beside something else which looked — in the poor rendering of the photocopy — more like a stick than anything else. It took a moment to work out that it was its wing, folded (*all skin and bone*, Max had said). I remembered the protesters I'd spotted outside Ian's chapel. The leaflet claimed there were bats at the site and that the females would be giving birth to their young in the summer. It said the building work should stop. I wondered why Martha had put this on her board and how Ian's daughter Liv might feel if she saw it. I flexed left and right, twinges ricocheting around my torso. Time to get back on the horse.

CHAPTER
FIFTEEN

"You want to learn how to fight."

"Yes!" I said, and Mac raised an eyebrow. The others turned to look at me. Waiting for the class to start, we'd introduced ourselves. The woman who took notes was called Beverley, the one who giggled was Anne. There was no one else this time; the teenaged girls had dropped out. The three of us who remained sat on the crash mats, trying to look populous. When Mac had come clanging down the iron stairs she'd looked at us, and then at the door, and then she'd set her mouth and told Beverley to put down her pen.

"You want to learn how to fight," she said again, standing beneath the dojo skylights, bouncing on her toes. "But that's not what I'm going to teach you. Not today."

I nearly said something then. If Mac hadn't been so stolid, so impassive, so frankly scary, I would have. Sometimes, when I remembered Johnny, I became a bag of blood and organs, something you could nick with the smallest blade and spill. When I thought about him, I didn't want to look people in the eye. So stop farting around, I wanted to tell Mac. You said we have a right to feel safe. Show us how. More than ever, after

Johnny, I just wanted to learn, and I wouldn't have minded how hard it was or how long I'd need to work. Nothing was as hard as feeling scared. I was hacked off that Mac couldn't see this for herself. But, instead, I just sighed and covered even that by clearing my throat, while she went on talking.

"Today, I'm going to teach you how to *avoid* fighting."

Beverley raised her hand. "But we want to learn how to fight. That's why we're here. I can *avoid* fighting at home."

Lucky you," said Mac, and the room went quiet. She sniffed. From the gym came the piston sound of exercise machines. I remembered how she'd killed the bird, her ruthless compassion, and wondered what had brought her to this point. I wondered whether she taught self-defence because of what she'd seen as a copper or for other reasons. Late thirties, I reckoned, not much younger than me. Enough time to have seen what the world was, to have worked out what to do about it.

"You want to fight, there's plenty to keep you busy," said Mac. She gestured over to the display in the waiting area, to the knives and nunchuks, to the blade-edged stars. "Just sign up with the martial arts boys," she said, and I wondered whether that would have been a better option in the first place. Beverley assessed the door.

"I'm not here to teach you to fight," she said. "I'm here to teach you to survive. Most assailants are male. They will be bigger and stronger than you. You do not want to fight an assailant. What you want to do is find his weak point. Watch."

She made all of us stand up but she picked out Anne, getting her to play the part of the attacker. "Grab me as hard as you can," she said. "When it hurts, shout *stop*." Anne mugged at us. She grasped Mac by her upper arm and grunted. Mac did something quick with her hands; I couldn't track her movement properly, but she twisted herself free somehow, and then she placed her fingers into the soft hollow at the base of Anne's throat and pressed down.

"Oh!" said Anne, and crumpled to the floor.

"Stop?"

"Yes!"

Mac released her and she coughed a bit. Beverley reached out to Anne and put an arm round her shoulder. She leaned in close and I heard her muttering in tones pitched between concern and outrage. Mac shook herself out.

"How did you get your arm free?" I asked. "That twisting thing you did?"

She pulled me forward and showed me, clasping her hands together and swinging them round my arm — under, then over — so that my hand was twisted the wrong way and I was forced to let go. Then she plunged her fingers into the centre of my clavicle and I too fell to my knees and coughed, my bruises singing. I wanted to thump her. I wanted to learn how to do it.

"Find the weak point," she said, as I spluttered.

We all practised. I stayed with Mac, trying the move twice, three times more, until I had it down pat, like the steps of a dance: clasp, swing, pull, stab. Her arms were taut with muscle, sinewy. Once I'd got the technique down, I took account of the way she was moving. She'd tighten up, then relax a little. I thought about Johnny and the mugger and all the people like them, how they could attack me when I was shutting up shop after a late night, when I was walking through the railway tunnel or across the empty shopping centre (a risk map of the town charted in my head, all the possible places and ways I could be hurt). I'd have no time to accustom myself to the quirks of their particular violence. It would happen so fast, they would move in ways which were inconvenient and unpredictable.

"Don't give me chances," I said. "Make it difficult for me."

"Your call," she said, and I spent fruitless seconds wriggling in her grasp. I tried again and then again, and then overcame her — one time only, my body a clench of pain, hers hardened against me — before she stopped us.

"Find the weak point," she said again, as the group sat panting at her feet. "Here's another one. Beverley — up! Approach me."

Beverley eyed Mac, keeping a pace away from her. "Oh, come on!" said Mac, stepping forward, holding her finger horizontally against the base of Beverley's nose and pushing upwards. We watched, incredulous, as Beverley jerked away from her hand. Then Anne and I tried it on each other, retreating quickly under the prickling pain.

"What about afterwards?" I said.

"What do you mean?" Even when Mac wasn't demonstrating, she was never quite still. She would stretch her shoulders, lift her feet one after the other, rotate her wrists. Now she rolled her head, left then right.

"What about after you've done the nose thing? How do you make the attacker go away for good?"

She looked at me narrowly and I thought again about that night with the mugger, that long minute when we'd been within touching distance. Had she guessed? Had she known my identity all along and not said a word? She was unshakeable enough, I thought, but she followed the rules. Wouldn't she have taken me down to the station to make my witness statement the minute she realised? Or, would it look bad for her, having let me go in the first place? It was public knowledge I'd been at the scene, but maybe not that she'd taken her eye off the ball and let me slip away. Perhaps she knew exactly what I'd done but was protecting herself by not saying anything. She held that narrow gaze for a second or two and I wondered what was coming next. But she just pinched her lips together and said, "This lesson is Weak Points," and turned to correct Anne's stance.

At the end of the class I watched the other two leave. Mac moved around the dojo, tugging the crash mats into line. I laced my trainer slowly. There were weeks left of this course, week after week of being with Mac and not being sure what she knew. The uncertainty would be intolerable. Better to clear the decks and be certain, once and for all, even if that certainty came with risk.

"You're in the police, aren't you?" I asked her.

"Yep," she said, crossing to the waiting area.

"I read about that superhero person," I said, at once a mass of clichés: pounding heart, quick breath, my face heating up. "Did you hear about that?" I prompted, watching for the clichés to rise in her too so I could see them. The slightest, tiniest flinch would tell me.

Mac snorted. "I attended the scene," she said, and when she looked at me again there was not a trace of recognition, I was absolutely certain of it. Still: that snort, the dismissive tone, irked me. I'd been the one to rescue the woman. Mac had come too late for that.

"You don't sound impressed," I said.

"I'm not." She paused at the foot of the stairway, one foot on the bottom tread. "Want another weak point?"

For a moment, I didn't understand, still reaching for a smart comeback. But Mac strode onto the mats and I saw what she meant.

"OK, then."

"Right. Grab me from behind." She turned her back on me. The label of her T-shirt was sticking up. "Come on," she said. "Hard as you like."

I did what she said: as hard as I could, my arms locked round her barrel squatness, my hands fisted between her breasts.

"Harder!" she said. "You're attacking me!"

I clenched my muscles, all of them, arms, legs, face. Her hands moved over mine and I gripped tighter.

148

"But the police can't be everywhere," I growled, between gritted teeth.

"No," she said. "We can't." She sought my little finger. "If someone's at risk, they should defend themselves with reasonable force," she said, lifting it. "Then call us. Vigilantism is a stupid, dangerous hobby."

"Hobby?!" There's so little strength in that smallest finger. I couldn't do anything about it. She levered it back until I cried out and let go of her. I had to drop down to the floor to stop the pain.

Mac adjusted her T-shirt. "You don't have to be bigger and stronger," she told me, as I panted my way to a standing position. "They'll always be bigger and stronger. You just need to know their weak points."

Neck, nose, little finger.

CHAPTER
SIXTEEN

I could hear Martha, settled on the bottom stair, murmuring to Liv, or Izzy, or whoever, the acoustics of the hall amplifying her voice so perfectly that she might as well have stayed in the kitchen.

"Hannah might not go ... She *might* not ... because she's still freaked out about that man ... I don't know."

I was reading a letter at the kitchen counter, the only win after a tedious morning at work in which I'd tried to address myself to sorting through a vast donation, found I just didn't have the staying power, and given up after ten minutes. The books remained where they were, slumped in piles over the workbench, in their stained boxes, in the overflow cage. I let someone else get on with the till work and pulled a copy of *Notre Dame of Paris* out of the wreckage, its spine too damaged for resale anyway. One paragraph in and it was the Feast of Fools, 6 January 1482, and I was miles and centuries away, exactly where I needed to be (Sanctuary! Sanctuary!). When my volunteer told me her shift was over, I had shoved all the other books into recycling sacks and this beauty had slipped out of

William Morris's *The Story of the Glittering Plain*, slithering onto the workbench like a landed fish.

It was a letter dated January 1978, the address a road not far from ours, the phone number a quaint four digits. The writer, wrestling with a fountain pen that pooled ink in the downstrokes, was thanking his teacher, a Mr Stanley, for "giving me a second chance".

"Now I have a good opportunity with the catering course and I am on the right road and I WILL BE BACK to visit, but DON'T ask me to talk about Chartism again!!!

Yours sincerely,

Ken Bullen."

I looked up. Outside, in the garden, Elliot was lugging a slab of wood across the lawn. He set it down then stood with his hands on his knees.

"I don't know," said Martha now. "I wasn't there . . . Like, just looked up at her window and then left . . . I don't know! Ask her . . . No, because —" She dropped her voice. "Her dad would totally go off on one. He was probably just walking his dog."

The man, the off-on-one father, Martha's lowered voice: all of them rang alarm bells for me. I kept very still and listened out for what came next. Martha was silent for a while — or, nearly silent, letting go of odd consonants, abortive words, as the person on the other end talked. Then, finally, she let loose a laugh of surprising fruitiness. Come on, I counselled myself. You're jumping at nothing. The whole world isn't out to threaten you or her. Let this be what it is: another gossipy, overdramatised chapter in her social life.

I forced my attention to the window. Out in the garden, Elliot had returned to the shed. Then I looked at the letter again. Mr Stanley had kept it for over thirty years. I wondered whether he'd just used it as a convenient bookmark, or whether he'd kept it close by so he could re-read it from time to time. I wondered, most of all, how Ken Bullen's life had worked out, and whether he was happy now. Alone in the shop, I'd searched for him online: Ken Bullen. Kenneth Bullen. Kenneth Bullen restaurant. Ken Bullen chef. There were no obvious hits, so I'd gone to one of those phone directory sites, where there had been an embarrassment of Kenneth Bullens.

"Fuck Zoe," whispered Martha, and remembering that bully and Martha's anxiety about what she was doing, I felt another kick of adrenalin. "She's just a sad little bitch. She's just . . ." The rest was lost, Martha whispering still lower, her words obliterated by the sound of her clambering off her stair and climbing higher. I traced her footsteps across the landing, into her own room right above me where her voice, no longer whispering, became a series of muffled hoots.

There had been more Kenneth Bullens than you could shake a stick at. He could have any future he wanted.

Graduated top of class

Went to Mexico for work experience

Fell in love with Canadian waiter

Owns "The Chartist", a Mexico City cantina

Happy.

152

Elliot emerged from the shed carrying a transparent plastic crate, exercise books sliding inside as his legs knocked against the box. I knew what was in there, knew the lid's neatly printed label and the reverse-chronological order of the contents. When he got to the back door and saw me he paused, a slight but unequivocal hesitation. I'd noticed this over the last couple of weeks: a reticence, his language more minimal than it would usually be. I remembered our conversation about holidays. Were things at work trickier than he was letting on? But this thought had led to others (Elliot's perennial need to shield me from financial worries, my perennial annoyance at him for doing so, my perennial annoyance at myself for not earning a more equal share of our money), until I worried that the whole discussion would be overwhelmed by his need and my annoyance, and I didn't want to open my mouth at all.

Somewhere in all of that, it did strike me that I never used to be so strategic about conversations with him. I'd just dive in and if I got it wrong, we'd work it out together. I tried to remember when we'd stopped talking normally and which of us had stopped first. I wondered if it had pre-dated the costume. I wondered — and even as it came to me, I rejected the thought — I wondered if secrecy was viral.

Elliot, canted back under the weight of the box he was carrying, came into the kitchen.

"You're not throwing those out," I said. "Don't even think about it."

"This is for the loft," he said, taking it over to the table and setting it down. He'd ducked back out before I could join him.

Martha's Schoolbooks (Primary), her early letter formations buried at the bottom of the crate, ill-disciplined queues of them straggling across the broad lines. In the upper layers were projects we'd sweated over together, stories she'd written and curled posters, their corners bearing Blu-Tack grease-marks. Squashed against the side of the box was the 3D model of the rainforest canopy which Elliot had helped her engineer (though this, of course, is utter parental duplicity — Elliot had engineered it *for* her). The paper branches were folded every which way. The toucan which had sat on the topmost layer had dropped off its perch and now languished on the floor of the crate, its beak bent at a right angle. I wished Elliot had stayed so that I could tease him about that model, about how quickly Martha had lost interest, about how late he'd stayed up to finish it, and then maybe he would tease me back about how assiduously I'd hoarded it.

By the time I went outside, Elliot was back in the shed. "Hey," I called. "That toucan's bitten the dust."

"What?" Something clattered to the floor and I heard him say, "shit!"

"Her rainforest project," I said, peeking in. "Do you . . . what are you . . .?"

He'd gutted the shed. The few things it had contained on the Dashwood Stores night — the Johnny night — were now gone. The slab I'd seen him heave onto the lawn was the workbench, wrenched from its

154

moorings, a line of clean wood where it had been fixed to the wall. He was the muckiest thing left in there, stripes of dust across his T-shirt, a dark smear down his arm.

"I'm clearing everything out," he said.

"I can see that," I said, feeling the prod of an unaccountable sadness. It weighted my voice and came out sounding, not like itself, but like the worst sort of pursed-lipped disapproval.

"I'll find somewhere else for all this rubbish, he said. "I'm going to paint the walls. White, to make it lighter. I'm putting in proper shelves for my stuff, and a drawing table."

It was exactly the sort of thing he'd usually have discussed with me first in one of our desultory familial chats: did I think it was a good idea? Did I mind not having access to the shed? I was surprised he hadn't mentioned it at all. Come to think of it, though, when was the last time we'd shared any of our plans? Weeks maybe. I was taken aback to realise it. Nevertheless here he was now, and I didn't want to spoil the moment so I made myself smile and said: "Shed de luxe?"

"Well," he put in almost before I'd finished speaking. "It isn't exactly a shed any more, is it? I mean, I know, technically it is. But . . ." He held his hands up in a gesture which encompassed the peeled roofing felt, the slatted walls, the concrete platform on which it stood. "I thought we could call it a studio." He cleared his throat. "I've got electrics," he went on. "I'm getting a heater for the winter. I just need some space. For my projects. You know."

Of course: the secret comic. I *did* know about his projects — more than he realised. After wearing the superhero costume I could even understand why the comic might obsess him, why he might be compelled to create a proper space for his work. I bet it's more than just a hobby, I thought (and Mac's words came back to me, unwelcome: *a stupid, dangerous hobby*). This was his other life. Vermilion was standing there, right in front of me. I clothed Elliot in his cape, placed Vermilion's mask on Elliot's face. I guessed that it kept pulling him back and back, that he'd started with one idea, a sketch or two, and it had transported him so completely he wanted to keep going: a few inked frames, then the story I'd seen, then others. I guessed that when things were dull at work, at home, he wouldn't be there at all but in the world he'd created, fighting crime in glowing colour.

I almost said all this, almost told him that I'd found his comic, and then I remembered that he'd taken great care not to involve me. I couldn't be found anywhere in its pages, and he'd never said a word about what he'd been doing. The thought of the not-woman niggled perpetually. I stepped inside the studio and he picked up a paint tray. When I reached out to him he said, "Better not. I'm filthy," which had never, ever bothered him before. And because of that perpetual niggle, and because he hadn't shared his plans with me, I didn't do what I probably should have done, which was to touch him anyway and tell him that I didn't care if he was filthy, that I just wanted to be part of what he was doing.

156

"OK," I said after a moment. "Henceforth it's a studio. By decree!" (and even I could hear how laboured that last part sounded). Elliot nodded, his face set, and we couldn't get any further, because at that moment Martha yelled from the back door ("Mum! What's for lunch?"), Elliot offered me a look that was perilously close to dismissal and, for lack of any better response, I left him and went to her.

In the kitchen, Martha had cracked open the crate and pulled out her Year 6 Cornwall project. *Logres* it said on the front, a reference to *Over Sea, Under Stone*, a book she'd read in a term-long Susan Cooper frenzy that year. She'd decorated the cover with a revolving Celtic cross, the segments between the arms revealing a succession of stereotypical Cornish imagery (a pasty, a surfboard, and so on). When I came in, she was spinning the cross round and round.

"What's for lunch?" she said again.

She'd sat at that same table at two years old, patiently converting rusk to glue as I toiled away with my copy of *Healthy Food For Toddlers*, the family on the cover boasting American smiles, the recipes offering forgiveness for a multitude of parental sins; if I could undergo courgette gratin, the Wotsits would be wiped from the record. Halfway to the fridge, gearing up to cook once more, I thought of an alternative.

"I don't know what's for lunch," I said. "What are you making?"

"Yeah, right," she said. Then: "Really?"

"Yes, really."

"Can't I just have what you and Dad are having?"

"No," I said. "We'll have what you make us."

"God!" she said. "I'm really busy. I've got loads of homework. Do you really want me to cook instead of doing homework . . ."

As her rant played out, I remembered the skills I'd learned with Mum: making a roux for sauce, baking blind, painting pastry with egg yolk. We used to make quince jelly, peeling the fiddly fruits, ball-hard and tiny, watching the yellow slop of the juice going through its alchemic transformation, petrifying into amber. I don't think Mum ever envisaged a future for me in which these skills would be surplus to requirement. Perhaps I'd thought I could save Martha from domesticity by keeping her out of the kitchen. But it occurred to me now that her adulthood would actually happen, that it was imminent even, that she would need to eat past the age of eighteen.

"We'll cook together," I said, when she'd finished venting. "I'll teach you something easy. Macaroni cheese, how's that? I'll show you how to make a roux."

She did the requisite humphing, but came over to the counter anyway. We washed our hands together at the tap. Inside the shed, Elliot was working away at the windowsill. I noticed that, despite the paint fumes, he'd fastened the door firmly shut.

CHAPTER
SEVENTEEN

It was Tuesday morning, and Allie and I were gazing through the shop window at the square outside. A regular customer appeared from the back of the Pepperpot, her Scottie dog trotting alongside her. We both grimaced. Rachel came to us at least once a week and every time, she took it upon herself to root out our failings: books mis-shelved, over-praised novels given undue prominence, forgotten classics underpriced. Allie had once made a sign saying "HELP!", so that afflicted staff could hold it up wordlessly when Rachel wasn't looking.

Behind the till my volunteer Uschi counted, her immaculate English only failing when it came to numbers (*vierundzwanzig,* I heard her whisper to the money, *fünfundzwanzig, sechsundzwanzig*). Allie and I watched as Rachel paused in front of the nail bar on the other side of the square, plunged her hand into the pocket of her waxed jacket and pulled out something. The dog sat down and opened its mouth.

"She's not in the mood for books today," announced Allie. "She's going to have a manicure instead."

We tracked her movements over the window display Allie had done for me. She'd set up a Cluedo board right at the front. Piles of detective novels rose around it to different heights, the colours of their spines matching the suspects: reds for Miss Scarlett, yellows for Colonel Mustard, and so on. A replica revolver sat on one of those piles, a spanner leaned against another. She'd set a candlestick on a small table next to an open, leather-bound book. The noose dangled over the game board, right over the dagger placed in the centre: not a real knife but a fake one, the sort you get from a joke shop.

"I can't bear that woman," muttered Uschi.

Rachel made her way through the landscape beyond our window, the same unremarkable vista I'd seen week after month after year, ever since I'd arrived here. Shoppers browsed market stalls, mothers ushered children — all the usual non-events. Now, they barely registered. Instead, more and more, I found myself searching compulsively for the aberrant, the unexpected.

"No, Usch. You're alright," Allie said. "Rachel's having a manicure this morning. Some nice acrylics, bit of nail art. Oh — hang fire. She's moved on to the solicitors now. She needs an injury lawyer. She's been hurt at work. She's had a trip, or a fall."

"I wish she would!" said Uschi.

"Now, that's unkind."

Bad things were happening all the time, I knew that now. They were happening right in front of us, slipping into the spaces between normal. I'd developed a sort of hypersensitivity to anything that might signal trouble: a man running, people stepping too close to each other. Trouble left its mark all around me. There was a rectangle of chipboard set across one of the windows at the bank over the way and I saw — with a rush of fright — a new graffiti tag painted on the wall of the Scout shop. Johnny, I thought. His big friend Max.

"Hey," said Allie. "You OK?" She kept her voice low, the dog whistle for secrecy. We were close enough that I breathed in her perfume, one of her breezy marine fragrances. "Jenny?"

"Yes?"

She glanced in Uschi's direction (*zweiundfünfzig, dreiundfünfzig*) "It's no good keeping things from me," she said, thumbing something away from my cheek. "Don't be an idiot."

The heat rose in my face, and I spooled back through all the things that might have given me away: leaving the shop in costume, or coming back, or — I glanced towards the stockroom, towards the lockers — the costume itself, a few steps away, calling out to be discovered. I touched the bridge of my nose where the mask had rested and the irrationality of this made me even more flustered.

"There's nothing, honestly . . ." But Allie was following my gaze and I could see the locker, its padlock rendering it horribly conspicuous.

"Uh-uh," she said, shaking her head. "Something's up, I know it. Even if I couldn't look at you and see it, I'd know from this place." She flung out her hand in a gesture imprecise enough to encompass the shop floor and stockroom, the shelves and desk and workbench. "The mess isn't like you," she went on, and I realised we were treading quite different ground, that I was reprieved. "And the disorganisation isn't either. Do you know your vollies keep coming to me for things? Forms you'd usually give them, recycling bags you'd usually order."

Oh, I thought. Only that. She was exaggerating, though. Things weren't as out of control as all that. "Well, tell the volunteers to come to me," I said. "We've had a busy time. I'm on it now."

"I'm not nagging," she said. "I'm concerned. I'm —"

"Look," I said, noticing Rachel heading our way, and glad of the interruption. "Incoming."

Allie scrunched her eyes up in mock irritation. At least, I hoped it was mock. "I'm offering to help," she said. "How about we get in early before opening tomorrow? Do the lot together, clear that stockroom completely, cull the shelves, get up to date on the admin?"

If I'd had the luxury of being offended, I might have said something sharp at that moment, but I couldn't because something much more pressing had occurred to me. Among the minor untidiness in the stockroom was Max's rucksack, which I'd shoved under the desk after coming in on that terrifying night. I hadn't opened it since then, had been almost scared to, worried about how I'd react. If Allie insisted on "helping" tomorrow she'd find it in five minutes flat. She might even open it (and — God! I remembered — she'd find the cocaine). Then she'd want to know everything.

Outside, Rachel made the dog sit again. She talked to it, saying the same thing over and over, delight on her face. I watched her lips move: "Good girl! Good girl!" (Cougar, cougar?). I needed to get rid of the bag. Even as the thought formed itself, this one followed: that my reflex was for concealment rather than openness, just as it had been with Elliot. Not a reflex, I corrected myself, but sound and sensible reasoning. That reasoning still held true. Nevertheless, I had the odd sensation of floating off, of being in a small boat bobbing further and further away from shore. I felt this, but I did nothing to alter my course.

"That's a great idea," I told Allie. "How does 8a.m. sound?"

With Uschi distracted by Rachel and Allie in retreat next door, I reckoned I had a couple of minutes in which to remove the rucksack unseen. I grabbed a black bin liner from the workbench and dragged Max's bag out from under the desk, feeling just the tiniest blip of guilt for throwing away his things. If he'd wanted to hang on to them, I thought, he should have chosen his friends more carefully. I pulled it out: black and red, the logo of a sportswear company, and suddenly it was sitting on the tarmac in a wash of streetlight and I was being hit and hit and hit and I couldn't stop it and it would never end. I was right there, everything bigger than normal, all the colours saturated. There was terror, and pain, and astonishment.

Just get the rucksack in the bin bag, I urged myself, but for a few seconds it seemed impossible to do anything. Out in the shop Rachel was querying something with Uschi. I saw Johnny pulling back for the blow, the skateboard already in motion. I saw the scuffed wheel, the Day-Glo decoration, the pale smudge where Johnny's feet had worn down the surface.

He beat me, I thought. He really did. I let myself remember it completely. It had happened. I couldn't change that now. He beat me and it had hurt like hell, but I was still here, and I'd had worse pain, actually, hadn't I? It wasn't childbirth. It wasn't a ten.

The rucksack was halfway into the bin bag when I pulled it out again. The top zip was open. Had I left it that way? I didn't think so.

I unzipped it fully and rummaged through the contents: wallet, keys, paint, energy drink. Poking my head round the edge of the doorframe I saw Uschi reading a cookbook at the till, Rachel sitting cross-legged on the floor in front of the vintage Penguins.

I looked again. Wallet, keys, paint, energy drink. The thing was, I couldn't find the coke. I thought I'd left it where I'd found it, in the front pocket, but — I stuck my fingers down inside and felt right down to the seam — nothing.

"Jenny?" called Rachel.

"Uschi!" I shouted.

I looked in the wallet. I looked in the pocket again. Then the light from the shop floor was blocked and I glanced up. Rachel was standing in the doorway, her grey bob framing her face like parentheses.

"I didn't want to yell," she said, eyeing the rucksack. "Have you seen this?"

She held out the book and I grasped the bag, sealing its mouth. The novel was Henry Green's *Loving*, the original price printed on its cover: 2/6. I slipped the rucksack off my lap and kicked it under the desk, Rachel watching all the while.

"Well, I must have seen it," I said, after a glance at the codes on the flyleaf. "I priced it up."

"It's in your one ninety-nines," she said. "Do you know much about Henry Green?"

"Rachel, I'm so sorry. I'm in a rush . . ."

"Well, this won't take a minute. He's hideously overlooked. Modernist. Look, Jenny, I'm going to buy this from you. I'm going to pay my one ninety-nine and it's an absolute bargain because it's actually a first thus. Do you know what that is?"

"Yes . . ." Uschi's footsteps bore down on us.

"It's a first printing in a new format. First Penguin in this case. It's worth a few pounds more than you're charging. I did feel I should tell you."

"Rachel, really, I just have to . . ."

"And hopefully you're getting something of a lesson in this because, God knows, Famaid needs all the money it can get. There are a few discrepancies in the Literature section, too."

"Uschi, can you ring this up, please?"

"One ninety-nine then," said Rachel, turning away. I jabbed my nails into my palms. On the other side of the partition, Uschi tutted.

I grabbed the rucksack and went outside into the empty yard. Beyond the gate, the church tower was golden against the summer sky, the trees fat with leaves. Wallet, keys, paint, energy drink. I must have missed the baggie. I held the rucksack upside down and shook it. Coins bounced against the concrete. Fragments of sweet wrapper floated out, drifting over the path and onto the grass.

"Oh God," I murmured. Ohgodohgodohgod.

I knelt on the path and pulled everything out of the wallet: Max's ID, his debit card, the money, all of it.

Oh no. Oh no.

I turned the rucksack inside out. I knelt down on the path in the mess and clenched my fists. "No!" I said, banging them on the concrete either side of me. "God . . . bloody . . ."

The drugs had gone.

For the rest of the day I was only half-present, caught up in narratives which might account for the missing coke, the intact wallet. I thought of the bag, now rammed into a bin on the High Street, and formulated reasons why the drugs couldn't possibly be traced to me, before being assailed by certainties that they would. After closing up I put on my music and tried to distract myself with admin. I was staring at an email from Head Office, skidding across the words, trying to get some purchase on them, when Laurie Anderson's "O Superman" came on. Then I knew exactly what would calm me down.

In her last lesson, Mac had progressed from "weak points", outlining a new scenario — the dark alley, the sudden attack. She'd choreographed a series of moves we could use to protect ourselves. They went like this: the villain grabs me, but I don't struggle. Instead I drop down, slipping from his grasp. Before he can react I slam my arms upwards, knocking his away. Then I do something Mac referred to as "applying a technique". I drive my elbow into his belly. I slip my foot behind his. I drive my hip against him so that he unbalances, then I knock him to the ground with a punch.

I got up from the desk and went into the shop, Anderson's panting metronome marking time as I walked through it, slow and precise. Drop, arms up, elbow out, step, shove, punch. I mouthed the words. It helped to imagine the attacker in front of me. He was about to hurt his victim, grabbing me because I was getting in his way. Drop, arms, elbow, step, shove, punch. At the end he sprawled on the ground, helpless. The left arm for the elbow, the right for the punch, my knuckles slamming into his mouth. When I'd done it five or six times it started to come smoothly and everything else began to fall away, a kind of moving meditation. I dipped and rose and twisted again and again, lulled by repetition. If anyone had been in the square outside, they'd have assumed I was dancing.

"O Superman" lasts eight minutes and twenty-one seconds. I closed my eyes and dipped and rose and twisted, and he fell to the ground and sprang up again unharmed so I could do it to him all over again. I stopped having to say the words, stopped being conscious of what I was doing, didn't care if there was talking or just a beat, didn't care when the beat broke down so there was no rhythm to rise and fall to. There was just me and him, and he fell, and fell, and fell, because I wanted him to. Because I made him do it.

CHAPTER
EIGHTEEN

Let me say first that I never consciously intended to read Martha's text messages. It happened by mistake, and that mistake set off everything that came after.

It was breakfast time and I was looking for my diary, missing from its usual place on the kitchen counter. Elliot was showering, Martha was in danger of running late again, and I had less patience than usual.

"Need to get a move on *now*," I told her.

She unwound from the chair and slouched past me, head bent over her mobile. I stopped her at the door. "Bowl."

She swivelled to scoop up the cereal bowl with her other hand, depositing it on the counter. Then she huffed. "God!" she said, holding up the phone in front of me. An indecipherable icon filled the screen. "Look what you made me do!"

"Right," I said, short-circuiting her complaint, taking the phone between thumb and forefinger and slipping it into my dressing gown pocket. "I'll have this till it's time to go. Thank you."

"So you can just take my property?"

"Twenty minutes, M."

"God!"

There was a wet circle where her bowl had been, a new addition to the collection: rings of dried milk, drops of sauce, a cereal hoop welded to the wood. Upstairs, she yelled through the bathroom door for Elliot to hurry up. My pocket vibrated.

When I pulled out the phone, the screen was still lit. At the bottom, a "I" hung next to the little speech bubble. I touched the screen thinking — honestly — that I'd be turning the phone off.

Well, not entirely honestly.

What I thought, precisely, was this: I think this might turn the phone off. Or it might not. If it doesn't and if I end up, by mistake, having a very quick look at Martha's texts, it might just help me get an overview of how she's doing.

And if I thought any more, I might have thought something like this: she only understands the tiniest part of the world she's operating in. She needs me, even if she thinks she doesn't. So I touched the screen, and a message popped up, the sender a string of numbers, no name. It said: *stop wining lezza your a total inadiq8*.

There was a subsidence within me, something falling through my centre. *Lezza*. I cannot tell you the fury. Nothing — not the mugging, not the graffiti, not even the encounter with Johnny — nothing matched up to what I would do to this little shit. And that last word. Once I'd unravelled it, I wondered what kind of enemy Martha had, this person who used *inadequate* as a noun. I would take her apart. I would go into school with Martha and take this little shit by the collar, and —

Just above the text, on the opposite side of the screen, was the message Martha had sent just moments before, as she'd been sitting at the breakfast table, the message which had prompted that stream of insults: *Leave Izzy alone u troll.*

Blooming in my memory: Martha aged three, being chewed out for something I thought she'd done. She had looked up at me, head tipped right back because she was so small, and proceeded to explain why I was wrong. I got ready to chew her out all the more, and then I noticed that her hands were shaking, her little frame shuddering. This tiny and frankly terrified person holding her ground, and suddenly, I couldn't give a monkey's whether I was right or not. "You're such a good girl," I told her, squashing her in a hug, kissing her temple as she held still, wary and baffled. "You're such a good, brave girl."

Upstairs, a door opened and closed. Elliot called, "Time to go, Bo Bartha." Martha replied in her higher register, the words indistinct. The next bit wasn't a mistake. I fiddled about on the screen until I found a list of previous messages.

From Liv: *Be-ATCH! fucking zoe. Dan sayz every1 laffs at her anyway off her face dancing at the edge*

From Izzy: *Thx gorge! POS*

Martha thudded down the stairs. I heard her dropping her bag, scrabbling for her shoes. "Check you've got your science folder," I shouted through, trying to work out how to close down the messages.

"I have."

My fingers poked at the front of the phone until finally something worked, some electronic Open Sesame, and the texts were replaced with rows of icons. From the hall came the rattle of keys being slipped off the rack. "Double-check your science folder," I called. "Look in your bag."

I pressed every button on that thing. When I reached the top, the screen went dark. I dropped it into my pocket.

Martha came through from the hall and stood in the middle room. On the windowsill behind her, I spotted my diary, in a place I knew I'd never put it. "Phone?" she said. "Mum? You OK?"

"I'm fine," I said, thinking, who moved that diary? I looked at Martha, hand outstretched, weight on one hip, expression halfway to arsey. I looked at her and I thought of the nasty bigot who was waiting for her at school. I cast about for the magic bullet, the pep talk which would send her into battle equipped. She was fourteen and she'd heard it all from me, a meaningless string of sounds, a background hum. What I wanted to give her now was not a lecture, but that feeling of confidence that would make her lift her head and meet Zoe's eyes unafraid.

"Hang on," I told her. "I've got something to show you."

In the middle room I made her face me.

"I'm going to be late," she said.

"Don't worry about that. I'll drive you in," I told her. "This is important. I'm going to teach you how to protect yourself."

"What?"

"In case you ever need it. I'm going to show you a great self-defence move, and then I'll take you to school."

"Um . . . weird much?"

"Put your bag down."

She hesitated before dipping her shoulder so that the bag slipped off to the floor. I kicked it towards the wall.

"Concentrate," I said. "It doesn't matter if your opponent is bigger than you."

"Yeah," she said. "My opponent."

"Imagine one," I said, and I waited for her to do that. When she did — when I could see she had someone very clearly in mind — I told her: "It doesn't matter if they're bigger than you, or stronger than you. The only thing that matters is their weakest point."

I made her grab me. I made her hold as tight as she could. Upstairs, there were footsteps across the landing. A door closed. I found Martha's little finger and prised it up with extraordinary care, and after a moment she said, "Ooh? Ooh! Stop." She looked at her finger, and at me, and she pushed up her sleeves.

"OK," she said. "My turn."

I circled her with my arms and squeezed, setting my cheek against the back of her head, so that her hair tickled my face and covered my eyes. She did a bit of puffing and panting. "Don't waste your energy," I said. "Just find my weakest point." I kept holding her, even after she'd found my little finger and bent it up too far for comfort. "OK," I said, buckling at the knees. "Stop."

That's it, I told her. You've got it.

CHAPTER
NINETEEN

The dress was red and clingy, the type of garment I'd always looked past when I went shopping, but it had found its way into my hand, and I had found my way into a changing cubicle, found myself wriggling out of my clothes, pre-emptively stockpiling excuses for how ridiculous this was going to be, how — in Martha's parlance — *sad* it was: I was just trying it on for something to do, I knew it would look awful, I was playing dress-up.

From the cubicle next door came a flat little "Oh!" of disappointment, a rummaging, a rustle.

Actually, I remembered as I wrestled under the uncharitable lights, I hadn't always looked past clothing like this. I recalled Elliot's sister years ago — this was at Uni, before she'd even introduced me to him — going through my wardrobe in a last-minute panic before a party. She had come up with a Morticia Addams stretchy black velvet thing I used to wear with a low-slung belt. It amounted to little more than body paint. She'd tried it on in my room, tilting unsteadily on the bed so she could see herself full length. "Do you really wear this?" she'd asked me. "Do you wear it *out*?"

And I had. I wore everything out, a roster of facepalm trends which now lurked in family photograph albums, ready to ignite hilarity: legwarmers, puffball skirts, oversized T-shirts standing in for dresses, a selection of jaunty hats, arab pants, bodycon, crop tops, combats. I wore them carelessly, not appreciating what I had, my own body wasted on me. I never gave a thought to holding in my tummy or pulling back my shoulders, or how to stand or how to sit, or any of the myriad ways I now routinely used to create the illusion I wasn't fat. In truth, I hadn't actually known that other people needed to do those things.

"Oh!" said the woman next door, happier this time, an upward inflection in her voice.

If I could go back now (I thought, reaching behind me to pull up the zip of the red dress), if I could go back and try on that body again, that pre-Martha, pre-eating-for-comfort, pre-I-don't-get-much-exercise body that I used to inhabit, I would do everything I could to deserve it. I would revel in it.

When I looked in the mirror, expecting the worst, I saw that the fabric had wrapped itself around my breasts, revealing a deep plunge of cleavage. It came in tight across my ribcage and clung to my hips. I had a shape after all, in normal clothes, not just the costume. It was a rough out-in-out which might be called hourglass, if you were feeling generous. I thought I might step out of the cubicle in it, have a look in the bigger mirror at the end of the changing room.

We emerged simultaneously, me and the woman next door. She was wearing a satiny summer dress, the fabric printed with a photographic image of feathers. I let her go first and stood back near the entrance to the changing rooms while she scraped her hair up on top of her head and smiled at herself, switching profiles periodically. White-legged though I was, barefoot and devoid of make-up, I still edged a little closer to the entrance, wanting to be seen.

Outside the changing rooms were the shoe displays, and the seating which went with them, occupied here and there by shoe-buyers, or the bored partners of shoppers. I pulled my shoulders back, waited for someone to look my way and . . . was that . . .?

A moment's dislocation, but it was her. Mac in civvies — long, multi-pocketed shorts and a polo shirt. She was sitting side-on to the changing rooms, a pair of utilitarian German sandals discarded beside her. Two things struck me immediately. The first was that she had a scar on her right calf, a tangled line of flesh about four inches long. The second was that she was wearing my shoes. The vigilante shoes. The glossy red heels, the ones I'd had on when I'd intervened in the mugging.

Against the neutral shades of the carpet and Mac's clothing, they were a shocking spike of colour: the drop of blood in your underwear, the wicked stepmother's apple. And Mac herself, like a character in one of those mix-and-match books kids have: two-thirds ordinary, one-third fabulous. But they can't be mine, I thought, and then I spotted the box they must have come from, the pop socks she'd been lent to try them on with, their "American Tan" line across her ankles. Not mine, of course, but just like them; thousands of identical pairs in shops all over the country.

She was leaning forward, swivelling her legs to see the shoes at different angles, her expression speculative, calculating. As I watched she walked her feet away from her a few steps, then back again. It looked all wrong, Mac doing anything that wasn't the shortest distance between two points. She seemed wholly absorbed, and I wondered where she was now — back in that alley maybe. I wondered whether she was still herself, or whether she was imagining what it might be like to be a superhero.

The woman at the mirror came past and I stepped back to give her room. She leaned into the shop, her fingertips holding the wall, and called to Mac.

"Classy!" she said.

Mac's voice: "Give me a minute, Cath."

"Shaz!" said the woman: "Come here. I need you to say something encouraging."

Shaz? Those shoes wouldn't lead her to me; I hadn't even bought them in Bassetsbury. Still, I went through a perfunctory mime designed to suggest that something was not quite right with my dress, and retreated to the cubicle. I was Jenny Pepper, Mac's student. No reason why she shouldn't see me. But still I locked the door as she came in and leaned back against it. In the mirror, I saw myself wincing.

Wincing, but in a great dress.

"Take off those pop socks, or I'll pretend I don't know you," said Cath, and I thought, lady, you are playing with fire. I waited for Mac to crush her, but all

176

I heard were two soft snaps, as if she were doing the very thing Cath had told her to.

"Were you having a mad moment there?" said Cath.

"I've seen those shoes before," said Mac, and I tingled with fright. "They were worn by a witness at a mugging I attended. Do you remember me telling you? The one wearing a superhero costume?"

There was silence from outside, while I let bliss shoulder out the fear. *Do you remember me telling you?*

"Why were you trying them on?" said Cath.

"Just curious," said Mac. "Look, I'm off in a couple of minutes. I'm on at two today."

"I wish you weren't," said Cath. "I know I'm a big baby, but I wish you weren't."

"We've talked about this," said Mac.

I won't lie. I was torn between embarrassment that I should have ended up hearing this and utter fascination. Fascination won, of course. It was like reading your teacher's diary. The intimacy — *we've talked about this*. It was the way you spoke to your partner, not your friend. It made me think of Martha. I imagined her being this comfortable with someone one day, doing something this mundane.

"Then you know what I'm going to say," said Cath. "Go on. Get something in private security. Or fraud work. Better hours, better money. You'll have loads of time to encourage me in changing rooms."

"It'll be different next year. I'll be trying for Armed Response," said Mac and then, maybe in answer to some face Cath had pulled, some silent gesture: "I think there's room to change the culture."

"People say that, but the culture doesn't change," said Cath. "Or it changes too slowly. Too slowly for you. I want you to be happy."

Someone else came in then. There were sorrys and excusemes, and a door closing at the far end.

"It's a lovely dress," said Mac.

Cath sighed. "I think it's gaping at the back."

"Looks fine to me."

"Fine is the worst word. Say a better one."

"I'm no good at this. You always look nice."

Cath tutted. "Dress," she said, in a knuckle-dragging voice. "Blue. Pretty."

Mac called time and told Cath she'd see her at home. There was the crumple of fabric (hug?) and something that sounded like a kiss.

When they'd gone I waited a good long time before coming out. It had never occurred to me that Mac was anything but happy, or that her happiness and her ambition might be in conflict. She wanted to change the culture, but to me Mac *was* the culture. In fact, I'd never imagined her as anything other than a representative of the roles in which I knew her: a police officer, and a police officer thinly disguised as a self-defence instructor.

I stood in front of the mirror and watched myself, twisting left and right, facing away and looking back. If I were a superhero, I thought, this is what I'd wear on my day off.

CHAPTER
TWENTY

Two nights later, hanging on to Elliot's arm for balance, I tip-tip-tipped up the driveway to Martha's school. It had been dropped on the crest of the hill sometime in the late fifties, a slab of concrete and glass. Squares of sticky coloured plastic adhered to the windows, picked at by generations of pupils and eroded to form abstract shapes, the focus of Rorschach speculation in double Maths. I kept looking sideways at the glass. There I was, curvaceous in the ravishing dress. There was Elliot, James Bond in a black suit, white shirt open at the neck, bow tie — undone — and mirror-shiny shoes. Elliot kept looking sideways at me, too. He'd been doing it all evening, since I'd come downstairs and he'd been in the kitchen chugging a beer. He'd spluttered just like they do in films, and had to put the bottle down.

"Wow, Jen," he'd said, wiping his mouth, and a succession of emotions had passed across his face. Surprise, and (I thought) an edge of lust; he'd started forward before stopping abruptly and closing his expression right off, sealing himself away from me. I couldn't place it, that last look of his, but if pushed I'd have said it seemed remarkably like sadness. As for me,

I'd felt a crushing disappointment that we weren't already snogging.

"You like?"

"Yup," he said. "I like. Now come on, we're running late."

At the entrance to the school, I stumbled and steadied myself against him. Something in his jacket knocked against me.

"What's this?" I touched his chest.

"It's just a prop."

"Oh, yes?" I opened his jacket. Inside, heat and cologne and Elliot-smell, all the warm solidity of him. I checked his response, an assessment I performed more and more now, his mood shifting in ways that were increasingly hard to predict. But he made no attempt to stop me. Inside his jacket there was a sort of harness, wrapped round his shoulders and coming down low across his ribs. Not a harness. A holster.

"Oh. You really have got a gun in your pocket."

"I was going for authenticity."

A couple came up behind us and we executed a shuffled sidestep, pressed close to each other. I kissed his chin, Bond-smooth, and nipped at his earlobe.

"Do you want to shake me or stir me?" I said, and immediately wished I hadn't, because he said nothing *at all*, just glanced back down the drive, and I felt stupid and clumsy and leery. Had I misread that look of desire earlier? Did he fancy me at all any more?

"Come on," I said, shaking him. "Come on, come *on*. Have some fun with me. What's wrong?" There were more footsteps behind us and he pulled away, drawing out the gun as he did so. "What's up?" I said again. "I'm sick of this. Tell me!"

He nodded towards the newcomers and said, "Forget it. Not now. Nothing's wrong." He raised the pistol and levelled it at me, and I thought how violence simplifies everything. There is no ambiguity, no struggle to understand what is going wrong in a relationship, or why. Just knock the gun askew, land a punch to the jaw and a knee to the balls: bam, bam, bam. Sorted in three frames.

"Hey!" I said. "Aren't you never meant to —"

He swung it away across the vista of the school, taking in the fence and Leylandii boundary, the caretaker's bungalow and car park.

"It's a fake," he said, and I took it from him.

The pistol was black, and heavier than I would have expected. I settled the grip in my palm, slid my finger *behind* the trigger — just in case — and pointed it away from me. There was a notch at the trigger end of the barrel and a red dot at the other end to line it up with. When you have no hand-eye coordination to speak of, you always assume you'd be a rubbish shot. I got the door of the bungalow in my sights, the letterbox on the door. I noticed a wobble in my hand. I imagined a shot across the car park, the *ting* on the metal of the letterbox, the dent they'd find there later. Then Elliot reached across and put his hand on the barrel. The gun dipped and my focus shortened again. He slipped it from my grasp and holstered it.

"Come on, Bond girl," he said, and I knew it was a softening of sorts, and regretted the thought that came to me unbidden: what a poor substitute it was, being a Bond girl, when all we ever really want to be is James Bond.

We entered through the canteen, soused in the mingled fragrance of yesterday's lunch and teenage sweat. Above us, I could hear voices and music, something Rat Pack-ish, echoing out of the hall and down the stairs.

"Mack the Knife," said Elliot. "Not Bobby Darin. Robbie Williams, for Christ's sake."

One floor up, there was a queue to get in, uniformed girls flanking the doors, their blonde hair swept into fiddly dos. I recognised one of them as Hannah, a girl in Martha's class. We weren't the only ones dressed up for Casino Night. Ahead of us, the women wore maxi dresses and diamanté, one of the men a full tux. After the door girls had checked their tickets, the tuxedoed man steered one of the women inside by pressing on the small of her back, the gesture tripping a memory: Ian Donaldson, Liv's dad, guiding me in the darkness of the ruined chapel.

The woman turned and I saw it was Liv's mum, Helen.

"Thank you, Zoe," she said to the other ticket girl — the one I didn't recognise. The girl pretended to bow.

Zoe.

Hannah greeted me and Zoe took our tickets. She was a hand's reach away. I had a sudden, terrible vision of enacting one of Mac's walk-throughs on her: destabilise, topple, apply a technique. I would never have done it, but the idea came to me just the same.

Zoe had a taste for ultra-thick eyeliner, a mole high up on her left cheekbone, a double-piercing in her right ear. One of the holes was unoccupied, the other had a demure stud in place. Her wrists, when she passed the tickets back to Elliot, were garlanded in charity bracelets. Her nails were painted pink and raggedly bitten.

"Here's your fun money," said Hannah, handing Elliot a wedge of paper. "You buy your chips at the table. The person with the most chips at the end wins a prize."

"How did you get roped into this, then?" Elliot asked.

Hannah grimaced. "Mr Grafton." She stretched out an arm to push open the hall doors, and we walked into the makeshift casino.

There's no disguising a school hall, but someone had tried. The walls were decorated with posters of playing cards, the stage with a stack of outsized dice. The PTA had raided their lofts; wrapped round the projector mount and straggling out from it, uneven lines of flashing Christmas lights stood in for the glittering ceiling of a Las Vegas casino. They were joined by the winking slot machines standing along the windows, their electronic tings and trills and flourishes audible between the spaces in the music. And the music was loud, once we were inside. Monster speakers had been set up on the stage, raised high on skinny tripods. In the centre of the room, two crowds were gathered. We'd been promised professional gaming tables, blackjack and roulette. As we watched, a cry went up from one of the groups.

"Drink?" said Elliot.

"White wine!" In the hubbub, I exaggerated my lip movements and knocked back an imaginary glass.

The bar was a line of trestles covered with paper tablecloths. Behind it, Bill Grafton was playing barman, his boyband hair like a wing folded across his forehead. He was dressed in a suit, passing a bottle from one hand to the other. When he saw Elliot approaching he tossed the bottle up in the air, end-over-end, then scrabbled for it with both hands as it fell back down towards him.

Onstage, a screen displayed an endlessly revolving roulette wheel. I stared at it for a while, trying to see the join, the jump-cut. There was another shout from one of the gaming tables and the group ruptured, a woman coming away laughing, a man pushing in through the gap she'd left. I went over to see what was happening.

The players were standing at the baize, a circle of onlookers around them. Penny, the PTA chair, sporting chandelier earrings and a plunging neckline, pushed two chips onto the 16. "Bang goes the humanities wing," said the man behind her, and she laughed. There were other people I knew, or who at least looked familiar; faces from other meetings, parents I made Martha thank when I picked her up from parties.

I felt a tap on my arm and Elliot was there. He pushed a glass of wine towards me and pointed at the next table. "Blackjack," he said. "See you in a bit."

184

Just in front of me, Helen Donaldson twitched her pendant into place and scratched at the nape of her neck. The clasp had rubbed at her skin, leaving a pink blotch.

"Jenny!"

"Hi."

"You're looking lovely." She reached up to pat her hair, a sixties bouffant.

"You too."

"Just watching Ian lose our life savings!" She tipped her head towards the table and I noticed Ian then, running his fingers down a tower of chips, nudging them forward onto the 34. She placed her hand on his shoulder. He turned to smile at her, then saw me, and winked.

"There's Gill," she said. "I promised to have a quick chat with her. Back in a mo."

When she'd gone Ian offered me a smile, and I realised that this time he had not glanced away, but allowed his gaze to linger. I remembered the surprise of his muscled arms, the erotic *ping* they'd set off in me. I drew myself straighter and smiled back.

"You betting?" he asked.

"Not yet." I pointed at his pile of chips. "How much have you got left after all that?"

"Nada," he said, grinning. "If you're going to lose, lose big."

There was a croupier, a young woman in a black waistcoat. She set the wheel spinning, and the attention of the table was suddenly on her. With a flick of the wrist she cast the ball into the outer rim. It streaked round in the opposite direction — "No more bets!" — and we fell into synchronised attention, trying to see it as it was, not blurred nor stretched, trying to track it. After a few seconds it slowed and tripped into the chambers of the wheel, skittering between the numbers, the watchers crying out in hope or disappointment, until finally it kicked up one last time and settled.

"Six black," said the croupier, and there was a cheer from the other end.

"Right," said Ian. "I'm done." He pushed himself away from the padded edge of the table as Helen returned with drinks for both of them. We stood between the roulette and the slot machines, shuffling back and forth when people needed to get past. We talked about our daughters, about GCSEs. Helen started to tell me about Liv's behaviour.

"It's getting hard for us to trust her," she said. I thought about my own child, as parents do in those situations, and prepared to calibrate Martha's activities against whatever Helen was about to reveal.

"I've started having to double-check what she tells me," Helen went on. Ian took a swig of his beer and placed a hand lightly on her shoulder. A quick glance passed between them. "He always tells me I worry too much," she said, giving a tight smile.

"We'll see Liv right," said Ian. "She just needs boundaries." His hand stayed where it was. Over at the blackjack table I caught glimpses of Elliot, seated with his back to me, and it was hard not to feel a pang of jealousy at Ian's attentiveness, at the unspoken connection he had with Helen.

"How's your chapel coming on?" I asked Ian, remembering the leaflet I'd seen in Martha's room and the protest over the bats.

"Great," he said.

"They've had to stop the development," said Helen, and the corner of Ian's mouth twitched.

"Oh dear."

"Temporarily," he said, taking his hand away from her shoulder. "There's a system. You just need to work it."

"Well," I said, struggling for something non-committal. "I'm sure you'll —" but he cut me off. "Look out," he said. "Here comes Tom Cruise."

Bill Grafton had left the bar and made his way over as we hid our guilty laughter. "If it isn't the high rollers of Year 10," he said. "Lost your shirts yet?"

The others gave appropriately amused replies and said polite things about the entertainment. I glanced towards Elliot again, but there was a fair crowd around his table now, and he was hidden. Just for a second I slipped my feet out of the precarious shoes, one at a time, and flexed them.

"We're not best pleased," Mr Grafton was saying. "We've had a DVD player and a load of laptops stolen. That's two burglaries in one month. The police can't work out how they're getting in."

"You amaze me," said Ian.

(Right, I thought. There'll be a dodgy door.)

"If you're expecting the police to sort it, you'll be waiting a long time," Ian went on.

(It might be a loose window. The ones in this place are ancient.)

"We're a school," said Mr Grafton. "We can't take our own action."

"Why not?" I asked.

"We have to do it by the book."

"Seriously though," I said. "Who'd stop you? Who'd know?"

Ian flashed me a grin. "Just stick up a couple of cameras," he said. "If they've come twice already, they'll come again."

"Oh, well . . ." Mr Grafton laughed. "You wouldn't believe the hoops we'd have to jump through to do that."

"We should get that vigilante onto it," said Helen. (And my heart pounded! And my face flushed warm! And I could feel a hot white spotlight trained right on me!)

"Which vigilante?" I said.

"Oh, God, it was great," said Helen, suddenly animated. "She actually stopped a mugging, in that alley at the back of the churchyard. She was wearing a Superhero outfit: cape, mask, the works. Didn't you hear about it?"

"I don't think . . ."

"There was a picture in the *Examiner*," said Helen. "Someone had a mobile. You'll think I'm nuts, but . . ." She glanced at Ian and took a step closer to me. "After I saw what she'd done, I wanted to do the exact same thing. I wanted to try it and see what it felt like. Does that sound odd?"

"Not a bit," I told her. "Not even slightly."

There was such a joyful turmoil in me, I couldn't believe she hadn't spotted it. I snuck glances at the others, watching to see if they were sneaking glances my way too. But they all just carried on as normal. Mr Grafton reminded us about the upcoming raffle then moved away. Elliot was still engrossed at the blackjack table. So, perhaps what I'd done wasn't crazy, or stupid, or unbalanced after all. Helen didn't think so, and neither had the *Examiner*. Maybe Allie and Mac were the ones in the minority. Maybe, to everyone else, what I'd done had been bold and admirable. Then I remembered that I'd promised myself never do it again, and my joy curdled.

I didn't catch what Helen said next; someone had just turned up the music again. I cupped my hand behind my ear.

"Do you fancy a go on the slots?" she shouted. "Bit of fun?"

"OK," I yelled.

My slot machine was decorated with cartoon characters. Helen's had an Arthurian theme. She shook a handful of coins from her purse and fed them in, moving her fingers over the bank of buttons until the machine lit up, the reels spinning and clunking into place. That set off yet more noise, an electronic glockenspiel, and it was suddenly all too much: the pounding Sinatra, the shouts from the tables, a phoney medieval lay battering at my ears. Helen gave me a thumbs-up and I smiled, and then, the moment she turned away again, shut my eyes. The flashing lights played against my closed lids.

This was not Vegas. This was a school hall in Bassetsbury. We were spending fake money in a fake casino and my husband, with his fake gun, was not James Bond. He wouldn't be saving anyone tonight. And it was fake that I pretended to like Mr Grafton, and it was fake that I had smiled nicely at Zoe. I wanted to leave right now, and my excuses for doing so would be fake, too. My life had been an extended method character immersion, and I'd just remembered I was only doing it for a role.

I opened my eyes and leaned across to Helen to tell her I was off. I looked past her, back down the hall. There were the two groups of onlookers clotted round the gaming tables. There was the bar and the screen and the playing cards decorating the walls. There were people in the spaces between all of these things. And there was something wrong with this picture.

I scanned it again, checking for the anomaly. And then I found it, the tiniest detail: one of the speakers on stage was out of line. It had moved — was this possible? — closer to the edge, as if it had crept there on its spindly tripod feet.

The horn section was laying it on thick at the end of "Come Fly With Me", the notes buzzed and I watched as the speaker, shuddering, inched forward a little more. Beneath it Mr Grafton was talking to a parent, oblivious. He leant in and touched her arm. She laughed and turned to walk away. The front leg of the tripod reached the edge.

190

I kicked off my shoes.

"You OK?" called Helen, but I was already plotting my trajectory through the room. I took a breath and began to run.

There was a line between the gaming tables but it wasn't clean. A man strolled away from the blackjack crowd, the croupier stepped back from her wheel. I shouted as I ran, my feet slipping on the polished floor: "MOVE!" The music obliterated my yells, but the man saw me anyway and veered out of my path. I pushed the croupier aside.

One tripod leg slipped off the stage, the speaker jerked forward. It swayed above Mr Grafton's head, straining at the leash of its flex, a taut line between the plug and the jack. There was movement in the crowd, people staring at me, staring — as Bill Grafton did now — with a convulsive social horror. I was the only one looking in the right place, at the sharp-cornered bulk dangling over them, at the jack which just —

Popped!

Out of the back. At the flex, which fell to the floor, limp.

At the speaker, which was pitching over the edge.

I hit Mr Grafton hard, ramming him with my shoulder. A yell, a shove, and he went sprawling out of harm's way, and I hurled myself on top of him. I slapped my hand over his eyes, scrunching mine shut, and never saw what happened next. There was a hollow *whump* as the speaker landed, a clatter, a communal shout of alarm. Something hit my hand which would have hit his face, had I not been protecting him. When

I opened my eyes I saw screws revolving on the floor next to us. There was a splintered black box an arm's-length away, wire mesh buckled at its front, a metal cone ejected from its innards. The speaker had embedded itself in the parquet floor, slats smashed or levered up where it had landed. By our heads was a single block of wood, thrown clear of the impact.

Bill Grafton shook me off. "Oh, God," he said. "Shit. Oh, God."

"Are you hurt?"

He was patting himself, feeling his chest and face. I looked him over: no injuries, but his skin was pale, his eyes shock-wide. Onstage, the remaining speaker had started pumping out a Michael Bublé song.

"You're fine, Bill." My skirt had ridden up during the rescue and I tugged it down. Elliot was there, reaching out to me. At his feet were bank notes, dozens of them, fun money carrying the school logo. I heard applause.

"Jenny?" said Elliot. "Jen?" As if he was unsure. As if he was checking.

Behind him, Ian Donaldson was waving away help. The sleeves of his tux strained at the seams as he hefted the remains of the speaker onto the stage. I grasped Elliot's hand and started to get to my feet. "Amazing," he was saying. "Unbelievable."

The gaming tables were empty, the slot machines abandoned. There was a crowd around us, and all the faces in it were looking my way. At that instant, before they went to clear up the mess, or took a sip of wine, or returned to what they were doing before, every single one of them was gazing at me.

I rose, ecstatic, borne on the updraught of their admiration. I wanted to shout, I wanted to punch the air, I wanted to run out into the dark and be mighty all over again.

CHAPTER
TWENTY-ONE

That night I lay awake for hours, buzzing. I relived every moment of the rescue: the way I'd noticed the problem with the speaker when nobody else did, how decisive I'd been, my headlong dash towards danger. I thought about how, afterwards, the room had arranged itself around me; I'd been congratulated, drinks were thrust into my hand. On the way home Elliot and I had retold the story, gleefully anatomising it (". . . you made this running leap . . ." ". . . I just thought: *protect his face* . . ."). There was nothing like it, I decided, as Elliot's snores crescendoed beside me and I reached across to joggle him into silence.

I considered the sort of things which, over the past few years, had thrilled me. I'd recognised a rare book at the shop, a signed first edition of Vonnegut's *Jailbird* which had netted us over £500. Elliot's design award; Martha playing Sheila Birling in the Year 9 production of *An Inspector Calls* (she had talent, a chip off the old block). No one could say these weren't lovely things. But then, there was how I felt when I took on the mugger, and how I felt when I saved Mr Grafton, and they knocked all the lovely things right out of the park.

Just before I'd rescued Mr Grafton, I'd had the thought that my life had been one long character immersion. But the role wasn't the person. I could detach from one and take on another. I'd berated myself for wanting to step away from my responsibilities to Elliot and Martha, but I was already more than one character, I had been for years: wife, mother, friend, worker. Would it really be such a terrible thing to put on the costume from time to time and take on one more role, when doing it would make me feel so transcendently marvellous?

In the street outside, a lone walker passed by, the click of high shoes rather than the scuff of flats. A woman, coming home late. I waited until she'd passed out of earshot, listening for any falter in the regular tap of her heels. When I was out there, being a vigilante, I felt a roaring exaltation but there was danger too, real and terrifying. I couldn't edit out the beating I'd taken, the fear it had instilled in me. But even that was a bit different now, wasn't it? It had taught me a lesson and I was alive to those dangers, less likely to stumble into trouble. Besides, Mac had finally got round to teaching us something useful in our classes, so I wasn't defenceless any more.

I thought about dressing in the costume and leaving the shop. Falling towards sleep, I saw myself walking dark footpaths as if I owned the place, striding boldly through my town, the cape flaring behind me.

When I woke up, the first thing I did was to repudiate everything I'd thought the night before. I reminded myself you should never act on anything you decide at 3a.m. and got on with my morning. I went to work. When Martha called to ask whether she could stay the night with Liv, I realised that there would be nobody at home that evening; Elliot would be with Ian up at the school, helping to clear classrooms before the summer holiday renovations ("Calling all fathers!", the email had said, as if women couldn't lift a table). I made myself imagine an evening at home alone in a tidy house. I reflected on how calm and grounding that would be. When a customer brought six boxes of useless books into the shop I thanked him warmly and hauled each one through to the newly organised stockroom, my T-shirt grey with dust. I looked through every single box, just in case there was something of value.

I watched the clock.

I glanced at the locker in which my costume lay.

When the jobs ran out, I sat at the till and searched a pile of children's books for the treasures they might contain. Everything I found — a feather, a bookmark, a photo — triggered fantasies of audacious rescue.

A dandelion was pressed between the pages of *Rousing Stories for Girls* (the girl on the front waving, apple-cheeked, from her bicycle, clouds haloed behind her head). When I parted the pages, the seeds stuck to one side in a clump, the stalk to the other. A memento left by a plucky wartime spy, I decided, slipped into her daughter's book while the girl slept. In the dark of night the child stirs and sees the book on her bedside table. At that moment, a dandelion is blown in the cold skies over Germany and a parachute floats to the ground. The girl never knows it, but her mother will rescue a family from the Nazis.

She'll rescue several families.

She'll liberate hundreds.

She'll slaughter the SS guards and set everyone free.

I looked up from the book and it was as if the colours around me had dimmed. Outside, a woman was dumping some bags in our doorway without bothering to bring them in. Judith, an hour and a half late for her shift, was stepping over them to enter the shop.

And I thought: Really? *This* is what I'm choosing to do with my life? My meagre, half-finished-if-I'm-lucky life? *These* are the experiences I'm choosing?

And I thought: Stuff this.

Closing time came and I couldn't wait any longer. Still too bright outside, but I wanted to get dressed anyway. I'd spent my lunch hour buying two extra items: a wig, to give myself one more layer of anonymity, and a new phone. The mobile I would use only when in costume, in case I needed to call the police. It was untraceable: pay-as-you-go, in a false name (Jo March), and bought with cash. I told myself I needed to dress early so I could get used to the wig, but I don't know why I bothered with the excuse. I was just desperate to get into costume.

Buttoning the blouse, I saw through its sheer sleeve a trail of darkened skin, the shadow of the bruise from Johnny's skateboard. I prodded it a couple of times and

197

pressed my ribs, where there was still an ache, and fear roared past me, a blast of noise and air. I shut my eyes while things were blown every which way. There was a streaking Doppler whine and then it was gone. I put on the tights and the skirt. I laced up my corset and tucked the cheese knife into my tool belt.

I put on the new wig, a sleek red bob. Positioning the mask, I thought of Johnny trying to remove it, the rage it had triggered. I put on my lipstick and my red mouth said: "Don't hurt me," and there was a tremor in my voice. I said: "No one hurts me," and it sounded like a question. Then I told him: "Don't fuck with me. Don't even think about it."

A door slammed in the yard and I jumped. Footsteps headed for my back door — my unlocked back door, my stupidly neglected back door. I dropped the lipstick into the basin with a clatter. I reached to turn the key but the handle was already moving.

I made it into the toilet cubicle just before the door banged against the wall. I fumbled with the bolt, all fingers and thumbs, Allie calling my name.

"Hey, Jen! Fancy a drink?"

"I'm in the loo!" I said, breathing slow and low so she couldn't hear me panting.

"I'll hang on," she said.

"No! Don't. I mean — don't bother. I really can't come. I shouldn't."

I leaned my head against the door. Her feet scuffed the concrete. "Oh!" she said, warily now. "You rushing back, then?"

"Yes." I waited. "You know. Saturday night."

"Of course. No worries."

But she didn't make a move to leave. She was suspicious, I could hear it. Allie was equipped with an unfailing bullshit detector. What's more, this was *me* trying to bullshit her; she knew all my tells. Very, very gently, I banged my head against the door. The wig rustled as it made contact. I could reveal myself and hear her judgements all over again, or I could carry on lying and she'd never let it rest. Or maybe I could cobble together a half-truth, to fend her off.

"Allie, the thing is, I don't want to come out. I've done something a bit stupid. I've . . ." I cycled through the possibilities: I've dyed my hair a terrible colour, I've tipped paint down myself, I've had a massive row with Elliot and need to be alone. "Allie, I've . . ."

"I know what you've done," she said. "Hon, I'm not the police." A prickling heat broke out on my skin.

"I found the coke ages ago," said Allie, so close that the wood vibrated against my nose and forehead. We were, I guessed, face to face, the door between us. "I haven't said anything to anyone." It took a moment to piece it together. Coke — rucksack — Max. I wanted to laugh with relief.

"That was you?" I said.

"Yep."

"Did you flush it? I don't care. It doesn't matter. It's not even mine."

Allie uttered a snort. "Can we skip to the part where we're straight with each other? Don't lie to me, Jen. You'll break my heart."

"Oh God, no. Don't get upset. Seriously, Allie? I'm not lying, I promise. It really isn't mine. Did you look at the rucksack? It belonged to a customer. His ID was in it. Didn't you find it?"

"Listen to me." Her voice had an edge now. "This isn't some moral panic. We've all done it. But maybe I can see the things you can't." She paused, both of us so silent for a moment that I could hear a crow cawing in the churchyard. "You've been acting weirdly, letting things slide. When you ... when people get ... dependent, that kind of stuff happens and they don't even notice it."

"Don't be silly," I said.

"Come out," said Allie. "Let's talk."

In those final seconds I looked, absurdly, at the walls, at the floor, hoping for an escape route. But there was none, and I knew it. I would open the door, and Allie would see me, and after that I couldn't control anything anymore. She could tell Elliot or the police, and then Mac would know and everyone, *everyone* would know. This was Allie though, I reminded myself. She loved me. She possessed an imagination and a decent supply of empathy. It would be a trust game. I'd just have to spread my arms wide and fall backwards, and hope that she caught me.

"OK," I said finally. "I'm coming out, but it's not what you think. Listen, just be supportive. Please don't laugh. And please don't tell anyone."

I checked my mask was straight. I adjusted my wig.

"OK," I said. "You asked for it." I opened the door.

"Shit!" said Allie. She was standing so close, right up against the threshold, her hand clamped over her mouth. I kept my head high. She looked at bits of me: my hands, my feet, my chest — her eyebrows rose — my face.

"What the actual?"

"You mustn't tell anyone."

"Are you going to a party?"

"It's not for a party!" I was still in the cubicle, the backs of my legs squashed against the toilet. As I came out, Allie took a step back. "I help people," I said.

"Oh my days." An amalgam of shock and amusement and — what was that? God, not pity? "You go out . . . on the streets . . . dressed like this?" She bit down on her lower lip. Was that pity? My jaw clenched.

"Yes I do," I said. "I go out exactly like this. I stopped a mugging."

"That was you? That was . . . Oh, my God!"

"Yes, and I —" But then I thought, maybe don't tell her about the fight with Johnny. I could imagine just how she'd react, her concern, the warnings. She wouldn't see the whole context like I did. "Go on then," I said. "Have a good laugh. Get it over with."

Allie drove her teeth down into her lip one more time. "You can't blame me for being a bit . . . this isn't . . . I thought you were in there hoovering up a line of coke."

She moved closer and touched my cape, rubbing the satin between her fingers. She ran her hand down the ladder of ribbon at the front of my corset. She kneeled, and knocked the steel caps of my boots. "I'm torn," she said, "between Complete Nutter and Slightly Fantastic."

My heart soared.

"And I'm not even on Class A drugs," I said.

CHAPTER
TWENTY-TWO

Allie and I talked until dusk came. I perched on the office chair, sweaty under the wig, the corset cutting into my hips, and at first she crouched in front of me as you might with a hurt child. She frowned as I talked, rubbing at my arm, and I squirmed inside until she retreated to the workbench. There she sat, swinging her legs, really and truly caught between complete nutter and slightly fantastic. The latter reaction was such a kick that I gave up a bit more to her. I told her about what had happened at Dashwood Stores, tweaking the story to deflect her anxiety. I presented it as a fight rather than a beating, me holding my own somewhat more than I actually had, and recasting the shop owner as a grateful recipient of my vigilantism. His cricket bat I edited out, and the extent of my injuries, and the way I'd been feeling ever since; the way terror would sometimes ambush me.

I knew I was deceiving her but I knew, too, that I'd go out there again no matter what she said. I wasn't blind to her arguments, but she hadn't done the things I had. She wasn't in the best position to judge. I wanted to keep her from worrying, so I packaged the whole thing carefully and when Allie talked about the risks I was quick to minimise them. Still, she was unsettled. When she wasn't warning about the danger, she kept going back to what she saw as my distractedness, to me being "off-beam". I wanted to tell her: you think I'm off-beam? This is what fixes it. This is what makes me feel OK. The problem isn't what happens when I'm wearing the mask; it's what happens when I take it off. Even as I said it inside my head it seemed to lend more weight to her argument than mine.

She left with a hug and turned to watch me from the front door, as if I might take off right there and then in front of her, a jump-jet vertical whoosh: through the ceiling, through the roof. Up, up and away.

I left through the back, shutting the gate behind me and taking a minute in the churchyard to gather my thoughts. No loiterers there, no smokers grabbing a crafty one, no dog-walkers or snogging adolescents. Then I set off, stomping up the alleyway fast enough to put all the other thoughts out of my mind. Halfway up I stopped to catch my breath and saw movement above me — a bird? A quick black shape sweeping across the disc of sky. But its flight had a different signature, its wings flickering as it banked and then dropped in a sudden descent. It climbed again then dropped lower still.

A bat. I watched as it shot away from me, towards the town centre, towards — I supposed — its home in the old chapel. I remembered the leaflet on Martha's noticeboard. It said the bats would be giving birth to their young in the summer. Maybe this was a mother getting food for her babies. I watched as long as I could, until she had disappeared from sight.

Things were easier once I reached the top. Busier roads, the pubs full, people spilling out onto pavements. I tracked a wavering course, keeping my eyes out for trouble, for fights and petty crime, for anyone who seemed vulnerable. I would get it right this time, make myself do all that *noticing* Mac was always on about. I'd control my temper and only intervene if I could do it in absolute safety. On the move I felt calmer, more grounded. When people spotted me they called out, or whooped, and I'd wave at them and think: what does Allie know?

Darkness began to spill across the sky, leaving a crack of untouched brightness west of town. When I heard the thumping bass note of the club, I realised I'd been here before. I'd seen the girl staggering out of the back exit into the alleyway where a taxi now idled, its driver trailing a hand out of the open window, fingertips tapping to the rhythm of the Bhangra he was playing inside. The two beats — from the club, from his car — knocked against each other, off-kilter. The driver caught sight of me and rolled his eyes as if I were patently hilarious, and I was buoyed up enough by then to let the idea slip away without disturbing me one bit.

At the club entrance, people straggled across the front of the building in something approximating a queue. The bouncer had set up a rope in front of the door, a token barrier anchored at both ends by stanchions, which would simply have tipped over had anyone chosen to push through. As I rounded the corner he was unhooking the rope and letting in a group of girls. The music swelled and subsided as they entered. Above them, the neon sign had lost another letter: *he dge*, it said. I peered up to see what was missing, an unlit T and E at the start of the words. The Edge. I remembered Liv's text about Zoe, and suddenly it made sense: *off her face dancing at the edge*.

Sniggering rippled down the line: boys in their clean T-shirts, shivering girls in heels. How old were they, these kids? The queue edged forward, stop-start. The bouncer rejected a couple of lads, who barracked him until he took a step closer. He let in another group and they crowded into the darkness of the lobby, wedging the front door open. Deeper inside, I could make out black walls and ceiling, a paybooth, double doors swinging open into the club itself. I caught a glimpse of the inner room, blue light dousing the punters, someone dancing, a girl leaning across to shout in another girl's ear. Was this a regular thing, these underage clubbers? Why weren't the police all over this?

"Nice one," said the bouncer, and I realised he was talking to me. He wasn't tall, but he didn't need to be. He carried himself with a lazy confidence, an assumption of his own strength. I saw why the boys had backed off when he stepped forward. "You come to save us, then?"

"Something like that."

Inside the club, the double doors swung open again. A man pushed through, heading out towards us. In the narrowing rectangle as they closed, blue-washed under the lights of the dance floor, I saw Martha.

Martha, who had told me she was at Liv's for the night. I was sure it was her. I couldn't see her features but I didn't need to; her head dipped a little to the right, her hand stiffened, splay-fingered. Then I saw Liv just behind her. The doors clapped shut.

The bouncer looked me up and down. "Over forties night is Wednesday."

"Just let me in," I said.

In the lobby, music blotted out everything else. An insistent electronic pulse, it hammered at my chest and made my eardrums shudder. A young woman slouched behind a desk in the paybooth, a half-eaten Mars Bar in her hand.

"Do I just go in?" I shouted.

She pointed to her mouth, nodding as she chewed, as if nodding would make her chew faster. I started towards the doors, but she banged on the desk and shook her head.

"You have to pay," she yelled finally.

All the things I'd packed into my tool belt, but no money.

"It's a tenner," she shouted, taking another bite.

Martha was in there, doing God knows what. I considered rushing the doors, but I was conspicuous; I'd be caught before I could do anything. The woman pointed to my shoulder. "Like the costume, though. Great cape."

They always liked the cape. I remembered the girl I'd found drunk behind the club. Her other comments had been less complimentary. The doors opened again and there was a blast of noise, a whiff of smoke. Martha was nowhere to be seen.

"I'm on a hen night," I told the woman in the booth.

"Oh yeah?" She posted in a last mouthful and crumpled up the wrapper. "No money, no entrance. Sorry."

"But I need . . . I'm the . . . mother of the bride. It's my daughter's hen night. I'm meant to be surprising her. Her mates set it up. I'll get them to give me the money. Two minutes, OK?"

Her cheek bulged, her tongue burrowing for some neglected remnant of food. Then she picked up a stamper, tamped it down on its pad, and held it out to me. I offered her my hand and she rolled it across with some force, tweaking the bones below my knuckles. When she'd finished, the club logo was there in black ink, dulling as it dried: "The Edge", the tail of the "g" a blade, a knife driving down from the name.

"Two minutes," she said, holding up two fingers to make her point. Then she reached for a second Mars Bar and started to tear the wrapper open.

Right, madam, I thought, bursting through the doors on the cusp between songs, you and I are going to have words. This was exactly what Helen had been trying to tell me about at the casino night. I assumed she'd been hoodwinked too. I looked about for Martha but the crowd was shifting constantly and she'd dropped out of sight. Already people were turning to glance at me, and — were they laughing? — nudging other people, and it

208

struck me that I was stuck, pissed off and stuck. If I hauled her out, she'd know what I'd been doing. If she even caught sight of me here, regardless of the wig or mask, she'd identify me the way I had her, from a dip of the head, a raised hand. And where was she, anyway? I scanned the club. There were scores of girls in here, all wearing high heels and short dresses, packed around the perimeter of the dance floor.

The music made it hard for me to think clearly. I reached for my phone to ring her but remembered that it would carry, in the background, the noise of the same club she was in. I scrolled through possibilities, each one rendering me more pissed off, all the while pushing my way to the margins of the room through a corridor of double-takes. I couldn't leave Martha vulnerable, couldn't pull her out without her recognising me, couldn't call Elliot without blowing my cover. I'd ground her for a bloody month.

Then I saw Zoe. Out of her casino uniform, she wore a silver mini dress which glittered in the moving lights. She was talking to a boy at the bar, touching her hair, letting her hand rest on his upper arm. They were laughing. In her other hand she held a drink, some concoction which required a straw. As I watched she sucked deeply on the straw, maintaining eye contact with him in a gesture she might have learnt from TV, or online porn. I'm sure this pantomime fitted well enough with the boy's preconceptions. For me, it was a reminder that Zoe, too, was just a kid. She gave the boy a tap on the arm and turned away from the bar.

Martha had been right about the uselessness of telling the school about the bullying. I knew she was right because I'd been fourteen once; the first thing teachers did was to let the bully know you'd complained, and the second thing was bugger all.

I watched as Zoe tottered to the back of the room, through the doorway which led to the toilets. Partway down the short corridor, all I could see of her were the last few flashes of silver from her dress.

Lezza, I remembered. *Inadiq8*. Kids don't tell bullies where to get off because they're too scared, and parents don't because they're too polite. But I wasn't too polite. I'd give her a piece of my mind. I could feel the exact piece working itself loose as I straightened my cape, as I settled my mask squarely over my eyes. I'd tell her what I thought of her. Then I'd get her and Martha and Liv — all of them, somehow — the hell out of there.

Cool air funnelled down the corridor. Halfway along was the women's toilet, "Edgettes" it said. But inside — no Zoe, no one in the stalls, my voice echoing in the empty room. There were no windows. There was no other exit. Out in the corridor again I found I was panting, a flush of heat settling damply across my chest and arms. It had been cool here before. At the end of the passage, a green and white sign crested the emergency exit. It had been cool here before, and that door had been open.

As I stood there I felt rage gathering inside me, rage at the whole lot of them. At Zoe, for being a bully, for managing to disappear before I could do anything about it. At Martha for being here, right where she shouldn't be, for forcing my hand and limiting my options. When I launched myself at the exit door, my boot slamming against the bar and tripping the mechanism, I carried all my rage with me. I let out a yell of frustration and landed in the alleyway.

And there, on the ground, was Zoe. She was lying face down, her arms pinned behind her back. A man was kneeling over her, and he was holding a knife.

He flinched and looked up and I was strapped into my runaway anger, carried along its trajectory. Without it, I might have flinched, too. Because his mouth and nose were obliterated by a white mask, and his eyes were shaded by a baseball cap he'd pulled down low, and the knife in his hand had a short blade which curved like a talon. Down on the ground amid the broken glass, Zoe was trying to peel her head away from the debris, looking straight at me. Her dress had ridden up.

I got to him before he could get to her again, rushing him, drawing the cheese knife — my only weapon — from my belt. Wordless, he jabbed his blade towards me, my skin suddenly flayable, my blood dammed and pressing for release. His knife came at me in close-up, his own throat in the unreachable background. I hopped aside so that he turned, the claw flashing too close, streetlight-yellow slicked across us. I kicked him and it was useless, so I kicked again, higher, aiming for his balls, but missed. Behind him, Zoe curled into a crouch and shuffled towards the alleyway entrance.

"Come on!" I shouted to him, heading deeper inside the alley, pulling him away from her. His blade wove and leapt as he advanced towards me and I watched it, biting down on the soft parts of my mouth. Zoe had now staggered to her feet, the sole figure in the frame of the entrance. Empty space stretched around her: empty enough for her to get away, empty enough for her to be safe.

Then I stumbled against one of the dumpsters and he was right up against me. He was grunting now. I could feel his breath warm on my cheek, filtering through a valve set into the front of the mask.

It happened fast: his hand locked onto my right arm, my left went up in defence. I blinked and there was a thump in my palm. The pain came a moment later, burrowing deep, streaking along the nerves, battering at the skin to get out again. I staggered into the arc of streetlight, bellowing. There was a second of blindness as my eyes adjusted, and then he came after me.

Chaotic with terror and fury, I lashed out, my hand slapping at his head, trailing gouts of blood. I was aware of muscle and bone and body heat. I drew back my own knife, but someone else was coming through the door. The attacker turned, my red stamped across the white of his mask. He started to run.

Something leapt in me then, something that made me charge past the bouncer who'd emerged from the club, made me hurl myself out of the alleyway, my lungs a stone in my chest. Out of the alleyway, off the pavement, tearing between cars towards this horror, this fleeing monster. Nearly at the corner, and when I thought I might lose him I launched my whole self, knocking him over, not caring how I might land or what would happen next. He sprawled beneath me, his knife sliding across the pavement. "Don't you touch her!"

There were voices around us. In a room far away, behind a locked door, there was the thought that I could stop. It was a flimsy thing, that thought, and no argument against the here and now: this man, who could get up, who could run off, who could leave and do it again if not for me. If not for this knife, which I brought down between his shoulder blades as he bucked, if not for the whole weight of me behind that knife. If not for this, again and again, while he roared and twisted, shaking it off, and I stabbed down into his jacket, barely denting the material. There was not one part of me, then, which noticed that I wasn't even cutting him, that people were shouting at me to stop; nothing which asked what was happening to me as I raised my arms and something spun loose inside, something which was not about the blade or flesh or incision, but about the dogged lift and fall, my willingness to go on whatever else happened, whatever he did, however it ended.

Someone caught my arm. The man heaved, tilting me off-balance. A tangle of legs and elbows, the bouncer tripping over me and falling as the attacker grabbed his weapon and got to his feet. A moment later, I was after him again but he was already gone, halfway across the road in the path of a hooting car, his hand up to his mask where it must have been knocked out of place. The bouncer rushed by in pursuit and I became aware of the things I hadn't noticed before: my own laboured breathing, a siren heading our way. The anaesthesia of rage was starting to wear off and my hand hurt badly.

Martha, I thought.

In bed later, I lay under the covers and shook. I was flat-out scared, and I was scared of everything. I told myself it was the shock, the injury, the medication. It was like the aftermath of a near-miss on the road, when all you can think of is what might have happened. I kept laying out the facts and trying to focus on them. On *it*, the one fact that mattered: I had saved Zoe. And then other thoughts would start to sneak in, and make me shake and pull the duvet around my shoulders — how it might have been Martha, how the man had got away and it might still be Martha. I told myself I was a hero and told myself I was a fool. I'd put myself at risk, even after Zoe was safe. And him — I'd needed to hurt him. I'd wanted to kill him. This was the thing I couldn't get past: the man running away, other people coming and me possessed with a bloodlust, a madness . . .

Unbalanced. Nutter.

Did I have . . . was that some sort of *episode?*

Co-codamol fuzzing my mind. I wasn't thinking straight. I needed sleep, and time, and for this bloody hand to stop hurting. And I needed, I thought (clenching my eyes shut, baring my teeth), to lay off the costume. It was time to stop. I pulled the covers over my head and curled up, knees to belly, a terrible pressure in my throat.

When I finally slept, my hand still throbbing, the medication ushered in a procession of sweating visions. In one, I moved through a dark alleyway with that even, resistless motion peculiar to dreams. A figure stepped out of the shadows and I was very afraid, and unable to move. It stepped closer and I knew it was coming for me. I tried to call out, but was mute.

It lifted a blade, which flashed in the dark, the tip black with a substance I knew to be blood. There was blood across the hand that held the knife, blood sailing down the elbow and dripping onto the ground. The hand would come down, and I knew it would not stop, that it would lift once more and come down again, and again, and again . . .

I was already kicking towards the surface of consciousness when I saw the face. It drew closer, so that the last thing I saw was the mask which obscured it, the sparkling swirls over the eyes, the pillar-box hair, and the red lips as they advanced towards me, opening wide. I didn't know if it would kiss me or bite me, and my terror of both was so great that in one last effort to escape I convulsed and turned away, and — finally — woke up.

CHAPTER
TWENTY-THREE

VIGILANTE SAVES GIRL FROM KNIFE ATTACK

[Caption]. **DANGEROUS: An artist's impression of the attacker. Police have appealed for witnesses to come forward.**

A fifteen-year-old girl was subjected to a terrifying ordeal at the hands of a knife-wielding assailant outside a Bassetsbury nightclub — and saved by the town's vigilante superhero.

The victim, who has not been named, was assaulted in an alleyway behind The Edge nightclub in Fenton Road, late on Saturday night. Police believe the man gained access to the club via an emergency exit. But when the vigilante appeared she distracted the attacker and chased him from the scene.

[Caption]. **INVESTIGATION: Police search the alleyway behind The Edge nightclub, where the attacker struck**.

FEAR

DCI Hari Kumar told the *Examiner*, "This is a highly dangerous individual, and we are expending

216

every effort to find him. We would ask members of the public to contact the police if they have any information that could lead to his capture.

He may be a local man. Someone may have noticed unusual behaviour which has alerted their suspicions, and I would appeal to them to inform the police immediately. There is the fear that he may strike again. Young women are advised to take reasonable precautions when out at night. Stay safe, stay with your friends."

Of the vigilante DCI Kumar said, "She showed great courage in challenging the assailant and put her own safety at risk. She may have prevented worse harm befalling the victim. However, we strenuously discourage members of the public from taking the law into their own hands."

[Caption]. **COURAGE: The only known photograph of the Bassetsbury vigilante**

The vigilante first came to public attention when she rescued a woman from a mugging and restrained the assailant until the police arrived.

Following Saturday's attack, the girl is said to be shocked but unharmed, and is recovering at home with her family.

Readers with any information about the incident are asked to contact the police on the following number. All calls will be treated in confidence.

CHAPTER
TWENTY-FOUR

"Explain that again?"

I repeated the story, queasy with deception but nervous of the alternative; if I came clean Elliot would think I'd been lying to him for weeks, when in truth everything had come about haphazardly, more cock-up than conspiracy. And it seemed pointless to wrestle with his response just as I was renouncing it all for good. (Renouncing it all for good *again*, I thought uncomfortably, and for a moment I wondered: is there a pattern here? But no — it was different this time.)

Elliot took a pull on his mug and stared out of the window. "Where's the knife?" he said.

"I did it at the shop."

I'd awoken that morning lagged in duvet, my breath a gasp, my wound still at its tireless drumming. My first thought was of Martha. I remembered seeing her leg it out of the club when the sirens came, Liv and Izzy legging it behind her, and me knowing my work was not yet done, not till I'd tracked them home, dragging my hand which flashed pain pain pain all the way across town till I'd seen them back to Liv's house.

I'd concocted a rubbish story to tell Elliot, a piece of nonsense involving a knife and an apple. It was all I had to show for my night-long opportunity to make up something better: an hour at the shop, peeling off my bloodied costume and stowing it in the locker, rinsing my hand and rinsing it again, watching the strip of my exposed flesh become a runnel of blood, then empty, and then fill up again in a perpetual cycle until I had to kneel by the basin to keep from fainting. A further two hours in A & E, my hand wrapped in a toilet paper bandage which turned scarlet as I sat among the Saturday night drunks. I watched their faces for the weals of a tight-fitting mask, caught myself doing it and suffered a moment of doubt. Could this really have happened? A man with a claw knife, like someone out of a comic. A man who didn't belong here.

Elliot had been spark-out when I got to bed. I was loaded up on Co-codamol, dipping in and out of sleep, borne to the surface by pain, lowered again by fatigue, thinking: apple, bloody apple — can't you do better than that?

"We finished up late last night at the school," said Elliot. "But you were even later. *At work*." He turned to me, hard-faced. "On a Saturday."

"I know." My hand lay on the table between us, Exhibit A. "I got involved and then I didn't want to stop. There's so much admin. And then the wait at the hospital . . ."

A pause. Then: "Bollocks," he said, the word smacking into the silence.

The muscles in my neck solidified. "What?"

"Tell me what really happened." He leaned back in his chair, put his feet up on the table and my shock thawed into annoyance. I could see how fake he was being: settle in boys, this'll be a doozy. But I was too tired and in too much pain to wonder what he was covering up with that fakery.

"Are you saying you don't trust me?"

"I'm saying it's an odd story. And I'm asking you to tell me the real one."

"You work late," I said, and I could hear how unfair that sounded — the defensiveness, the misdirection. I could hear myself placing a new deception on top of the first so I could stand on higher ground.

"You're right," he said. "I do, sometimes. When there's a pitch to prepare, or when we're behind deadline, and I do it because I know if we lose that piece of work that's our mortgage left unpaid, or Martha's clothes, or the gas bill, or the food bill." He gathered speed as he talked, striking a finger for each burden he counted, their names piling out of him as if they'd been waiting for a good excuse. "I hate it," he threw out at last — such a terrible thing to hear, even then — and I didn't know which part he meant: my bollocks story, or working late, or the infinite ranks of his responsibilities.

"Hate?" I said. Elliot must have been disinhibited by anger; it was such an exposing word to use. If I put one foot wrong, he'd disown it. "What do you hate?" I reached out and realised I was reaching out with my injured hand. "What's going on?"

Elliot looked away, and for an instant everything was suspended, everything was possible. Then he turned back and said, "This isn't about me."

220

"Tell me!"

"Don't lie to me," he said. "It feels like shit."

What an awful thing, that he would *feel like shit*, and that he would feel enough like shit that he was prepared to admit it. For an instant I considered telling him everything, but the idea seemed so unworkable, so sticky with consequences, that the thought was immediately followed by a rush of denial. I felt myself flounder about, looking for a way to feel less rubbish about the lying. What I came up with was lame, and it was this: I wasn't the only one keeping secrets. And so I persisted.

"It's not a lie," I told him. "Please don't feel like shit. I did cut myself on a knife."

He sighed. But I really did, I thought, and felt a prod of shame. In an attempt to neutralise the rising guilt, I made a deal with myself, and I knew I'd be getting the worst of the bargain: his tiny secret for my colossal one. He tells me, I'll tell him.

"What's going on with you, Elliot?" I said. I looked right at him and willed him to talk about the comic. I pictured Vermilion, put him front and centre, and waited for Elliot to see him too. But he didn't say a word. "Well then," I said, as if in some way I'd proved a point. There was a clatter at the door and we both twitched towards the sound. Martha.

She was unpacking in her room when I came in, music so loud that I had to do it in dumbshow: the friendly smile, the frown as I caught sight of something on her hand, pulling it towards me as she snatched it back. I turned off the noise.

"What's this?"

"What's what?" It was barely there, just the tip of the d pointing up her arm, the bit she'd missed when she was covering her tracks.

"This is an entry stamp," I said. "For a nightclub. Do you think I was born yesterday?"

After the almighty row that followed my "discovery" of her behaviour, Martha was grounded for a week. Her incarceration coincided with the start of the summer holiday. Sealed in with me as I nursed my injury, she maintained a fuming non-communication. In the lounge the next day (me on the sofa, her on the chair scrupulously separate), she channel-hopped, flipping through cartoons, reality shows, property porn, the early evening news.

Her thumb stalled. There was a reporter standing outside The Edge. When she came to the part about the vigilante ("Some say courageous, some say foolhardy, but everyone agrees, without her prompt action, things would have turned out very differently for the teenaged victim") Martha forgot, for just a second, that she was angry with me. Her face opened in delight and she turned to share a mutual thrill, before catching up with herself and shutting off again.

I cannot deny how good that felt. I want to deny it, because what sort of person would find any pleasure in that situation, given what Zoe had been through? The thing is, this was my last flare of glory. Everything

222

around us was so humdrum — the telly, my slippers, me — as if it were a stage set and a designer had chosen everything in it to represent the unremarkable. And there was my daughter, glowering at me in her unremarkable resentment while thrilling to my escapades: who *is* that masked woman?

"Did you see her at the club?" I asked. Martha shook her head. On screen, the camera panned along the alley. I remembered Zoe, shuffling out of it to safety. The police may not have released her identity, but the grapevine had. The morning after the attack, Martha knew exactly what had happened.

"Do you know how Zoe is?" I asked, and Martha gave me a death stare.

"How would I, if I haven't been out?"

"You might have texted someone?"

But she was already off, a belated flounce. I reached for the remote and turned up the volume, to find nothing new, just the same old horrors: a knifeman, a mask, a warning to young women. I'd watch Martha like a hawk, I decided. He'd been right here in Bassetsbury, a few steps away from the kebab van, just down from Cheeky Charlie's Chicken. And there would be no vigilante to catch him now. Would the police do it? I'd got closer than they had.

I scolded myself for the thought. My heart started to hammer, and I had to get up and move around the kitchen, pushing back at the voice (*my* voice) saying that I'd wandered into the wrong story by mistake, that I didn't know what on earth to do now that I was here.

Over the next few days I dosed up as often as I could and the pain would recede for a couple of hours, its shape visible but not its features, like someone moving behind a net curtain. I had to change the bandage daily. Each time, I unwrapped it with a prickle of fright in my groin, nervous in case it stuck to the wound and pulled it open. The stitches lay whiskery in my palm, the cut — which would soon be a scar — a new lifeline tracking across my hand.

I texted Allie to tell her I was OK. *I need to see you*, she texted back, and I promised I'd be in soon, and hoped she wouldn't take it into her head to come round to my place first. I knew she'd have some ripe things to say about the attack, and didn't feel strong enough for that yet. One thing at a time.

I started doing normal things. I shuffled from room to room, adjusting to the unexpected inconvenience of operating with only one hand. I struggled to open bottles and jars, I enacted a clumsy Dance of the Seven Veils after a shower, draping the towel against my body and flicking it upwards. Everything was a performance: using the toilet, getting dressed, eating.

I tackled the laundry with the heavy feeling of picking up where I'd left off. There was a weight in my chest as I scoured the bottom of the basket for stray socks, an itch of impatience as I opened a new box of colours tablets because, as I knew only too well, the ordinary powder would fade the clothes, and that was unacceptable in a well-run household.

When I'd cleared the backlog from our room I moved on to Martha's. She'd been downstairs watching telly all morning while I dragged through this tedium with my wounded hand. Nevertheless there, in the bottom of her laundry basket, was an immaculate pile of clean clothes — the very same clothes I'd washed, dried, sorted and returned to her the previous week, the same ones she'd assured me she'd put away. I looked at them, still folded in amongst the dirty stuff, and remembered how I'd gone to the trouble of separating her printed T-shirts from the rest, how I'd air-dried them so their designs wouldn't be damaged in the tumble-dryer.

I shut Martha's door and before I knew it I had shaken everything out of that basket and was slamming it against the floor with my good hand, whisper-shouting while I banged it again and again, and when banging it wasn't productive enough, stamping on it till the carpet was scattered with fragments of wicker. "You lazy little shit!" I yelled mutely, kicking it against the wall. "I'm nobody's fucking servant!" Then I charged downstairs, puffing, and snatched her mobile from her.

"Hey!" she barked.

"No phone," I said. "No TV, no screens, no music. You've got housework to do."

Often Elliot was working, but even when he came home he'd spend more time in the shed than the house, the distance between us now visible. It had grown with tectonic slowness, a continental drift. We can fix this, I kept thinking. There's time. When I'm myself again, I'll have the energy to tackle it. Sometimes he'd look at me, poised on the brink of something, and I'd feel sure he wanted to fix things too. There would be a standoff, each of us waiting for the other to speak first. But when we spoke it always seemed to be transactional: practicalities, logistics. He and Martha had divvied up all the household chores you couldn't do with one hand, and sometimes we talked about where the iron was, or which food needed finishing up, the very politeness of our exchanges a red flag. Then he'd disappear into his shed for hours. At the end of that first week, I found out what he'd been doing in there.

It was Martha's fifteenth birthday. In the normal way of things, I'd have been organised weeks beforehand. We would have, in fact; her birthday was an annual project we'd always planned together. Gutted, I rang Elliot at the office with three days to go.

"I feel awful about it," I said. "It's just caught up with me."

"It's sorted," he said, and this felt worse somehow.

"You've bought her something?"

"I've made her something." He sounded . . . I would characterise it as business-like. It made me wonder, for the first time, just how far apart we were, and how fast we were drifting.

In our household, you get to choose what you eat on your birthday; you can have anything. Martha chose lasagne, with pavlova for dessert. Elliot stopped by the supermarket on his way home and bought them ready-made. This was the last day of her confinement and I thought she might baulk at spending it with us but she said no, that was fine. She'd have a proper celebration with Liv and Izzy once she'd been let out.

226

When it was time to give Martha her present, Elliot made us close our eyes while he disappeared into the kitchen. The back door opened and he scuffed away down the garden path. I let my eyelids relax until I could watch Martha through a hazy letterbox, sitting there with her own eyes scrunched shut like a good girl.

"Fifteen years ago," I said, and almost had to stop right there, poleaxed by the smile she gave when she thought I wasn't watching — instant, unmediated, guileless. "Fifteen years ago, I was in so much pain I wanted to jump out of the window."

She tipped forward so her elbows were on her knees. She shook her head. "I knew we'd have this."

"I remember thinking it. There were these big windows you slid open, aluminium edges. The car park was four storeys down. I looked at it as another contraction started, and I thought to myself —"

Martha sighed, then joined me in the chorus: "I would *literally* be relieved if I could jump now."

"Every birthday," she said.

"I have never been in so much pain."

"TMI."

"And as for the fluids . . ."

"Don't say fluids! I'll puke!"

The shed door banged shut.

"Fuh-loo-ids," I said, stretching it to three syllables.

There was a clank and a thud: Elliot was back. "Keep them closed," he said, and then I knew what he'd done for her. Martha turned her head towards the noise, still grinning. I think she'd guessed, too. I remembered his own Steampunk outfit — the tight trousers, the breastplate, the gun — and imagined what hers might be like.

"OK. Open your eyes."

"Oh, my God!"

At first I couldn't work out why he'd brought his own costume in. Two hangers' worth of it, and the gaiters and gauntlet, top hat and glasses, which he ferried in from the kitchen separately.

"It's in your size," he told her. "You liked mine, so . . ."

Oh no, Elliot, I thought, you idiot. All the work you must have done, but she'd want a skirt, wouldn't she? She'd want a bustle and a leather corset or something. The sweetness of it touched me; he'd tried so hard.

But Martha had gone over to the costume and was running her hand over the breastplate. "This is so cool," she said. She picked up the glasses: metal rims, circular lenses suspended inside, the glass a deep blue. She put them on and looked at herself, reflected in the window.

"Sick," she said, and I was cast adrift by her enthusiasm. I wondered how Elliot had guessed what she wanted, and how I hadn't. Then I thought of Martha's pending declaration, her coming out, and of how I'd always assumed I was the custodian of that secret. Now it occurred to me that Elliot might be capable of guessing it, too. I felt a bit ashamed of having doubted him (of having patronised him, in fact). Fathers were meant to be bumbling things, emotional klutzes, good-natured enough, but missing half of what was really going on. I tried it as a thought experiment: imagine if the whole

228

household didn't rest on my shoulders. Imagine if I ever let things slip, Elliot would be capable of catching them.

"I made you this," Elliot told her, fetching a last item from the kitchen. I knew, from the way he was controlling his mouth, not letting it smile too much, from the way he averted his gaze as if this last gift was a trifle, that he'd spent hours in the making of it, that it was his favourite thing.

It was a gun, a tricked-out Victorian pistol whose barrel was stacked with a grey tube, rounded at the ends like an airship, clasped by tentacles of gold filigree.

"Cool!" Martha took it from him and weighed it in her hand. "Hey, it's heavy."

"It's quite solid."

She drew a bead on him. "It doesn't work, right?"

"The pistol's a toy. But it's a . . . you know . . . I've based it on . . ."

She posed with the gun, holding it up near her face, extending it double-handed, pretending to shoot at her own reflection.

"Thanks, Dad." She went to cuddle him. He dipped her head and kissed the top of it. She treated me to a perfunctory hug, and I felt chastised. I'll make it up to her, I thought. When the birthday fuss is over, I'll get her something wonderful.

Martha wanted to try on the costume. I went upstairs to help while Elliot put our food in the oven. At the door of her room, she told me, "I'll see you in a minute," and closed it, leaving me waiting on the landing. After a bit, I knocked and she said, "Yeah, alright."

When I came in, her gaze didn't shift from the mirror. In the costume she stood differently, swaggering in trousers, foppish in her cravat. The breastplate androgynised her, ironing out any latent principal-boy sexiness.

"Tomboy warrior," I said. She pulled back her bobbed hair then let it fall around her ears again.

"I look like a girl," she said, sharply. "This is what a girl looks like."

I hadn't meant anything by it. It struck me again how impossible it was to get it right with Martha these days; one word out of place, and she'd come straight back at me, quick as anything. "You look great," I said. "I didn't mean . . ."

"I hate *tomboy*," she told me, levelling a drop-dead look at my reflection. I counselled myself not to engage with this, to change the subject. It was her birthday after all. I remembered that the next day she'd be free to go out again, and I knew she was longing for it.

"We should talk about tomorrow," I said.

"What about it?"

"Well, you won't be grounded anymore."

Martha put the gauntlet on her arm and tried to balance it while she fastened the catches. Every time she turned her wrist to reach the buckle, the gauntlet slid off.

"Learn from what happened to Zoe," I said. "Make better decisions. Keep yourself safe."

"It was *one* time," she said. She sat on the bed and laid her arm in her lap.

230

"Budge up. I'll do that for you." Shoulder to shoulder with her, the breastplate warmer than I'd thought it would be. I tapped it with my fingernail. "Plastic?"

"Well, metal would be too heavy, wouldn't it?"

"I suppose so. Look, M, there are times when Dad and I tell you off for our convenience — yes, I admit it," as she raised an eyebrow. "Or to stop you doing something which would be bad for you in the long-term." I fiddled the strap through the buckle. The holes weren't properly open yet, so I had to wiggle the pin through. "This is different. This is isn't about the long-term and it's not about things being easier for us. This is about your safety, right now, and it's as serious as it gets." Martha kept her eyes on her arm and I knew I'd gone wrong already. I wasn't striking the tone I'd wanted, but now I couldn't let it go without setting her straight. I couldn't fail in this, of all parental duties.

"A man with a knife!" I prompted, when she didn't react. "He just took her. He just grabbed her, as easy as that."

"I know."

"I'm just saying — be sensible."

"I am sensible."

"Really? Sensible enough to be under-age in a club?" (There it was! Louder, shriller — off I go!)

She shot me a look. "When will you stop going on about it?"

This — the dissonance between the danger she was in and her lack of emotion about it — set up a jangling panic in me. "I want to be sure you understand this," I said. "I had no idea where you were that night. And do you realise it could have been you, out in that alley? Actually you?"

Martha, expressionless, reached behind her for the top hat and — as if she'd performed some kind of magic trick with it — my anxiety became anger.

"I can't keep you locked up, Martha," I said, my voice moving up another notch. "That's what I'm saying. As of tomorrow, you're free to do any number of stupid, stupid things. You have to . . . you're not indestructible! You have to make good choices."

She ran a finger under the rubber strap of the goggles, stretching it free of the brim.

"Well?" I demanded, but Martha just scraped up her hair and put on the hat. "Say something!" She slipped on the sunglasses. I thought her hand might have trembled, that she might finally be starting to understand, but she turned the flat blue discs towards me impassively.

"OK," she said shrugging.

For the next few moments I wasn't in control at all. A stream of words left me: contradictory, tautological, verbal shakes and smacks, hot button words to put the fear of God in her. "OK? Have you been listening to any of this? You have absolutely no idea, have you?" I said, I shouted, getting to my feet. "You are so . . . you are . . . he had a knife!" Sifting her expression for remorse, for fear, for anything that might comfort me, anything but apathy. "You think in some magical way it won't be you next time? Really? Well, she was *just like you!*"

Martha stood too, and I thought for one moment she was going to hit me, and then I saw that she was trying to get out, that I was blocking her way. "I need to know you've heard me," I said, but she pushed past anyway, knocking me against her desk and running downstairs: a Steampunk Fury in socks.

CHAPTER
TWENTY-FIVE

It was mid-morning but Allie's shop was in shadow, lights off, a customer just leaving as I came in. On the counter was the latest *Examiner*, news of the attack already old, the update (**KNIFEMAN: POLICE SEARCH CONTINUES**) trumped by a promised crackdown on fake ID cards in local pubs and clubs. Allie was up a ladder, her head wedged into a niche in the ceiling. Bits of deconstructed light fitting leaned against the surrounding shelves: a long metal plate, two fluorescent tubes striped with dust. She popped her head out of the hole. When she saw it was me, she let out a long breath.

"Go on, then," she said. "Show us the damage." I held up my bandaged hand and she shook her head. "Look at the state of you."

"I'm fine."

She retreated into the hole, working away with her screwdriver. A glint of silver dropped out of the ceiling and into her waiting hand. Just before she pulled her head out again, the same hand nipped up to swipe at her cheeks.

"You OK, Allie?"

"Stupid light," she said. "Grab this." She passed down a black metal box which I placed on the counter, skimming the paper as I did so (urgent, witnesses, fear, warn). "The new one's next to the till," she said. "Can you get it for me?"

I expected her to say something else, but after I'd handed it up she applied herself with a ferocious concentration. I climbed the first two steps of the ladder until I was face-to-belly with Allie. A pair of pliers poked its nose out of her trouser pocket.

"Say something!" I said.

"Hold this in place." She raised my bad hand and I pulled away, offering her my right, which she used to support the box. "Got it?"

"At least I'm not a cocaine addict," I said, waiting for her to laugh, but she ducked down so her face was level with mine.

"Not funny! You scared me stupid. Compulsive gamblers always win the first time. Did you know that? You won the first time, not getting the shit kicked out of you by that mugger." She tapped the handle of the screwdriver on my head, harder than she needed to, and I shook it off. "You can see it, right?" she said. "Tell me you can see it."

"See what?"

"You need to stop."

"I won't do it again," I said, hating the note it sounded, like a chastened child. "I'd decided that anyway."

She pulled the pliers from her pocket and let them ravage the wires hanging out of the disembowelled fitting, their jaws closing on each one, stripping the plastic sheath. The shop door rattled and a man came a little way inside, holding the door ajar with one hand.

"You open?" he asked. Allie shook her head.

"We're just fixing the light," I told him. "Give us . . ."

"Ten," said Allie.

"Ten minutes," I said. "And we'll be up and running."

He left and I bent to pick up the curls of plastic littering the base of the ladder. Allie stepped down a rung. I thought she looked a little mollified.

"So," she said. "What was it like, then?"

I thought about the mask, and how everything seemed possible when I was wearing it, and about how I had felt barely any fear or pain while I was fighting. I thought about all the things you can do when nobody knows who you are. Then I remembered those frenzied final moments with Zoe's attacker, when I didn't know who I was either.

"When I look back, it seems scary," I said. "But in the moment itself, everything else disappears. You can only see forward. There's something . . . liberating about it."

Allie thought about that for a minute. "What do you need liberating *from*?"

"It was just an expression."

"You chose the expression," she said.

I was torn, then, between resenting the way she was calling me to account and feeling that, really, it was bleedingly obvious what I needed liberating from. I was amazed she couldn't see it for herself.

"Come on," I said. "Seriously? You get a chance to exchange all this," I gestured towards the gloom at the back of the shop, "for thrills and excitement and people thinking you're fantastic. Wouldn't you find that liberating?"

Allie placed the pliers on the top of the ladder with considerable care. "When you say *all this*," she asked, looking down the shop to where I'd gestured. "What do you mean?"

"Oh!" I realised, too late, that how I felt about my life could implicate hers. "You know I don't mean . . . there's nothing . . ." I desperately wanted to backtrack so she wouldn't feel hurt, but I could feel myself heating up, unsayable things hammering at my teeth to get out. Every single one of them would only hurt her more.

I could say: You can't really be satisfied with this? Is it truly enough for you?

Or I could say: it's not you, it's me. It's being a mother, the state you so desperately wanted and can't have. It's being a mother, for which I am wholly grateful, which transforms me every day into a duller person.

Or I could say: is this all you think I am? Is this all you think you are?

"I just meant our ordinary lives," I told her instead, craven. "Don't you sometimes want something more?"

She looked at me for a beat, and I had the sense she was hearing every one of those unsaid things as clearly as if I had said them after all. "Maybe," she said. "But not that. A knife! A fucking knife. You were stabbed. It scared the shit out of me."

"Unharmed," I said.

"You were *not* unharmed!"

"No." I raised my injured hand again. "But she was."

CHAPTER
TWENTY-SIX

Dusty heat rolled down from the loft hatch, intensifying as I climbed higher. Halfway up the ladder, I entered a sweltering dimness. Elliot crouched under the eaves, staring through the lid of a transparent storage box. I was here to show willing, to take an interest in his activities. The thought was a corny one, like the kind of boyfriend advice teen magazines used to dole out, but I was more and more preoccupied about the growing gap between us. It might have been corny, but it didn't seem like a bad place to start.

"How's it going?" I said.

He started, as if I'd caught him doing something embarrassing, and rose to pick up another crate. Immediately, I wanted to know what he'd been looking at. "Fine," he said. I hoisted myself up through the hatch lopsidedly, favouring my good hand.

"Do you want some help?"

He dropped the new crate on top of the first one. "I'm nearly finished."

LETTERS, it said on the box he'd been studying, PHOTOS on the one he'd just stacked on top of it. Glorious letters, Elliot used to write me, in the days when people still did that kind of thing. He illustrated them most of the time: caricatures of himself driving his rackety Beetle, sketches of me as a Modigliani woman, as a Chagall circus girl atop a feathered pony. He wrote as he spoke, the lines clogged with idiom so that he was right there with me when I read them. Me, scrunched up in the back of Jules' van, transformed by Elliot into Rousseau's Snake Charmer, my dark pelt velvet in the moonlight, the whites of my eyes shot wide. I'd kept it all in that box, his effusive creativity, my alter egos. I remembered the not-woman in his comic and the petty, petulant thought rose that he could have chosen any one of these Jennys to be a part of it, if he were still thinking of me in that way.

Elliot shifted a carrier bag of CDs on top of the crate and I picked out a couple. Beneath us, in the bathroom, water was running. The girls' voices echoed against the hard surfaces.

"*Trailer Park*," I said.

"Yep." He took it from me and put it back.

"I used to leave the room when you played it, do you remember?"

He sealed the mouth of the bag in a double-knot, the second pulled so tight the handles started to stretch.

"Way too melancholy," I said, when he didn't answer. "Do you remember the Treatment? I'd give you the Treatment afterwards."

"Don't, Jenny," he said, and in his voice I heard a single, clear note of utter misery. He nudged a box towards the eaves, a bit of cobweb trailing from the back of his head.

240

"Elliot," I said. "What's happened? What's going on?"

"Stop!" he said. He made shooing motions with his hands. "I can't do this. Don't try to soften me up. Don't talk to me about what we used to do. Don't use it as currency."

I opened my mouth, doltish. I looked for some recognisable landmark by which I could navigate. "Soften you up?" I managed.

"It's actually worse than the cheating," he said. "No — bollocks to that. It's not. But it's an insult."

"Cheating?" My nose began to tingle and I held up my hand to delay his response while I sneezed three times in quick succession. Between the second and third sneezes it hit me. "*Cheating?*" My first reaction was a dunderheaded shock, my second an urge to hug him really hard. (And tucked away somewhere inside, there was another response — a small, troubling pleasure: that he would think I *might* have an affair, that he even thought it was possible.)

"I'm sick of this bullshit," he said. "You're no good at it. No charity shop has a stocktake of donations, does it? And who gashes themselves like that cutting an apple? And why *the fuck* do you not answer the shop phone when you are, apparently, working late? You're a shit liar, Jen."

Below us, the bathroom door opened. "Be quiet!" I said.

"I will not be quiet!"

"Yes you will," I said, stepping onto the joist beside him and clapping my hand over his mouth. He shook me off, and we waited in a sudden *pax* as the girls trooped across the landing. Through the hatch I saw them picking their way between the legs of the ladder, Liv in jeans and a bra, her hair wrapped in a stained towel.

"Are you kidding?" I hissed, once Martha's door was shut and the music had been switched on. "I'm not having an affair. There's no one. Honestly. Have you been . . . how long have you thought this? Why didn't you say something?"

"You're lying."

"I'm not!" From Martha's bedroom below us, a burst of laughter.

"The late nights, the . . ."

"I am not having an affair! Why would I do that?"

He looked wary and, of course, I thought in that moment of telling him the truth. All of it.

Years previously, Elliot and I had gone camping on the Gower coast in a storm. I remembered the wind getting inside the tent as we were putting it up, lifting it and pulling it about as we scurried around trying to secure the guy ropes in place. Every time we attempted to loop the ropes onto the pegs, a new gust would come along and the tent would buck and kick and threaten to take off. And now, every time I thought of coming clean, I thought about that tent. I had pondered — in the wake of that unsettling conversation with Allie — over what the truth really was, how violent and unmanageable it might be, about how I'd struggle to keep it under control and peg it into place. Elliot would want to know what had driven me, why I'd lied, why

242

our life was not enough for me. I couldn't imagine how to fix those problems, so there they would be: unsolvable, immutable and, once I'd articulated them to Elliot, they would be his problems, too.

I might have been holding out on Elliot, but I was emphatically not cheating on him. The idea was a ridiculous one. I spent the next few minutes telling him this in lavish detail, both of us subsiding eventually until we perched side by side on a joist, our knees touching.

"The thing I don't get," I said, when I thought he was convinced. "Is why you just sat on this for so long. Why didn't you say something?"

He looked exhausted, the kind of tiredness that descends when you've been trying to hold things together for ages, then find out you can stop. "I hoped it wasn't true," he said. "It's not a conversation you want to have with your wife."

"This is not bloody *Othello*," I said. "Talk to me!"

He waved his hand in front of my eyes as if testing a blindfold. "It's not as easy as it sounds," he said. "You've been very . . . distant."

I immediately thought of Allie, and her comments when she'd caught me in the costume — even before that: *acting weirdly*, she'd said. Both of them were exaggerating, reading too much into it. Maybe I had missed a few things here and there, at work and at home, but that only amounted to a bit of daydreaming, a couple of neglected chores. It didn't merit this armchair psychology.

"I've been right here," I told Elliot. "You've been out of it for weeks. Don't look so offended. I've tried to talk to you loads of times. That casino night, at the school. I just wanted us to have some fun together."

"That dress," he said. "I wondered who you were wearing it for."

I beat my fists against his chest in mock fury, a vintage heroine just before she is kissed. It wasn't entirely and absolutely true, but I said it anyway: "I wore it for you, you bloody idiot. And you didn't say a thing! I thought you didn't care anymore."

His hands closed over mine. I didn't know whether he was telling me to stop or beginning to soften.

"I'm your girl," I said, and that really was one hundred per cent true.

"Alright," he said. "Then what were you doing when you were out so late?"

I must have hesitated for a second, no more. "The shop's doing badly," I told him (and realised, as I spoke the lie, that it probably wasn't far from the truth). "I didn't want to worry you. It's made me paranoid. I keep staying late to sort things out. I keep changing the displays. Stuff like that."

"The displays in the shop? That's what you're doing?" He let go of my hand and folded his arms across his chest.

"Not always," I said. "Sometimes I'm next door. I use Allie's office for putting books on the website. She's got a quicker computer. She's got a scanner."

I can't honestly say he looked fully satisfied. I wanted to see relief, to watch the penny drop, but it didn't

244

happen. Elliot opened his mouth as if he were about to say something and when he didn't after all, when he finally let me hug him and when, after a moment or two, he hugged me back, I knew he was just giving me the benefit of the doubt. But it was OK. It would be fine. I was knuckling down, and if the thought of that made my heart sink, it wasn't his problem. He'd soon see, when I went back to normal and made chicken pies and got through the laundry without breaking things, and opened post and cleared the kitchen table. He'd see I was the person I'd always been. I reminded myself he had his own secrets, that there was a *quid pro quo*. I told myself that the remaining lies weren't even worthy of the name.

CHAPTER
TWENTY-SEVEN

My head in the oven, I worked at a residual stain, a treacly deposit eroded to a brown nub. It was sticking to the cloth as I rubbed, coming away a little at a time. The apron pulled tight against the back of my neck. The acidic edge of oven cleaner pared away at my nostrils and windpipe, slicing down to my lungs. The tumble-dryer roared. When it stopped and changed direction there was a clatter of buttons on metal. In the silence, a snatch of music. I think it might have been "Young Americans".

("Young Americans", and I'm seventeen again. It's playing from a cassette recorder on the teacher's desk in the room we used for changing backstage. There's brown paper taped across the glass panel in the door so the boys can't see in. My friend Becky, Celia to my Rosalind, strokes a dollop of green hair gel through her fringe. "I'm off to look at Orlando's arse," she says.)

Elliot was still with Yaz at the office. They'd broken the back of their pitch, he said. They were ordering pizza. Don't wait up. Under the cloth, the blob of burnt food flattened. I pressed harder and felt it give, finally, detaching from the metal and skidding free.

When the phone rang again, I emerged.

"Jenny? It's Helen. Are the girls with you? I'm here at the cinema and I can't see them. Have they come back to yours?"

"What?"

I was upstairs before she could answer, bolting into Martha's room, the bathroom, our bedroom. All as empty as I knew they would be, Helen spooling out her fears ("I've looked everywhere, the cinema staff have looked. They're not there. She's not answering her phone . . ."). A Prozac voice in my head told me to dial it down. They were together, she'd be somewhere sensible. I hung up. Martha was fine. She'd be . . .

She'd be out front. I peered down towards the end of the road where she'd turn the corner any moment now. I ran a little way along, barefoot, just to see further down the street, to see her coming. And then she didn't come and it was obvious she'd arrive from the other direction, so I ran the other way, but still no Martha. It was OK. She'd be fine. They'd taken a bus. They'd missed their stop.

I called Martha's mobile. It went to message. I texted. Maybe she'd walked along the footpath at the bottom of the garden and couldn't get the gate open.

I ran back through the house and up the lawn, unlocking the gate, listening for voices along the dark of the path before realising that of course she wouldn't come this way.

When I called Izzy's mum, Carrie, her voice went tight.

"I've just been for a run," she said. "They might have come back while I was out."

There were footsteps across a wooden floor. "Isabel?" she called, her Manchester accent untempered by Seattle. "Izzy?"

I slowed my breathing. I tried to keep a lid on my heart rate. Elsewhere in their house I caught the sound of a radio. It must have been tuned to a panel game, or a comedy programme; when Carrie came back ("I'm just calling her on my mobile. Wait a minute") there was laughter, and a flutter of applause.

"*Pick up, pick up,*" she whispered. There was another swell of laughter, and then silence.

"Jenny?" she said. "They're not here. And she's not answering."

In the car, I realised I still had my apron on. Its stripes were leached of colour in the darkness and there was a horizontal band of grime where I'd leaned across the oven door. We'd had supper before she left, Martha texting while we ate dinner, me biting her head off about it.

I had never really wanted superpowers until now. I tried to will them into being: super-hearing which would catch her voice across the clamouring town, X-ray vision that would tear through walls and reveal her to me. I would leap tall buildings in a single bound, I would anchor a line of silk to the furthest point and swing across and carry her off to safety.

None of the people on Bassetsbury's streets were Martha. Outside The Edge, I drew to a halt, the engine idling. There was no queue of clubbers shivering along the wall, no quixotic bouncer or token barrier. The windows and doors were covered in chipboard. Already someone had added graffiti, an extruded cartoon which crossed from one window, over a slice of wall, onto another. The illuminated sign had been switched off for good. The Edge was closed.

I turned into the side street and drew level with the deserted alleyway. Under the streetlight the tarmac flashed with broken glass. I could see it again: Zoe lying there, her eyes looking to me for rescue, and then it wasn't Zoe anymore, but Martha, and I had to get moving. While I drove, I called home: nothing. I rang Martha again, but her phone was still turned off. I looped through the streets, haphazardly, called Helen, called Carrie, but no one had heard anything.

I had just crawled up the hill, my eyes sweeping left and right, when Martha rang.

"Mum," she said. "Help me."

CHAPTER
TWENTY-EIGHT

The girls were huddled in a bus shelter on All Saints Road when I got to them. I'd expected tears but they were grim-faced, as if committing to an emotion would trip a switch and make worse things happen. Martha wouldn't meet my eye.

On the journey home — first Liv's house, then Izzy's — I was angry with relief, barking questions at Martha, which she dispatched impatiently. When it was all out (the party they knew they'd be forbidden to go to, the cinema ruse, the arrangement to meet in the bus shelter) Martha pressed on.

"Hannah was going to get us in. But Mum, she never came!"

"What do you mean?"

From the back, Liv said, "She called us and said she was on her way. But she never arrived."

I tried not to betray the havoc of anxiety that started up in me at that moment. I made myself concentrate on the next task: getting the girls home as soon as possible. Then I could think about Hannah. At Liv's house, I waited in the car while she got out, watched as her front door became a block of light, her mum a silhouette inside it. I drove off before Helen could come out and exchange commiserations. We dropped off Izzy in silence. Back in our own road I switched off the ignition and we sat in the car, the engine ticking into coolness.

"I know I shouldn't have done it," said Martha.

"I'm livid," I said. I pulled her across and she resisted. Her hand was over her face. I hugged her close and fisted my hands, bouncing them off her shoulders and arms, feeling the resistance, the physical fact of her.

"I'll deal with you later," I said. "Tell me everything you can about Hannah."

"It wasn't that she didn't turn up," said Martha. "Something's happened to her. I know it has. That's why I called you. That's why we kept waiting and waiting and didn't go back to the cinema. She wouldn't just not come. She was on her way when she rang. I heard footsteps. I heard cars."

I remembered Hannah at the casino night greeting parents at the door: big smiles.

"Are you sure she hasn't just gone to the party without you?"

"Liv called Dan. He's there. He says she isn't."

"And you're certain she's not back at home?"

"We called. She's not there. Her dad sounded really worried. Mum —" She turned to me and I could see the workings of fear, her lips pressing and releasing, her shoulders tensed. "There's something else. There's this man who's been standing in the street, looking up at her window. He did it, like, twice. Her dad went off on one about it and told the police."

"OK," I said, trying to keep her calm, but nothing was OK, nothing at all. I thought about the attacker I'd fought outside the club, Hannah in his sights, him knowing where she lived. But the police had a lead now. "So the police know about him? That's a really good thing. Was she able to describe him?"

"They never came round," she said. "They were going to come tomorrow, after school. Mum, I don't know what to do."

I left Martha on the sofa with orders not to go out for any reason, to let in no one but Elliot, to call the police and to keep trying Hannah's mobile. I asked her for Hannah's address. I said her friend would be fine and I told myself the same thing, as I left the house and set out on foot, along our road and into the tunnel, emerging on the other side near the station.

A train arrived at the same time I did. I stood at the end of the footpath and watched passengers being disgorged from the entrance. They continued their separate journeys: up the hill, or down it and into the High Street. I thought of the hundred different places they might go, of all the places where Hannah might be, and the impossibility of knowing which was the right one. I considered going home, but she was still out here — somewhere — so I started walking again, a panicked ramble, a directionless wandering, no system to it.

Then I found myself opposite the churchyard. I could see the gate to our shop just twenty paces away. Twenty paces over the road, down the path, across a patch of grass and there it was, ivy crawling over the brick frame, rampant in the summer warmth. The key turned smoothly. The gate swung back, and I was in.

I hadn't looked at the costume since the fight at The Edge. I'd returned from the nightclub and bundled it into a locker, padlocked it and dropped the key into a mug of cable ties, where it had remained ever since. Opening the door now, dragging the clothes from their bag, I could see time had done nothing to improve them. The blood was dry, garments crackling with it as I shook them out. The left glove, petrified in supplication, carried a neat slash down its palm.

My heart tripping over itself, I looked from the glove to my hand, each a version of the other, the glove's sheen dulled with powdery rust, my hand clean but for the purple track that was merely an absence on the glove. I prodded my palm, damp with sweat. The cut had healed enough to hold together. I could press on it and there was tenderness rather than pain.

It came back to me in flashes: the man's mask, his strength, his utter lack of hesitation. The way all reason had slipped from me in his presence so that I was barely a thinking person at all, but a relentless body, arm, fist, a beast lumbering roughly in the direction of Good. I shouldn't let that loose, not even with Hannah out there, and the minutes passing, and her not found. Not even if I had only to slip on the mask to see clearly, to know what to do next. Not even if Hannah had been my own daughter.

That thought clarified everything. If Hannah were my own daughter it wouldn't have been a cluttered decision but a clean one, my safety of minor importance, my latent . . . proclivities . . . a risk worth taking. I shook out the cape and laid it across the back of the chair. Maybe she is a beast, I thought. But she's my beast, and I need her.

I climbed into the costume just as it was: holed, slashed, bloodied. My skin showed white through the ripped tights and the cut glove flapped open to reveal my scar. I loaded the tool belt with both phones: mine so that Martha could reach me, the vigilante mobile in case I needed to call the police. The knife was foul, blood-dipped, its pouch stained dark at the bottom. I held it under the tap till it was clean and wiped it off on the tea towel.

When I put on the mask, everything else fell away: the endless hypotheticals, the fear. I looked through its narrow aperture and let go a lungful of air. I saw that there were some places it made sense to look, and that if I didn't find Hannah there I could keep searching. I saw that one of me out there looking was one more than there had been half an hour previously. It was time to go.

I knew where Hannah's journey had started, and I knew where it was meant to finish. I slipped out of the back exit and cut through the churchyard, striding up the alleyway I'd wandered down a few minutes previously. At the top I caught movement, the sky flickered black on indigo and it was a bat again, and then another, then several, loping high above me in switchbacks and dips and glides.

Hannah's road was built on an incline, the houses stepped up the side of the hill, basement garages tucked under street-level front doors. I half-expected to see police cars parked outside her home, but everything seemed normal: a car pulling out of a drive further down, a man pushing a buggy. "Please," I heard him mutter as he trundled past me. "Just go to sleep . . ."

From my vantage point in the bushes opposite, I could see the lounge exposed on the ground floor, its picture window lit up, curtainless. Above it were two bedrooms, looking out over the park below. Stickers blotched the corner of one window. In the dark behind the glass something moved. A moment later I saw it again: something pale, rising slowly, remaining aloft for a few seconds. I shifted so that the streetlight fell on a different part of the window, and saw that it was a hand, a man's face behind it as the hand rose up once more to cover his mouth, and drop away, and return.

There were three possible routes between here and the girls' meeting-point. I searched them all, one by one, cars and vans switching past me. I stared into each windscreen, looking for Hannah. Sometimes the drivers hooted. Sometimes they slowed and rolled down their windows. I memorised number plates and kept each string of data in my mind until it was elbowed out by the next one.

I ran alongside the station fence, looking across three platforms for a girl who might have decided to take a train out of Bassetsbury that night. Perhaps it was just that: not abduction, but escape. I ran until the platforms gave way to open track, and ran back in case I'd missed her the first time.

I thought of Mac and the lessons she'd taught me. What would she say? Something irritating. She'd say: take an attack alarm, shout loudly. I'd covered all the ground and there was nothing. No call from Martha to say her friend had been found. Mac would say: notice things, be aware. I walked back into town, to the junction with the High Street. Right, I thought. I'll notice things. There must be something.

I noticed everything. Litter, parked cars, graffiti, lit and unlit windows, people going into places, people coming out, and none of it carried any significance. I noticed for all I was worth, until I'd come full circle and was standing halfway down the High Street with Famaid in sight, wondering where to go next. And then I noticed something else, the smallest sound.

It was a soft whoosh, like a long sniff. It came from behind me, down in the cobbled yard where I'd once left my cape to be dry-cleaned. I stepped into the passageway, my footfall echoing against its walls, and there was a new sound, a muffled keening. When I emerged into the yard, a security light clicked on.

Hannah had been placed up against the florist's window. She had on a T-shirt of some kind, ripped at the shoulder. Below the waist, she was naked. When I stepped closer she turned her face towards the noise and shouted again, tape over her eyes, tape over her mouth mutating the cry into a formless moan. She kicked at the ground, both feet together where her ankles were bound.

"It's OK, sweetie." I told her. "I'm here. You're safe."
She shook her head violently.

"I'm going to take the tape off your mouth first," I said. "Then I'll do your eyes. I won't hurt you, I promise. You're OK. You'll be OK."

When I began, she pulled away, so I stopped. I told her again what I was going to do, exactly which part of her I would touch. I told her I wouldn't touch anything else. The tape wrenched at her skin, prising it upwards. Her mouth free, she cried out.

"I want my dad," she said, her voice hoarse.

"Let me sort you out, then I'll call the police," I told her, very slowly uncovering her eyes, my fingers keeping gentle pressure on the lids as the tape tugged at them. The security light turned off again, and I remembered what she'd see when it came back on.

"Don't be scared when you see me," I said. "I'm in costume. I've got a mask on."

"Not a mask!" she said, shrinking away from me against the wall. I remembered the attacker's mask: a white dome, the valve set into the front.

"I promise I'm safe," I said. "My costume might look a bit . . . strange, but I'm safe."

When she'd let me remove the rest of the tape I stood up and the light triggered, a flash of red and black as it lit me up. I looked down at my clothes, at my ripped tights and my slashed glove. Hannah stared at me and I knelt again to free her wrists, then her ankles. Afterwards she curled forward, holding her hands over her groin.

"Let's get you covered up," I said, undoing my cape.

She spread it out over her naked lap like a skirt, her breathing loud and shaky. I sat next to her and she shuffled away until she was beyond my reach. While I called the police on my anonymous mobile, she set her fists on either side of her legs, anchoring the black satin. The light switched off and she told me to put it back on.

"You're bleeding," I said. "Did he cut you anywhere?"

She shook her head. "He hit me. He said he'd cut me."

I looked at the clean cobbles. "Did it happen here?"

"I want my dad," she said again, her voice a little stronger now.

"The police are coming," I said. "Very soon. They'll take you to him."

I listened out for sirens. He'd done it under their noses — the police station was just round the corner — but still they weren't here. They hadn't got to her in time to do anything about the man outside her window, and they were nowhere in evidence now.

"Please," she said. "Just take off that stupid mask."

My hand went up to my face and touched the mask, its braided edges rough under my gloved fingers. I could see it was horrible for her, that after her ordeal at the hands of a masked man compassion required me to take it off, and yet when I started to lift it, when I thought who I'd be revealing — the head-ducking me, the insult-absorbing me, the appeaser — I faltered. That person wasn't the one needed here. What would I do, if I had to face this horror without the mask? Snivel and panic and be no good whatsoever. I didn't want to compound Hannah's suffering by keeping it on, but I'd be no use to her if I took it off.

"I just . . . I can't," I said. "I'm better for you like this. Please, trust me."

From elsewhere in the High Street there was a sudden rise of voices, drinkers piling out of the pub probably, but Hannah jumped. I shifted a little closer and she let me. The voices moved towards the yard.

"They won't come in here," I told her. "The police will arrive any minute now."

Level with the yard, a shout — "my size!" — channelled down the passageway to where we sat. Hannah made a fractional movement and I lifted my arm and put it round her shoulders. She'd be freezing, I thought, and started to rub some warmth into her, but she said, "Don't," so I kept still. The light went off and we waited in darkness together. She shuddered against me. Finally, with a draining relief, I heard them: sirens that seemed to start far away, further than the police station.

"Here they are," I said. "They'll look after you. They'll take you to your dad."

I put the lengths of tape in a pile next to her. I brushed down the back of her top, dusty from the cobbles, and rested my hands on her shoulders while the sirens muscled down the High Street.

"When they arrive, I'll go," I said.

"Please stay."

"I'll stay till they're here, I promise." I crouched, keeping one hand on her shoulder. In the High Street a car stopped and there was a double-slam. I tried to stand but in a sudden burst of energy Hannah gripped my wrist and pulled me back down to her. "Get him," she said. "Fucking kill him."

The shock made me slow. It took me a moment to work out what she was asking. "What?" I said. "No. The police will help you now. Listen." Footsteps clattered in our direction. "They'll get him," I told her and then, worried that I hadn't sounded convincing enough, "They really will."

Hannah snorted. "No," she said. "You will."

"I . . . I can't."

"You can. You helped Zoe. You found me. Promise you'll get him."

You've got the wrong woman, I wanted to tell her, but Hannah was staring at me with a fierce urgency, her nails digging into my glove, hurting my arm.

"I can't lie to you," I said. "I can't promise to catch him."

Two figures clattered into the yard, two lengths of darkness, and Hannah sucked in air between her teeth. I tried to pull free but still she clung on.

"Don't promise to catch him then," she said. "Just promise to try."

The light clicked on and for a moment the police were too dazzled to see me. I checked it really was them — a man and a woman, blue and white, stiff in their stab vests. In that final second, desperate to get away, feeling the weight of Hannah's suffering and the smallness of the thing she was asking me to do, I told her: "Yes. I promise I'll try."

She let go and I ran, pelting down towards the rear exit, into the loading bay, across the road which fed the shops, and out into the back street. A man was there, something held out in front of him and I thought — gun, knife! — and raised my fist. A flash and he'd pocketed his phone, and I'd run past him, diving into the darkness of the underpass, pressing myself against its rough wall. I stayed there, hearing the cars roaring overhead, shaking.

I waited and then waited some more, long past the time when they'd have given up looking for me, when Hannah would have been taken to safety, but the shaking didn't stop. I wrapped my arms around myself and shook all the more. I couldn't identify its source, and at first I thought it must be fear or rage, both so enmeshed in me that I didn't know how to prise them apart. I let them do their worst, and when they had subsided a little I could see more clearly what was left. I could see a clean, white anger.

I would try. I would try and try and try. I would stop him if I could, before he touched anybody else.

CHAPTER
TWENTY-NINE

In the days after Hannah's rape I spent hours online browsing weaponry, nervous every time someone came into the kitchen or the stockroom. I looked at websites intended for cooks and martial arts practitioners, for hunters. I found knives whose unflinching purposes were advertised in their description. There were neck knives, skinning knives, gut hook knives. There were knives named with cheerful inventiveness: the Zombie Slayer, the Brooklyn Slicer. In calmer corners of the net I found sensible, sanctioned opinions which gave me only the briefest of pause. It was dangerous to go out equipped, they said. Your own weapon could be turned against you. I thought of that, and then I thought of going out there unprotected. It was unlikely, I felt, that anyone giving that advice had ever found themselves cornered in an alley with an attacker who would breathe in, stab you, and breathe out unperturbed.

He wasn't the only one who scared me. The cheese knife had dented the man's jacket. Zombie Slayer and its ilk would slice right through. After that strange, dissociative episode — not *episode*, I corrected myself. Too medical, too psychiatric a term — after whatever had happened to me when Zoe's attacker had run away,

I wasn't entirely sure I could guarantee where the blade would land, not completely certain I could stop it once it had begun its descent. At times like that I worried that I was a kind of weapon myself, a gun at half cock, an unexploded bomb, something outside anyone's control.

Mostly though, I dismissed these fears as squeamishness. I had promised Hannah I'd try. And even if I hadn't, this ... thing ... could have happened to my own daughter. (And *Oh God*, I'd think, when that idea came to me, as it did ceaselessly: when I awoke in the night, the weight of it compressing my chest, when I walked down the road where I'd found Martha in the bus shelter, and imagined not finding her after all, when I stared out of the shop window across to the yard entrance and thought of Hannah, and felt grateful it hadn't been Martha, and hated myself for it.) At those moments a part of me peeled away from myself, a cartoon soul after a cartoon body has died, and ran screaming through the streets of Bassetsbury, Brooklyn Slicer held aloft. I contemplated fascist solutions and found them to be just the ticket, a curfew for every man, and me a one-woman army patrolling to keep everyone safe. A knife? Why thank you, I think I will.

When it came I unwrapped it and laid it on the work bench in the stockroom, the hilt scarlet and black, the blade sharknosed, a curious serrated section underneath. Even under slight pressure, its edge was keen.

There was no pretence now that I wouldn't be wearing the costume again. In fact, *costume* was the wrong word, I thought. You put a costume on to act, but I wasn't acting any more. This was my uniform, and it needed bringing up to scratch. Some of it was easy: spare gloves, new tights. Replacing the cape was a pain, because it had been so distinctive. I ordered a new one from a costume maker in London who produced enough specialist things that she wouldn't notice mine. I was currently looking at handcuffs online, using the shop computer, jumping at every noise Uschi made behind the till, minimising the window in case she came in, expanding it when she didn't.

The front door opened, footsteps banged across the floor towards the stockroom and I entered my card details just as Allie came through. She held up a copy of the *Examiner*. I caught a quick glimpse of Day-Glo vests, candy-striped police tape, the cobbled yard in merciless daylight. I caught words from the headline: *rape, girl, vigilante* and at the bottom of the page an eyeful of red and black — me: teeth bared, fist raised.

"We need to talk," she said. *Transaction completed*, said the screen.

Outside, the air was all bacon and chips from the Stag. A pile of flattened cardboard boxes had toppled and fanned out over the grass next to the shed. The grass was confettied with stubs from Allie's fag breaks.

"So," she said. "How are you doing? That must have been absolutely horrible."

It was fatal, that kindness. My chin and lower lip began quaking immediately, as if she'd thrown a lever. My heart began to push at the walls of my chest so that I needed to sit down.

"It was," I said. "It was just awful. Poor lamb. I can't
. . . give me a minute."

Allie parked herself in the other chair and placed her
hand on my back. While I wept and my mouth made
strange shapes, and I tried to push all the crying back
into myself so I wouldn't make any noise, she chattered
about nothing and gave me time to recover, using that
tact which was her version of tenderness. "We need to
tidy up out here," she said. "The place is a tip." Her
hand rubbed my shoulders. "Cut the grass," she said.
"Plant some bulbs."

"Narcissi," I said wetly from inside my hands, feeling
my forehead contract, my eyebrows nudging at my
fingertips.

"Yeah. Crocuses."

I waited a little longer then swept my knuckles under
my eyes, wiping the moisture off on my sleeves.

"My lovely," she said after a moment. "You are going
to stop now, aren't you? Please?"

I looked at my knees.

"Really," said Allie, her finger tapping at my back. "I
think you see that, don't you? It's time to stop. The
police are on this. They're serious about it."

"Don't you think it's weird that both girls are from
Martha's school?" I asked her. "Did you notice that?
Don't you think that's . . . unsubtle . . . like he wants to
be found out?"

"It's not my job to think about that," she said. "And
it's not yours either. The police have got this."

"They've done nothing!"

"They've done loads. They're not going to tell us every time they make progress, are they? This stuff happens behind the scenes. Think about it. Think about other crimes. They're not in the papers every five minutes, are they?" There was something a bit . . . off about Allie's tone, I realised. I'd been expecting a certain amount of prickliness from her, given how serious things had become, given how difficult it had been the last time we'd talked about it. But she spoke with a sort of measured care, almost wary.

"The police can't be everywhere," I said, wriggling so she took her hand away.

"Neither can you."

"Yes, but . . . but I can be where they're not. And I've actually seen him, remember. None of them have."

"Great," she said. "So go and tell them what you know."

"They already know what I know!" I could hear myself getting agitated. Allie could, too. I watched her mentally stepping back a couple of paces. When I spoke again I tried to sound calmer, more reasonable. "They've interviewed the girls, who have seen him as well. Seen — oh God — seen more than I have. There's nothing extra I could tell the police. Do you understand? I know less than Zoe and Hannah. I just know a bit more than anyone else."

Not quite anyone else. Somewhere, someone — another woman, probably — was noticing odd behaviour in her partner, starting to get suspicious. I knew less than her. I wondered whether she knew about the attacks, whether she had a daughter herself and was trying to protect her. I'd be prepared to bet her suspicions never went close to the truth. She'd think of mundane things — affairs and work problems. She'd have no idea about the horror she went to bed with every night.

So I knew enough to justify pursuing him and not enough, I was sure, to make me turn myself in. Besides, if I did that I couldn't fulfil my promise to Hannah. I couldn't put the mask back on and keep trying.

"Anyway," I said. "The police already knew Hannah was in danger. Did you know that? Bet that wasn't in the paper. Hannah told them someone was watching her bedroom from the street and the police couldn't come to see her till the day after the rape. They didn't get there in time. So you'll understand why I'm not massively confident about their contribution." As I said it, I felt a twinge of guilt about Mac. I couldn't imagine her letting down Hannah.

Allie barely reacted. "Just listen to this," she said. "When my sister had anorexia it was the weirdest thing. It was like she'd been cursed by a bad fairy. She couldn't see the world the way it really was. I don't mean metaphorically. I mean real, physical things. She'd look in the mirror and she was a bag of bones, but the person she saw was fat. It was bizarre."

"I don't know why you're telling me this," I said, with an uncomfortable suspicion that I did in fact know. This measured approach of hers, it was just the way you'd treat someone who was ill, someone who couldn't help themselves. It was the way you'd treat someone if you thought that a tougher approach might make them flip out and suddenly run mad.

"You put on a cape," she said. "It changes how you see things."

"It's the mask, really," I corrected her, trying to sound relaxed and rational, but she spread her hands as if I'd proved some kind of point.

"OK, so you put on the *mask*, and that seems alright to you, but to the rest of us it's . . . unusual. You're out there unarmed against a dangerous bastard, and I'm worried about you. I'm really not sure you're having the effect you think you might be having. And I'm kind of hoping you'll . . . just stop. Right now."

She said it with heavy emphasis, and a second horrible thought occurred to me.

"Allie, you're not thinking of . . . are you going to tell people who I am?"

"God almighty, hon," she said. "I don't know. Who are you?"

Most of what was in the paper I already knew, or guessed. I went over it later that day, sitting at my kitchen table surrounded by breakfast detritus. Hannah's attacker was the same man as I'd seen at the club: mask, baseball hat. The *Examiner* didn't mention the strange hooked shape of the knife blade, and I wondered whether that was something the police were withholding to help them identify genuine leads. He'd abducted Hannah as she walked to meet the other girls, taken her somewhere and raped her. When I thought of that — of the word itself — I could feel myself repelled from it, two magnetic norths bouncing away from each other.

I didn't know if Hannah was being shielded from all this coverage, or where she was now — police station, hospital, home? I had no idea how these things worked. I hoped she'd be OK. I hoped her dad was alright.

The yard was just the place he'd dumped her, which explained why it was so clean. I made myself think about the not-cleanness of the other place. I thought about the things which might be in it, and whether Hannah had seen it all, or whether he'd already taped over her eyes by then so that she could just hear it, echoing or dulled, feel its chill or warmth. I found I couldn't abide the thought of her terror. I forced myself to reconstruct what might have happened, hiding my face in the damp hollow of my hands when it got too much. I told myself I was looking for clues but, if that was the case, I didn't find any. It felt, instead, as if there was a strong hand at my back, shoving me forward. There was a voice too, not unlike my own, right behind me. Look, it urged. Look, you coward. Open your eyes and look.

There were warnings to the public. There were appeals for witnesses and — a bit of a shock this one, though it shouldn't have been — a call for the vigilante to come forward. I reminded myself that they already knew far more than I did. Police were linking the attack to a third incident — or rather, a first one — an attempted abduction back in March, a girl from Heathland School who'd fought back and fled. So his territory was wider, his reach longer, he wasn't only targeting Martha's school. I didn't know whether this made him more or less frightening, and I remembered I'd heard about the abduction before. A woman had brought a flyer into the shop months ago, on an afternoon when the only thing I cared about was Martha being late to meet me. It had stayed up for a couple of weeks in our window, carrying the same photofit which was reproduced now with the caption, **SEARCH: Police believe this man may be responsible for three recent assaults on teenage girls**.

It was the only picture I had of him in which he wasn't obscured by a mask, but it was a face of devastating averageness, as if the features had been arranged for the sole purpose of evading recognition. No glasses or beard, no dimple or cleft, eyes and nose and chin evenly distributed, a face that was its own mask. And I didn't know whether this really was the attacker, nature colluding to conceal him, or whether it was an approximation the girl had come up with in the petrified aftermath of her ordeal, dishing out likely features to the police artist so she could go home with her mum.

You fucker, I thought, and for a moment it was as if I were wearing the mask, because everything else slid out of view and my vision contracted, just a shrinking white dot in the middle of the blackness. I looked at the man and I knew I would keep my promise to Hannah. More than that: I knew I wouldn't just *try*. I would hunt him down. I would get him, and it wasn't even a choice. It was the destination of the rails I was running on. I would go wherever they were taking me.

270

CHAPTER
THIRTY

I left the house after an early tea. Martha raised a hand blindly as she finished eating. Elliot, stacking the dishwasher, frowned a question.

"Self-defence class," I said, and when he looked doubtful: "You want to come?" He shook his head.

I walked fast, heading out along the road west of town. Where the clothes shops and cafés ran out and the tyre-fitting places began, I got tired. On the low wall round the Kwik-Stop car park I sat for a minute, hot enough to whip off my sweatshirt. For a second I was muffled in its darkness while the fleece slid past my mouth and nose. When I came out into the light again, the rapist was there.

He was on a bike, barrelling down the street. Settled over the handlebars, his face blocked by the white cup of the mask, he pressed forward into the wind. Before I could process what I was seeing I'd charged out in front of him, the flag of my sweatshirt waving. At that moment I didn't care if the bike went into me, or if he was carrying a knife, or if we both got hit by a car. I just knew he couldn't be allowed to get away. There was a squeak of rubber on tarmac. A van swerved past, hooting. Oh no, I thought: of course . . .

The cyclist stopped a foot away from me, momentum carrying him forward out of his seat.

"What the hell are you doing?" He pulled off his mask. He was too blond, too short.

"I'm sorry."

"I nearly crashed into you!" He was too skinny.

"I said I'm sorry!" I was shaking, suddenly feeling very exposed. "I thought you were . . ." But he got back on the bike and cycled off before I'd finished speaking.

I retreated to the pavement. A woman further down turned away and started walking again. I thought of all the witnesses staring at me from alleyways or pavements or windows. What a stupid, hair-trigger reaction, not a moment of thought behind it. I had a sweaty sense of hurtling downwards, no brakes, no steering. I would be useless like this. I needed to get some control. Mac would help with that, I knew it. For ten minutes I just sat on the wall until I felt better, calming myself down by taking account of the normal, unthreatening things happening all around me. Then I moved on, trying to look ordinary.

When I arrived at the dojo, the door was unlocked. The room was silent and dark, all texture: bristling carpet, pudgy crash mats. My shoulder hit a padded pillar. On the other side of the swing doors the gym was lit, squeaks and thuds against a pumping bass line. Through a glass panel I saw a man lifting weights, his jaw vibrating with effort.

Next to the doors was a panel of switches. I put them all on. Blocks of reluctant light dallied and flickered before stamping across the waiting area, the dojo itself, the mezzanine above. I waited there: three minutes, five, ten, but no one came.

When I reached the pavement outside, I heard her shouting. She rounded the corner from the gym, slowing her jog to a walk. She was wearing tracksuit bottoms and a T-shirt which said, "667, the Neighbour of the Beast". Her cheeks were splotched with exertion. I looked down at her feet, remembering the red shoes, and found — of course — trainers.

"You looking for me?"

"There's no one at the dojo," I said. "Isn't this the right time for your class?"

"The others . . . I thought you'd dropped out," she said. "A phone call would have been appropriate."

"I haven't been well," I said. "I wondered whether you might consider teaching me a few extra skills, one-on-one. I know it'll cost more. I don't mind."

She turned and made her way back towards the gym, so that when she replied, I could barely hear her. "I'll give you an hour," she said. "You can pay me in cash."

When I told her what I wanted, Mac shook her head.

"Please."

"No. Knife defence? Why would you want to learn that? There's better things you can do here." We faced each other on the mats, lunging forward to stretch our calf muscles.

"Well, that's what I want to learn."

"Why do you think you need it?"

"Why does it matter? For my interest. For my peace of mind. That rapist, he has a knife . . . doesn't he?"

"Triceps," she said, and we each sent a hand down our upper backs, our elbows pointing skywards. My head pillowed against my arm, I craned to look at her.

"Teach me," I said, and when she didn't reply: "Look, you're probably right. I'm sure you are. But . . . show me why I'm wrong. Let me see for myself." She was impassive. "Empower me," I tried, and she let loose a proper guffaw of laughter.

"Right," she said. "I'll empower you. Half an hour. We'll see how much empowering you can take."

She returned half my money, and then clanged upstairs to the mezzanine office. Muttering, she emerged with a knife.

"It's rubber," she said, as she came back down, bouncing its tip on her palm to demonstrate. "It's what the martial arts boys use."

Mac choreographed the move for me. An attacker approaches, blade raised, slicing down from above. I block his downward arm with my own, grabbing him above the elbow with one hand, below the wrist with another. I tilt him backwards, using my knee as a fulcrum so he topples over. I punch him in the face.

We walked through it a couple of times: me as attacker, me as victim. I could immediately see how rubbish this was. Only a cinematic villain, I thought as I approached her, knife held high, would attack like this. Hammer Horror with a stake in your hand, or Norman Bates. The sounds of our tussle — my huffing, the tacky lift of bare feet off plastic mats — echoed against the walls of the dojo. Then there was the sinewy

274

grip of her hands, the twist, the tilt, and I fell backwards onto the mats with an "Ow!"

"Ow?" Mac leaned down to retrieve the knife. "*Ow?*"

For a few moments my breath marked time. I pushed my hands into the squashy surface of the mat, raised myself a little, then fell back. "It doesn't work," I said.

"No."

"It's too fast, too unpredictable. When you block, you get hurt."

"Correct," she said. "So . . . you really want to understand this? Get up."

Standing in the centre of the room, I straightened my top. Mac glanced beyond me, into the gym. "I'll stop when you tell me to," she said, and though I knew how she loved these theatrics, how she relished teaching me a lesson, I felt my throat tighten just a little.

"OK." My hands opened. My arms moved in front of my chest. Mac shifted her grip on the knife handle.

"Look at the clock," she said, and I did.

I flinched before she even reached me. The blade was coming at my belly, and then my chest, and then my neck, and I couldn't take stock of any of it because Mac was shouting as she came, shouting in my face: "Is this working for you? Is it? Is this *empowering* enough?" There was a thud at my back which I registered as the wall I had retreated to, and it was all I could do not to put up open palms against the snub tip of the knife, but instead try to block the blows with my arm. "You've got no chance!" she shouted. "You're dead already!" I curled up, offering her my neck and back, protecting my head with my hands. The knife jabbed at me amid her bellowing, and the only thing I managed not to do, in that whole relentless attack, was to tell her to stop.

And then she did.

I crouched against the wall, heaving in and out. "Look at the clock," said Mac again, squatting next to me.

"What . . .?"

"Do you see?" she said. "Twenty seconds. That's how long it took to finish you." We both slid down on to the mat. She was out of breath too, pink across her cheeks and down her neck.

"They come at you fast," she said. "They come at you full of rage. It's not just the attack, it's the anger. It's crippling. Nothing works." We sat quietly for a moment. There was enough vehemence behind her words to make me wonder what exactly she'd been through. I thought of the scar I'd noticed on her calf, now hidden beneath her trackie bottoms.

"What if I had a knife too?" I asked.

"You've watched too many movies," she said. But I could see her in my peripheral vision, frowning. "The thing to do is run, if you can," she told me. "Call the police."

"Imagine that's not an option."

She didn't say anything. When I turned to look at her, she was staring at my hands, open in my lap. "What's this?" she asked. The scar in my left palm was clean and pink.

"I did it cutting an apple," I said.

"There are refuges," she said. "The police will render aid . . ."

"God, no! It's not that."

"There are ways we can protect you."

"It's not that!" I stood up, struggling to keep a clear head.

"Listen!" I said. "What if you had to fight back anyway, even though your chance of success was almost nothing?" Oh God, I was nearly crying. Just like that. "What if you didn't have the option of not trying? Imagine you had to do it, Mac. What would you do? Not all this . . ." I mimed the balletic overhead stab, the slo-mo block and turn. "What's the stuff that nearly works, or partly works, or might just work?"

Mac trapped her bottom lip between her teeth and chewed on it for a few seconds. "Well," she said. "There's one thing I've seen."

It was another block, both fists intercepting the stabbing arm. When I took the assailant's role, I could see how it might be effective. I hammered my arm against the little rocks of her fists. It gave me pause. But you have to be quick, she said, you have to aim the block just right. Otherwise you're back where you started, stopping the blade with your own skin.

"So this works?" I asked.

"No," she told me. "Not usually."

We switched roles and I tried the manoeuvre, slowly at first. I told her, just keep stabbing away, I'll work on it. I got her to approach me from different angles and I anticipated her strike. The manoeuvre had much in common with catching a ball and, like that elusive skill, it improved with practice. I watched Mac's arm: its angle, its speed, the small hesitations that preceded a change in trajectory. I got used to the impact of her arm against my fist, the jarring shock travelling up to my shoulders.

I looked at the clock. Nine minutes left.

"You'd grab me, wouldn't you?" I said. "With your other hand? To hold me in place?"

"Yes."

"So do it."

She paused for a second and her eyes narrowed just a fraction. She reached out and grasped the front of my T-shirt, yanking me towards her: sweat against a base note of Imperial Leather.

"Like this?" said Mac. She drew back her hand and we started again.

Our combat became a cramped and messy thing, all tight corners and guesswork. Close in, it was harder to see the blows coming, and they came quicker. I missed two for every one I blocked. But after a while I got better, and missed only half of them.

"Now shout at me," I told her.

"Stop holding your breath," said Mac. "Breathe."

"Shout at me."

She shouted. Despite the manufactured nature of her anger, despite it coming at my own request, it triggered a destabilising jolt of adrenalin. The first thrust after that went into my belly, the next into my chest. I stumbled sideways and she stabbed me on the arm.

"Keep shouting," I told her. "Make it bad."

She frowned and I thought she was going to object, but instead she started yelling again, stepping it up. "You will never win," she shouted. "You cannot do this!" She turned up the volume and I kept trying to block, and then actually blocked — sometimes. "You are fooling yourself." Then I stalled — unaccountably, in the midst of all that abuse — and glanced up. Her mouth was tight, her eyes devoid of rage. The knife tip nosed between my ribs.

We stared at each other, catching our breath, and then started again. I missed and missed and blocked, missed and blocked. It finished swiftly. Above her cries and my puffing there came a sequence of alien sounds: a voice, bracketed by two thuds. Mac twitched towards the noise, her hand briefly stilled. I grasped her above the elbow, below the wrist, my palms slapping against her skin. There was time to register that the music from the gym had swelled and retreated as I hauled her round and heaved her over my knee. She tumbled onto the mat and a man's voice said: ". . . in here?"

"We're fine," she said, not taking her eyes off me as I delivered the final leisurely punch, my arm drawn back at an exaggerated angle, my fist steaming towards her towing me behind it. Its leading edge nudged her cheek. Behind me there was a grunt. The music rose again and was muffled. The door banged shut.

"That's your half hour," said Mac from the mat. I checked the clock. She was precisely correct, the second hand swinging up towards the twelve as she spoke.

She left without acknowledging me, pushing through the doors to the gym. After they closed, I leaned against a viewing panel, my damp fingers braced against the wood. She steered a course between lumps of machinery that perpetually folded and unfolded around her. As my breath started to obscure the view she reached the door to the women's showers, lifted a clenched hand and shook it in a gesture — of annoyance or triumph, I couldn't tell which.

CHAPTER
THIRTY-ONE

"I'll be back after my self-defence class," I told Elliot. "Keep an eye on Martha."

Since we'd talked, there had been a peace of sorts between us. The anger seemed to have gone from him. At dinner time, we'd stay at the kitchen table after Martha left. In the evenings, we'd pause the TV to make waspish comments about the programmes. We had started, tentatively, to make each other laugh again. For all this, things weren't quite the way they used to be. Elliot was still a little reserved, and I'd catch him watching me from time to time. Buoyed up by our reconciliation, I dismissed his guardedness as a habit he'd got into, a hangover from his previous suspicions. If pushed, I might have remembered that he had his own secrets to keep, and put it down to that.

Now, as I was on my way out, Elliot swallowed the last mouthful of his pasta. "This attacker," he said. "This rapist. He's flattened every liberal impulse I've ever had."

"Keep a close eye on Martha," I repeated. "I mean, actually check on her."

"All that anti-capital punishment, restorative justice, rehabilitation bollocks, and all I want to do is kill him. I'd do it myself."

Upstairs, the bolt on the bathroom door shot home. I pictured the rapist at the centre of a seething crowd, all the mothers and fathers of all the girls in Bassetsbury dismantling him. I could see Elliot there, armed with, for some reason, a baseball bat popped into my mind.

"You and me both," I told him. Above the lounge, water thundered into the bath. He cocked his head towards the noise.

"She won't be going anywhere in a hurry," he said. "I'll be lucky if she's out within the hour."

When I got outside, dusk was already falling. Trees and roofs stood black against a backlit sky, the longest day long past. I was halfway through the railway tunnel when I heard, between my own echoing footsteps, a scuffle at the entrance. I glanced back, but the mouth of the tunnel was empty, no sound now except for a motorbike in the road ahead. I hurried through, then paused at the exit. I stopped for a good, long time, looking back down its gullet, and listening for the sound of amplified breathing. But there was nothing at all.

I went into the shop the back way. Turning my key in the gate I heard another noise behind me, a rustle among the bushes, and this time I spun round, to see . . . an empty churchyard. Not again, I thought. This had been happening more and more, and it wouldn't do anyone any good, this constant jumpiness, this nervy expectation of disaster. It made me less effective. As I had to so often these days, I reminded myself of all the things it was more likely to be than a rapist. Just a bird, or a cat, or a dog off the leash. A couple of kids sneaking a fag or a snog. Still, I put the door at my back and scanned the area, switching off the peripheral noises, trying to isolate the sound I'd just heard. I reached into my bag, pulled out the new knife in its sheath and stood there holding it like a talisman until a minute had gone by, and nothing remotely unusual had happened. I reminded myself what I was here to do. I would start making good on my promise and return to all the places he had attacked, to see if there was anything I could learn. If there wasn't, at least I'd be one more person on the streets, keeping an eye out for trouble, and ready to act.

I put the knife back in my bag and soothed myself with simple actions. Open the door. Lock it behind you. Get that uniform on, quick.

The curtains were all closed at Hannah's place, the bedrooms upstairs dark, the lounge window a glowing rectangle. The house had the look of a ship bound tight in anticipation of a storm, every loose thing lashed down: the car off the drive, bricks on the lids of the bins, the windows shut, even on this warm night.

I waited for a while in the cone of shadow between streetlights. I had a list of places he had struck: the nightclub, the florist's yard, and now, Heathland School. But I wanted to start here, at the centre of the damage. The man had staked out Hannah's house before he'd raped her. He'd stood right where I was, probably. The thought should have been chilling, but actually it made me stare with a fierce concentration at the space beside me, as if I could conjure him into being. I wished he'd left some sort of impression of himself, a ghostly print that would give him away. Or maybe — maybe he'd return here. It was possible.

I checked the street, down towards town, up to the crest of the hill. I imagined him on his way, dressed in ordinary clothes — a suit? jeans? — his cap and mask waiting somewhere else. I tried and tried, but I couldn't give him a face. His superpower was his ordinariness: his ordinary height, his ordinary build, vanilla and beige moving among us unseen. I remembered how he'd been at the nightclub. Was there a limp, a slouch of the shoulder? What were the whorls and loops of his movement? I had recognised Martha by a dip of her head, but the rapist was just mask and knife to me.

They'd taken down the police tape in the yard where I'd found Hannah. Just being there made me sweat. Heat built in my skin, as if someone had turned up my thermostat. The florist had re-opened for business; behind the glass, there were fresh blooms. I eased onto the ground and sat as Hannah had, my back against the window. This could have been Martha, I thought again, and then pushed the idea away. It was unbearable. I wouldn't have let it happen. Somehow, I would have rescued her. How though? When he could just snatch her, just do whatever he wanted? Usually, when these tormenting thoughts came and I wasn't in uniform, I found the way to blunt them was to imagine myself wearing the mask. Now, in full kit, I waited for the real thing to take effect, but all I could think about was Hannah's first words when I took off the gag: *I want my dad.* I imagined Martha terrified, screaming for me, and me not coming, and I felt myself getting close to panic.

I concentrated hard, thinking about Zoe and how I'd saved her. I could do that for Martha too — more so, because she was my girl. I'd heard about people being able to lift cars off their loved ones, do things they'd never be capable of doing normally. I was quick and decisive in uniform. I was fearless. Whatever dark place he took her to, I would find her. I could see my boot kicking in the door, his shock and her relief. I could see myself fighting brilliantly with clean punches, *Thwak! Pow!* I'd come to the rescue and he wouldn't know what had hit him.

Under my hands the cobbles were smooth, the channels between them damp. Hannah's hands had been bound. I placed mine in my lap. I closed my eyes — Hannah's had been taped shut — and listened to the sounds of the street beyond, the swell and fade of footsteps and voices. His breath would have been in her ear, his threats. (In the High Street a car rolled to a halt, a squeak as it rubbed against the kerb.) She would have felt the knife against her skin. Her vagina would be burning raw, she'd have wanted to be sick but been scared of doing it, her mouth sealed shut by the tape. Her ambitions would have shrunk irreducibly to survival.

He would never do it again. I wouldn't let him. I stood, slipping the knife out of my belt, its hilt snug against my palm. On the blank wall opposite the dry cleaner's, the serrated underside ripped lines across the brick: two swooping downward curves, peaks rising above them. I carved slanting elliptical eye-holes and filled them in with rasping scrapes, grinding the brick to powder at their centre. I looped curlicues across the brow and cheeks and then it was done: my mask, gazing down at the yard. Out of breath I finished, wiped off the blade on my glove, brick dust on black satin.

The victims might see this. The rapist might. I applied myself to the wall again, scraping three words underneath. Then I holstered the knife and strode through the covered passageway into the High Street.

Mac was there. On the pavement right next to the passageway. I backed up, retreating towards the yard, but just as I approached it the light flicked off and I was left in darkness. One more step back and it would switch on again, revealing me. Forward, and I'd end up right behind her. I stayed where I was and listened to the soft echo of my breath.

She wasn't alone; the vehicle I'd heard was a police car. It was a hulking thing, an MPV sitting low over its wheels, the bonnet washed sodium-yellow in the streetlight. A front tyre rested on the kerb: half-on, half-off. Inside the car, two faces floated above dark uniforms.

". . . Time for a new challenge," Mac was saying. "I'll be applying early next year." She stood a little back from the vehicle, hands grasped behind her, legs apart.

I didn't hear the reply, the window open just the tiniest crack, but I saw her right hand grip her left, bunching the fingers. A white straw rose towards the lips of the officer nearest. His cheek convulsed.

"No worries there," said Mac. "I'm in good shape. And I learn fast."

The driver's door swung open and she took a step back. "Yeah," said the copper who emerged — black-clad, his scalp showing shiny through blond hair — "There's all of that. But Armed Response isn't just about shooting straight."

Private security work, Cath had suggested in the changing room. Fraud investigation. The driver walked away and Mac followed for a few steps. I crept forward and watched her watching him as he marched past the bank and the electrical shop towards McDonald's, carrying his cup before him like a suspicious package, repelling the kids on the pavement: a drop of detergent in oil. Inside the car, the radio squawked. He dropped the cup in a bin.

As I watched, something tugged at my memory, something about Hannah's story, which I hadn't got quite right. I tried to catch it, but it evaded me, something glimpsed out of the corner of my eye.

"There's all sorts of factors," the officer said when he returned, glancing at Mac briefly as he levered himself back into the car. "Psychological suitability. You know that. Whether your face fits."

The culture doesn't change, Cath had said. I thought about Mac's rectitude — look at the way she was standing now, with that alert stance. I couldn't imagine her parking the police car sloppily, or enjoying it when kids were intimidated by her, or breaking eye contact with another officer just so they'd know they weren't in the clique. Her face would never fit; she was a stickler. I saw that Cath was trying to protect Mac when she encouraged her to leave, and I could see why. I wished she was less obviously keen, less hurtable, because I understood that she might be the best officer for the job — maybe better than any of these wide boys — and that she still would not succeed.

The wide boy slammed the door and slid the window up. "Cheers, then," he said, as the glass sealed. I could see Mac's face reflected in it, her mouth closing, as if she'd been just about to reply. The car bounced down from the kerb, nosing through pedestrians on the closed road, sirens winding up and quickly down to get people scurrying. Mac watched it leave and I thought she'd leave too. Instead, she turned until she was facing down the passage. I thought of what she might see if she took a step closer: the pale of my face, the glittering gold embellishment on my mask. She peered into the arch and I turned and ran — across the yard into a flash of light, the cobbles giving way to tarmac as I rounded the side of the florist. I ran on, leaving her behind me in the empty space, looking at the wall, at the mask I'd sketched on it, at the message beneath the mask: *I am watching.*

CHAPTER
THIRTY-TWO

"This one's from Liv. The Incredible Bulk." Martha waited. I could see her out of the corner of my eye, mouth half-open in expectation of a laugh. "What? What's the problem?"

"OK," I said (measured, careful). "Think about this woman. Can you think of anything about her more significant than her looks?"

Martha sighed. "OK," she said. "Izzy's sent one. Blunderwoman."

Did they really think these things, or was it just the best they could come up with? "But she hasn't blundered, has she?"

"We're just joking. Stop being so . . ."

"I'm not being so. I'm just saying — tell the truth about her. Think about how she helped your friend and find a name that fits. You can do better than this. You could come up with something really good."

She turned to face the window and mumbled.

"What was that?"

"Nothing."

"I'm just — hang on. There's a space." A half-space in fact, my back wheels overshooting onto double yellow lines. "Get a carton, one of those four pint ones. Green top."

"Can't you?"

"No, I can't. I might have to move. There's my purse. Tell Sue hi from me."

Martha pulled the seatbelt out with her, letting it ping away from her hand at the last minute; I had to yank it back inside before the door slammed. While she was gone, I stared blankly at the vista (steering wheel, road, pavement), my thoughts untethered. I squeezed my upper arms, prospecting for muscle. Minutes went by, and I shifted my gaze to the shopfront. Shadowy through the glass, Martha shuffled forward in the queue, head bent to her phone. Then she disappeared behind Sue's policeman, and I laughed out loud.

The policeman was one of those life-size cardboard figures which act as a warning to miscreants. It was lodged in the window, a presence so familiar I'd ceased to see it. But in the past few days, Sue had tinkered with her policeman because now a red wig perched on his cardboard helmet, a black cape hung around his shoulders.

When Martha emerged from the shop, she turned to look at him. His cape was lifted at the shoulder by the aerial of his cardboard police radio, lending him a one-sided hunch. Sue had slipped a mask round his face and painted his lips red. His helmet elevated the wig and there was a Mekon-ish air about him, a bit grotesque, to be honest. There was a speech bubble stuck to the window. If I'd been a little higher — if I'd been standing in front of it — the bubble would have seemed to emerge from the copper's mouth. It said, "I am watching."

Martha got back into the car. "*I am watching*," she said, nodding towards the window. "There's a thing about it in the paper."

"Really?"

"Yeah. Pictures."

"Go back and get me one, will you?"

She opened the plastic bag and tilted it towards me, a copy of the *Examiner* already tucked inside next to the milk. Above the masthead there was a photograph of the wall in the yard, my mask scratched onto it. *She Is Watching*, said the teaser. Pictures inside. On the front page there was an interview with a forensic psychologist, addressing the question I'd asked myself, many times: why were the victims from such a narrow group, and in such a small town, too?

"This is one of several common patterns we see," Dr Patricia Moss told the *Examiner*. "This man thinks he's smarter than the police — in fact, he thinks he's smart enough to take enormous risks in terms of how he chooses his victims. This fits with the real motivation behind rape, which is that it is a power-grab, a demonstration of dominance. But what's interesting is that power-grabbers are people who actually feel they don't have any power, or don't have enough.

The gratification they get from rape, from that feeling of power, drives them to do it again, but their insecurity shows in aspects such as the fairly small areas — comfort zones — they work in.

Residents should be extremely vigilant, but they should also remember that these perpetrators end up being caught precisely because of that desire to push their luck."

So he was a risk-taker, arrogant enough that there was no limit to what he might do. The thought turned me cold, but I knew Dr Moss must be right. Almost daily on the news now, stories were emerging about celebrities in their seventies pomp, raping with impunity in a studio, or a hospital, or an office.

I was aware of Martha reading over my shoulder and got ready to reassure her, but when I looked in her direction I could see that she was reading a different article, one at the bottom of the page about a local B&B owner who had banned gay guests. She saw I was watching and glanced away quickly. Her expression was unreadable, but I could guess what she was imagining: herself at the door of the B&B, being refused entry.

"That woman's completely out of order," I said. "You see that? That's history."

Martha made a non-commital "hmm?" noise.

"Give it ten years," I told her. "Ten years, and those attitudes will be quaint, like not wanting women to have the vote, or slavery. We'll laugh at people like that."

I waited for her to say something. I waited to say something perfect back. Martha stared out of the windscreen. "Wasp," she said eventually and I frowned in her direction, trying to crack the code. "Wasp!" she said again, more vehemently. Three cars up from us, a traffic warden tweaked at something on a windscreen. Wasp, her father's word.

I started to reverse — carefully, there was another car parked behind me now — and a curious ululation came from the pavement. Then a double-rap on the boot of the car, and I stamped on the brake. In the back window I could see a man standing at the edge of the kerb, holding up his hand like a traffic cop.

When I got out, he actually looked surprised.

"What are you doing?" I said.

He glanced down at my back wheel. "It's a tight one. I thought you might like a bit of help."

"Why? Because I can't drive my own car?"

He closed his eyes. "Look, if you don't want any help . . ."

"Don't present it as a kindness. Would you ask him?" I gestured across the road to where a young bloke was getting into his car. "Or him? Or any man? Any man at all?"

"Listen . . ."

"Because I never see blokes doing it for other blokes. Never." The traffic warden glanced between us nervously. "Have you any idea how patronising it is? All this *to me, to me* crap, all this —" I adopted a crouched stance, a dunce expression, and beckoned him on. "Next time, wait till you're asked."

I didn't even look at Martha when I got back in. I rammed the seatbelt into its buckle and nudged the car backwards and forwards, keeping my eyes where they needed to be, editing out the man, the warden, the onlookers. Martha put her face in her hands. On the final turn, as I edged out into traffic, I — ever so slightly, hardly at all really — clipped the bumper of the car in front.

"Shit," I said, and Martha let loose an explosive laugh, a throat-scraper.

"Shit, shit, shit," I said, and Martha said, "Mum!" She snorted as we pulled out, then turned to look behind us, where the man was still standing, palms skywards, a told-you-so glee writ large on his face.

I was giggling myself now. The last thing he saw as we left, framed in the back window of the car: Martha's face gurning at him, Martha's hand sticking up two fingers.

Almost home, but to reach it we had to go the long way round, through the complex of mini roundabouts, the cogs in the clockwork of Bassetsbury town centre. Martha was quiet for a while, head down over her phone. When she next looked up I glanced at her, wanting to laugh about the *to me* man again, but she looked leaden.

"Liv wants us to go and see Hannah," she said. "When I'm allowed out again." Her mood had changed, just like that, an emotional sleight of hand.

"Well . . . I think that's a good idea. I hate the thought of her being isolated. One more week, Martha. And there will be conditions. Parental supervision, spot checks . . ."

"You don't know what it's like!"

". . . Lifts to and from . . ."

"Don't! You could not even imagine a worse punishment than this!"

I'm not a shouter, but at that moment I had to stop myself yelling at her, something sharp and quick to discharge the sudden fury. She was facing out of the window again. Beyond her, I saw our left turn slip by. "Oh, believe me, I can," I said. "Two weeks in the comfort of your own . . ."

"No! Not that! A worse punishment than *this*." She held up her phone. I caught a few words of the text: Hannah, school, police. "I mean thinking about Hannah, what happened. Knowing . . ."

"Martha?"

"She was raped!"

"Love . . ." I reached out to her, stunned at my own idiocy, but she pushed further away, wrapping her arms around her knees.

Neither of us spoke while I drove on to the next junction, a fiddly network of Victorian roads, clogged with parked cars. Impossible to turn in any of them, so I pressed on.

"Avenger," I said finally, reaching for her head, cradling its curve in my palm. "Ferocity."

Martha curled over, forehead to knees, so that when she finally spoke I nearly lost what she said.

"The police are in school."

"But it's the holidays."

"Liv said they called the teachers in. They're interviewing them."

"Why?" A pedestrian stepped out onto a zebra crossing; I spotted her almost too late and put the brakes on, a little hard.

"All the girls he has hurt have been to our school."

We looked at each other. "No, love. That's not right. Heathland, one of them . . ."

"No, Mum. It was . . ."

"I read about it. He tried to abduct her. She got away. Definitely Heathland."

"Mum, you're not listening. Izzy's just told me. It was Naomi."

Behind us, a car hooted. The pedestrian had landed safely and was trotting down the opposite pavement.

"Who's Naomi?"

"She's at Heathland *now*. Her parents moved her there last year. But before that she was at my school. She was in my year."

The driver leaned on his horn again, but I didn't move. I was looking at Martha. There was a sudden, cramping pain in my guts. I tried to remember the way your face is when you're not very frightened. I tried to make it do that. All the victims were from the same year group of the same school, attacked off school premises by a man who must have known exactly where to find them. Martha was looking at me frankly, her face open with fear and that terrible, yearning edge that children have: a little bit of hope reserved, just in case Mum says the right thing and makes it better.

"Naomi was in my year," she said again. "They all were."

CHAPTER
THIRTY-THREE

That evening was a quiet one, Elliot home early and spread out at the end of the sofa, beer bottle beside him, drawing pad on his knees. In recent days things had continued to change for the better; there was a fluidity between us, Elliot seeking out my company with a new enthusiasm. No, I corrected myself. With the old enthusiasm. We were talking about trivial things again — and as soon as I noticed that, I realised how much I'd missed those idle conversations: anecdotes about customers' oddities, unedited passing thoughts, lame jokes, the very same things I hadn't appreciated when they were easy to come by. The change came from him and I didn't know why, and didn't want to ask in case the act of asking tilted things out of true once again.

The sight of the beer reminded me there was a half bottle of wine in the fridge. When I got back with my glass, Elliot had started scribbling. I tried to look, but he flipped the pad over, grinning, and reached down for a swig. On the coffee table was the pile of DVDs I'd trawled for in Allie's shop, the ones I'd thought Martha might like. I was trying everything I could to make staying at home seem like a good option to her, and in choosing the movies had used a Venn diagram approach, isolating films that were romantic *and* a bit arthouse *and* featured indie music.

"You mind if I watch something?" I said.

"Go ahead," said Elliot. "What is it?"

"*Gas Food Lodging.*" I waited to see if he'd remember but he just smiled, turned the pad back over and started drawing again. I picked up my notebook, angling it away from him.

Teacher?
Pupil (sixth-former)?
Worth watching school gates? Snooper?
Someone who lives near the School?

Four possibilities, the rest of the page empty. I'd kept thinking about the rapist, about his certainty that he'd never be caught, about the mistake that would reveal him — most of all about who he could be. I found myself returning to him at random moments, as if in some way I might surprise and capture him unawares. After a bit I wrote:

Caretaker?

I stared at the page for a while longer, until I heard Martha's step on the stairs. She came through and I snapped the notebook shut.

"What's this?" She was holding a novel, *Code Name Verity*, one of the haul she'd bought with the book token I'd given her — finally — for her birthday. A

298

friendship bracelet stuck out from between the pages a third of the way through.

"It's called *Gas Food Lodging*. You want to watch it with me?" I sneaked a glance at Elliot: oblivious.

"Never heard of it."

"I saw it when it first came out. You'll like it."

Against the soundtrack of the movie, I heard Martha's own as she put down the book on the counter, went to the fridge, poured a glass of milk. Returning, she dallied by the doorway.

"You coming in?"

She shrugged. "For a bit." She excavated her mobile from a pocket and sat in the chair opposite us. I put my feet up on the coffee table. Incy-Wincy, Martha used to call it when she was small, the wooden legs touching each other like fingers and thumbs. Elliot would pretend offence. The table was a design icon, he'd inform us. It occurred to me now that it might have been genuinely disconcerting for him to see the glass surface marked with Martha's smudgy fingers, its edges protected with plastic guards, a flotsam of Lego washed up against its base.

"We saw this on our first date," I said, nodding towards the TV. "Me and Dad."

Elliot uttered a soft, "Oh" and brought his hand to his mouth.

He'd taken me into London. We'd sat in the back row of an artsy fleapit and he'd reached across, taking my face in both hands as if he were going to pluck me. When we kissed I had anchored my palm to his neck, thumbing at his jaw, the seat arm digging into my hip.

"I still haven't seen the whole thing," said Elliot. He scooted his feet over and nudged mine. I nudged back.

"Get a room," said Martha, raising a hand as a blinker. On screen, Fairuza Balk made unsound romantic choices. Martha wriggled sideways so that she was lying across the chair, feet over one arm, head resting on the other. I sent a packet of biscuits skidding across the table to her.

When they were both absorbed, I snatched the *Examiner* from the table. This edition was wall-to-wall rapist and vigilante. The interview with the forensic psychologist was on the front and there was a piece on page three about a local dad organising a "fathers' army" to patrol the town. The centre spread — the pictures promised in the teaser — carried a photo of the wall in the yard where I'd left my message for the attacker. Around it were arranged readers' contributions, low-res snaps taken at locations across town, in all the places I'd left my mark that night: the back of the nightclub, the entrance to the school Naomi attended, and on Martha's school, several — on the pavement at the side, on the fence flanking the driveway, on a stretch of wall out by the prefabs.

I made sure my face was set to nonchalant and glanced at the pages as if I'd just happened upon them. When I looked up to see if the others had noticed what I was reading, I found Elliot watching me.

"What?" I mouthed, my face heating, but he just smiled, a full-wattage world-beater. I frowned a question, he shook his head, and I didn't want to make a single move to disrupt this harmony. We gazed at each other until finally he looked away and we sank once more into what we'd been doing.

There was one more article, a vox pop: **MENACE OR MARVEL? WHAT DO YOU THINK OF BASSETSBURY'S SUPERHERO?** I'd read it earlier and kept returning to it, trying to work out how I felt about it. Contributors had been snapped in the High Street. The thumbnails showed them squinting into the sun against a backdrop of town centre landmarks. Lee (student, 20) thought it was a harmless laugh, but Angela (credit controller, 52) suggested it was "trivialising an important issue". Mahesh (29) was convinced it was a hoax and Richard (75) thought it was dangerous, but I was most interested in the opinions of Allie (36, Famaid manager).

She was pictured outside the shop, at just the right distance and angle for part of the sign to be seen behind her. Unlike the others, she wasn't smiling. Her head was inclined towards the camera, her lips pursed, and I don't think it is pushing credibility too far to say that she was looking straight at me.

"Whoever's doing this is playing a dangerous game," she told the *Examiner*. "They'll only stop when they get hurt — unless someone reveals their identity first."

It was so grossly out of character I still couldn't believe she'd done it this way rather than just talking to me. I could imagine how hesitant she might have been, speaking to the reporter. She'd have had to force herself to do it, surely, because Allie wasn't a game-player. *Who are you?* she'd asked me. Maybe she thought I'd given up listening to her. I wanted to feel offended and righteously angry, but I knew she wasn't wrong;

nothing she said would have pushed me off-course. I wondered just how worried she must be to threaten me. I wondered if she was worried enough to make good on her threats.

Martha laughed, a *hoo-hoo-hoo*, which took about six years off her.

"I remember this part," I said.

"They're sleeping together?"

"Yeah. But the daughter doesn't know. She thinks she's set up a blind date."

Elliot nudged my foot again. He raised his index finger, pointed to the ceiling and mouthed something.

"Tidy?" I whispered.

He shook his head and whispered back, leaning on the *s*. "Study."

I detoured via Martha's room to make my regular check. It was as chaotic as ever, her floor as uneven with discarded clothes. On this August night, one window was open. I stuck my head out into a grey dusk, the air damp and warm, a weight in it which promised thunder. Martha's windows, thin and assailable, opened her up to the gaze of the houses opposite. Down below, the alleyway at the bottom of the garden provided access between the pub and the station, or a shortcut into town, or a quiet back way for someone to stay off the roads and out of sight. I pulled the window shut and locked it, and tested the lock. I put the key on the windowsill, where she could see it.

In Elliot's study I looked round all his nice things, the photos and posters, the clean unused fireplace. I couldn't work out why he'd wanted me to come up here. Then I noticed the wedding album, in the same place as before but front-facing this time. The extra pages stuck up out of it, a tease of Vermilion's red and black. In the shop, this was how we got books to fly off the shelves; face them to the front and everyone wants to pick them up. I pulled out the comic and found a whole new story. *For Art's Sake*, it said on the cover. I realised, in a happy rush, that this was what Elliot wanted me to find, that after all those times when I'd silently urged him to let me in on his secret, he was finally doing so. I remembered his grin downstairs and recognised it, in retrospect, as encompassing the twin pleasures of concealment and imminent revelation. But the pages weren't on the desk, or in the middle of the floor where I couldn't miss them, nor had Elliot simply presented them to me. Instead he'd left the comic in the wedding album because — it dawned on me at last — he knew I'd found his previous one there. I'd been busted. I closed the study door and turned the page.

Vermilion's alter ego, artist Edward Porter, has hit hard times. Wealthy collectors are buying work from a mysterious new talent. And those collectors are found murdered just after they have installed their paintings. While Porter struggles to pay the rent, earning extra money in a down-at-heel café, Vermilion prowls Metro City searching for answers.

At night he creeps into the homes of the rich, leaping from roof to roof before slipping in through an attic window, darting through a briefly opened front door or climbing the glass walls of a skyscraper. Across two pages, Vermilion stands in the corridor of some ancestral pile, the red of his cape in the foreground, the corridor stretching ahead of him, its darkness punctuated by illuminated paintings, each one in a different style, each one meticulous: the rich greens of Rousseau, a precisely-rendered Jackson Pollock and, right at the end, a Lichtenstein plane exploding in scarlets and yellows.

On one page, Vermilion stands in an apartment high above the twinkling city. The room is bleached white and cream, but above the fireplace there's colour: a painting, a splash of red on a white background, red which breached its boundaries, dripping off the canvas and onto the frame, pouring down the white, white wall, flowing across the mantelpiece and onto the floor. But Vermilion isn't looking at that and, after a moment, neither was I. He isn't looking at the man's body, twisted in its death agonies on the pale rug. He is looking — and so am I, so am I — at the woman who has burst in on him.

She's curvaceous and flame-haired, clad in black and scarlet, her body shaped with the usual comic book brutality. Short skirt, high glossy boots and a cape which flies out behind her, revealing a flash of red lining. And she is wearing a black mask, decorated in golden swirls.

[Speech balloon]: **What the . . .?**

[Speech balloon]: **looking for something, Vermilion?**

She is called Scarlet and she, too, has been investigating the murders. She tells Vermilion her story as they stare out at the city together, speech balloons packed black as she reveals her quest: to catch her

304

father's killer. Before I turned the page I thought, this could be even better. We should see this in flashback, her alter ego (let's call her . . . Jessica Jennings) grieving over the death of the first victim, her own father. We see her weeping in her bedroom at night and, through her open door, in reversed viewpoint, we glimpse Vermilion himself. He's standing in that long corridor full of paintings, unaware of her presence. In the next panel she turns and glimpses him too, and above her head we see: *!*

Downstairs, the lounge door opened and closed. On the page in front of me, silhouetted against the nightscape, Scarlet tells Vermilion she has vital evidence. She'll share it — if he allows her to work with him and avenge the death of her father.

[Extreme close-up, speech balloon]: *I work alone.*

[Close up, speech balloon]: *Then you will fail.*

They stand in the darkness within kissing distance, a sliver of air separating them, her hand on his cheek. In the next panel there's suddenly light, yellow on their faces, and they both turn, mouths open in surprise.

[Spiked speech balloon, unseen speaker]: *In here, officer! I heard noises!*

Scarlet vaults out of an open window.

[Speech balloon]: *How will I find you, Scarlet?*

The final panel is breathtaking: a full page. We are standing at Vermilion's shoulder and can see, as he does, through the transparent wall of the apartment, out onto the city. Reflected in the glass is the police officer who has just burst into the room. A cable snakes from the open window, down the long drop to the streets below. At the end of it, light flashing from her hand, is Scarlet, airborne like a spider paying out silk behind her.

[Speech balloon]: **Don't worry, Vermilion. I'll find you!**

I stared at that final image, at the flash from her hand, and I turned back a couple of pages to the moment where she and Vermilion nearly kiss. There was her glove, black-clad, alighting on his face. And on the third finger, slipped over the satin, a ring.

My ring.

My engagement ring.

I saw the red hair, the same red as my wig, and the redlined cape just like mine, and the ring which could only be mine, and the superhero who was me, incontrovertibly. Elliot knew everything.

I closed my eyes and could picture the horizon rolling away from me as I released myself off the edge of the building. Motion lines streamed out from my arms, my feet, the buildings tumbling around me, but I was not scared. I knew there was a rope to hold me safe. I knew I would not hit the ground.

Then Elliot came in. "J," he said. "You are magnificent."

He came to me and we looked at each other with what-next expressions, and we both laughed. We touched each other's arms and shoulders with little squeezes, as if we were making sure we were still solid. A part of me was panicking — what if this was the end of it all? What if Elliot knowing made everything harder? — and another part was delighted, amazed that the sky hadn't just fallen in.

"How did you guess?" I asked him. "Was it the paper? Someone took a picture."

He shook his head. "I followed you."

"Oh God!" I knew exactly when he'd done it. I remembered the noises I kept hearing on my way to the shop, the sly rustles and scuffs, the state they'd put me in.

"You know I heard you?" I said. "I was bloody scared."

"I'm sorry," he said. "I thought you were lying to me — which you were — and following you was . . . kind of exciting."

Well, I couldn't fault that. "You were in the churchyard, then?"

"Yes. I saw you come out in your costume. You were astonishing. You were incredible."

"You didn't freak out?"

"For about three seconds. Then I thought, oh my God, maybe she's found the graphic novel. Maybe she's . . . I thought, she's doing this for me. And you looked . . . you were . . ."

"Doing it for you?"

"Yes."

We sat down, our backs against the door, and I told myself there would be time to correct his misapprehensions. He wanted to know, of course, why I'd kept it all secret. We slid further down till we were lying side by side on the carpet, heads pillowed on bent arms in mirror formation, elbows levelled at each other. There were lots of reasons why I hadn't told him. I'd rehearsed them ad infinitum. He might have jeered, he would definitely have worried. I'd told myself it would never happen again. And —

"I didn't want . . ."

He had everything that was cool and fun and admirable, and all I wanted was this one thing. All I'd wanted was to wear the uniform and go out into the streets without anyone knowing who I was, so that I could decide for myself who I might be. I hadn't wanted Elliot to see me from the outside and tell me what I looked like. (And I hadn't wanted Allie to, and I didn't want the police to either.) I had a horrible feeling they might say I looked like a fat middle-aged woman in a funny costume, and the thought of that was unbearable, because it wasn't like that from the inside at all.

That was the truth, but how absolutely impossible to tell him. What a rejection it would have seemed, with him so thrilled by it all, telling my story in the pages of his comic, making it a heroic one. Elliot's hand touched mine gently.

"I didn't want to shock you," I said finally. "I thought you'd be shocked."

"I was," he said. "But that's no bad thing."

The more we talked about my secret identity, the more I strayed into quite different areas: how it frustrated me that I did the hard yards with Martha and he got to be the fun one, how alien I sometimes felt in my own life. I muddled through, and I lied to him a little to save his feelings, and probably a little to myself as well, and if that seems dysfunctional, I can only say that in my experience of human relationships,

308

muddling through is all we can do. If you want a clean line of cause and effect, watch a Hollywood movie. Read a comic book.

After a bit, we stopped talking and started kissing, still lying on the carpet as if we were grabbing a quickie at someone's party.

"You ever thought about selling those comics of yours?" I said, my nose nudging his cheek, the edge of a shelf digging into my arm.

"Graphic novels," he corrected me, and I swatted at him. "No, of course not. I'm just some bloke drawing in his shed, aren't I?"

"Studio."

He paused. "Yes," he said. "I'm just some bloke drawing in his studio."

"But . . ." I said, and he kissed me again, and then I wasn't interested in talking for a while.

CHAPTER
THIRTY-FOUR

The nun in the photograph was smoking. She was smoking and laughing, pushing her free hand towards the camera to block the lens. The wind tugging at her veil also tugged the smoke, in a synchronised skew. Hard to work out dates, with a nun. I'd never thought of that before but — no make-up, no hairstyle, no telltale fashions. Behind her lay a backdrop of olde-worlde urban deprivation: black-rubbed tenements, a cobbled street. A kid in long shorts and a pudding basin haircut balanced on the edge of the kerb, staring. The photograph had slipped from *God's Smuggler*, a 1967 first edition.

So, a mischievous nun who wasn't afraid the photographer would give away her crafty fag, an audacious nun who risked discovery by hiding the photo in *God's Smuggler* (a witty nun?) or — the photographer had kept the photo. A photographer secretly in love with the nun?

He was a snapper for the city newspaper, the nun a visitor from a convent in . . . Buenos Aires. Together, they exposed the wrongs committed by slum landlords. The snapper brought his local knowledge and a camera to record the evidence. The nun brought her passion for social justice and her habit, that impeccable camouflage. Because who would ever believe a nun could be a threat? Well, this one was. And at the very moment the picture was taken, she realised that the photographer was in love with her, and she with him. Bound to her vocation, she left that night. By morning, she was gone, leaving only a thwarted lover and an image on a roll of film, sealed in a dark canister . . .

The phone was ringing. I looked up from the workbench, wondering if Judith was likely to answer it, but she didn't shift her attention from the cookbook she was browsing. Allie was standing outside, arms folded, staring at her own window. I ducked out of sight and ploughed towards the phone through the rubbish on the desk.

"Jenny? Maria from Events. You're a hard woman to catch."

The more I thought about what Allie had said to the paper, the more unsettled I became. I wasn't public property, and I didn't appreciate her threatening me like that. She wasn't being malicious. She was worried about me, that was all, but after so much *BAM! SMAK!* I didn't know if I could talk to her about it without breaking something.

"Jenny? I haven't heard from yourself about LitFest. There was a form. Should I send it again?"

"Uh, OK. Yes."

"It's just we're really pushing it this year. You know the dates? Between September twelfth to the nineteenth. Have you taken receipt of the posters?"

I peered round the corner again. Allie had shifted her attention to my window.

"It's all good, Maria. I'll sort it. Listen, we've got quite a queue of customers building up. Can I get back to you later?"

Allie knocked on the window, but I wasn't ready for a conversation. "Judith," I said, putting down the phone. "I'm going out. You know what to do, don't you?"

"Well actually, Jenny, I was rather hoping to leave a little —"

Just before the back door closed behind me, I heard the rattle of the front door opening. I legged it across the yard and out through the gate.

Since the night in Elliot's study, he and I had spent more time together, talking late as we had in the early days, when the urge to be together was a kind of amphetamine keeping us up past the point of exhaustion, our mornings furred with the dopiness of the newly besotted. Back then, I could talk to him with the light off and forget I wasn't talking to myself. Now I trod a little more carefully, but something of that early excitement had returned. Maybe it was just the pleasure of secrecy, the two of us sharing things other people didn't know, but I found myself seeking out his company more and more. Now I thought I might see if I could tempt him away from work for an hour and hire a boat in the park. We could bob about in the middle of the lake, the oars drawn up, and just talk.

Elliot's agency occupied a detached Edwardian house with a few other businesses. Its metal-canopied veranda, beautiful and showy, seemed out of place in Bassetsbury's grey drizzle. Its front entrance faced the park. When Elliot hosted a client meeting he'd let the visitors in that way, so they could take note of the immaculate garden and climb the sagging stone steps to the front door. But everyone else came in through the back, as I did now, past the shed, through the infrequently cut grass, past the plastic garden chairs and table where people spent their lunchtimes in good weather.

The reception area was pristine, in yellow and teal, the receptionist, Polly, restrained in black. Across the wall, in lower-case, the company's name was inscribed: *lemonade*. There was a yellow mug half-full of tea on Polly's desk, a teal bowl of lemons on a floating shelf. Elliot had always displayed awards on that shelf before. I remembered that on the night I'd found his comic, he'd come back empty-handed from the prize ceremony. Now that I thought about it, he hadn't come back with his hands full in quite a while.

"Long time no see," said Polly.

"I wanted to surprise him," I told her. On my way to Elliot's office, I passed the bigger room in which Yaz worked with a few others. There were a couple of empty desks, which surprised me. No Yaz, just one designer talking low into a phone, his desk scattered with the usual paraphernalia: a piece of foam board on a cutting mat almost — but not quite — the same colour as the teal in reception, a metal ruler, a scalpel. There was a subdued feeling to the place; less chat, less energy than usual.

I stopped at the open door and watched Elliot for a moment before going in. He was alone in the room, the other desk empty. On the screen in front of him, the words *Reese Engineering* had been transformed into the shape of a screw, the downstroke of the R the screwhead, the g finishing in a point which made me think immediately of the nightclub stamp on my hand. A couple of years back, Elliot's clients had all been iconic brands or edgy, design-led startups. I'd found it a bit poncey sometimes, how they'd only pitch for those prestigious accounts. Yet here he was, designing something for Reese Engineering, a logo lacking all his usual finesse. It was an ugly, crude thing and, looking at it, I knew that its production would have caused him no small misery. Or maybe, I thought, this is what you produce when you're miserable.

I was used to envying Elliot his job, or rather, not the job itself, but the things it conferred on him: financial independence, an aura of cool. In contrast — and, God! It was frustrating — when Martha was smaller and I used to tell people I looked after her full-time, I'd see them downgrading their estimate of my IQ before I could say another word. I'd see them scanning the room for someone more interesting to talk to, and that someone was very often Elliot. Then they'd bang on about what an important job I was doing, their enthusiasm directly proportional to their relief at not having to do it themselves, while I smiled and imagined punching them. One night, Elliot introduced me to a client with the words: "Jenny's a full-time mother, but she's really intelligent." I kept on smiling till the event had finished, then yelled till my throat was sore (and besides, a "full-time mother". What other sort is there?). Managing Famaid elicited marginally more interest, but people's sense of other people's worth usually follows the money, and honestly there was a troubled, unexamined part of me that didn't blame them for that. So I reflexively envied Elliot his job and the status it brought.

But now I remembered his vehemence a few weeks back, when he'd listed all the things he was responsible for providing. *I hate it*, he'd said. It occurred to me, as I watched him at his desk, his attention roving from the screen to the window, that there might possibly be a downside to shouldering the greater part of a family's financial burden. Always the woodcutter, never Little Red Riding Hood. When I first met him, Elliot was going to be an artist: that had been the grand plan. It was something he never mentioned now. I thought about roving the streets trying to rescue people. I thought about searching for clues. I wondered how long I'd been missing what was right in front of me.

I'll find this bastard first, I thought. I'll keep my promise to Hannah and I'll make Martha safe. Then I'll see what I can do for Elliot.

I'll save them all.

CHAPTER
THIRTY-FIVE

I'd gone out on a few patrols since Elliot had discovered my secret, and each time I came back he'd be up waiting for me, the light from our bedroom a pale rhombus on the street. When I got in, a tautness would go out of him. I'd undress and he'd pull me under the covers, patting me down tenderly, searching for injuries.

He wanted to know everything, every tiny detail. He asked about the precautions I'd taken, about what I'd seen, what I'd felt, until I felt cornered by his questions and I wanted to say, get out there and do it yourself; then you'll know what it feels like. More than once, I looked back with longing at the days when I'd enjoyed the liberation of total secrecy. Part of it was fear, I knew that. He was scared for me and I didn't blame him. Still, he never tried to stop me. I think his fear was constantly tussling with a sense of wonder.

Elliot was comforted by what I told him, which was that I'd wandered the streets and paths witnessing nothing, intervening in nothing, achieving nothing. For once, this was not a deception. There were fewer women and girls out at night now, but a lot more men. They waited in pairs near pubs and clubs, or walked purposefully through the streets. At first I was on high alert, and then I saw that many of them were wearing a sort of uniform themselves: jeans and trainers, fluorescent yellow T-shirts with FATHERS TAKE ACTION in red. I had my work cut out to remain unseen. I didn't know whether to welcome their presence or resent them. The rapist would surely be less likely to strike when they were on patrol, but I feared they'd make him more careful and cunning, harder to catch. As soon as I'd thought that, I realised what I was acknowledging; that a man like him would perceive them — but not me — as a threat. It made me feel diminished, but I also thought: let him underestimate me. Let's see where it gets him. In a bad moment, I wondered whether the rapist himself might be somewhere among them, hiding in plain sight.

The T-shirted men kept their lips pursed and their eyes narrowed, shoulders back in a quasi-military bearing. They were good people, I was sure, protecting their families. But it raised a new fury in me that the rapist could get away with this, filling the streets with men and wiping girls — all of them, even the ones he didn't hurt — right off the face of our town.

Returning home after each failed patrol, I'd take a moment at the foot of our stairs to straighten my shoulders and paste on a smile. I'd remind myself that it was just a matter of time before I turned up an important clue or spotted him walking the streets. I remembered that I hadn't promised to succeed, only to try. But trying seemed such a petty, puny thing. I'd tour the sites of previous attacks and stand passive outside the school gates, staring in. I'd wander streets and paths and find myself longing for the catharsis of conflict. Frightening though it was, it would have been preferable to this constant, agonised deferral.

Amidst all this, there were unlooked-for moments of beauty. Coming down the footpath from the school one night, I caught movement out in the street: a cat emerging from some unseen hole in a fence. As it loped across the road, I saw in its slender-legged gait, in the loofah bulk of its tail, that it was no cat but a fox, one of those urban foxes which had entered Bassetsbury myth but which, until now, I had never seen. It stopped in the middle of the road and turned my way, mouth open — a triangular face, the clean economy of its curving teeth. We stared at each other for a few seconds and then it startled at something and trotted away, the white of its tail tip disappearing into the dark.

In the daytime, I focused on keeping Martha safe. On the first day of term I drove her up to the school.

"Why can't I just walk?" Martha asked the car window, staring out across the opposite carriageway. On the pavement beyond, groups of boys were trudging up to the school, their bodies levered forward against the pitch of the hill.

"I thought you'd like a lift," I told her. "You don't usually want to walk. I'm going past anyway."

"Why are you going past? Where are you going?"

"You whine about walking most mornings. Is that Liv?"

"No. Her Mum's giving her a lift, too." She reached forward to switch on the radio. I turned it down, and she tutted.

"Martha, this party?"

She sighed. "It's fancy dress. At Josh's. His parents will be there. It's as" — sighing again — "safe as anything. Constant Adult Supervision."

I thought of her meticulous Steampunk costume; this would be its first outing. "Lifts there and back," I said. "Ten-thirty curfew."

"Ten thirty?"

"Yep."

"That's like a . . . do you *want* to humiliate me?"

"I want to keep you safe. Honestly, M, right now everything else comes second."

Kids pushed through the side gate. There would be more coming in via the footpath on the other side, some sneaking through the gap at the bottom of the field and others entering at the front, where we were heading. The school was vulnerable. Anyone could just walk in. I remembered Mr Grafton at the casino night, telling us about the computer thefts. The thought came that I shouldn't take Martha in at all, that I should keep her safe at home with me.

"Let me out," she said. "We're close enough."

I made her wait until we reached the lay-by right opposite the school gates. I leaned over to kiss her. She checked the pavement and let me, keeping her head close to mine for a second or two. Then she saw Izzy coming and was off, slamming the door, dashing across the road so fast that my hand hovered over the horn.

Over by the gate, Izzy and Martha were reunited. I tried to guess, from their gestures, what they were talking about. Someone with a big head . . . with a hat

. . . someone whose head was exploding? Then Dan and Josh came round the corner from the hill road, Josh cutting between the two girls and making straight for Izzy, hand to her waist, Izzy on tiptoes, reaching up to be kissed.

Didn't see that coming, I thought, and then I caught Martha's expression, her look of stunned and sudden grief. She glanced away from them and stared up the road as if she were intrigued by something approaching from the other direction. I knew that look instantly, knew it from the inside: the scramble to put together a game face. I just couldn't work out why she needed to. Martha's hands hitched up her bag strap, smoothed down her hair, folded over themselves. Maybe I was wrong about her being gay. Maybe she fancied Josh.

A car pulled into the lay-by from the other direction so that we were nose-to-nose. It was Helen Donaldson, offering me a comedy grimace as Liv scrambled for her stuff. Martha gave a final hoist to her expression. When Liv landed on their side of the road, I expected Martha to greet her, but she looked back at Izzy instead, and I finally recognised the peculiar blend of longing, and sadness, and desire in that glance.

Oh, my lovely girl. I didn't know which got the upper hand in me then, compassion or envy. I wanted to run ahead of her and make everything smooth, like those people in the Winter Olympics who sweep the ice with brooms ahead of a curling stone. I rewound all the times I'd seen Martha and Izzy together. The girls were so extravagant in their affection for each other, so tactile, their language so lavish (love ya grrrrlll! Thx gorge!) that it was easy to miss authentic desire. But the clues had been there: Martha's protective fury when Izzy was being bullied, the way she snuck glances at her even when — especially when — Izzy wasn't looking.

Martha turned with the others and walked into school, and I knew this was something that she would absolutely have to bear alone. The pain, the near-certainty that this particular love would be unrequited, it was the thing I couldn't mediate for her. In return she'd also bear alone the one glorious gift adolescence gives you, despite all its sufferings: the unfettered ability to experience a raging passion.

It was probably time to talk to Elliot about all of this. Tonight — no excuses. Ahead of the girls, the two boys turned in mirror image like an opening book, Dan yelling something. Martha rested her hand on Izzy's shoulder and Liv flipped him the bird. In front of me there was movement, and I looked round to see Helen face-palming. She laughed and I pretended to, eyebrows raised, mouth open, absolutely silent.

That evening, while Martha was getting ready for the party, I knocked on the shed door. After a moment the bolt clunked back and Elliot emerged, blinking in the light. I caught a quick glimpse of a pale interior, heard the woolly sound of a radio just off-station.

"I'm going out in a bit," I said. "Can we chat first?"

He frowned. "Are you . . . wearing the cape?"

"Is that a euphemism?"

"Are you?"

"Yes," I said. He opened his mouth to say something, and it didn't look like anything good. "I'm picking her up at 10.30," I said quickly. "We'll come home together."

Both of us looked up at Martha's room: curtains shut.

"Come on," I said, grabbing his hand and leading him further along the side of the shed. It tripped a sense memory, all those long-gone times when a boy had pulled me out of sight for something illicit. There was a tang of creosote and the hay-smell of grass spat out by the mower, drying in clumps at the edge of the lawn. I pulled him close and nipped at his neck and kissed him.

After a minute he drew back. "So, listen," I said, and at just the same moment he said, "Don't go out."

"No!" I unwound his arm. "You don't get to do that."

"What, I don't get to look out for you?"

"You know what this man can do, Elliot."

He chafed my shoulders in something that was only partly affection. For the rest of it, I think he wanted to give me a good shaking. Fleetingly, I wished I'd lied about where I was going.

"Trust me," he said. "I am constantly thinking about what he can do. Don't even call that into question. And that's the point, isn't it? He could do anything. He could hurt you."

"I can look after myself," I told him. "Really — you'd be surprised. I've had self-defence lessons."

"I thought that was just a cover story?"

"No. I've been going for ages. I'm prepared."

I wondered why he'd suddenly changed gear like this, and watched as one expression succeeded another: defensiveness, confusion, realisation. "No, Jen," he said, and a bastard pity was in his voice. "Babe, you can't fight him. I don't think you really believe that. That's not why you're doing these things."

Don't you dare, I thought, tell me why I'm doing *these things*. I opened my mouth to retort, but there was a clatter above us, Martha's window being hinged open. Any moment now, she'd come out there. I talked myself down from my annoyance: it was fear getting the better of him, that was all. It was love. I quelled the urge to snap back, but didn't have time to go the long way round, soothing and explaining and picking this apart. We needed to talk about Martha.

"Jen," he said, but I cut across him.

"I will be safe," I said. "I won't do anything stupid. Look, I'm leaving in a minute, but I really do need to have a word first. Can we go in the shed?"

He didn't answer for a second. Then: "Not enough room."

"We don't need much," I told him. I moved, but he got there first, blocking the gap with his body and slipping inside, closing the door behind him. A thump, a rattle.

"Just tidying up," he called, and then he opened the door again.

The shed was . . . well, it really was a studio now. A tight space, white walls and canny shelving to keep the floor clear, a warm-wood pungency with an edge of fresh paint. There was a drawing table like the ones in Elliot's office, its back edge crowded with kit: rulers, masking tape, jam jars filled with pens. In the centre of the desk, a sheet of tessellated panels waited to be filled. Tucked under the lip of the table was a wooden stool.

"Let's sit down," I said, and he switched off the radio and settled on the floor. I sat against the door opposite him, toe to toe. "It's Martha," I said.

He used to sing her "Martha, My Dear", plinking away on that piano in the middle room.

"There's a bit of a curveball," I said.

"Oh, God."

"No. She's OK. It's not a bad thing. It's a different thing. It's a . . . different's not bad. It's just . . . you have these expectations. When they're not . . ."

"Now you're worrying me."

"She's still her. She's still Martha."

His mouth opened in slow motion. "Oh," he said. "That."

"Say it."

"You say it."

I looked at the hand he was resting on his jeans leg, index finger scratching at the denim, a smudge of something red above the knuckle. "I think she might be gay," I said.

"Yeah," he said.

"God, I didn't think you'd . . . did she tell you?"

"No," he said, and my jealous heart decontracted. "But I think you might be right."

On the wall above the desk, a corkboard held a collage of night-time images. Elliot had been down the High Street with a camera. I saw our cobbled square, the Pepperpot, the Pound Shop which used to be the old Red Lion Inn.

"I think she's a little in love with Izzy," I said, and for a moment we mirrored each other, wincing with empathy.

"I did wonder if . . ." he said. "It could be a phase, couldn't it? An experiment?"

"Well . . ."

"She's quite young, isn't she? What do you reckon?"

"Elliot," I said. "How old were you when you realised you were straight?"

"Mum!" Martha's voice sailed out of her window. "Liv's on her way! I'm going!"

"Of course," said Elliot, nodding at me, continuing to nod as he looked down at the floor. "You're right. She's old enough to know, isn't she?"

I scrambled up and pulled open the door, squinting in the light. "Hang on, Martha!" I called.

"OK, then!" said Elliot, hearty and apropos of nothing.

"Are you alright about this?"

"Completely," he said, but I wasn't that dumb. I stuck my head out again and bellowed: "Martha, do not leave yet!" When I looked back at Elliot, he'd stood up and was making busy little let's-move-on gestures, brushing himself down, pulling up the blind a little more.

"Listen, J," he said. "I've had a mad idea. It's mad, but it's great. Let me go with you. Let's both be superheroes."

I worked so hard to make my face do the right things. I'd almost taunted him with it before, but now that he'd actually suggested putting on a mask of his own, all I could feel was gutted. I was shocked at the amount of resistance that flooded me in that moment. I think he saw it, even as I scrabbled to make it good.

"Elliot," I said (tender, tender). "It's a great idea. But I'd be terrible at it." Then I thought of something — a bit of whimsy, an *homage*. I winked and made my mouth smile. "I work alone," I told him.

By the time I got into the house, the front door was open. A car was waiting in the road, Ian leaning on the bonnet.

"Hello, stranger!" he called, and I raised a hand. There was rustling from Martha's bedroom, the click of her light being switched off. Out in the street, a van pulled up behind Ian and hooted.

"They're here, Martha!" And then I remembered; Elliot would want a photo of her outfit. I dashed to the kitchen to get my phone, switching it on as she descended, raising it as she thudded down into the hall: black and red, masked and caped, my twitch of shock triggering the shutter.

"What do you think, Mum?"

I couldn't possibly tell her what I thought, because what I thought was a Pushmi Pullyu of pride and jealousy. What really took me aback was where that

326

jealousy was directed: not, as I'd have expected, at Martha's youth and costume-appropriate body. Instead, I found myself irrationally jealous of the vigilante who, unlike me in my civvies — the joy-crusher, the party-pooper — had finally managed to inspire my daughter.

"Oh, Martha, look at you."

"I'm calling her Magnifica," she said.

It wasn't a perfect copy. The mask was accented in silver rather than gold, the corset was a black vest, the cape a standard-issue superman one she was wearing inside out — I'd caught the yellow lozenge on its lining as she landed. She'd made a decent job of it, though. Not Elliot's steam-punk costume in the end, but my uniform, and her name for me was Magnifica.

Outside, the van hooted again. Ian mouthed something at the driver.

"I knew you'd come up with a good name," I told her. "Be sensible tonight."

"Don't worry," she said, snapping the mask. "This will scare him off."

"No, it won't!" I followed her out. "Take your safety seriously, love."

Liv (shoulders bare, gold circlet on her forehead) was pressed up against the passenger window, sticking out her tongue.

"I'll pick you up at ten thirty on the dot," I said, and Martha threw me a glance of sudden malice. "Keep your phone switched on. I may call you." From the shadowed back seat Izzy cheered. The van driver rapped on the inside of his windscreen.

"You'd better go," I told Ian, who was still lounging against the bonnet.

"You think?" He grinned and started to stand, then settled himself back down. "Yes, I think I'll just . . . oh no — maybe not . . ."

The driver stuck his head out. "Get a move on, you wanker!"

Ian held up a placatory hand. "I'm on my way . . . not quite, though."

"Really, Ian —" But the next hoot came from right under him, Liv reaching across and leaning on the horn.

"I'm off," he said. "Give my best to Elliot."

As he drove away he put a hand out of his window. I lifted mine briefly, till I saw it was not for me but for the van driver: an unabashed V-sign held aloft all the way to the end of the street.

Back on the pavement, I looked at the photo I'd taken before Martha left: mainly wall and banister, a corner of her (blinking, midway through jumping off the bottom stair, cape lifting behind her). Magnifica. A girl dressed for a woman's job.

CHAPTER
THIRTY-SIX

After I'd put on the uniform, I brought my fists down onto the toes of my boots to feel their solidity. I checked the knife, and then I checked it again.

I'd planned a frictionless route, slipping through the town centre and up the opposite hill unseen. Footpaths, disused yards, empty car parks — I tracked a tangential course across them, ducking out of sight if anyone came close. I took the hill at quite a lick, pounding up the footpath, mindful of the limitations on my time. Puffed out near the top, I slowed, and as the school buildings came into view I heard deep laughter, a lad shouting "Get off!" Two lads, a smaller one bent double, his neck gripped in the crook of the other's elbow. He called out again, "Fuck off!" A second or two later the bigger boy saw me and let go of his mate. The other lad frowned at him, then followed his gaze. As I passed, they let loose snorts of laughter.

"Get over it," I said, tramping past the side gate, past the netball courts and the sixth form block.

Beside the main entrance, my message was still scratched into the fence: *I am watching*. Someone had filled the cuts with black so that it stood out clearly, a warning and a promise. I checked the empty pavement for witnesses, clambered over the gate, and was in.

A Saturday night, an empty school, the only gatekeeper the caretaker whose bungalow squatted in the car park. I passed it, crouching low, watching the windows and door until I was safely out of sight. The school was the centre of everything, Martha had said so. All those fruitless patrols waiting outside the gates, and I'd finally remembered there must be a way into the building. The police couldn't work out how the thief had got in, but I could if I looked carefully enough. Mac would say: find the weak point.

It took half an hour of window-pressing and door-rattling, hugging the walls of every building, before I found the weak point, a back way into the kitchens of the school canteen. It was screened from sight by a clump of conifers, a half-full Coke can on the step. Above the canteen, the hall, the staff room, classrooms, access to the glass-sided bridge which led to a second building. I rose on reverberating stairs, through the smell of floor polish and cooking fat.

In the staff room I checked the noticeboards for clues and found only messages about staff birthdays, student allergies, union posters. I was about to leave when Elliot's name jumped out at me from the PTA newsletter, pinned next to the kitchen rota. Special thanks to Elliot Pepper for his sterling work at the end of last term, it said. Our hardy team of classroom-clearers finished the job in double-quick time, thanks to his military organisation. You little sod, I thought, remembering how late he'd claimed to have finished.

330

He'd had the hump with me the next morning, had stretched the truth to make a point about my own late return. There was a photograph in the newsletter too, a bunch of the dads lifting desks one-handed, their free arms curled muscle-man style. Elliot was at the front, raising his arm high, his T-shirt riding up, a glimpse of belly above his jeans.

Nothing in the classrooms, nothing relevant in the drawers of the teachers' desks but I pressed on, knowing that in the next place I looked, I might find something significant. I jogged across the glass bridge towards the main block, watching the wall of windows ahead of me for any movement. No luck in the gassy Science corridor, every lab shut fast. A floor above, in the Humanities area, displays of tea-soaked documents curled on noticeboards. The Humanities office bore a still from *Monty Python and the Holy Grail* and a notice saying "PLEASE do not knock between 1p.m. and 2p.m. unless is it an EMERGENCY. Your teachers need their lunchtime too." Clearly, the signs were considered enough of a deterrent. The office was unlocked.

There were three desks in the room, a Goldilocks feel about the place: one workspace meticulously tidy, one messy, the final one just right. The tidy and messy surfaces abutted each other in a face-off, Baby Bear set slightly apart. The wall carried an outsized planner and a poster declaring that "Historians Do It For Old Times' Sake". There was a Blu-Tacked collection of Thank-You cards and a portrait of Thomas Cromwell cut out of a magazine.

Three drawers to a desk. I went through them all, sifting through pens and fags and battered make-up, through elastic bands and a selection of half-finished handcreams. On the desks themselves, an abundance of paper was stuffed into trays, in piles, in folders. All the time, I was trying to keep my mind loose and open, waiting to spot any kind of connection between the school and the attacker. The Baby Bear desk carried a pile of exercise books, the top one pulling me up short: Martha Pepper / 11H / History / Mr Grafton.

Bill Grafton's top drawer boasted a start-of-term neatness, a stash of chocolate bars pushed to the back, a rainbow pack of highlighter pens.

Nothing, nothing. Bloody nothing.

I took off my mask. I put it on again. No difference at all.

What did superheroes do to find the clues which broke open the case? They were just there, in the right place at the right time, or their superpowers kicked in, or a helpful policeman called them to the scene. A stupid, dangerous hobby, Mac had said. A *hobby*.

The head teacher's office was locked and for some reason this made me furious, as if it were a personal slight. I kicked the door and kicked it again, the shock jarring my leg. I kicked the office doors of both the deputy heads. I went through the reception desk, harvesting paper clips and Post-it notes, pens and half a cereal bar, its wrapper secured with an elastic band.

Notice things, Mac had said. But what was there to notice here, in this abundance of detail? I felt a tremor of doubt. Was it possible, after all, that I really was . . .

332

ridiculous? Was I just a figure of fun, a fat woman in a too-tight corset, in a fancy-dress mask? Was it possible that when people laughed at me, they were responding appropriately?

The thought nearly got the better of me. It took a moment or two to remember what a self-indulgence it was. So what if I looked silly? So what if it was a bit undignified? I was doing this for Hannah. The girls in this school were being targeted, and the tiniest piece of evidence could keep them safe. Once more, I summoned the memory of the fight behind the club and the way I'd protected Zoe. That was the thing to keep hold of.

I ran up to the top floor. In the first classroom I entered, chairs were stacked on desks, a school jumper crumpled on the teacher's table. On the white board, in red pen I wrote: *I Am Watching*. And then the next classroom, and the next, and then I thought of all the watching I was doing, all the seeing I was failing to do, and I gave that up and checked the bins instead. They were all empty.

In the movies there was always a basement room, unlit, always a wall covered in photographs and newspaper cuttings. When you found it, you knew you'd caught the villain. I clattered downstairs to the bottom floor, a windowless den of changing rooms and lockers. In a few weeks' time, after the weather turned, the walls outside would be stamped with mud, pupils bashing clogged boots against the brick.

A fug of stale sweat. Posters of Olympians curving their bodies over poles, airborne above beams. In a corner by the lockers was a door marked BOYS SHOWERS, a pile of boxes in front of it telling me the room was out of commission. I bent to the keyhole and saw only darkness. I moved the boxes, kicked at the door a few times, but my heart wasn't in it. Besides, I needed a pee.

Afterwards I squeezed soap out of the honking dispenser and stood in front of the basin with my gloves tucked under my arm, staring at myself. Everyone could see straight except her sister, Allie had said. She was a bag of bones till she looked in the mirror. I straightened my wig. "Amir is fit", someone had scrawled on the wall. Just under it, in a different hand: "He farts in class", to which had been appended: "through his nose". Nonsense and truth, the same as you'd find on any toilet wall. I glanced at the rest of the graffiti: "French is boooooring", "Mr Cooper fancies Miss Dooley", "Men are like tights: they run or they cling, but they never fit right in the crotch". This was the real inner sanctum of a school. This was the place they'd never show you on open evening. You'd meet the head teacher, but you'd never meet the cleaner.

I hitched up my corset and rubbed at a smudge of lipstick, wiping the red off on my palm, wiping my palm off on a paper towel.

Blunderwoman. The Incredible Bulk.

Martha.

With a jump of fright, I yanked the mobile from my belt and checked the time.

It was eleven o'clock.

CHAPTER
THIRTY-SEVEN

Two days later I was still furious. I swept the shop floor while my volunteer Stan sorted through a donation in the stockroom. I could see him taking some really good stuff out of those books and binning it, but actually it just felt better to keep sweeping, digging that broom right under the bottom shelves, flicking dust out of every corner.

The truth was, if the police had done their job I wouldn't have been needed at the school at all, and I wouldn't have let the time slip, and I wouldn't have been late for Martha. None of it would have happened — the dash from the shop to the party, rubbing at my face to remove the imprint of the mask, the certainty bearing down on me, even before I'd pushed past the teenagers on the front lawn, before I'd shouted into the wall of music, before I'd run upstairs and searched the bedrooms, that my trip was in vain; Martha had gone. If they'd done their job, if this bastard had been caught, I wouldn't have had to make myself breathe slowly against the canter of my heart and pull out my mobile phone to get help, and see the text from Ian Donaldson, left hours before: *Sticking around having a jar with Graham. Will bring M back.*

A phone was ringing in the stockroom. I bent to pick up a crisp packet which had got stuck under the card stand. Stan (twenty-three, but with the name and cardigan of a man fifty years his senior) called from the shop.

"Jenny, is that your phone?"

Martha was safe, anyway. She was in bed by the time I got home, and absolutely fine. Elliot had been visibly relieved when I got back, although he was a little cool towards me. I was at pains to tell him how uneventful the evening had been, how frustratingly inconclusive. I wasn't sure how far I'd convinced him but the next morning, things felt almost normal. The worst thing that had happened in my absence was that Martha's mask had gone missing. She'd taken it off at the party to eat, she said, and couldn't find it afterwards; now she'd have to get a new one.

I moved the little armchair out of its corner and swept out all the crap: clumps of hair and dust, a tattered book which had found its way under there. The phone stopped ringing, then started again.

"I don't think it's mine," I told Stan. "Not my ringtone."

A customer kicked our door open with her foot. "Donation?" I said. "Stan will help you. Have you signed up for Gift Aid?"

The woman frowned and set down her box on the floor. From somewhere in the back, the mobile started ringing again. "I've just read about this," she said, dusting her hands off against each other. "If I sign up,

I'm legally liable for those books. If something happens with them, I could be sued."

I looked at the woman's hands, and a memory poked at me. I looked down at my broom.

"It leaves me wide open," she said.

"Jenny?" called Stan.

I'd been in the yard before . . . before Hannah, when I'd picked up my cape from the dry cleaner. The cobbles had been washed. When I was with Hannah they were wet, and it hadn't been raining.

"Jenny? I don't know where that ringing's coming from."

But there was dust on Hannah. I'd brushed it off her clothes. I'd thought it was from the yard, but it couldn't have been. The dust must have come from the place where she'd been raped.

The phone stopped ringing. "I won't be signing up," said the woman, tapping me on the arm. I shook her off, wanting her gone, Stan gone too — all of them.

"What do you think might happen?" I asked the customer. "What health and safety threat do you think your books pose? Do you think someone might trip on a carelessly constructed metaphor? Do you think they might cut themselves on a sharp observation?"

"Hey," she said. "I'm giving them to you as a gift. I could have taken them anywhere. There are some nice books in there."

The ringing started again. I marched into the stockroom and picked up my phone from the desk. The screen was dark, the handset silent even as the sound continued elsewhere, further back.

"We really appreciate it," called Stan, but the woman had left and I was still listening to that perky waltz coming not from the workbench, not from the stockroom at all, but from the bank of lockers next to the sink — from the only one whose door was locked. My vigilante phone was ringing and it was no wonder I hadn't recognised it; no one had ever called me before.

Stan had paused at the workbench, baby wipe in hand, a clean path carved through the spatter of brown on a recipe book. Beyond him was the closed locker.

"Everything alright?" he said.

"I could use a coffee," I told him, making myself say it nicely, unhurried. "Would you mind getting it? And one for you — my treat."

When he'd gone I dug out the locker key, two-way checking (back door, front door), then I slid off the padlock and rummaged for the phone. There were a lot of missed calls — how did anyone even have this number? — and a string of messages.

The first was from Mac. At the sound of her voice, I got such a fright I curled over and had to lean on the desk. She said the police needed to talk to me; if I came in myself it would be easier for everyone. In a fluster, I cast about the stockroom as if she were watching me at that very moment. Then she said, "We will find you," and I realised she wasn't talking to me at all, but to the vigilante. She said: "We will find out who you are, make no mistake," and then the second message started, and I was so het up I didn't even catch the name, just my own voice murmuring, "shitshitshitshitshit." It was a reporter from the *Bassetsbury Examiner*. She said she'd keep my identity confidential. She said: "Those things the police are saying? I've got my doubts. We want to hear your side of the story."

My phone — my untraceable phone. And what were the police saying? After that, there was a male caller, quite young: "Yeah, we're really in trouble here. We need rescuing . . ." In the background other young male voices sniggering. "Shut up," whispered the caller. I remembered the process of getting the phone, tried to work out how my privacy could have been breached, searched for the mistake which had led to this. I hadn't used my own name when I bought it. They couldn't identify me. "We need some of your big . . . oh, get off . . . I can't . . ." He giggled for a second or two, then hung up.

The next woman spoke very, very quietly. "Is this for real?" she said, then silence. "OK," she said. "I saw your number in the paper. Do you come when you're called, or what? Hang on." There were footsteps. An opening door. A closing one. "I don't know if you're really there," she went on. "I don't know if you'll listen to this." I heard breathing and swallowing, the ambient sounds of an inside space. She sounded so nervous, and the silence stretched for so long, that I blurted out "I'm here! I'm listening." At the front of the shop, Stan's back appeared against the glass door. He pushed against it, swinging inside with the coffees. Down the phone, the last of her message played out. "My husband . . . He —" But then a child's voice called from a distant room — "Mum?" — and the message ended.

The last caller, also a woman, asked, "Is this a game to you? I just wanna know. We're all really scared and you're poncing around like . . ." She produced a mock-laugh. "I'm asking you to stop it. It's an insult to those girls." I squashed the receiver close to my ear so none of it could escape and reach Stan. "You look like shit and you're not all that," she told me.

"Stan?" I said, turning off the phone. "Would you mind very much getting the *Examiner* from Allie's shop?"

COPS SEEK VIGILANTE
SUPERHERO "MAY HAVE CRUCIAL EVIDENCE"

As tension mounts in Bassetsbury over the rapist still at large, the town's police tell the *Examiner* they have a new target: the vigilante who came to the aid of two victims.

The eccentric law-enforcer has been criticised by police in the past for helping members of the public. Now cops say she's under suspicion herself.

"We are very keen to speak to this woman," said P.C. Sharon MacIntyre. "Vigilantism is never something we would condone. In this case, a vigilante's actions are preventing us from bringing a dangerous criminal to justice."

VICIOUS
The costumed crimefighter fought off the attacker after he assaulted a teenager at the

340

former Edge nightclub. She found the second victim in Bodger's Yard, behind the High Street, and alerted police. The girl, who cannot be named for legal reasons, had been raped.

P.C. MacIntyre said the police were "intrigued" as to why the woman was on the scene so soon after the attacker struck. She added that there was evidence the second crime scene had been contaminated.

"If anyone knows who this woman is, I would urge them to come forward," she said. "She may have crucial evidence that could lead to the capture of this vicious rapist. We will pursue her vigorously."

With the town living in fear of another attack and many parents keeping teenagers at home until the rapist is caught, P.C. MacIntyre said the police were "expending every effort" in finding him. There will be more police on the beat in Bassetsbury until the man is found. Meanwhile, the controversial "Fathers Take Action" group established by local dad Harvey Cox continues to patrol the town centre at night.

There was one more item on the page, a sidebar:

SUPERHERO: WE'VE GOT HER NUMBER
The *Examiner* has received a tip-off about the mobile number the vigilante uses to alert

the police — and we're passing it on to our readers.

So far our calls have been unanswered — will you have more luck? If she comes to the rescue — or makes a supersized blunder — tell us on our dedicated vigilante webpage: www. bassetsburyexaminer.co.uk/vigilantetracker

And that number? It's . . .

Allie was upstairs at her desk, in a doorless cubicle off the main room where two volunteers, girls in their late teens, were steaming donated clothes. The air was damp with it, the steamer galloping under their talk.

"I need a minute," I called, pushing past them into Allie's office.

She had cleared a space on her desk and placed an L.P. in the centre of it.

"I'm up to my ears," she said, but I was already holding out my mobile to her.

"Go on then," I said. "Call the police. Tell them."

On cue, it started ringing again. There was a yelp from the other room. Allie frowned. "*Never* put your hand behind the clothes when you steam them!" she shouted through. "You'll be burned. I'll get done for it. The admin's a nightmare."

"Call the police," I told her. "Stop flirting with it. You've already given out my number. Just do it and get it over with."

Allie looked at me and blinked once. "You've lost me," she said. She reached for a fat cylinder of bubble wrap, lifted the album and unrolled the wrap beneath it. "Are you going to answer that phone?"

"No, I'm not. But don't worry — there'll be another call straight after it. It's been ringing all morning."

"So . . .?"

I pulled the paper from under my arm and shook it at her. "Tip-off!" I said. "Tip-off!"

Allie peered at the page and then at me, stony-faced. "You think *I* did that? It's not even your number."

"It's my . . . it's my . . ."

"Oh, it's your *other* number? Your special superhero number? Your batsign? And how would I get hold of that, then?"

The moral high ground shifted beneath my feet. I held the button and the phone shut down. Allie folded the bubble wrap over the L.P. once, then flipped the record end over end to cocoon it, slapping it flat onto the desk each time.

"So, what?" she said, ripping off a length of Sellotape. "You think I called the paper?"

"You said that thing in the vox pop."

"That was your first thought, then? You thought I'd dob you in?"

"I'm trying to help people," I said. "Really help them." Allie glanced out of the door. In the main room the steamer crackled.

"I don't know what *real help* means," she said. "I thought we were offering real help here. Is that the kind of help you mean? Or did you mean, *visible* help. Help with everyone looking at you and taking pictures and writing about you. Is that what you mean?"

"Allie!"

"Because I may not be attracting attention over here, in my boring little shop, with my boring second-hand clothes, but I'm pretty sure I'm managing to help people."

"Don't! Don't make this . . ."

"What an idiot I've been," she said.

I tried to make it seem like anger, turning on my heel and storming off, facing away from the girls as I hurried through the main room so they wouldn't see my face quaking. As I banged down the stairs, footsteps clumped out of Allie's office and across the ceiling.

"If you've used that phone to call the police they'll have the number, won't they?" she yelled. Between my opening the door at the bottom and it slamming behind me, I caught her parting shot: "It was the cops who dobbed you in. Great work, Sherlock!"

That night, I worked hard to keep things normal. I made a fish pie, a complicated one which demanded infused milk and sieved potato, and all sorts of other sophistications that kept me anchored to process. Martha came in and we had a decent conversation about her day, by which I mean we actually had a conversation, that she told me things I didn't already know. A classmate had been suspended for jerry-rigging a vending machine to dispense free chocolate. Martha suspected that Izzy was already tiring of Josh (and yes, I watched her closely, and yes, I saw the clumsy hotch-potch of hope and fake casualness she presented). Then she wandered off into the lounge and switched on the telly, and I half-listened to a re-run of *Friends* while I finished the pie, ploughing lines across the butter-puddled mash.

We will pursue her vigorously. I thought about the necessity of remaining unseen, about the hue and cry that could be mustered. What could the police do to find me? Eyewitnesses could contact them, or Elliot could, or Allie, or anyone close to me who had guessed. I'd have to watch out for CCTV cameras. They had my phone number. All the thrillers I'd seen, where the criminal only has to turn on his phone for the police to find him — was that possible here, in Bassetsbury?

While the pie cooked I went into Elliot's study and typed *police track mobile phone* into a search engine. I found, quite quickly, that it's easy to track a mobile in real life. The police need sign-off, but they'll get it, especially — said one site, in a statement which drained my appetite — in cases involving serious crime, such as rape. You switch on your phone and twenty minutes later there's a knock at your door.

I imagined coppers running to catch me and I knew my own innocence, and how useless I'd be to them. I knew they'd run towards me and away from the rapist. I thought back to the argument in Allie's office and was sure I'd switched off my mobile. I'd kept it off. I'd shoved it into a zipped section of my handbag and it had stayed there.

When I heard Elliot's key in the door I slipped out of the study and went to greet him, waving from the top of the stairs when he came in. Normal, normal, normal.

345

"Dinner's in the oven," I said, smiling. "Can I fix you a drink?"

We ate at the kitchen table and Martha protested as usual, and we talked in a desultory way about our days, like an ordinary family. Then I made tea and Elliot cleared up without being asked (and it struck me that this, too, had become ordinary, and I wondered how that had happened). On a full stomach, after a few glasses of white, it was easier to keep Allie's comments (and Mac's, and some of Elliot's) at bay. Going to the police would be worse than useless. I'd tell them nothing they didn't already know, and they'd stop me from patrolling ever again. Instead, I was keeping my promise to Hannah and, yes, it involved me doing something . . . unusual, something daring and risky, and of course that was going to freak people out, people with less gumption than me. I'd reclaimed the night! One more woman out there, one more active, responsible citizen, could only be a good thing for Martha and her friends. Couldn't it?

I went up to bed early (a little randy, quite tired), leaving Elliot downstairs watching telly. I would make it up with Allie and I would continue to elude Mac. I'd done very well. I was bloody marvellous.

This exaltation lasted all night and into the next morning. It lasted until breakfast time, when Martha, eating her cereal in the lounge, suddenly cried out, and I went in to see what was wrong. "Oh no, Mum! No!" — tickertape streaking across the bottom of the screen behind her: BASSETSBURY GIRL MURDERED.

346

CHAPTER
THIRTY-EIGHT

The girl was Iona Thomas, aged 15, from Martha's school, in Martha's year. Twin brothers aged ten, a mother and father displayed for the cameras in the throes of their grief, begging for information.

"Someone must know who this is," said her dad, resting between words, water swaying in the glass at his elbow. "If you've noticed anything suspicious . . ."

Iona was resurrected in the photograph her parents had provided. They hadn't used a school photo, but one of her in a garden, laughing. You could just see a little bit of another person in the background — a bare elbow — and a sparkle of water droplets. I wondered if the other person was one of her brothers. I wondered if she'd been turning the hose on him one hot afternoon, just a few streets away.

Martha and I sat in blank incomprehension, watching news reports, flicking channels when Iona's segment ended on one station, starting the story again on another as if, somehow, we'd stumble on a channel where she wasn't dead, where there had been a mistake. She'd been strangled, they said (and Martha put her hand up and touched her fingertips to her own throat). The reports showed flowers piling up at the school gates and at the entrance to the road where she'd been found. "This quiet community," they said, and "a town in shock."

God forgive me, I kept thinking of reasons why it wouldn't be Martha, why she and Iona were different. Maybe he only liked girls with long hair, or maybe Iona was out when she shouldn't have been, and Martha didn't do that anymore; she'd learned her lesson. Or maybe it wasn't actually him, but someone closer to home, because that's what everyone says: you're likely to know your rapist. I sat there being a bastard, formulating ways in which Iona had been marked out for this, pushing her away from us, and I hated myself even as I did it because I knew, really, that it was all rubbish. She was Martha. She was me.

After a while I couldn't take it. I switched over to *The Simpsons* and went into the kitchen to make us macaroni cheese. Neighbours would be visiting the Thomas family with cling-filmed casseroles, depositing them on the doorstep. Iona's mum would take five sets of cutlery out of the drawer and then realise what she'd done.

Cutting butter for the sauce, I took the knife and laid its edge against my arm and pressed, and dared myself to press harder, and when I found I couldn't, called myself a coward. While the water boiled I braced my hands on the wall and knocked my head against it, gently at first and then harder, till it made a thumping sound like far-off hammering, till it properly hurt. I clenched my teeth and kept banging away, as if I could

348

transmute all my guilt and fear into something as manageable as a bruise.

Martha stayed on the sofa in her pyjamas for the rest of the day, texting, chain-watching, flipping between innocuous comedies. She talked intermittently.

"I didn't really know her," she said. "But she was nice. She was funny. She did Assembly Bingo." And, when I was a little too slow in responding: "I'm not just saying it because she's . . ."

Dead. Raped. Murdered. We hesitated before the words. Such attention-seekers, those words, such conversation-stoppers. They didn't fit in our world.

"How do you stop it being you?" Martha asked, and then I was filled up by the desire to kill him, just like Hannah had told me to, just like I hadn't done. And I told Martha a BIG BLOODY LIE. I said: "It can't be you." I gave her self-defence tips to empower her, and then disempowered her by explaining that she wouldn't be going anywhere, ever, unaccompanied until the man was caught. She didn't raise a single objection.

She locked her own windows.

She looked up the superhero's phone number online and programmed it into her mobile, and I was beset by shame. I watched her visibly relax, placebo-calmed.

"If you're ever in trouble, don't call that number, will you, love?" I said. "Call the police."

She said: "I feel funny about going back tomorrow."

"Don't, then," I said.

I searched the net for every last detail of the crime, for information which might not have made it to the television news. I checked back hourly for updates, but there was nothing I hadn't seen on TV that morning. Despite the news reports, despite my own shock being corroborated by Martha's, it was hard to believe it was real. I thought of the man I'd fought behind the club and I thought of a girl murdered, and I just couldn't make them fit together. It couldn't have happened. But then I googled it all over again and it had. It really had.

I anatomised everything I'd done — or failed to do — since Hannah's rape. Should I have talked to the police after all? Did I miss a clue at the school? Was there something I'd overlooked when I'd been with Hannah? Why hadn't I asked her more questions, then and there, when I could? But she'd needed comfort at that moment, not the third degree.

As for Martha, I never wanted her to leave the house again. I'd take a sabbatical from the shop and home-school her until the killer was caught. Or, if that wasn't possible I'd chaperone her everywhere she went, only leaving her once she was in the care of the school or another trusted parent. She'd be drilled on this: known and trusted adults only.

I lay on my bed and reached up, gripped my own neck and squeezed hard, feeling the cartilage in my throat click out of place, feeling the thump of blood against my thumb.

That night, when Elliot got home from work, he went straight to Martha's room. They were up there for a while, his low murmur buzzing through the ceiling in the kitchen. Afterwards he came down to me, wrapping me in his arms so completely that there was just a tiny gap through which I could breathe.

"That poor child," he said, and he pushed me away so we could look at each other. "You cannot go out there again. You can't. I'm shit scared."

"I'm lost," I told him, and to my amazement he said nothing to press his advantage, just held me until I'd stopped crying.

He made dinner. He did a tidy-up, which at one point in my life would have cheered me immensely. When Martha said goodnight he made her come over. He put a hand on the nape of her neck and bent her head, placing two kisses on her forehead. Iona's dad would give *anything* to do that, I thought. You do it every day as a parent, you do it so carelessly, and he would never, ever be able to do it again.

On my way to bed I detoured into Elliot's study. I was pretty sure he'd been working on some new pages since he'd sent me to find his comic. I was sure, too, that Scarlet had stuck around despite Vermilion's misgivings. I don't know what I was looking for: the comfort of seeing her triumph, or the catharsis of hating myself when she did.

He'd displayed the new comic on a shelf at eye-level. Vermilion was on the cover. He stood high on a roof overlooking a dark street, his cape triangled behind him. I knew that roof. I saw it every day out of the window of my shop. It was the dome of the Pepperpot and he stood on its flank, gazing out over a town which was so precisely Bassetsbury that I could recognise every alleyway, every shop, every sign and bin and lamp post. Vermilion watched over all this, a tiny figure in the distance. But the eye was drawn away from him, to a single, glossy black boot towering huge in the foreground, its treads lodged on the back of a red stone lion.

The lion was real too, a Bassetsbury landmark overlooking the high street: fur serrated, tail stretching back like a pump handle, its sweep echoed in the ripple of a cape, caught by the wind and flicking up at its hem: Scarlet. Behind the gold-swirled mask, her implacable gaze mirrored the lion's. They both stood sentinel over the High Street, chins up, unmoving. Most arresting of all, she was . . . me.

Her face had morphed to become mine — my jawline, my nose, the slight downturn of my lips, attentions so intimate and unsentimental that my throat felt blocked. Scarlet's tiny waist and unlikely curves had gone. Now those red ribbons were holding back real flesh. She was mighty and magnificent, and she stared out over the town and the swashing letters of the comic's title, which had also changed. The comic was now called: *Scarlet*.

In the story Scarlet — with her sidekick, Vermilion — trawls the streets of Metro City for her father's killer, the vicious criminal known as The Artist. After a tip-off about one of the fatal canvases, she enters the dingy storeroom of a low-life art fence. Amongst dim sculptures in browns and blacks, the paintings glow with their own light. Stacked up against the walls, there's the corner of a Van Gogh here, the edge of a Keith Haring there, fragments of an unlikely haul.

At the front of one stack was a Craigie Horsfield. I felt a leap of recognition; I knew this piece and loved it, a black and white tapestry of a captive rhino, horns a pale glint amidst the grey textures of undulating ribs, pleated hide, walls and straw. The real piece was huge — we'd seen it together a few years back, the gallery a venue for some work do of Elliot's. I'd stared at it for ages while other people milled round us, till even Elliot had become bored and moved on. It was one of my favourite things.

A superhero should have a name, something she can brandish as she goes into danger. In the movies they were gifted by awestruck townspeople or in sensational headlines, but I found I didn't hate myself quite enough for Fat Girl or Blunderwoman, and the *Examiner* hadn't bothered to name me at all. Scarlet didn't seem quite right somehow. Magnifica, I thought — but the name, in my mouth, was a brutal swagger.

Avenger. Ferocity. Words as unyielding as a mask.

And then I remembered what it had felt like the first time, stripping off my fleece and stepping into the vigilante's red and black. I remembered the way the mask had liberated me. I had walked out into the streets of Bassetsbury, freed from my own life.

I struck a clean line through the title. Underneath I wrote: Liberty.

Inside the comic, one of the statues moved. Liberty hadn't seen it, her gaze fixed on the rhino canvas, but in three successive panels the statue turned, stepped forward, came up behind her. It wore a Roman soldier's helmet, its face obscured by side-flaps, its eyes glowing red. Its stone sword had become a blade which flashed in the dark. In the final panel of the triptych, the tip of that sword was levelled at Liberty's neck.

At the last moment she turned and swung her foot until it connected with the helmet (CRAK!). The statue stumbled against the paintings and she followed the kick with a POW! to its belly. Around Liberty more statues mobilised. She SMAKed and OOFed and BAMmed a path through her enemies, and there was a comfort in that, in her metronomic dispatching of the wicked. She didn't flinch. She didn't fail.

CHAPTER
THIRTY-NINE

The next day Martha still couldn't get out of her pyjamas, so she stayed at home. It took twenty-four hours of umbilical texting with Izzy and Liv before she was ready to go back. All the kids were scared, the parents more so. School buses ran half-empty; morning and afternoon, cars clustered opposite the school gate like platelets at a wound site. When I picked her up, she told me that three girls in her class had gone on spontaneous family holidays.

School — home — school — home, all of us waiting for the other shoe to drop. I spent my time at the shop avoiding Allie because I didn't feel equipped to make peace. Furiously, I pulled stories out of the air using anything I could find (bookmarks, receipts, shopping lists) as waymarks to a happy ending. I spent my nights staring at town centre maps, making notes. In all that time I came up with only one decent idea.

On Friday night Martha and I went to a residents' meeting hosted by the police. They used the Town Hall theatre, a room with the aesthetic of a seventies working men's club, yellowish walls and red carpet punctuated with patches of stiffened brown. We spotted Izzy and her mum Carrie standing near the front and made our way over to them. Martha would be staying at Izzy's that night.

"You walking or driving them home?" I asked Carrie.

She wrinkled her nose. "Don't worry, I'm driving. I won't let them out of my sight."

We both looked behind us, to where the girls had sat down in a row about halfway back.

"OK," I said. "And in the morning, just call whenever she's ready to come home. One of us will collect her."

Carrie bobbed her head towards the seats. "You joining us?"

"Oh, no," I said. "Thanks, but I'd better stay at the back. I might have to leave early."

I leaned against the wall and watched people as they came in. Some of them were parents I remembered from PTA functions. There were teachers and the odd student too, younger ones sitting next to their parents and others, like Martha and Izzy (heads now bent together, looking at the inevitable mobile phone), keeping their distance. On stage, a line of worthies sat on chairs in front of an art deco backdrop: *Fat Sam's* said the sign. Two coppers, their shoulders heavy with metalwork, and three civilians; I recognised Martha's head teacher, Ms Murray. I thought Mac might have come but I couldn't see her, not even amongst the officers watching from the edges of the auditorium, unsmiling, arms folded. I knew what they were doing. I was doing it too.

He'd come, wouldn't he? He'd come to suss out the opposition, to feed off the fear, to get a kick out of being powerful and secret, his secrecy the core of his power. I was pretty well-qualified to know how that might work. The seats filled: Martha's form tutor, Liv's dad, Josh with a woman I assumed was his mother. And all the strangers, the unknown quantities. Even at that point, before anything official had happened, there was a screwed-down intensity to the room, people talking in pairs, low and close, movement restrained. I watched for anything that struck an odd chord, for someone who was ... who was doing what I was doing, probably. Looking outwards, scanning, observing. There was a bloke who kept jumping out of his seat and looking round at the room, but he wasn't the attacker: too beefy, too built. Bill Grafton was standing near the door, bouncing lightly on his toes. He exuded officiousness and I wondered whether he was here to support Ms Murray, both of them in suits.

I glanced at the nearest copper to see if she'd spotted anything untoward, but her gaze was sliding over the room, undiscriminating. Izzy had got out of her seat and was talking to Josh. He touched her arm and she pulled it away. Martha was doing a not-very-good impression of someone curious about the whole room and not especially interested in the couple by the windows. Then one of the officers on stage stood up. Izzy took a step towards her seat, but a latecomer was already sliding into it, so she retreated again, sitting next to Josh, but not touching him.

The officer introduced herself as Detective Superintendent Stephanie Lockshaw. Blonde, mid-fifties, a gesticulator. Occasionally she'd clap a hand to her chest and hit her mic, and an explosive report would boom from the speakers. She talked about the Thomas family and their dignified response to Iona's murder. It occurred to me — as she talked about staying calm, about trusting the police to do their job — that I was standing in the wrong place. From the back, I couldn't see people's faces. I waited until the questions began and tiptoed down the other side of the auditorium out of reach of the lights. Three hundred people here, maybe. As I passed alongside them I watched their reactions: the angry ones, the baffled ones, the frightened ones. There were plenty of frightened ones. I switched my gaze from one face to the next, and each time I settled on one, I became convinced I was missing something vital in another. It was bound to be here, the dead giveaway. I just had to be looking in the right direction.

In the front row local hacks hunched over notepads, blank-faced and scribbling. Carrie sat with her elbows on her knees, her hand over her mouth. Some people looked bored. That was suspect, surely? And what about those who asked questions? He'd do that, wouldn't he, getting a buzz from being right under their noses?

How many more bobbies have you put on the beat?

What have forensics turned up?

How close are you to catching him?

Was it suspicious, to check your mobile phone while such things were being discussed? Because there was a lot of that going on, and for the space of a question or two I sought out the phone-checkers and assessed them for signs of not giving a damn. Then a man stood up, and the tension in the room cranked up a notch. He said: "It's simple. If you've got a daughter, keep her inside. Keep her safe."

Lockshaw opened her mouth to speak, but before she could a woman got to her feet. I knew her — Patsy someone, a daughter in Martha's class.

"Whoa there, Dobbin!" Patsy shouted (and three hundred heads turned her way). "That is *not* the answer! Our girls will be safe when the men are off the streets. We're not liking a woman for this, are we?"

Liking.

The man hadn't sat down. "Right," he said. "You're going to rely on this bastard staying inside when he's told? Good luck. I'm going to rely on effective parenting."

The room fell apart. The head teacher and the copper both started talking, their words bumping against each other. They did a bit of after-you, but by then the man was being berated by two people sitting near him, each of them monologuing with no reference to the other. Patsy worked her way out of her row and started towards him. Bill Grafton, I noticed, was watching it all impassively. Lockshaw said, "OK, OK," and waited for silence, but didn't get it.

Over by the door, Izzy had become very still. She pursed her lips and clenched her body smaller, her left hand grasping her right. Josh touched her tentatively on the shoulder.

Lockshaw tried again: "I know this is a very stressful time," she said.

The effective parenting man flicked his hand, dismissive, and sat down. Two seats along from him, a woman was still telling him to *piss off*. Josh put his arm around Izzy and she didn't push him away. Martha looked down at her lap.

At the back of the theatre, a door banged shut. Mr Grafton had gone.

"Events like this place a community under a great deal of stress," said DS Lockshaw. "But let's be clear: the offender is the one to blame. That said, there are some common-sense actions you can take to protect your children . . ."

Common-sense actions. This was sounding more and more like one of Mac's early lessons. I wondered what had made Mr Grafton leave so quickly. I skimmed the audience, getting nowhere. "Ensure their mobiles are kept charged," said DS Lockshaw. "Encourage them not to go out alone." Residents sat or stood, shifting from foot to foot. They made notes, or didn't, or waited with their hands up to speak. I glanced at the door, but Mr Grafton hadn't come back. I remembered Hannah telling Elliot how she'd got involved with the casino night: "Mr Grafton," she'd said, and she'd grimaced.

The exit was reached through a small bar, empty now as I came through it. Glass-panelled fire doors gave onto a balustraded landing, the double-sweep of its staircase lending it an incongruous Busby Berkeley air. Grafton was out there on the landing, near the top stair, and there was a girl with him: dark hair, flat pumps, a long thick cardigan which must have been far too warm for her on this mild night.

So many people to keep an eye on. I didn't know whether the girl had been sitting in the hall and left, or whether she'd just come in. She had her back to me and he was facing my way, but his eyes were fixed on her. The heavy door muffled their speech, a repression of vocal highs and lows, a broken rhythm. As I watched, she pulled the cardigan tight and wrapped her arms around herself to pin it shut.

Grafton leaned in, and a flush of adrenalin flooded my system. I looked down at my feet, naked in sandals, and — just to steady myself — I imagined them clad in my glossy steelies.

The girl was talking now, fast and animated. Grafton tried to speak once or twice, frowned. He narrowed his eyes and I thought I saw something cold in that gaze.

My heart rattling in my chest, my breath coming quick. What's the timetable here? Do you wait till they've done something bad? Till you think they're just about to? Calm down. Put on the corset. I closed my eyes till I could see it, stays radiating down its flanks. I laced it tight and it straightened me up. It muffled my heartbeats.

There was something nerveless in that look of Grafton's. And I could see now that the girl had become distressed, her arm movements jerky. She kept shaking her head. He took a step towards her. She took a step away. From the theatre came a screech of feedback.

He stepped closer to the girl and placed his hand on her arm. I could almost feel the hilt of the knife. I summoned the mask and settled it in place. She looked

361

at his hand, and then at his face. I watched through the eyeholes. There was no periphery.

The doors brushed against each other as I eased them open, and I heard clearly what she said. She said, "No."

I roared — "Don't you fucking touch her!" — then rushed him, and he snapped into a defensive crouch, right at the edge of the top stair. The girl yelled and he took a step back. Just one step, but by the time I pushed him (the girl's hands raised to her face, eyes wide), Grafton was already unstoppable. He fell, flipping at unlikely angles, an astronaut in zero gravity you'd think, if you couldn't hear the *crump* and the *oof* of gravity engaging mercilessly with flesh and bone. He tumbled down until he came to the curve in the stairs and caught hold of a banister.

"Are you OK?" I asked the girl.

"Don't hurt me," she pleaded, eyes red, cheeks spidered black.

"He can't hurt you now," I said. "You're safe."

I stepped towards her, but she started to back away.

"I don't think —" Grafton was panting. "I don't think I'm the one she's scared of."

"Shut up!" I said. He groaned and sat up. "Get the police," I told the girl. "Quick! They're in there."

She was glancing from Grafton to me, exercising exactly the sort of careful control over her body that you do when you're beside yourself with fear: locked muscles, slow movements, blank face. I felt a pang of unease, a glimpse of something untoward at the edge of my vision.

362

Gratfon reached for the banister again. "I was . . ."

"Shut it!" I told him, confused by the girl's responses. "You have no idea who you're dealing with!"

He pulled himself onto his knees and I came down below him, cutting off his exit.

"I know exactly who you are, Mrs Pepper," he said. "Leave her alone. She's Alice. She was Iona's best friend."

Alice was still backing away, eyes fixed on me. "I'm doing it now," she said. "I'm getting the police."

I looked at Grafton's face and saw no anxiety at the prospect of their arrival. I looked at the girl and saw that it was not him she feared. I looked down at my clothes — my real clothes, blouse and jeans and sandals — and knew I'd landed in a looking glass world where Mr Grafton was not a murdering predator, but a teacher trying to offer help, where Alice was not a doomed victim but a grieving friend. Where I was not a hero. And I knew that the strangest thing about this world was that it was the real one.

There was a *bang* as the theatre door crashed open, running feet through the bar, and a second *bang* as two coppers burst out onto the landing. I pelted down the stairs, the thud of their boots behind me, making it out of the front before they did, out into the night, and I ran, and I ran, and I kept on running.

CHAPTER
FORTY

The musty smell of rotting carpet, the corner of the lockers digging into my back, the drip-drip-drip of the basin tap. Welcome to my lair.

I was the newest terroriser of young girls in Bassetsbury. I was a dispenser of judgement rather than justice. And the things Allie and Mac and Elliot had been trying to tell me — that I couldn't catch this man, that I had flapped about the town achieving nothing — they were all true. My knife had only ever been used to graffiti. A prop, that was all it was. I had thought there was another part of me, someone who could do extraordinary things. In this I'd been a fool. Certainly, I'd never been a superhero. I'd been — I was — ordinary and unremarkable and almost sick with wanting to be different.

I saw it all dry-eyed. Most of it. I will confess that the only part where I couldn't quite hold it together was when I thought about what I had *not* done, the thought of Hannah shaking in the yard, of Iona cold and undefended. Then I did lose it, briefly. In the end, Hannah really had got the wrong woman; and trying wasn't good enough. I got up and unfastened the locker that held my uniform. My costume.

There was a bin halfway down the High Street — far enough away, I thought. It was one of those black metal things with a postbox mouth. I put the corset in first. I sensed myself hesitating for a moment, so I bent the stays irretrievably then stuffed it right in. After that it was easier. I posted in the tights and the skirt. I posted in the gloves.

The boots wouldn't fit. Those fat, air-cushioned soles, those domed steel toecaps, they were just too big for the opening. I let myself consider the possibility of keeping them. And then I legged it across the road to the Save The Children shop and dumped them on the doorstep. So glossy, I could still see the streetlight reflecting off them when I was back on the other side of the road. The knife clanged into the bin. I shoved in the tool belt and the cape (they'd always liked the cape).

I don't know how I failed to hear the woman coming out of the insurance shop. Maybe I heard noises but I didn't register their significance. Or maybe I knew what they meant, and I really, truly, did not give a stuff anymore.

I think she'd been standing there for a while. But at the point I turned to see her — leaning in the doorway, tabard on, bin liner gripped in a rubber-gloved hand — at that point, I was holding the last piece of my costume. My mask, with its lovely baroque curlicues, my mask, which had made me believe I was seeing straight.

Her hair was in a ponytail, just as it had been when I rescued her from the mugger. She looked at me, and the look said: ker-*ching!*

"Do it," I told her. "Call the police."

She guided me inside, and I let her. She settled me in a chair and fixed me there with monosyllables. (You sit there. Drink this. Here.) She went on with her work, tidying, spraying, wiping, and I told myself I'd get up in a minute and leave.

"So," she said finally, coming over to the desk where I was sitting. "You're not superhero anymore?"

"I don't want to talk about it," I said. She reached across me to wipe the screen. On the inside of her arm, a tattoo: Olenka 2007. *My Olenka*, she'd said to me, as she held up the little girl's photograph on the night of the mugging.

"I keep your secret," she said.

"What's your name?" I asked.

"Ay-va," she said, spelling it in the air: *Eva.* "You say it like in Poland."

"Eva," I said. "I need a wee."

They had tried to make their toilet as nice as possible in that office. Nice handcream, *pot pourri* like vegetable crisps. There was a proper towel and two different kinds of tampons on the cistern. I remembered the toilet at Martha's school, how much it gave away about the place. When I came out, Eva was dusting the desk I'd been sitting at.

"This one?" she said, pointing to the chair I'd been using. "He loves her." She indicated another desk. "And she's married, and she loves him too."

I knew how that worked, stories creating topography in a flat landscape. But maybe this one wasn't made up. Cleaners saw everything.

"When you clear up after people, you know it all, don't you?" I said. "You see what they throw away, all the private stuff." I pointed at the desks, at the bins, and she said quickly, "I understand when you speak. Please don't patronise me."

"I'm sorry," I said. "Not done well today, all told." I dropped my face into my cupped hands and held it there. I breathed out, hot and damp. "OK, Eva," I said. "I'm done. Thank you."

I'd reached the door when she finally answered me. "I see it all," she said. "Everything! And nobody sees me. I am —" She waved her hands in front of her body, wiggling her fingers.

"Magic?" I said.

"No!" She slung out a line of Polish and looked at me expectantly. "I am air for them," she said. "They treat me as air."

I turned the latch. From where I stood at the window, I could see straight across to the shadowed arch of the passageway, a few steps from the yard where I'd found Hannah. Eva was invisible, but this was the view she had, working after everyone else had gone home, looking out on the High Street at night. When I asked the next question, it was only to assuage the niggling doubt which would come if I didn't; I was just tidying up the last few things before leaving the room.

"Eva," I said. "Have you read about that man who's attacking girls?" She flinched, and I thought nothing of it. Who wouldn't flinch, being reminded of that? "He raped my daughter's friend," I told her, and she brought her hand up to her mouth.

"No," she said.

"He killed a girl."

Eva shut her eyes and her fingers crept higher to cover them. "I know," she whispered.

"Eva?" I said. "Are you OK?"

She nodded and lowered her hand, driving her fists into her ribcage.

"I just wondered whether you might have seen anything that night. My daughter's friend, he left her right there. Look! Just over there . . ." I stood back so she could see past me, across the road and over to the covered passage.

"Oh!" she said, and I was certain I heard relief. "No, I see nothing. Really." Her face relaxed, and she pulled the door open.

"Eva?"

"Time to go now."

"You didn't see anything, the night Hannah was raped?"

"No. Time to go." She gave me a little shove, not quite friendly, and I was out on the doorstep.

"You've seen something though, haven't you? What have you seen?" Eva shut the door. For a few seconds, as she locked it, we were face to face through the glass. "What have you seen?" I shouted, and she turned to go back into the office.

368

I ran up and down the front of the building and hammered on the glass. I found myself looking round for something I could use to smash the window, a vestige of the superhero stirring, a last-gasp urge to fix everything with my fists. Eva kept her back to me, gathering up her cleaning gear, and I thought of her stubbornness on the night of the mugging. Then I remembered why: the photo.

"What if it was your daughter?" She'd started to strip the gloves from her hands, tugging the tip of each finger. "Hey! What if it was your daughter? It could have been *my* daughter! Just tell me what you saw!" She paused, a glove half off, her hand monstrously extended. I rummaged in my handbag and found my purse, which popped open as I dragged it out, a patter of coins spilling into the bottom of my bag. When I found the photo, I slapped it against the glass.

"Hey!" I shouted again. "Here she is! Look at her! What do you know? What can you tell me?"

Eva turned and looked at the picture, and I didn't know what I was seeing in her face then, whether I'd done enough. For an instant there was anger, and then a sort of tremulous fear, like a nervous diver on the edge of a high board. She came to the door, looking up and down the street, checking the pavement opposite. Then she pulled me inside.

"I don't know," she said. "I don't *know*."

"But you suspect something, don't you?"

"I see things all the time. I can't tell police everything." When it seemed that she would stop there,

369

I held up the photograph of Martha. I pointed at the tattoo on Eva's arm. "Olenka," I said.

For just a second, her mouth became flaccid, her chin lifted. Then she said, "It's maybe nothing. I don't tell police because I don't know for sure. I think, if it is not him, I lose my job. If it is him . . ."

"Don't tell the police, then," I said. "Tell me."

CHAPTER
FORTY-ONE

I headed out along the high street. Any minute now, I thought. Any minute now Eva would come running after me, shouting that she'd been mistaken, that there had been some linguistic mix-up. On the edge of the hill road I waited, to give her a chance. I looked behind me, but the pavement was empty. I crossed.

The things Eva had found — a hanging file containing clippings about the attacker's crimes, a knife with a very distinctive hooked blade — were kept at one of the other offices she cleaned, a nice place opposite the park. But it was probably nothing, she said. There was lots of equipment in that office. It had a nice garden, a nice — her hand performed a ski-jump descent, kicking up at the end — nice . . .

I offered her the words and waited for her to reject them as patently outrageous: "Canopy? Metal roof?"

She nodded. "But most people, they go in back."

I threw up in the toilet she'd just cleaned. I asked if I could sit down again for a bit. She finished up while I wrestled with what she'd told me, asking her the same question, over and over again: are you sure?

Elliot's office. Elliot. It was impossible. I'd fought the attacker hand-to-hand outside the club. If I could spot

Martha with a single glance, surely I'd have recognised him? And there were plenty of offices in Bassetsbury. Eva and I had communicated awkwardly enough. I might have misunderstood. It couldn't be him. I should just go home. I should —

All the wives of all the rapist-murderers I'd ever seen on the news, coming out of court protesting their ignorance of their husband's crimes. Idiots, I'd thought. Idiots or wilfully ignorant. But that was them. I was different. I'd go home and tell Elliot about this mix-up. He'd have some ideas about what Eva had really meant. He could help.

I imagined telling him all about it: how he'd laugh it off, how I'd watch his face for the slightest hesitation. If I believed him and the attacker struck again I'd torture myself with the possibility that I'd been wrong. Unless I knew for sure, everything we did would become toxic. Could I even sleep next to him? The girls were always at our house; it was a safe place for them. They dropped their guard when they were there, disinhibited, wandering round half dressed.

I forced myself to consider the evidence, for Zoe and Hannah, for Iona and Martha. For me. The thing that was making me feel sick, the thing I was trying not to think about, was this: Elliot had lied to me about what he'd done the night Zoe was attacked. He'd said — with some vehemence — that he'd left the school late, but I knew he hadn't, because the PTA had thanked him for getting the job done quickly. I'd known it was a lie for weeks, well before Iona. It had never occurred to me it was intended as an alibi. (Another rise of nausea, my gullet convulsing — I tried to breathe deeply so I wouldn't throw up again.) Elliot knew Hannah — hadn't I been with him when we met her at the casino night? He'd tried to stop me patrolling. He'd offered to come with me. (I felt faint and tipped forward in the chair, resting my head in my hands until the humming stopped and my vision cleared.) I recalled, with a charge of relief, that he'd been home on the night Iona was killed — and then, a moment later, my going to bed early, half cut and drowsy. I'd fallen asleep before he came up. But surely . . . surely, I'd have *known*?

On the way to Elliot's office I listened for Eva's footsteps. I bargained with a god I didn't believe in: let it not be Elliot, please, and I'll go straight to the police. I'll turn myself in and tell them everything. Let it not be Elliot and I'll be content with what I have.

The building was empty, the burglar alarm on. I disarmed it (the code was Martha's birthday, set years ago when lemonade was the first to rent space here). Getting into their rooms was no problem; I always carried a spare key for Elliot. Eva had described the file: at the back of a grey cabinet four-drawers deep. Not a top or bottom drawer — a middle one. I didn't ask how she came to be looking there. But Elliot's office had cabinets in yellow and teal, the company colours. So did Yaz's. I ran from room to room, yanked out the clanging drawers, shoved my hand down into each file, felt for a knife.

Accounts, Alarms, Bank, Business Link, Chamber of Commerce, Data, Debt Collection, every file in Elliot's office as dull as its label promised. Nothing at the back

373

of the drawers, nothing unlabelled. Every time I didn't find what I was looking for I'd feel a swell of hope, and then I'd stamp down on it and force myself to press on, searching all the files, and all the drawers and — eventually — every cabinet in every office. And then the desks, and then the bins, and then every spare bag and box in every neglected corner of every single room. There were a few scalpels for cutting paper; no hook-bladed knives. When I came up dry, I told myself I wasn't looking hard enough. I went into the communal kitchen and searched the cupboards.

Until I got to the kitchen, I hadn't really thought about the other companies which shared the building. But emptying crockery from a top shelf, I could see the eclectic mix: Pantone mugs for Elliot's lot, some jokey retro ones ("Oh no! I forgot to have children!"), a mug carrying the logo of a plant hire company. In the fridge, food huddled together on segregated shelves.

Eva hadn't said anything about Elliot's business, just his building. And there were other people here, of course there were, smaller firms with offices off the narrow corridor. I was already out on the landing, determined to bash down every door, when my phone vibrated. The number on the screen was Martha's.

For a few seconds there was just the quiet rumbling of an accidental call: her mobile, shoved into a pocket or handbag, must have been nudged awake. I probably gave a little smile at Martha's clumsiness. I know I hung on, hoping to hear her laugh or chat with Izzy. She was definitely in a car. Someone switched on a radio a little way off. She must have been in the back. I was just about to shut down the phone when I did hear Martha. She wasn't talking. She was — making an odd kind of sound. A sort of humming, in short bursts, up close to the receiver, but unmistakeably Martha: her pitch, her timbre. The humming had an urgent quality, like something being expelled. I'd heard that sound before, on the night I'd found Hannah, when she'd tried to shout with the tape over her mouth. There was a dropping-away inside me, as if my blood pressure had suddenly crashed.

"OK," I said. "Joke over." Then the humming ceased and all I could hear, against the rumble of the car and the noise of the radio, were snotty nasal breaths.

"Martha! Speak to me! Stop mucking around!"

There was the ratchetty crunch of a handbrake, and someone silenced the radio. A door slamming, footsteps, a long metallic slide, a clunk. Then a man's voice, only just audible.

"Fucking mobile!" it hissed. "How the fuck did you —"

"I'm coming!" I shouted. And then the phone went dead.

CHAPTER
FORTY-TWO

Briefly, I was immobilised, invaded by visions of Martha fearful and alone. I saw Zoe lying on the ground in that alleyway, Hannah tied and gagged. For just a moment I let myself imagine my daughter with a killer so arrogant that he would snatch a girl in a town suspicious and twitchy, a town clogged with vigilantes and police. I imagined her with a man driven to risk more and more each time he attacked. It was bigger than me, all of it, and it stopped me moving or functioning, or working out what to do next, so I closed my eyes and pushed it all away till there was only Martha, and only me to save her.

Then something gathered in me, and I knew the world would buckle under my terror and rage, and time would bend, and I would wrench things out of how they were and make them how they should be.

The other doors in the building: Hartley Associates Financial Advisors, ISD Holdings, SoftKey Software. Quick, oh God, pick the right one. I was poised to try the first door when I looked again at the second — ISD — and remembered the board outside Ian Donaldson's new development (ISD Holdings, it had proclaimed). Coincidence that he would be here too, I thought, and then I realised: no coincidence. Elliot would have recommended the office building to Ian, at some school event probably, all of us passing through each other's lives so often.

There. I placed my palm against the wall. The police had been "intrigued" as to why I'd found Hannah. It only occurred to me now that I should have been intrigued too. I'd found both Zoe and Hannah, and the only reason I'd found them was because of Martha. They didn't just go to the same school; they were in the same social churn: friends, acquaintances, boyfriends, even enemies, even bullies, that whole crowd. Hannah and Zoe and Josh. Martha and Izzy and Liv. And their parents. Elliot and Ian, turning up at the school to clear the classrooms, Elliot getting them all to finish early.

So Ian had left early, too.

I was a white ball skimming around the edge of a roulette wheel, waiting to leap into a chamber. I kept speeding past the right number, the one I needed to end up in. They said I'd contaminated the crime scene when I found Hannah. I'd put my cape on her, I'd held her, I'd brushed her down before the police arrived.

Brushing her down. Brushing off dust when the cobbles weren't dusty, when they were clean and wet. Red-black, red-black, red-black spinning past me. And suddenly I was back in my kitchen, in a time before I thought I was a superhero, when I was Martha's mum coming home from Liv's dad's chapel, hacked off and knackered in a coat covered with white powder. Dry cleaning, and ten quid down the drain. I'd brushed dust off Hannah, but I couldn't have brushed off all of it. Forensics would have found that dust; they'd know by now that it was from a construction site. They wouldn't know which one, though. You had to be in the right place at the right time to know that. You had to go so unnoticed that you were like air. And you had to be a superhero.

I was running down the stairs. I was out of the building and halfway down the street, I was pounding down the footpath, my lungs heaving, my heart hammering. I was flinging myself across the hill road, fumbling with my phone, dialling 999, misdialling, trying again.

I was at the chapel gates and Martha was in there with him. Two minutes, to call the police and talk them through it; two minutes too many. And then I remembered that I had not, after all, disposed of the last piece of my costume.

I searched in the zipped section of my bag, pulled out Liberty's mobile and turned it on. Please God, I thought. Let them be tracking me. Let them come.

CHAPTER
FORTY-THREE

Inside the gates things became simple, the edges of the world out of focus, the centre clear and sharp. He hadn't even locked them. They were pulled to, a chain casually looped round the uprights. His van was parked in the scrubby mess of the garden, its back door facing the rear of the chapel.

Front door locked, back door too, the kitchen sitting dusty behind unboarded windows. I hesitated with the brick in my hand, knowing the smash would alert him and put her in danger. So, instead, I pressed it against the glass and pushed.

Two clean sounds: a sheet of ice breaking, a bell-high tinkle on the floor below. I reached through and opened up. There was a sting across my arm as I struggled onto the sill. A snap as I landed, the pane giving way beneath me. I made my way into the total darkness of the side hall.

I walked blind, hands out in front of me. I wanted my knife more than almost anything. Now, from inside the chapel proper there came a raised voice — his — and scuffling. I moved faster, fingertips brushing the wall, feeling the space around me open up as I reached the front of the building. I drew back the locks on the great front door and flung it open for her, for when I'd saved her and she could escape. Streetlight flooded in. I dumped my handbag on the floor.

From the inner chapel came a muffled keening. I opened the door.

These things:

A cone of light, standing lamps trained on —

My girl on the floor, face down next to a stack of ripped-out pews.

Ian jumping up in the act of undressing, jeans round his ankles, pants still on.

Martha turning to me, her mouth taped, her face covered with a mask just like mine had been. Only — not quite mine, silver glinting from it; Magnifica's mask, the one Martha had lost at the party. The guilt almost too much then, almost gumming up my limbs, almost gluing me in place until —

Ian looked at Martha, at me, a claw-bladed knife suddenly in his hand. "Two of you, then," he said, his voice echoing, a shadow of doubt in his face.

Terror and fury possessed me, my body a single clenched muscle, my teeth, fists, nails — everything I had — ready to be thrown at him. I looked at Martha. "I'm here," I said. "You're going to be OK." Poised to go berserk, but something pulled me back, something cool-headed and calculating. I looked at the pews, at the lines of yellow flex crawling across the floor, at the lights, at where he was in relation to them. I saw chunks of wood scattered and I took account of where they were. I saw that Martha was bound, hands and feet. I

380

saw that Ian was bending to pull up his trousers, and then — then I went for that fucking bastard.

There was noise. He might have shouted. All I could see was him and all I needed to do was to get him before he could touch her one more time. I balled up my fists, kept an eye on that knife arm, caught it mid-arc as it swung towards me, slammed against it with both fists, just like I'd been drilled to do with Mac, and he didn't cut me. He pulled back for a second stab, his ankles tethered by the trousers, and I saw his centre of balance shift.

My fist rammed into his face. His blade missed my arm and sailed free of his hand. Ian toppled to the floor, his head catching the edge of a pew and juddering into stillness.

"OK, I'm here. You're alright." I went over to Martha, sat her up and pulled off the mask. I kissed her temple. (There was blood in her hair, a graze on her face.) I fiddled at the tape binding her hands, picking at the edge before I could unwrap it and free her. I pulled the gag off her mouth, so gently slow, so careful. She turned away from me and spat on the floor, spat and spat. Discarded next to her, a skirt, sliced right through. Her top was ripped, her pants wet with pee. She stopped spitting and started to cry, and we sat in the stink of timber and I covered her with all of me that I could, my hands my legs my hair, patching her with blood from my arm, where the window had cut me.

"Izzy was with Josh," she said, moaning it, a string of vowels. Through the door of the inner chapel I could see the open front door, the rectangle of light beyond it: freedom.

"I didn't want to go home with her any more and he offered me a lift. I said OK. I thought . . ."

"He did this," I said. "You didn't do anything, Martha. But we need to leave." I grabbed a weapon, one of the pieces of wood I'd seen on the floor, a pew-end.

Martha got to her feet slow and unsteady, walked a few steps, then froze when she drew level with Ian. I listened for sirens.

"Come on," I said. "Now." At the edge of the spotlight, he stirred.

"OK," said Martha. "I'm OK."

We almost made it out, while he writhed to kick off his trousers. Then there was a puffing behind us, and his footsteps, and I swung Martha towards the door. But she stumbled and he sidestepped, and then he had her, Martha's neck locked in the crook of his arm, her body bent double. I heaved the pew-end high above my head.

"Really?" he said. He slid his hand down to her neck and pulled her upright and she coughed once. "Two seconds," he said. "You know I can do it." His grip was effortless, jerking higher so she began to whimper and I let out a whimper too.

In that suspended moment he looked at the door, and at me, and at her, and I knew the assessment he was making: two dead women and no one left to talk, him so strong and us so weak. Panicked, I was assailed by visuals: me going at him, arms windmilling,

382

smashing the plank towards them, hitting Martha, his hands clenching tight, Martha dropping lifeless to the floor. Then, amidst the images, something like an idea. Clear black lettering in a thought bubble. Martha's eyes rolled to meet mine, and I knew what she had to do.

"You're bigger than her," I said. "Bigger than me."

Ian gave a curious spasm, as if he was about to shake her off. "Don't beg," he said. Her hands scrabbled at his.

"You're stronger than both of us, isn't he, Martha? Do you remember what we said about that once?" I shifted the wood in my hand. "Do you remember what we do, when an opponent's bigger and stronger than us?"

"Opponent?" said Ian. "Stupid bitch. She's not my . . ."

I stepped forward. One step, and he gripped her a little harder. "Listen to me, M. Because it doesn't matter if they're bigger than you, or stronger than you, does it? The only thing that matters —"

Martha red-faced, a slow blink which could have been a *yes*.

"The only thing that matters is their weakest point."

She stopped scrabbling, and went still and — oh, God — for a second I thought it was all over.

"No!"

Then, at her neck, a fluttering movement: her hand patting at his, feeling for his little finger, touching it so softly he didn't pay her any attention.

"Yes," I said. She hooked underneath and yanked back hard.

A snap, a shriek from Ian. Then both of them were down and my weapon arced towards him, towards his penis, his balls, the softness of his belly.

"Get out!" I yelled to Martha. She was on her hands and knees, dragging air into her lungs. I raised the bludgeon again and brought it down on Ian's head. He ducked the blow and kicked, sending the wood skidding across the floor.

"Get out. Now!" I hauled Martha up and shoved her towards the door. Ian came after me, bellowing. I was the only thing between him and my daughter.

It rises up, pure and whole and implacable, like desire, like the urge to push. It takes hold of me as you stagger towards safety, as Ian screams that I'm a bitch, that he'll show me, that he'll fucking kill me. I am a superhero as he drags me to the ground, as I reach out and worm my fingers into his eyes, as he cries out and pulls my hair, as he bangs my head against the floor.

I cling on to fingerholds (ear, T-shirt, arm) because that way I'll stop him reaching you. I cling on and his hands close around my throat. I drag air into my expendable lungs. I hear the thump of my disposable heart. You're almost there.

The last thing I hear is Mac. She's yelling. She's saying: stop.

The last thing I see is you, stumbling out into the light. The last, best thing.

Epilogue

I was a mother living in Bassetsbury. I was the one who always cleaned up after breakfast — remember that?

I was an actor. I made my name in a cut-down *Romeo and Juliet* in your school gym, the one your teachers chose because it fitted with the curriculum and wasn't overly expensive. You may have tried to leave halfway through to use the toilet.

I was a charity shop manager. You know the compensation lawyers in the square off the High Street? Look just to the right — the shop with the predictable window display? The peeling paint? That's mine.

I was a woman of average looks.

I was a compulsive story-maker.

I was a friend.

I was a wife.

I was a superhero.

This is how it ended.

I kept my promise to Hannah. I kept on trying, even after Ian was arrested. Once Martha had been released from hospital, once we'd given our statements to the police and she was back home safe with Elliot, I slipped out and went down to the station to find Mac. She came through into the waiting area.

"How's that girl of yours doing?" she said, and I told her, it's going to be a long road. Then I said: I've come to confess.

Ian pleaded not guilty to all his crimes — including the attempted rape of Martha — so she had to go through the hell of giving evidence, with all that entails. I lobbied hard to be called as a witness first so I might be in court to support her when she had to go through it. They agreed to that, at least. In the witness box I was Martha's mother, the one who'd rescued her, but I was also the vigilante. When that part came up, there was a gasp from the courtroom, just like you see in the movies. In my superhero days I'd have got quite a kick out of that.

Once I'd been released as a witness, I could come in every day. When I'd imagined it beforehand, I'd vacillated between competing visions of Ian: hunched in the dock a beaten man, or lounging there arrogant and untouchable. In the event he just looked like a reasonable bloke; he must have worked hard on his body language. It was better that way. It reminded me he was not yet defeated.

I stared at him almost the whole time, aiming curses at his head, concentrating so much hatred into that stare that afterwards, I'd feel exhausted. Almost the whole time. When Martha gave evidence (her sexual history, what underwear she had on) I kept my eyes on the screen she was speaking behind. I didn't shift my gaze for a moment, even with Ian constantly in the periphery of my vision. They wouldn't let me stay with her, but I'd told her I'd be right there, even though she couldn't see me. I wasn't going anywhere, I told her. I'd never leave.

Elliot sat next to me, and all around us were the swells and eddies of other griefs: a creak, a sigh, a groan. Ian's parents were a couple of seats behind, and the victims' families — Iona's, Naomi's, Hannah's — further back. We were all sealed into our own private suffering, but sometimes it was hard to contain. When Ian was called into the witness box, Iona's mum shouted that he was a monster, a fucking monster, that she hoped his own daughter would die like hers.

In the end, forensics did for him — the traces from Hannah's and Iona's clothing a perfect match for the dust at the chapel — as well as Helen's own, courageous testimony, in which she refused to corroborate his alibis. She shivered as she spoke, gaze fixed on the rail in front of her. When he was found guilty on all counts, I don't think there was anyone in the public gallery who wasn't crying, but still I didn't take my eyes off him as he was led away. Later, after sentencing, I watched unblinking to the end just in case, at the last moment, he made a run for it. Just in case I was needed for one last act of violent abandon: to chase him, to bring him down, to finish him once and for all. But Ian's final defeat occurred without incident, a humdrum shuffle down the stairs below the dock, a descent into the darkness step by step until the only part of him I could see was the back of his head, and then that too disappeared and he was swallowed up entirely.

I never understood why Ian did what he did, but after the verdict we learned more about the pattern of his behaviour. The court was let in on the background information which had been inadmissible as evidence. Ian had been convicted of sexual assault as a young man. Helen had made a call to the police alleging domestic abuse, retracted as soon as they'd come to the house but reasserted now. The papers were full of things that hadn't been printable before the verdict. There was an ex-girlfriend who'd alleged rape, and a primary school playmate of Liv's who spoke up to say he'd assaulted her. These stories pointed to a history of increasing violence, of misogyny that had drawn him on to the next act, and the next, and the next. I worried about what he might have done to Liv, but that was one part of the story we would never learn. Within weeks of Ian's arrest, Helen had reverted to her maiden name and put her house on the market. By the time the trial came, she and Liv had moved away. Martha received a card in the post not long after, with Liv's new address, but to my knowledge she never wrote back. I know Martha still misses her. They say Ian will be in prison for forty years. If he ever gets out, I'll kill him myself.

A week after the attack on Martha, when her injuries were starting to heal and we'd opened the curtains for the first time, Allie came to visit. She said nothing about our last row or what Ian had done, or my part in it all, but she did bring presents.

For Martha there were comfort offerings, chocolates and a blanket, and a cuddly dog, which Martha claimed she was too old for, but which she took to bed with her that night, and every night for months. For me there were ... well, for me there were comfort offerings, too. I think I've said that Allie was no reader; she must have gone to a lot of trouble to choose these.

There was *I Capture The Castle*, *Summer Lightning*, *Miss Pettigrew Lives For A Day* and one I'd never heard of called *Miss Buncle's Book*, about a woman living a secret life in a mundane place. Nothing very terrible happened in it, and after the gentle vicissitudes of the plot, there was a happy ending. I read *Miss Buncle's Book* and kept an eye on Martha, and Elliot kept an eye on both of us. The world went on, and the calls from journalists went straight to message.

It's a warm day, so we've left the studio door open. We're sitting on the floor, leaning against the cushions I brought in after those first tentative, bone-aching collaborations. The desk won't be used till the pencil stage and we're not there yet. Elliot has to do that alone anyway, hunched over the Bristol Board, feet tucked behind the legs of his stool. This is a different phase. This is the part where we find the story. He has a drawing pad on his knees and his hand keeps moving, moving over the paper all the time we're talking. I work better with objects; today it's a dandelion seed head. I'm having to hold it very carefully, because when I gesticulate it starts to shed, hanks of it detaching, shaking out onto my lap and the floor.

I catch myself reaching up to touch my neck. I've been told I do this a lot when I'm thinking. There's a patch of darker skin an inch below my right ear, one of Ian's thumbprints which has never quite faded. I look at my bruise often, and I think of those other, unfadeable marks on Martha, on Hannah, on everyone who loved Iona. Liv, too — I never forget her. I'm still shocked that it happened in such an ordinary place, to such ordinary people, but I tell myself that's where it always happens.

There are dandelions all over Norway, vast meadows of them. I can see these three things in my mind: a dandelion letting go of its seeds, the Northern Lights flexing emerald, a superhero. It is an origin story, and I don't yet know how it's all going to work. I can't see how to pull these elements together. But it will come.

From the kitchen there's a howl of laughter, Leah's voice shouting: "Oh no, that's cold! Oh no — that's really . . ."

"Sorry?" says Martha, giggling. "What's that? I can't hear you."

Leah's in Martha's Maths set. They've started coming back together after school, to do homework. (That's them now, *doing their homework*.) When Leah's attention is elsewhere, Martha forgets herself. She becomes absorbed in Leah's profile, the nape of her neck, her hands. Sometimes, when they really are working, when Martha's head is bent over some intractable equation, I catch Leah's gaze resting on her for a beat longer than is usual for a study buddy.

There's a shriek from the kitchen, but it's alright; they're just pretending. Elliot watches me carefully. I've never told him that once, for a few minutes, I entertained the idea he might be a monster (though, how pervasive this language is! Not a monster, of course: a wicked human). When he finally told me what he'd been doing on the night Zoe was attacked, when he confessed to checking up on me, visiting the shop and finding it empty, racing home and hunting through my things for evidence of my infidelity, I looked him straight in the eye and told him, with only the merest pang of guilt: that's OK.

I love this part. We drink lots of tea — the studio's filled with unreclaimed mugs — and I send ideas half-formed across to him, and they return a bit different, and I change them again, and send them back. If we get stuck, we talk about something else for a while. There's no hurry.

"Dad?" Martha's calling from the back door. "Mum? Can we have this chicken?"

There's a standoff for a second and then Elliot's up, stepping over me and out of the studio, past the shelves of graphic novels, past the squat bottles of ink with their rubber-bulb lids, past the glass case containing a single glossy red shoe. When he shuts the door behind him, I look at the logo he painted on the back.

It's a single letter, scarlet like fire or oxygenated blood. There's a sensuousness about it which I like to think was inspired by the edge of a cape in the wind, the base furling back at its tip, the swash whipped about the summit of the sweeping, capital L.

For Liberty.

And then I can see it. I can see a woman walking out of her kitchen, leaving a pile of junk on the table, a spread of mess on the counter. I can see Liberty falling to earth in a strange country, dropping through a green vortex of charged particles. I can see her land in a field of dandelions, the seeds rising and spinning around her as she touches down. I can see the troubles that will come, that she'll mess up, cack-handed and misguided and wrong, that she'll keep going anyway.

I can see the happy ending.

Acknowledgements

Thanks to my agent Jo Unwin, for her multiskilled professionalism, and for kindnesses which would fill this page on their own: you are utterly coolio. Also to über-editor Kirsty Dunseath, whose talent continues to astound me. Thanks to Sophie Buchan and everyone at W&N for being both brilliant and Top Fun.

Some of the material in this novel came from very close to home; it was no mystery to me how a woman standing in a messy kitchen might dream of becoming a superhero. But once that idea had taken root there was still a vast amount of knowledge I lacked. As ever, I'm gobsmacked by people's generosity with their time and expertise, helping me learn those many things I didn't already know. So thank you, thank you, thank you to:

Lee Harding, Comic Geek Extraordinaire, for cluing me in.

Seth & Caleb Harris-Reeve for bringing their considerable expertise to bear on the creation of Elliot's superheroes and villains.

Daniel Clifford, for talking me through the niceties of the comic book cottage industry.

Julie Hoggan, for being Alfred.

Ian Sutton & Milestone for their patience in dealing with my endless queries about the minutiae of running a design agency.

The girls of Sir William Borlase's School & Aylesbury High School, for telling me what it is to be fourteen in the twenty-first century.

Carmen Haselup, for helping me understand how it feels to be a gay teenager.

Tom Wright, author and forensic psychologist, for lending his expert voice to my own forensic psychologist.

P.C. Jo Wilson of High Wycombe police station and Inspector Hannah Wheeler & Sgt. Eve Woodroofe of Twickenham police station. Eve, thank you for taking the time and trouble to arrest me; getting locked in the police cell was entirely my own fault.

Lawrence Kershen QC and Sarah Williams, Clerk to Aylesbury Crown Court, for advice about trial procedure.

Ben Tominey for expertise in the construction industry (and nasty knife blades).

Magda Adamska, for all things Polish.

Del Hoggan & Amy Enticknap, for letting me in on the life of an actor, and sharing the joys of Theatre In Education.

Phil Parker, for the bats.

Gillian Stern for her keen eye and generous spirit when I needed a second opinion.

Isabel Rogers, who gifted her name to Izzy and in doing so benefited the Authors for the Philippines appeal.

Professor Ann Oakley, for generously giving me permission to use a quote from her brilliant *Housewife* as the epigraph for this novel. Forty years after publication, her seminal work on domestic labour is still — shockingly — relevant.

Finally, Al and the boys: I think we all know what a nightmare I've been while writing this book. Thank you for putting up with me.

Other titles published by Ulverscroft:

JUBILEE

Shelley Harris

It is 1977, the Queen's Silver Jubilee, and a photographer captures the moment: a street party with bunting fluttering in the breeze. In the centre of the frame, an Asian boy stares intently into the camera. The photograph becomes a symbol of everything that is great about Britain. But the harmonious image conceals a different reality. Amid the party food and the platform shoes, there is tension. Fast forward to the present and the boy, Satish, has become a successful cardiologist. When Satish is asked to take part in a reunion of those involved in the Jubilee photograph, he must confront the truth about that day.

UNDER A CORNISH SKY

Liz Fenwick

On the sleeper train down to Cornwall, Demi can't help wondering why everything always goes wrong for her. Having missed out on her dream job, and left with nowhere to stay following her boyfriend's betrayal, pitching up at her grandfather's cottage is her only option . . . Victoria thinks she's finally got what she wanted: Boscawen, the gorgeous Cornish estate her family owned for generations, should now rightfully be hers, following her husband's sudden death. After years of a loveless marriage and many secret affairs of her own, Victoria thinks new widowhood will suit her very well indeed . . . But both women are in for a surprise. Surrounded by orchards, gardens and the sea, Boscawen is about to play an unexpected role in both their lives, as long-buried secrets are uncovered and a battle of wills begins . . .

BITTER ALMONDS

Lilas Taha

Omar is an orphaned Palestinian born into chaos, displaced by violence, and driven by forces beyond his control to find his place in the world. He only has one thing to hold on to: a love that propels him forward and gives him hope. Nadia is maturing into womanhood in a refugee community in Damascus. She tries hard to cope with the tough realities of her world, but she is confronted with a cruel load thrust upon her by a selfish brother. Will she break out of her traditional social mould to create her own destiny?

SLEEPING ON JUPITER

Anuradha Roy

A train stops at a railway station, and a young woman jumps off. She has wild hair, sloppy clothes, a distracted air. The sudden violence of what happens next leaves the other passengers gasping . . . The train terminates at Jarmuli, a temple town by the sea. Here, among pilgrims, priests and ashrams, three old women disembark — only to encounter the girl once again. What is someone like her doing in this remote place? Over the next five days, the old women live out their long-planned dream of a holiday together; their temple guide finds ecstasy in forbidden love; and the girl is joined by a photographer battling his own demons. As the lives of these disparate people overlap and collide, Jarmuli is revealed as a place with a long, dark past that transforms all who encounter it . . .